Flash

Tim Tigner

This novel is dedicated to the Beta Readers from my early years: John Chaplin, Christophe Martin, Janet Nelch, Cheryl Rennecker, Elena Tigner, Gwen Tigner, Rob Tigner, Steve Tigner, and Mark Tower, with everlasting gratitude.

For more information on this novel or Tim Tigner's other thrillers, please visit timtigner.com

Chapter 1

Spoons

TROY AWOKE to the sound of screaming. That was not unusual for a combat surgeon, but hearing soprano was.

He opened his eyes to utter blackness and a monster headache. What the hell was going on? His memory was failing him and he felt oddly unsure of … anything.

He self-diagnosed a concussion, but sensed that it was the least of his woes.

This premonition proved correct a moment later when he tried to sit up—but could not. A cold steel ceiling pressed down on his left shoulder. He also felt walls abutting his back, head and feet. As Troy strained to wrap his mind around his baffling predicament, his nose upped the ante.

Hesitant fingers groped to confirm the stench.

He was lying in a pool of blood.

Troy knew that this was the moment most people would begin to scream and flail, their fight and flight reflexes tripping all over one another. He remained motionless. Analyzing. He had learned at a very young age the wisdom of lying low and keeping quiet. In orphanages things had usually worked out better that way. In the army they still did.

He reached a steady hand into the darkness before him. Cool flesh met his bloody fingers just inches from his face. He had found the bleeder—or at least one of them. He checked the flabby neck for a pulse just to be sure. Definitely dead. "Better and better," Troy whispered to himself.

Another soprano salvo erupted from the darkness, making his heartstrings resonate. Those were not wails of pain he realized, but cries of fear.

"Hold on! I'm coming," he shouted back. Troy did not know if he was coming, of course. Aside from being boxed up with a corpse he had no idea where he was or how to get out. But he knew that hope had a power all its own. Best to offer it for now and figure the rest out later.

The screaming stopped. Then the box shook with a familiar rhythm. The motion snapped the puzzle pieces into place. He was in the trunk of a car.

The sound of an opening car door confirmed his hypothesis.

Troy strained his ears.

"Who said that?" a woman asked, her voice soft but clear.

Troy stifled his habitual Captain Troy response, giving his alternative title instead. "Doctor Troy. I'm in the trunk. Are you in danger?"

"I'm not at a party. What are you doing in there?"

For a dumb question, that was a really good one. "I have absolutely no idea. Ask the Taliban. But please let me out first."

The woman remained silent for what seemed an eternity. He appreciated her dilemma. Curtain A or curtain B; the proverbial lady or the tiger. Picturing her trying to decide, he realized that if he got lucky and she pulled the trunk release rather than running off, his appearance might send her over the edge. He would look more like a feasting vampire than a valiant knight as he leapt to her rescue. Granted, she did not seem to be expecting a fairytale moment, but he decided not to risk it and added, "Don't be scared by what you see."

More silence ended with a cautious, "What do you mean?"

"I'm not at my best. I'm really much more charming than my present appearance might suggest."

The car jiggled some more and then the trunk sprang open with a thwang and a woosh. Brave woman, Troy thought, scrambling to climb out before she caught sight of the corpse.

"Freeze!"

Freeze was a command one quickly learned to respect when working in a country rife with landmines. Troy turned his muscles to stone, but shifted his eyes toward the source of the command. What he saw both pleased and disappointed him. A petite beauty stood by the passenger door, knees bent slightly in a classic shooter's stance, revolver leering at him from between two steady hands. She wore a white blouse, pink shorts, and white tennis shoes —all spattered with blood. Definitely not Taliban, but hardly Cinderella either.

They were in the corner of a parking garage illuminated only by emergency lighting. As he raised his hands up slowly over his head, Troy scanned the shadows cast by concrete pillars and parked cars. They appeared to be alone.

"I'm frozen," he said, trying to sound disarming.

She stared at him in silence.

He stared right back at her. It was not unpleasant. She was short, and slender everywhere a woman was supposed to be, while generously rounded on top. He was not sure how his mind could focus on attributes like that at a time like this, but it did and he was glad for it. Stop to smell the roses and all that.

She spoke at last. "You're all covered in blood."

"You noticed that too," Troy said. "But then it appears that you use the same designer."

She did not look down at herself. No doubt the sight of her blood-spattered blouse was what had initially sparked her screams.

Troy did look down in an attempt to appear less threatening only to find himself out of uniform. That was odd, but not his chief concern. Priority number one was pacifying the pixie with the gun pointed at his chest. Hardware aside, she did not look like a killer, but then mental illness could be a master of disguise. Looking back up he said, "It's not my blood," and motioned toward the trunk with his head. "Speaking of which, would you mind putting your finger outside the trigger guard?"

Tinkerbell craned her long neck to glance into the trunk but then looked quickly away. "What happened? Who is he?" she asked, her arms starting to tremble. Her finger still on the trigger.

"I'm a bit curious about that myself," Troy said, deciding to focus on the latter question first. "His uniform looks a bit like Marine dress blues, less the jacket. But he's much too ... squishy to be a jarhead, and that's not the Marine crest on his shoulder boards. Mind if I take a closer look? We've been sleeping together and I don't even know his name."

"Don't move!" she said.

"Sounds like you've got my headache," Troy replied. "I woke up with a real humdinger."

His comment mollified her expression. "Me too," she said. Then she beckoned with the gun. "Go ahead and have a look."

Troy pivoted back toward the trunk and went to work. The shoulder joint creaked as he moved the corpse's arm out of the way, indicating that rigor was setting. Troy knew that meant he'd been dead for three to four hours. Nice to have a timeline. For the moment he had little else.

He spotted two bloody holes and a name tag on the corpse's chest. "His name tag reads Evan Johnson, Detective Sergeant. That's an imperial police rank."

"Imperial?"

"As in British empire. A number of those former colonies are part of the coalition."

Her look did not telegraph comprehension, but Troy returned to the search anyway.

Evan was not wearing his utility belt, so he had no handcuffs, nightstick, or phone. Troy could guess where his handgun was—as well as two of its bullets. Still concerned about the possibility of experiencing the third, he kept his movements slow and steady before the woman.

He slid his hand gingerly into Evan's front right pocket and pulled out a set of car keys—Fords, like the car. Next he reached around and pulled Evan's wallet from his back pocket. He flipped it open and read from the identification card. "Detective Sergeant Evan Johnson, Royal Cayman Islands Police (RCIP). Boy is this guy a long way from home." Troy realized the obvious as he spoke. "But then, so are we I suppose."

"What do you mean, we're a long way from home?" Tinkerbell asked.

Troy turned back toward her. "Judging by your alabaster skin, green eyes, and state of dress, I'm guessing you weren't born in Afghanistan."

"What does Afghanistan have to do with anything?"

The look of sincere confusion on her face gave Troy pause. "Where do you think we are?"

"South L.A., I'm guessing."

"As in Los Angeles?"

"Of course."

Troy felt his stomach begin to constrict. He reached for his own billfold but found his pockets empty. He reopened Evan's wallet and pulled four bills and a receipt from the main compartment. The bills were ten-Cayman-dollar notes.

He took a step back to study the other cars in the garage. All had RCIP logos and right-side steering wheels. Strike two.

His stomach shrank to the size of a walnut.

"What is it?" the woman asked.

Troy ignored her and turned his attention to Evan's petrol receipt. Between juvenile detention and foreign tours, medical school and war, Troy had encountered some of the worst humanity had to offer. Nothing he'd seen had shaken him like the flimsy piece of paper he now held in his hand.

The woman spoke again, but all Troy heard was fuzzy background noise.

Not wanting to believe his eyes, he retrieved Evan's identity card in hopes of finding contrary information. Confirmation greeted him instead. Strike three.

Feeling dizzy, he turned his attention back to the petrol receipt. He mouthed the words as if testing to see if they were real. Thirty liters, forty-eight Cayman dollars, September third, two thousand … eight.

He had not just forgotten the last few hours.

He was missing seven years.

Chapter 2

Loss

EMMY WATCHED the man's face pale as he studied a document from the dead cop's wallet. "Will you kindly tell me what it is?" she repeated.

He continued to ignore her, even though she was the one holding the gun. She was holding the gun, Emmy repeated to herself. What was going on? Ten minutes ago she had awoken in the front seat of a cop car with the worst headache of her life, a huge silver pistol in her lap, blood spatter all over her blouse, and no idea what had happened. Then some guy locked in the trunk and claiming to be a doctor told her to "ask the Taliban." Was he insane … or was she?

Now she watched wide-eyed as he pulled his shirttails out of his shorts and began inspecting his own stomach. Drug addict was her first assumption, but his washboard abs belied the user life. When he wiped the blood from his flesh, she saw his jagged scar. It looked like the doctor had once removed his own appendix with a pocketknife. He spread the skin taut around the scar and poked at it as though trying to confirm its authenticity. Then he looked away and sank to his knees.

"What is it? What did you find?" she asked.

After a long tense silence he regained his feet and locked her gaze with disbelieving eyes.

She tried to read his thoughts but found only confusion.

"Will you answer one simple question for me?" he asked.

She wanted to say, "Hey buddy, how about answering my

question first?" But his grave expression caused her to nod in silence.

"What year is it?"

She knew then and there that she should run. She had hoped that the doctor would have some answers, be her defender, ally, and guide out of this mess. But he was talking gibberish. Still, something in those cobalt blues gave her pause.

She took a moment to analyze him as she would a client—from the outside in. He wore an olive safari shirt, khaki cargo shorts hanging from a silver-buckled belt, and running shoes. Practicality was clearly his chief wardrobe concern, but he knew what style fit him. Definitely ex-military. An officer.

At about six feet, he was taller than eighty-eight percent of his peers and would be accordingly overconfident. He was fit and broad of shoulder. A man's man, used to command. A ladies' man, used to getting his way. His face was handsome, but marred. Two angry v-shaped scars peeked down from above the thick dark hairline over his right eye. Probably a war wound. Possibly an accident. Definitely traumatic.

His most distinctive feature was a big dimple in the center of his chin. It reminded her of the actor who played Spartacus. But unlike Spartacus, she noted, violence was not Troy's default reaction. He used humor to defuse tension.

He was college educated, highly intelligent—although quite possibly demented, and a wisecrack. She put the odds that he was a doctor at fifty percent.

"What year is it?" he repeated.

She decided to chance a few seconds more to see where this was going. Keeping the gun pointed straight at his chest, she said, "It's 2002. June fifteenth or sixteenth."

"You're sure it's not November 2001?"

"I'm sure," she said, backing up a step.

"Or September 2008?"

"What's this about?"

"Check out your reflection," he said. "You can still keep the gun on me if you want, but crouch down behind the car door and take a good look at your face in the side mirror."

"Why?" she asked. "What would I be looking for?"

He stepped forward until the barrel of her pistol pressed into his chest. Then he held the receipt up before her eyes while placing his free hand softly on her shoulder. "Six lost years."

Chapter 3

Flat

THE WOMAN seemed to spend forever staring into the patrol car's side mirror. When she finally straightened back up to look at him, her posture drooped. The Colt dangled from her arm like a burdensome weight. Tinkerbell had run out of pixie dust.

She looked blankly in his general direction, tears flowing freely down her troubled face. Despite his own problems, despite their impending peril, Troy's predominant emotion was the urge to wrap her in his comforting arms. He was glad to find his hormones still working at the ripe old age of thirty-eight, but resisted the chivalrous impulse nonetheless. When a patient was in shock, it was best to tread lightly. Then there was the gun.

She opened and closed her jaw a few times before producing any sound. When at last she managed, her voice was but a whisper. "Two thousand eight. Are you sure? This can't be."

"My last memory is taking shrapnel from an Afghan IED. Now I have a scar that's long healed. What's the last thing you remember?"

"I don't know. Nothing as crazy as a terrorist bomb. Business as usual, I guess. I'm having trouble remembering. Everything feels hazy … forced."

"I feel the same," He said.

"Six years … Is that possible, doctor?"

"Medically speaking, yes. But it's highly improbable."

His bedside manner seemed to calm her a bit. She wiped her tears and none replaced them. "You think we're in Afghanistan?"

she asked, like Alice to the Cheshire Cat.

"I did when I first woke up. Now I think we're in the Cayman Islands."

Her expression conveyed the same *anything can happen in six years* acceptance that he felt. "Where are the Cayman Islands?"

"In the Caribbean. Between Cuba and Jamaica—I think."

"I've never been to the Caribbean. I've never even left the United States."

Troy did not know what to say. He shrugged.

"How did this happen?"

"I don't have a clue." He stepped forward and put a reassuring hand on each of her shoulders. "But whatever happened, happened to both of us. You are not alone."

He watched his last words pour life into her like a magic elixir. Her face blossomed and her eyes regained some twinkle.

She dropped cross-legged to the concrete floor, set the gun down in her lap, and began to massage her aching temples. "So what's our next move?"

Normally, Troy would have sat down with her, but this was neither a pickup bar nor a yoga class. "We run."

"Run? Where?"

"I don't know. Anywhere. We need to put distance between this corpse and ourselves. Nothing good can come from being discovered with a dead cop."

"You didn't …?"

"Of course not." He paused, catching himself. "At least I don't think I did. I can't be sure—and neither can you." She started to speak but he pressed on. "For that matter, we can't answer any questions, provide any alibi, or put up any kind of a legal defense. The I-have-no-recollection line only works if you're the president or someone in his favor. Now, maybe the last seven years have been really good to me … but I'm guessing not."

She did not get up.

He stepped toward her and held out his hand.

She looked up at him. Now that her tears had stopped he could almost see the processor spinning behind her clear emerald eyes.

"We need to run," he pressed, reverting to operational mode.

"That will only make us look guilty," she said, still ignoring his hand.

"I think we've already got looking-guilty covered. It's a question of getting caught. The way I figure it, either one or both of us did kill him, or—much more likely—someone wants it to look like we did. I'd say they've done a pretty good job."

He braced for blowback.

She just nodded in silence for a moment and then, much to his surprise and delight, completed his own thought. "And in either case, we're better off disappearing until we can figure things out. Okay, let's get moving." She took his hand and added, "With my luck it's time for a shift change and a division of cops is about to come barreling through those doors."

"If I were behind this," Troy agreed, "that's exactly how I would have planned it."

As he pulled her to her feet, Troy noted that she could not weigh much more than a hundred pounds, if that. There was no way she had lifted Evan into the trunk. Even drained of blood he was at least a deuce.

Troy started toward the garage door but she stopped him with "Wait."

He turned.

"Shouldn't we, you know, try to clean up? Get rid of fingerprints?"

"In an ideal world I'd like to take a shower too." He gestured the length of his blood-soaked body. "But we're a long way from ideal."

"We can't walk down the street looking like this," she replied, mimicking his gesture. "You look like you just sprang from the

Devil's womb and I don't look much better."

"It's after midnight," Troy said, pointing to his Ironman watch.

"So much the better. Let's take the car and solve two problems at once. We can drive to a car wash—pop the trunk and ride through on the hood. It will be a hoot."

Smart lady, he thought. Smart, cool, and quick to rebound. "You're right."

She looked surprised to have won without more of a fight.

He backtracked to the car and slammed the trunk. He pulled Evan's keys from his pocket and slid into the driver's seat. "Well let's go then."

The woman walked around the car and hopped in beside him.

Troy turned the ignition, but nothing happened. He tried the dome light and then the headlights. Nothing. "The battery is either dead or disconnected."

"You really a doctor?" she asked. "Not a mechanic?"

Troy guessed it was the first time in history that a woman had asked that question and hoped to hear mechanic. He gave her a wry smile and popped the hood. "I'm a combat surgeon. That's more like a plumber, but I'll see what I can do."

While looking beneath the hood with a beautiful woman waiting in the car, most guys pray that they will find a big red wire hanging loose from its connector. Troy found exactly that. "The positive terminal has been disconnected from the battery," he said, pushing it back over the battery lead.

The door chime engaged, applauding his efforts.

As he lowered the hood slowly back into place, his gaze fell on the front passenger tire. It was completely flat. A picture of the spare—lying in a blood-filled tire well beneath Evan's blubbery corpse—flashed before his eyes.

"What?" she asked, reading his grimace.

He walked around and opened her door. "Get out. We have to walk. We have a flat."

She did not move. Instead she said, "I can change a tire in five minutes. Surely you can manage it in three?"

He stared at her a moment, trying to pierce her resolve with his eyes.

She did not flinch.

"I'm not sure about three minutes, but I expect that I can change a tire faster than I can change your mind."

"You are quick."

"Soooo, as long as you're willing to help, go ahead and pop the trunk."

The word trunk made the connection for her. Her face puckered, but she quickly swallowed the lemon. She reached across the driver's seat for the release lever and then joined him around back. She had the Colt tucked beneath the waistband of her pink shorts where it looked ridiculously large. Her eyes avoided the trunk.

Troy rotated the body until he could grab it beneath the shoulders. Evan had definitely taken full advantage of the free-doughnuts perk. "Help me do this right," he said. "We need to flip him over onto his left side so he doesn't leave an enormous bloodstain on the floor."

"I'm not good with blood," she said, her eyes locking onto his like a life preserver.

"How are you with jail?" Troy asked, regretting the words even as they left his mouth. "Sorry. Look, you don't have to do any real lifting. Just keep his feet from flailing as I flip the body."

She nodded.

Troy was still trying to hoist Evan over the trunk's lip when he heard footsteps behind them and the overhead lights blazed to life. He turned to see a police officer walking carrying a can of Coke in one hand and jingling his keys with the other. Although he was dressed like Evan, the lean captain was the yin to the hefty detective's yang. He had a beak of a nose and an Adam's apple that was nearly as prominent. His straight sandy hair parted in the middle of his forehead and hung surprisingly long for a ranking cop. He froze mid-step as his eyes came to rest on what must have been an unbelievable sight.

Before the captain had a chance to react, Tinkerbell had the Colt leveled at him. She was good with that thing, Troy marveled. And for someone so petite, she could muster quite a commanding voice. "Down on your knees! Now! Hands behind your head!"

Chapter 4

Countermeasures

TROY HASTILY DUMPED the corpse back into the Ford's trunk. "And so the chase begins."

He had been hoping to clarify a few basic aspects of his situation before running from the law—things like the year, and what continent he was on, and whether or not the woman with him was a murdering psychopath. Looking over at his pistol-packing coconspirator, Troy knew that was not going to happen.

She held the weapon steady and pointed at the name tag on the officer's chest. Troy was glad not to be on the receiving end this time, but sorry to see all chance of an anonymous escape evaporate.

Captain Honey had instantly dropped his keys and his Coke out of shock. Now he was sinking to his knees as ordered. No surprise there. After seeing his blood-soaked captors pawing at his colleague's pale corpse, it was a wonder Honey's pants were still dry.

Troy shut the trunk—gently so as not to startle the woman— and walked toward the captain without a word. He arced his route to keep well clear of Tinkerbell's firing zone. She looked cool on the outside, but he knew from experience that she was panicked on the inside and thus likely to be jittery around the trigger.

Speaking in an Irish brogue, he said, "Ya do as ye're told, captain, and we'll be out of here in two shakes. Ya try to be smart, and we'll be with ye for eternity."

Honey nodded weakly.

After pocketing his gun, Troy used Honey's own handcuffs to

secure his hands behind his back. Then he grabbed the collar of Honey's shirt in one hand and lowered him face down onto the cola-covered floor.

"Use his shoelaces to bind his ankles together," the woman suggested, her accent suddenly Irish as well. "Then truss 'em to the cuffs. That'll keep him put. An' don't be forgettin' to stuff a stocking in his gob."

My kinda psychopath, Troy thought, as he followed her suggestion. Quick, decisive and bold.

Satisfied that Honey's bindings would buy them a modest head start, Troy ran back to Evan's car, slid in behind the driver's seat, and turned over the engine.

Tinkerbell slid in beside him. She still looked cool, but in the close quarters he could smell her sweat.

Captain Honey stared at them in silence.

Troy threw the patrol car into gear and hit the gas. The flat tire thunked but the car still rolled. They only needed a mile or two, and he prayed the spent rubber was good for as much. The garage door opened automatically as the car approached, revealing a curtain of wind-driven rain. "How did I know it would be raining," he said.

When no comment came, Troy looked over at the woman who had hitched her wagon to his. She stared back at him, eyes wide and blazing. This seemed a good moment to put her in the right frame of mind.

"The chase begins the moment we roll out that door," he said.

She did not seem to be breathing.

"They are going to catch us, eventually, you know."

She remained silent, but paled.

"Now that Captain Honey has seen us, our only chance of living out the rest of our natural lives beyond bars is to figure out what really happened. We've got to solve this before they catch us."

She nodded and finally spoke. "I know."

"It will likely take us weeks, maybe months."

"I understand."

"From this moment forth, we've always got to be thinking in terms of countermeasures: escape, evade, and confuse. We make one mistake, and it's life without parole."

"For chrissake, I'm with the program. That should already be obvious. Now hit it."

Troy punched the gas and the Ford surged out into the storm. He turned right to keep the weight off the bad tire and then gave the motor its head. The road was short and winding. The buildings around them were commercial in nature, but not in the Fifth Avenue sense. They were cheery wooden structures, gaily painted behind wide sidewalks. The scene reminded Troy of the Deep South. Definitely not Kandahar or L.A. Grand Cayman it was.

He heard a thud inside the car. He looked over to see that the woman had dropped the Colt on the floor. Darting his attention back and forth between her and the road, he saw her kick it away with her foot. So comfortable with the weapon just moments ago, she now seemed disgusted by it, like a reluctant actress whose tasteless scene was done.

"You did great back there," he said. "I was thoroughly impressed."

"We've got to get rid of this car," she replied. "The police will be looking for it in no time."

"I know."

"They can probably track us with GPS."

"On an island? I can't see the taxpayers springing for that expense."

"Maybe it's not so expensive in two thousand eight."

Troy caught her eye. He had not thought of that. "Good call."

Their road dead-ended at a T intersection, forcing him to hit the brakes when every instinct demanded that he floor the gas. A car shot past in front of them and the woman said, "We're driving on the wrong side of the road."

"Good thing we're in a cop car then," he said, turning left toward the ocean.

"Look for a big hotel," she said. "We can leave the car in a busy corner of the parking lot. If we roll down the windows and pop the trunk, the wind-driven rain should be as good as a car wash."

It was not a bad idea, Troy thought, but he had a better one. Seconds later they hit another T intersection, this one with a traffic light. Across the road a large pier disappeared into the harbor. He looked down the road to the right and then the left. Nobody appeared to be about, but then no sane person would be. "I've got another idea. Hold on."

He drove straight across the intersection toward the opposing curb. The deflated left side of the chassis bucked and protested loudly as it passed over the hump, but the wind swallowed the noise and the powerful engine barreled ahead, pushing the car forward with rear-wheel drive.

Like much of the surrounding architecture, the pier appeared to be constructed entirely of wood. Troy propelled the Ford out to the far end where it widened into a viewing platform. He put the transmission in park and looked back over his shoulder. Between the darkness and the rain, the only things visible on land were the streetlights, and they were a blur.

Looking forward again he inspected the railing before them— just boards and nails.

He turned to Tinkerbell. "Get out."

"You're not going to—"

"The tidal salt water will destroy our DNA and fingerprints." Troy pressed buttons to lower all four windows as he spoke. "Now for the tricky part. I really do suggest that you get out."

She did.

Troy threw Honey's Colt onto the floor next to Evan's, hoping to sever all links to both guns. Then he put the Ford in reverse and backed up until the front bumper was about thirty feet from the railing. Pressing his foot down on the brake, he shifted the cruiser into drive and pushed his door all the way open. This would be a first.

"It can't be as easy as it looks in the movies," the woman shouted.

"Nothing ever is—but we're doing okay so far."

Holding the doorsill with his right hand while grabbing the edge of the roof with his left, he shifted his foot from the brake to the gas. The car shot forward. He pulled with his left hand and pushed with his feet until he was standing up on the doorsill. He jumped backwards and away, hitting the boardwalk as the cruiser crashed into the rail. He heard the sound of wood splintering over his own grunts and groans, but by the time he had stopped rolling and regained his feet, the cruiser was already submerged.

The woman stood by the gap in the rail, watching the tail disappear beneath the waves. "It barely made it through," she said. "Then it dropped like a rock and flipped upside down. With the rail in this condition, they will find it come first light."

"The salt water will have done its job by then," Troy said.

"So, what now?" she asked.

"Now we find a hotel and go for a swim."

She stared at him with incredulous eyes. "Perhaps a massage while we're at it?"

"That would require registration," he said with a wink.

Her expression changed. "The chlorine … The bloodstains … Got it," she said.

"You need to do one thing first, though."

"What's that?"

"Tell me your name."

She smiled for the first time. It was a beautiful smile; one of those smiles that used to make men pick up swords and storm castles. "Emerald, my name is Emerald Green. My friends call me Emmy."

Chapter 5

Out of the Frying Pan

FARKAS CURSED the weather as he drew the emery board across his fingertips. First a few freak murders, now a tropical storm. What was next, swarms of locusts? He wished the police would get their act together so he could get back to business as usual. Tying up loose ends was not his forte.

He rubbed the pads of his fingers together, testing for the slightest ridge. Nothing. Smooth as silk. He returned the emery board to his shirt pocket without taking his eyes off the rain-soaked garage door. He would leave no prints on this job site, but then he never did.

As he slid back in the saddle, his satellite phone began to vibrate. Farkas cringed. He knew who it was without looking.

He removed the ear bud connected to the police scanner at his waist and gave the canal a scratch before activating the wireless satellite phone receiver in his other ear. "Yeah."

"Are we happy?"

"Not yet."

"Tell me."

"Call me back in an hour. We should be happy then."

"Tell me now."

Farkas was not in the mood for this, but he knew who buttered his bread. "A fight broke out at some hick bar named Moonshines. It ended with two dead teenage tourists and a roomful of drunken locals all pointing the finger at each other. The entire third shift of the George Town Police Department was called in early and asked to report directly to the scene."

"The entire third shift?"

"That's only half-a-dozen cops. Oh yeah. Did I mention the bloody hurricane?"

There was a long pause, followed by, "Where are you now?"

"I'm staking out the police garage from a bus stop across the street."

"A bus stop? You're not in a car?"

"They've been using a scooter, so I have been too. Only way to match their maneuverability. Bloody things are everywhere here, and fortunately they fit under bus stops."

Again a pause. "So our friends are in place, but undiscovered?"

"Right," Farkas said. "I expected discovery over an hour ago. Who would have predicted a double-homicide in paradise? I mean, what are the odds?"

"Tell me you set the flasher to max and erased the full twenty percent?"

"I did. These two are much too clever and resourceful to play patty-cake with. Troy will have lost about seven years of memory, Emmy six. Poor bastard will think he's still in the army. She'll believe she's still eking a living off the streets of L.A."

"Good. How long since the flash?"

"That's the problem. Three hours."

"Shit."

"Yeah. I've been monitoring the police scanner. They're wrapping up at Moonshines. I'm expecting a full house any minute, but we're cutting it close." As he spoke, the streetlight above the garage began to dance. For an instant Farkas thought it was an optical illusion caused by wind and rain, but experience quickly superseded. He cursed. His blood sugar had dropped dangerously low.

Farkas had passed out a few weeks back in a Chicago hotel lobby. He'd been waiting for the elevator after an early morning run when the room started spinning. Then the marble floor hit him in the face. He woke up in the hospital with a raging headache and a pancreatic tumor. An insulinoma. Benign but requiring regular and frequent anti-insulin injections to avoid hypoglycemia. Operable in the long term and not a big deal in the short. He already carried an insulin injection kit. Camouflage for the tool of his latest trade. All he had to do was exchange the insulin for anti-insulin and then actually start poking himself four times a day.

"I gotta go," he said, hanging up on his boss without waiting for acknowledgement.

The reminder alarm on his watch had startled him just as he was liberating the cop's soul from his body. He had twitched and nearly put a bullet into Troy as well. With Troy dead or injured, all his trouble would have been for naught. Farkas had slapped the beeper off without thinking—three hours ago.

Eager to correct his mistake, Farkas pulled a black leather pouch from the left cargo pocket on his shorts, unzipped it, and laid it open on the seat of the scooter between his legs. He selected the silver injector pen—not the black; even in a hypoglycemic haze he could never make that mistake—and cocked the mechanism.

His satellite phone began to buzz again.

He ignored it.

He was pulling up the tails of his black silk shirt to expose his favored injection site when the light across the street actually did start flashing and the garage door began ascending.

"Govno!" Farkas cursed in his native Croatian. He stuffed his shirt back into his shorts as he studied the opening door. Could Troy and Emmy really be escaping? He would prefer swarms of locusts.

The anti-insulin would have to wait.

He dropped the injector pen back into the pouch and stuffed the pouch back into his pocket without taking his eyes off target. He pushed the starter and brought the scooter to life. For what seemed a full minute the garage door stood open but empty, like a hungry mouth. Farkas was about to move in for a closer look when a squad car tore out and turned in his direction. Number thirty-seven. Detective Sergeant Johnson's. Flat tire and all.

As the car raced past him, Farkas caught a glimpse inside. Troy was no longer in the trunk. He was at the wheel, with Emmy once again by his side.

It was a shame, Farkas thought, pulling the scooter out in dark and silent pursuit. He had gone to some trouble to get the meddlesome pair life in prison. By fleeing the scene, Troy and Emmy were only outsmarting themselves. They had just upgraded their sentence to death.

Chapter 6

Radiation

THE RAIN DIMINISHED to a light drizzle while they bathed off their bloodstains, but the wind refused to let up. Now the gale threatened to blow Emmy over as they trudged the waterfront in search of safe harbor. She was tempted to walk behind Troy, to use his broad shoulders as a windbreak. But she had been burned before by taking the back seat, so she stayed by his side, confronting the elements head-on and taking three steps for every two of his.

"You're pretty handy with a weapon," he said, his eyes continuing to sweep their surroundings, his tone inquisitive.

Truth be told, Emmy was baffled by her own behavior, and more than a little scared. "To the best of my knowledge, that was the first time I ever touched a gun."

"Really? You fooled me. And Captain Honey too."

"I just did what they do on TV."

Troy shook his head. "There was more to it than mechanics. You radiated enough competence to bluff Dirty Harry."

Emmy debated how much to tell her accomplice as they crunched along the roadside stones. It did not take her long to conclude that the biggest secret of her life was already on the table. "I've been doing that since I was fourteen. Had to … to survive."

"Doing what?" he asked, turning toward her with a hint of understanding in his eyes.

His expression encouraged her to open up more than she generally would. "Radiating competence," she replied. She was about to elaborate when he grabbed her arm and pulled her further back from the road with a shush.

They crouched behind a cluster of palms.

Ten seconds later a police car drove slowly by, lights off. Troy obviously had excellent hearing. Or, she reevaluated, perhaps his mentor had focused on skills very different from radiating competence.

"How far do you think we've come?" she asked, as they resumed their trek.

"The swimming pool's just over two kilometers to the southeast."

"Sounds far enough to me," she said, pointing ahead to a pink neon vacancy sign.

The Seagull's Nest was on the cheaper side of the road, away from the water. To her it looked perfect. Not too big. Not too small. Not too fastidious.

Troy scanned the area before returning his gaze to her. "Too risky. The police will be checking all the hotels. Besides, I only have eighty Cayman dollars. I'm not sure what Cayman dollars are worth, but judging by the prices posted at the Gas-N-Go next door it's less than an American dollar. We'll probably need all eighty for food and a change of clothes." He nodded, implying game, set, and match, and turned to continue their march.

"Hold on a minute," she said. "You've been calling the shots ever since you got behind the wheel and I relinquished the gun. I've been happy to go along this far because you seem to know what you're doing and I didn't have a better plan. But now I do have a better plan."

He stopped and turned, thrusting his dimpled chin forward like a lance. "What's your plan?"

She did not really have a plan yet, per se. But she had needs. "I don't care about food or clothes. I need someplace to gather my thoughts in peace. I need to get dry and I need to get some rest."

"If you don't change your clothes, you're going to be gathering your thoughts in prison and getting nothing but rest. Those pink shorts you're wearing mark you. Mark us. Don't worry though," he said, his expression softening. "I will find us someplace safe to get some sleep. You'll feel better once the sun comes up. Then—"

Troy stopped talking as a couple emerged through the motel's lobby door twenty yards ahead. They faded back into the palm copse and watched as the young woman made her way to one car and the older man unlocked another. The couple was obviously done, with each other—and with their room.

Now Emmy had a plan.

"I'm going to get us a room," she said, leaving no uncertainty in her voice. "Anonymously. And I won't need any of your money." Without waiting for his reaction, she turned her back and began unbuttoning her shirt.

Emmy knew she looked a mess. She was still completely drenched from the rain and their blood-cleansing dip. Her hair was flat and damp, and she bore not the slightest remnant of makeup. But she also knew that most men would not notice those finer details if something more alluring was on offer.

She took off her shirt and then her bra. She gave both a good wringing and then donned her shirt while holding her bra between her knees. She fastened only the middle button and then tied the shirttails so that they knotted just under her breasts, augmenting her cleavage while exposing her toned midriff. Her breasts were not huge, but they were large and pert enough to make a wet white shirt an irresistible attraction for most pre-geriatric men. Checking the results in the reflection of a parked car's window, she decided that if six years had indeed passed, they had not been overly cruel. She turned back around to test her hypothesis.

Troy did not disappoint her.

"Hold this," she said, handing him her wet bra. "I should only be a minute."

Emmy turned back around before Troy regained enough composure to comment, and headed for the lobby door. She used the interval to put herself in the proper mindset. She was cold, drenched, exhausted, and beyond confused, but she needed to appear sexy and carefree. That would hardly be a piece of cake, but Troy's flaring irises helped to boost her confidence. And, after all, she had been there before.

Emmy gave the outside of the motel the once over. If this were a corporate hotel or normal operating hours, she would have done some reconnaissance before plunging in. She would have tried to get a look at the key rack, or the logbook, or she would have walked the grounds to determine which of the two-story complex's forty or so rooms were occupied. But she was too tired for that, and frankly, she did not feel the need. It was approaching three AM on a tropical island: amateur hour.

She breezed into the lobby and made straight for the bell on the counter. After confirming the location of the key-drop slot, she adjusted her cleavage while the air-conditioning did its trick. Then she slapped her cheeks to add some color, read the name plaque on the wall, and gave the bell a jingle. Twenty seconds after her second ring, a sleepy-eyed forty-something male emerged from the room behind the counter. The instant she caught his eye Emmy knew that her assumptions were correct.

"May I help you, Miss?"

Emmy put her hands on her hips, arched her back and shook her head in self-reproach. "I'm so sorry to disturb you at this hour, Anton. Problem is, I've been such a fool. I just tossed my key in the drop slot but left my purse in the room. Would you mind fishing it out for me?"

"Ah ... sure. What was your room number?"

She had no idea what room the prostitute and her John had enjoyed, but she suspected that a military-minded man like Troy would want the high ground if there was a choice. "Oh, I don't remember. Twenty-something I think. It's on the key."

She stood on tiptoe and leaned over the counter toward him while inclining her head toward the drawer that caught the keys. Anton pretended to be considering her request as he soaked up an eyeful, but then pulled open the drawer without further comment. After a second glance at her soaked shirt and a quick appraisal of her pouty lips, he fished out the only key. "Twenty-seven?"

"That's it. Thank you, Anton. You're a doll."

Chapter 7

Into the Fire

FARKAS SKIDDED the black scooter to a stop on the gravel lot of Whitfield's Fish Market & Restaurant. He dismounted in the shadow of Whitfield's delivery truck and removed his helmet. The air had gone sweet again after the storm but the smell of yesterday's fish lingered here. It was unpleasant, but nonetheless reminded Farkas that he was hungry.

He unslung a long slim case from his shoulder and slid it atop the truck. He was about to follow it when his satellite phone began to buzz. He checked the luminescent dial of his watch. Three AM. Luther had waited two hours—double the time frame promised. Farkas had to answer. He activated the wireless unit in his ear. "Yeah."

"Are we happy … yet?"

"Very happy."

"Tell me."

Farkas backed away from the truck for a slow three-sixty audiovisual scan before uttering another word. The wind brought him snippets of banter from a few distant beach bums, but no other signs of life. This section of the coast was delightfully deserted. "You will recall that the original plan was to have them caught covered in blood in the dead cop's car, with the murder weapon and corpse and gunshot residue on their hands?"

"But no alibi," Luther added.

"Right. A perfect frame but for the lack of witnesses and motive."

"Go on," Luther said.

"We now have a witness, an ideal witness—not to the murder itself, but close enough. They restrained another officer at gunpoint during their escape."

"Excellent. Did the security camera catch it on tape?"

"No. The cameras are on the outside of the garage, angled to capture faces as people enter and exit. But the officer they humiliated was a captain. Head of the second shift."

"Does he have them now?"

"Not yet. I'm about to see to that. Although from what I've been hearing between the lines on the police scanner, this has become a shoot first, ask questions later scenario. The captain's account of what he saw them doing to Detective Johnson really shook everyone up."

"How long until they're caught?"

"Fifteen minutes."

"No chance of their escaping—again?"

"Not a prayer."

"I want details," Luther said.

As a rule, Farkas never shared the details of his work with anyone, but the fresh taste of crow loosened his tongue. "I'll do you one better. You can listen in—quietly. It might do you some good to get a taste of life in the field."

"Listen in on what?"

"You'll see."

Farkas crossed the dark road to the pay phone in the Gas-N-Go parking lot. He practiced speaking with a raised voice and island twang before dropping in three coins. "Yes, hello officer, this is, well, I'm not sure I want to say. I've been listening to my police scanner—you see I have this condition that just doesn't let me sleep. My husband, he says that, well, it doesn't matter. I was calling to say that I just saw a couple whose description exactly matches the fugitives you described in connection with the 11-99. Clothes,

color, height, everything. They just walked into the Seagull's Nest
Motel on South Church Street. If you hurry, I'm sure you can catch
them."

He cradled the receiver without waiting for the inevitable
questions. Then he gave the receiver a superfluous wipe. No sense
tempting fate.

"Nice," Luther said. "What now?"

Farkas had been so focused on his work that he had forgotten
Luther was listening. "By my calculations, the first squad car will
arrive within three minutes. I've got to hurry into position."

"Position for what?"

Farkas said, "Plan B," as he jogged back across the street to
Whitfield's parking lot. He used his scooter as a step stool to climb
atop the delivery truck without leaving a telltale print on the hood.
Odds were, Mister Whitfield would drive his truck to the docks
before dawn, taking the crime scene with him, but Farkas liked to
be meticulous.

"I'll be using the new toy you bought me," Farkas clarified,
pulling the silenced Heckler & Koch sniper rifle from its custom
carrying case. Remaining prone on the roof, he twisted the stock
into place, then attached the trigger unit and Hensoldt scope. He
slapped in a five-round magazine, put a couple of beanbags under
his forearms for support, and sighted in on the Seagull's Nest. The
lobby's aluminum door handle looked close enough to touch. "If
our friends outmaneuver the cops again—there's no way I can
miss."

Chapter 8

Pride

CAPTAIN HONEY leaned over the pier's broken rail and watched the dark waves slap the barnacle-crusted supports. His flashlight revealed no sign of Evan's car, but he knew it was down there all the same. Honey reached again for the weapon that wasn't there and cursed. He crouched to diminish his profile, keyed his shoulder mike and spoke through gritted teeth. "Molly, this is Honey. I'm at the end of the harbor pier. Looks like our perps took Evan's car for a swim."

"You think they drowned?"

"I'm not that lucky."

"You want me to wake up Sherwood?"

"Oh yeah. Nobody's sleeping until that couple's in jail. Have Sherwood bring diving gear for me too. Tell him I want to be in the water in fifteen minutes." Honey would gladly get wet for the chance to recover his Colt before submitting his report.

"Will do," Molly said. "Does that mean we can release the suspect couple Huey brought in?"

"Hell no! Not till I've seen them. Give 'em coffee and tell them I'll be there as soon as circumstances—"

"Hold on," Molly interrupted. "I've got an emergency call coming in."

Honey stood and wiped the drizzle from his face with a soggy handkerchief. What a miserable night. His first week wearing captain's bars and he ends up with his pants around his ankles.

He looked back down at the water. In all likelihood, his former partner was down there sloshing around in the submerged trunk. A friend and family man with twenty years of service reduced to fish food. How fragile we are …

He shook his head. Esther was a widow now. Martha had nearly become one too; Honey wasn't kidding himself about that. That pixie of a woman had seemed eager for the trigger. If his bladder had not been empty, forensics would now be cataloging his puddle of piss. Retirement would have been his only escape from that humiliation.

"We got a break, Captain," Molly's voice came back on, all squeaky and excited. "A woman monitoring police channels just reported seeing a couple matching your description enter the Seagull's Nest Motel on South Church."

Honey's hopes surged for a second but then his brows narrowed. "That's awfully convenient," he said. "Let me guess; she called from a payphone and didn't tell you her name."

"Right on both accounts. What you want to do?"

Honey thought about it for a moment before answering. In all likelihood, it was a diversion. The woman who called was probably the perp herself. "Which payphone did she call from?"

"The one in front of Gas-n-Go, right next to the motel."

"Really? Well, all right! Tell Sherwood to dive without me. Have Leroy and Bobby join me at the motel. Tell them to come locked and loaded."

Chapter 9

Dive

TROY FELT the dynamic of their situation change as he swung the privacy lock into place behind the door to room twenty-seven. Until that moment, all his thoughts had been on escape and evasion. But now that he was no longer moving, he could feel his mind shifting gears. He was eager to begin unraveling the mysterious ball of twine that entangled him and his remarkable companion.

As he scanned the room hoping to find a coffee pot, an eruption of gushing water broke the silence. "I hope you don't mind if I go first?" Emmy said, her voice echoing off the bathroom tile. "I really need a hot soak."

"Don't you think we should discuss things first?" Troy asked— biting back an offer to join her in the tub.

"You already told me that you don't know anything."

"Yes, but—"

"I've got a six-year memory void," she pressed. "I don't know anything either—except that I'm in no condition to be playing Sherlock Holmes. I'm cold, tense, and scared. I doubt that there's anything you can say or do to alleviate the scared. A long hot bath, however, will do wonders for the cold and tense. So, I'm going to have a good soak, and then I'm going to get some sleep while my clothes dry."

Troy stared in disbelief while the mirror fogged, digesting this unexpected twist.

"Then in the morning," Emmy added, "when our minds are

fresh, we'll sit down over breakfast and try to figure things out. How's that for a plan?"

Troy searched for the right words, but apparently his muse was still stuck in the trunk. In frustration he voiced the first coherent thought that popped into his head. "This isn't British colonial warfare we're waging. We can't just lay down our sabers and muskets to enjoy a refreshing cup of afternoon tea, confident that our enemies will be similarly distracted. Captain Honey, the man you brought to his knees with your gun, you can bet that he's not taking tea. Nor are his subordinates. Nor are the people who left us with the corpse in the car."

"Look," Emmy said, hands on the curve of her hips, chin jutting forth in a defiant stance that seemed strangely familiar. "Thanks to some bold moves on both our parts, we are finally out of immediate danger. It's three in the morning and nobody has a clue where we are—ourselves included. Now, I'm no doctor or expert on British colonial warfare, but it still seems pretty obvious to me that the smart move is to use this time to recoup and reconnoiter so that the next move we make is not straight into a waiting trap."

Although her words carried weight and her posture remained aggressive, whatever spark she had shown the night clerk had extinguished. She looked to Troy like a half-drowned kitten. The sight punctured his resolve and he nodded. "Go ahead."

She said "Thanks."

Troy found himself looking into the mirror on the back of the bathroom door. His thirty-eight-year-old hair wasn't sprinkled with grey yet, but crows had begun scratching around the corners of his eyes. The big change was on his forehead. Two v-shaped scars descended below the hairline over his right eye, one for a centimeter, the other for nearly two. Their color was still an angry red, meaning they weren't more than a year old. He probed them with his fingers. A few months, he guessed. Half a year. They ran for another couple of inches under his hairline. "One more reason not to go bald," he muttered. Since he did not know his parents, he didn't know what hairline to expect as he aged, but so far, so good.

Turning from the mirror, Troy looked around their sparse room. It appeared darker without Emmy's presence. There was no television to offer company or news. He put the heat on high and set the blower to full. Since he was too wound-up to begin recouping, he slipped behind the curtains for a little of that reconnoitering Emmy had vaunted. The window turned out to be a sliding glass door. It opened into the waist-high railing of a faux balcony.

The road they had trudged in on was to his left, and there was a Gas-N-Go to the right. He did not know what lay further down the dark street beyond, but he should. He needed a map—and he knew where to get one.

He said, "I'll be right back," to the bathroom door, getting only a relaxed "Mmmm," in response. He found the lobby dim and quiet but for the night clerk's snoring. He was halfway to the rack of advertising brochures when a kaleidoscope of red and white lights erupted on the wall before him.

The sight sent another traumatic jolt down his spine. He snapped reflexively into a defensive posture, but quickly recovered his poise. He crept forward and peeked out the lobby door just as two police cars slid to a stop on the motel's gravel lot.

Troy reacted so quickly that he probably made it back to the room before the cops had set their parking brakes. He ran straight to the bathroom and threw open the door. Emmy was still in the tub, with only her face and knees above the water. Her eyes had been closed but now they were open wide. "The police are here! We have to go—right now!"

He grabbed her sopping clothes off the floor and bundled them up in a towel as he spoke. She was still lying wide-eyed in the sudsy water when he finished so he reached in, not knowing what part of her he would get. "We'll jump out the sliding glass door. The main entrance is already covered. Get your shoes on—the rest can wait."

She scuttled into her Reeboks as he pulled her toward the sliding door. They slipped behind the curtains and he carefully slid open the door. There were three police cars outside the lobby now, a mere fifty feet away. The few palms and bushes that haphazardly marred the parking lot between them promised pitifully little cover, but the Jeep parked below their window offered some hope. "I'll lift you over the rail and lower you down," he whispered.

Before he could act on his words, she jumped up and over the top rail, using her left arm as a fulcrum. She ran her right hand along a supporting rail to control her fall and then dropped seamlessly from the bottom rung. As she hit the ground, a bullet punctured the stucco where her head had just been.

Troy knew that the cops had not fired. After two tours in a combat theater he had a sixth sense about such things. He also knew better than to waste a single second searching for the sniper. He just dove.

Chapter 10

Opportunity

FARKAS PEELED BACK his eyelids to see stars. Real stars. As his vision adjusted and his mind sought solid ground, a dark face moved into his line of sight, replacing Orion's belt with a knit cap and dreadlocks. "You okay, mon?"

The peculiar dialect snapped Farkas out of his daze. Where was he? The last thing he remembered was taking a shot at Emmy from atop a delivery truck. Had he been flashed? Had Luther finished with him and decided to cover his tracks? No, Farkas concluded. If that were the case, he would have no memory of Luther or mind-flashing or the woman. "What happened?" he asked.

"You passed out, mon."

"That much I understand. What I want to know is why."

"I dunno fa sure," the Rastafarian replied, his tone more amused than concerned. "I was walkin' along mindin' my own business when I saw you lyin' besides da truck. I didn't see no bottle or smell no booze, so I went to check your pulse and saw da medical alert bracelet. I fightin' da sweet-blood myself." The Rastafarian held up a wrist to reveal his own red aluminum band. "So I guessed yous ran outta juice. It happens on da islands when people get to drinkin'. I gave you a dose from one of da needles in your pocket."

"Which syringe did you use?" Farkas asked, his eyes flaring wide.

"Calm down, eh. I understand dese mattas. De vial in da silva pen had a Lilly label. De vial in da black one had no markins at all, just de unusual red color. Never seen dat before, and I seen a lot."

"What did you—"

"I gave you da silva. Like I said, mon, no worries." The Rastafarian handed him back his pouch. "Perhaps you'd like ta share da black?"

Farkas accepted the pouch. It was zipped up, but he could feel both injector pens through the leather. He had been a fool to let this happen. If "Rasta" had not wandered along and taken an interest, he might have slipped into a diabetic coma. It was an amateurish mistake, getting so caught up in the thrill of the chase that he forgot to take his meds. He looked up and met Rasta's eye. "Thank you, friend. But believe me, you don't want to be sharing the black."

Rasta held up his hands. "No worries."

Farkas got slowly to his feet, pretending to be short of balance so he could scan the area surreptitiously. First he checked to be sure that the two of them were alone, then he swept the ground for signs of his sniper rifle. That eighteen pounds of fine German craftsmanship was worth a cool twelve grand. And it was nowhere in sight. Either Rasta had stashed it, or it had slipped from his grasp before he toppled from the roof of the delivery truck.

He reached into his back pocket and withdrew his wallet. The fact that it was still thick more or less confirmed that his rifle had not been purloined. First things first, right? He pulled out five one-hundred dollar bills and handed them over to his new friend. "This has been embarrassing," he said. "I'd like to forget the whole evening ever happened—especially if anyone should come around asking questions."

Rasta enthusiastically nodded his complete agreement. "I hear ya, mon. Consider it forgotten."

Farkas would, but not because he trusted in solidarity among society's outer fringe. Rasta would undoubtedly spend the next twenty-four hours smoking, shooting, or snorting his new wealth. For short-term memory loss, that was just as effective as a NATO 7.62 mm round—or a shot of Luther's 456.

Rasta left quickly once the money was in his hand, no doubt worried that Farkas might realize that the bills were hundreds instead of tens. Fifteen minutes later, Farkas, Heckler & Koch checked into the Starlight Motel as Mr. and Mrs. Smith.

The room's phone caught his eye the moment he opened the door, and he felt a twinge in his stomach. He looked at his watch. Four AM. What the hell.

Farkas had never met Luther. He did not know what he looked like or where he lived. He assumed that Luther called the United States home since all of their business was there, but in the electronic age he could just as well live in Australia or Switzerland. In any case, Luther's secrecy gave Farkas the luxury of ignoring time zones when he called.

Luther picked up on the second ring. "Tell me what I want to hear."

"I can't do that yet. I … had a problem."

"Spare me your excuses and cut to the chase. Where are they now?"

"I don't know."

"You don't know? Well, that's just great. That sounds like the same kind of carelessness that cost you your medical license. No wonder your people always lived under the heel of someone else's boot. Some folks just never learn."

Luther liked to hurl emotional barbs. Farkas was immune to them. He had seen too many bones broken with sticks and stones. "Relax, Luther," Farkas said, his voice as calm and icy as a frozen lake. "We have nothing to worry about. They have no resources, no clues, no idea what's going on. The only thing they do know is that they have to avoid the police. They are either going to get caught, or they are going to disappear and then do everything in their power never to be heard from again. Either way their investigation is kaput."

Luther chuffed. "Is that your stellar insight talking? The same prescient voice you've been listening to all night? Well, let me assure you that one can always find a third option if he gets creative enough. And since Troy and Emmy have shown themselves to be a cross between Sherlock Holmes and Leonardo DaVinci, here's what you're going to do. Are you listening?"

"I'm listening."

"Good. For the next two days, you are to keep your eyes glued to the entrance to Solomon's. The way I look at it, within forty-eight hours they're either going to get caught or they're going to flee Grand Cayman. There just aren't enough places on that tiny island for them to hide with the police believing that they've killed a fellow cop. So, if they don't show up at Solomon's by close of business Friday, then we'll assume they've fled. Until then, you're on lookout. Got it?"

"Got it. What then?"

"Then you're to get your ass on a plane to Las Vegas. Check into the Bellagio and wait for instructions."

"You got a new case?"

"I've got reason to believe one is coming."

"In Vegas?"

"In Vegas."

Farkas smelled an opportunity and seized it. "All right. But as long as we're painting by numbers now, why don't you tell me exactly what you want me to do if Troy and Emmy make a miraculous appearance?"

"We're done with half measures. You're to make use of your new twelve-thousand-dollar toy."

Bingo. "Fine. I'm willing to play it that way, if that's what you want. But given the potential need for clean up that might involve, you'll need to send me more 456."

There was a long pause on the phone before Luther said, "I'll send you the dose you'll need for the job in Vegas. That will give you two in hand. If you end up using both on Grand Cayman, I'll send another one to Vegas with the file."

Farkas knew that Luther hated to part with 456. His boss feared that he would set up his own business on the side. He was right to be paranoid, but wrong in his assumption. Farkas had grander plans.

Oddly enough, it was not the threat of competition itself that worried Luther. The market could absorb a thousand times what he supplied. He was just paranoid that word of his secret memory-erasing concoction would leak.

Farkas decided to play one fear against another. "That's not good enough, Luther. To guarantee that I can keep things totally quiet, I should have at least four doses at my disposal. Better six. We've never had to deal with a situation like this before. It's unpredictable. Without 456 it could get messy. Raise uncomfortable questions."

Luther forced another long pause. Farkas knew that he had him. "All right. I'll overnight you three more doses. But I expect regular updates. Every six hours. Agreed?"

"Agreed."

Chapter 11

Form

TROY AND EMMY did not speak during their desperate sprint from the Seagull's Nest. All oxygen went to fueling their legs, and fear froze their tongues.

After ten breathless minutes of putting turns and obstacles between themselves and their hunters, they emerged from a tropical forest onto a crumbling old access road behind a small strip mall. Troy slowed to a walk and Emmy bent over to gulp air with her hands on her knees. He was glad to find that he had maintained a marathoner's legs over the past seven years. Emmy, too, was in remarkable condition—not to mention spectacular form. "You're in better shape than most of the soldiers I know," he said. "I'm impressed. Really."

She shifted her gaze up from the ground to meet his. Her emerald eyes were skeptical but they brightened when she saw the sincerity on his face.

He smiled, adding, "You're much stronger than you look." He extended the bundled towel holding her clothes. "Slip between those dumpsters and get dressed," he said, gesturing. He pulled his olive safari shirt off over his head and held it out. "You can use this to wipe the muck off your legs."

"That's a nice gesture, Troy, but I can just use the towel." She waggled the bundle of clothes.

"Oh, right ... well ... I'll just climb up onto the mall roof then —make sure that they're not tracking us."

"Tell me one thing before you go," Emmy said. "How did you

handle it—waking up locked in a cold dark box full of blood with a corpse? I thought I was going to lose my mind and all I had was a gun and a bit of blood on my clothes."

Troy cocked his head. "Tommy McGuffin locked me in the kitchen dumpster on the eve of my ninth birthday—the start of Labor Day weekend. I spent two dark days and three darker nights terrified that worms would wriggle into my ears or I would suffocate from the gas of rotting cabbages. Can't say that I considered what Guffy did a favor at the time, but …" He shrugged. "Now clean yourself up. It may seem like we've been through a lot, but I suspect that our adventure has just begun."

When he dropped back to the ground a few minutes later, Emmy was dressed. "Coast's clear. We should get moving, but I'll need your watch first."

She handed her Tissot over with a query in her eyes.

"I assume we were simply followed to the motel by whoever actually killed Detective Sergeant Johnson, but we may have been tracked by electronic means." He threw her watch into the woods, followed by his own. "I also need your shoes."

Emmy's look turned to one of horror. She was no doubt imagining what their mad dash would have been like barefoot. "Don't worry," he said. "I didn't have the tools necessary to open the watches, but I can visually inspect the shoes. You'll get them back."

As he busied himself washing the muck off their shoes in a puddle, she said, "Who shot at us?"

"It wasn't the police. They use pistols and shotguns. That was a silenced rifle shot."

"You could tell?"

"I've been to war."

"Don't the police have snipers?"

"They do in big cities. I doubt they would have one here, not a pro anyway. Plus the cars I saw were obviously reacting to a tip.

Whoever shot at us was already in position when they arrived—no doubt because he called them."

"So our troubles have doubled—and just when I thought they couldn't get any worse."

"In the short term, perhaps," Troy concurred. "But this is actually great news."

She looked up at him with shock in her eyes. "By what convoluted reasoning is having a sniper after us good news?"

"I'll tell you later," he said, finishing with her shoes. "You can put these back on."

"No concealed tracking systems, explosives or microphones?"

Sweet and saucy, Troy thought. "No, nothing but foam. We can keep moving. Now that we know they can't locate us electronically, our best move is to put quick distance between ourselves and the Seagull's Nest. We're ahead of them for now, but that advantage will evaporate if they bring in dogs." He looked up from tying his laces. "Island cops probably have helicopters at their disposal too—commandeered from all the sightseeing tours."

"So where do we go? How do we hide from helicopters and fool dogs?"

"We double back in the direction we came from and steal some boardwalk bicycles from a beachfront hotel. Then we cross to the other side of George Town and head for Seven Mile Beach while it's still dark."

"And then what?"

"Don't worry. I have a plan."

Chapter 12

The Postman Always Rings Twice

FARKAS STUDIED the whitewashed four-story residence with an assassin's eye. Deep shadowed balconies with walled sides faced the wide avenue from every apartment, and the northern exposure meant the sun was always to its back. The building was perfect.

So were the people.

Unlike the guarded luxury high-rises that fought the hotels and restaurants for space along Seven Mile or West Bay, or the cheap-but-cheerful inland complexes rented by the poor-but-proud working class and secured by Smith & Wesson, number twelve Elisabeth Avenue housed the locals who had managed to climb to the middle rungs of island society. They were the shop owners, junior bankers, and real estate agents whose toil created the backbone of the Cayman economy. For the next two days, one of their quiet, undefended, unsuspecting homes would host his surveillance operation—and maybe more.

After a final glance at his watch, Farkas drained his espresso and stood. He had waited until nine-thirty to make his move so that most of the residents would be gone for the day. This left him only thirty minutes to get into position before Solomon's opened, but he liked working under pressure.

He had narrowed the selection to three apartments on the second floor. Each boasted a balcony that suited his needs, offering both the concealment and the alternate egress without which he would not operate. The final choice would depend upon the occupants.

His earlobes and fingertips began to resonate with a familiar tingle as he crossed the palm-lined avenue. The moment had come to pick the winner.

He timed his approach up the cobbled walk to hold the front door open for a housewife exiting with her dog. He gave her a friendly nod as she passed, and then stepped into the empty foyer. Certain that there were no security cameras inside, he removed his sunglasses but not his Kangol cap. Along with the beard, it would remain in place until he left the island.

He put his duffel bag down on the clay-tiled floor and set to work on the locks of the mailboxes for units 2A, 2B, and 2C. They were typical five-pin cylinder locks. Each presented not more than a few seconds' challenge for the tension wrench and pick held in his smooth, practiced fingers. Having warmed up on the first two, he even got the third plug to turn with nothing but the initial rake of the tumblers. Oh, that the rest of the day would go so smoothly, he mused.

Thanks to what must be the world's most ambitious postman, Farkas found letters in each of the first two boxes along with advertising flyers. The third had already been cleared out. He picked the three most personalized letters from the first two, returned the rest, and closed the boxes.

So far, so good.

He took the stairs to the second floor and then spent a minute listening at the doors of all three apartments. He heard a child crying in 2B, the unit that had already collected its mail, and ruled it out. Either 2A or 2C would have to do.

His knock on 2A was answered in short order by a woman whom he took to be the maid. "Mrs. Rocha?" he inquired, not sure if he should be pronouncing it with an h or a k.

"No," she said without further explanation. "What do you want?"

Farkas spotted a yellow banana peel in the bag of trash beside the door and decided that this was not just a monthly maintenance cleaning. Someone would be coming home this evening. "This letter was placed in my box by mistake. I'm new to the building so I thought I would take the opportunity to meet my neighbors."

"Do you not think that tactic would work better in the evening, when people tend to be home?" she asked, accepting the envelope.

Farkas's desire to fade quickly from memory overruled the impulse to crush her larynx, so he simply said, "Yes, I suppose you're right. Sorry to disturb you."

He turned and headed up the stairs, making enough noise that she could not help but hear. He waited on the third floor landing for ten seconds after hearing her door close and then walked quietly back down to 2C.

"May I help you?" asked the withered woman who opened to his knock. Before he could respond, an equally gaunt gentleman joined her. Mr. Wooten was naturally much taller than his wife, but osteoporosis had bent his spine into a question mark, so he peered out through the crack at shoulder level.

"Good morning. You must be Mrs. Wooten. I'm Warren Christopher." Farkas repeated his previous spiel and then proffered the letters with an expectant smile. With his peripheral vision he spotted a little cart for wheeling groceries propped off to the side of the entrance hall—evidence that they got by without outside assistance. Excellent.

"You get Jamison's old place?" Mr. Wooten asked, his voice crackling but friendly.

"I believe so."

"He was a good man, Jamison. Why there was a time—"

"How about a cup of tea?" Mrs. Wooten interrupted, opening the door wide.

"Why, thank you. That would be lovely." Farkas lifted his duffel bag up from behind the doorframe and entered. "Is it just the two of you living here?" he asked, setting the bag down inside before turning to bolt the door.

"For forty-two years now," Mr. Wooten said, obviously pleased to have the opportunity to take the lead in the conversation while his wife studied the bulky bag.

Forty-two years, Farkas repeated to himself. The teakettle wasn't even on the stove, and he had already learned everything he needed to know. "I'm afraid I have some bad news for you ..."

Chapter 13

Charles

FOUR HOURS AFTER their mad dash from the police and sniper at the Seagull's Nest, Troy and Emmy were looking at what he suspected was the finest hotel on Grand Cayman: The Imperial. A taxi had just disgorged an elderly couple dressed to the nines, indicating the arrival of the morning's first flight. As The Imperial's bellhop busied himself loading the extravagant vacationers' seven bags onto a trolley, the valet waited patiently by the curb, no doubt hoping that the next guests would arrive by rental car. Troy sympathized.

He rose from the park bench where they were seated, smoothed the front of his shirt, and said, "I trust you'll think of something clever if this goes wrong."

"Have I ever let you down?" Emmy asked, also rising.

"Not that I remember."

They both stood in silence for a moment, digesting the new meaning of that everyday remark. Then Troy rolled his thick shoulders, turned and made a beeline for The Imperial's valet as the bellboy followed his patrons inside.

Noting his purposeful approach, the valet came out from behind his gazebo. Troy realized his mistake a second too late. To the locals this was paradise, not a combat zone. He needed to act relaxed, to take the snap out of his stride. Of course, this time around the cat was already out of the bag. He had about a second and a half to find another way to keep the valet close enough to the wall that no one could spot them from the lobby. Recalling another trick from his youth, he held up his left hand in a vague gesture.

The bellboy paused, his face crinkled in confusion.

Once Troy had narrowed the gap to three steps he looked up at his hand, waving and flaring it like a magician making something disappear. As the valet followed the movement with his eyes, Troy closed the final step between them and put a crushing right uppercut under his jaw. The valet's head crashed back and his legs went limp. Troy caught Charles beneath the armpits as he fell and dragged him back behind the podium.

Troy quickly stripped off his own tired rags and donned the valet's pressed white clothes. He was halfway there. Now he just needed a rental car to arrive before the bellboy returned.

Looking across the street from behind the valet stand, he caught Emmy's eye. As she gave him the thumbs up from the park bench, his plan hit another snag. Two cars arrived at the same time.

Both guests drove rental Toyota Camries, one white, the other gold. Thinking fast, Troy went first to one passenger door and then to the other. White was in front, and it contained another elderly couple, well dressed and fit. Gold contained a couple much closer in age to himself and Emmy but with waistlines two to three times their girth. Troy then went around to the driver's side of each car. He smiled and handed each man a ticket stub while repeating the same phrase: "Welcome to The Imperial, Grand Cayman's finest resort. Please proceed to reception. I'll see to your car and have your bags in your room before you've stopped soaking in the view."

To Troy's relief, neither sleepy-eyed gentleman gave him a second glance. They just pressed ten-dollar bills into his hands and grabbed their wives by the arms. Since the security camera looked in on cars exiting the circular drive, Troy hopped into the gold car and backed out.

"Well done," Emmy said seconds later as they pulled out onto the A1. "Now what?"

Troy accelerated, eager as always to put distance between them and their last stop. "You tell me. Find us a map."

She did. "The island is shaped kind of like an elf's shoe. We're on the long curlicue toe now, also known as Seven Mile Beach. West Bay is north at the tip of the toe and George Town is south at the base. Savannah is on the ball of the foot and Bodden Town and Breakers are both on the arch off to the east. Looks like West Bay is the biggest town after George Town. And it's not far. Let's turn around and head there, get off the road." She tilted the map in his direction and pointed.

"No good," he said with barely a glance. "The toe is a dead end. Besides, we'll be okay for at least another fifteen minutes. Let's use them to buy fifteen miles. We'll go there." He pointed to Bodden Town. "Major roads to the east and west, minor ones to the north, and a port to the south."

"Okay. I'm guessing it will take us about thirty minutes. Perhaps while we drive you can finally tell me why you think it's great news that there's a sniper after us?"

Troy looked over at Emmy and studied her face for a minute before answering. The sun was up now and it added a sparkle to her pale skin, giving him the impression that it really was made of alabaster. She met his gaze with her sprightly green eyes. "Two reasons," he said. "First of all, it means that we didn't kill the cop."

"How so?" she asked with dubious intonation.

"Because it confirms that a third party is involved—a third party with a gun."

Emmy pressed the tips of all ten fingers together and stared into space through the tent they formed. After a minute she said, "You're making a lot of assumptions."

"That's unavoidable. But I'm also applying Occam's Razor, going with the simplest, most obvious explanation."

"That's why you were so quiet these past few hours," Emmy said. "You were working all this out."

"I gave it my best shot."

"How about cutting to the chase."

"All right. I think someone tried to kill us because their attempt to have us locked up failed."

Emmy processed his assertion for a moment and then asked, "Why not just shoot us in the first place? Why lock us up instead?"

"There are lots of potential reasons," he said, bouncing his head slowly from shoulder to shoulder as he recycled various scenarios through his mind. Picking a favorite, he asked, "Did you ever read the Count of Monte Cristo?"

"Of course."

"Do you remember why Edmond Dantes was imprisoned in Chateau d'If?"

Emmy thought about that for a minute. "You think someone wanted us locked up on an island to keep a secret?"

"I don't know, but that makes more sense to me than anything else I can come up with. Anyhow, this brings me to the second reason I said it was great news."

"And what's that?" she asked.

"Neither you nor I have any idea how we ended up in that car, or on Grand Cayman, or even what we have been doing for the past six or seven years of our lives. But we do know one thing for certain."

"What's that?"

"The sniper has those answers."

Comprehension dawned on Emmy's face like a mountain sunrise. "So how do we find him and get him to tell us without dying in the process?"

Troy shook his head. "I have no idea."

Her countenance darkened a shade. "Wonderful."

"But I do know where we should start …"

"Where's that?" Emmy asked.

Troy pulled off the motorway onto a scenic overlook and motioned backwards with his head. "In the trunk."

Chapter 14

Kanasis

OLIVER HORTON waited patiently for the willowy six-foot blonde to situate herself, his newfound appreciation for the simple-things-in-life attitude keeping his hand off the horn. First she stretched and leaned over her teal convertible this way and that, adjusting what must be Versace's entire fall collection until the shiny black bags lined up just so in the back seat. Then she moved on to set up her diamond-collared poodle with his treats and sippy cup in the passenger seat. Ridiculous displays like Miss Trust Fund's used to drive Oliver nuts, but now that he was faced with two-to-twenty behind bars, he lapped them up.

Oliver pulled his rented Mercedes into the parking spot as BRIANA3 pulled out, and then looked up at his destination's unlikely façade. Wendell had warned him that Kanasis was different. Different in style. Different in technique. Different in results. But aside from implying that Kanasis would charge him a seven-figure fee, Wendell had been uncharacteristically nebulous when pressed for details about the lawyer's work. It was as though his old Harvard roommate was at once proud and frightened, like a kid who found a loaded gun.

Dewey, Cheetam & Howe was not plastered high in bold letters as Oliver had imagined while boarding the plane in Vegas. Nor was Kanasis grandiosely displayed like the trademark of a French designer who had found a way to sell thread for more than its weight in gold. This Rodeo Drive address simply had KANASIS chiseled vertically into the black granite pillars that framed the armored glass door. Tasteful. Permanent. Proud.

Unlike the windows of its neighboring boutiques, which leading designers had painstakingly arranged to draw gazes and pull people in, Kanasis had fronted his office with mirrored glass. Passersby could still see in if the lights were on and they focused their gaze, but most of those who strutted past in their thousand-dollar shoes were no doubt pleased to see only their reflections. Oliver cupped his hands around his eyes and peered in.

Plants and sculpture occupied the foreground, bestowing a sense of virginal serenity. Not a bad tactic, he mused, given what Kanasis was selling. Beyond the Garden of Eden, Oliver saw legs. Two. Long. The perfectly sculpted flesh drew his eyes like a candle in the dark. His throat went dry as he followed them all the way up into the skirt of a twenty-something angel. She was sitting before a computer monitor typing away, oblivious to his stare. Two more points for Kanasis, Oliver thought. Having seen the reception, he was most eager to step inside.

He pried his eyes from the glass and took a firm grip on the thick brass cylinder that served as a door handle. His pull yielded no reaction at first, but after a momentary delay the heavy glass plate swung outward as though it weighed but a pound, and he stepped into an entry hall walled in mirrored glass. As a building contractor, Oliver recognized the system as one jewelers often used to inspect and approve their clients. The short, mirrored hallway ended in a second door, identical to the first except that it was hinged on the left. Again, he grabbed the brass cylinder and again the door released after a momentary delay. Another electromagnetic lock.

As the second door swung shut behind him, Oliver turned toward the heavenly receptionist. She smiled pleasantly back at him. "Good afternoon, Mr. Horton. I'm Kimber. Are you here to see Mr. Kanasis?"

Oliver stood there like a deer caught in halogen headlights, partly because Kimber was probably the single most beautiful woman he had ever met in the flesh, but mainly because the goddess knew his name. Apparently, Wendell had warned Kanasis that he might be coming. Kanasis had then passed that information along to Kimber, who had gone online to pull his picture off the Internet so that she would be ready when and if he walked through the door. Now that was the kind of service you expected for seven figures, not to mention a mark of great efficiency. Oliver was already thrice impressed and he had barely stepped past the threshold. This was a promising start. "Ah, yes. Mr. Kanasis. Is he available?"

"Just a moment and I'll check. Feel free to have a seat or enjoy the art." She made a sweeping motion with her long thin arm, forcing Oliver to rip his gaze from the natural beauty to the manmade variety.

As he was trying to form an opinion as to whether the watercolor in the opposite alcove was an original Renoir or a print, he overheard Kimber say, "I have an Oliver Horton here to see you."

He turned back around to find that she was again smiling at him. "May I ask who sent you?"

"Well, nobody, really. I—"

Kimber began shaking her head before he could finish. "I'm sorry. What I meant to ask was who referred you?"

"Oh, ah, Wendell Branson. But Mr. Kanasis obviously knows that."

Kimber's lips curled up as though reacting to an inside joke, but she just said, "Wendell Branson" into her headset. Then she nodded in agreement, giving Oliver the feeling of exclusive acceptance. "You're in luck," she said, standing as she addressed him. "Please follow me."

Oliver followed, working hard to keep his tongue off the Persian carpets that covered the hardwood floor. Watching Kimber, he was finally beginning to understand why a lawyer would spring for a

Rodeo Drive address. Aware that he risked meeting Kanasis in a state of full salute, Oliver gave himself a mental cold shower by diverting his attention to the decor. They passed several more alcoves, each adorned with an Impressionist watercolor, and several stately office doors, each flanked by pedestals supporting arrangements of fresh flowers. At the end of the hall, Kimber stopped before an elevator. She pressed a big brass button and stepped aside as the door opened.

Oliver thanked Kimber—most sincerely—before stepping inside and pressing the button labeled "K." The only button. Nothing happened after the door closed, at least as far as Oliver could tell. Either it was one of those incredibly smooth elevators, or it was just sitting there. He looked down at his watch. Fifteen seconds, thirty, a minute. He pressed the button again. Nothing. Two minutes. Three. Paranoia began to take hold. He sniffed the air for gas or smoke but detected nothing. He wanted to pound on the door and shout for help but did not want to appear cowardly to Kimber, so he focused on his breathing. In ... out ... in ... out ... After four minutes he backed into a corner and grabbed the handrails lest the floor should drop out to reveal a shark tank below.

After four and a half minutes, the doors slid silently open to reveal a palatial office. Feeling somewhat foolish but decidedly relieved, he stepped immediately inside.

Kanasis's workspace covered the same footprint as the entire first floor. A big hyacinth macaw greeted him with, "Welcome" from a perch directly across the room beside a granite bar. A floor-to-ceiling slate waterfall gurgled along the wall to his left between two exotic palms. To his right was a fireplace flanked with a suite of black calfskin chairs. Beyond them, beside a window that looked out over some of the world's most expensive real estate, stood Mr. Kanasis's enormous oak desk. It was unoccupied. The only person in the room with Oliver and the bird was another impeccably dressed assistant who was busy working the espresso machine behind the bar. This assistant was a good decade older than Kimber, and, alas, torn from the pages of Gentlemen's Quarterly rather than Harper's Bazaar.

"Espresso, Mr. Horton?"

Oliver looked at his watch. Ten fifteen. Normally he refused caffeine after breakfast, but he had been feeling pretty self-indulgent since learning that he was headed for the slammer. "Please."

The assistant nodded appreciatively and began brewing. Oliver noted that he moved with the grace of Baryshnikov and considered the possibility that he had studied to become a dancer. You couldn't walk your poodle from the spa to the psychiatrist in Beverly Hills without tripping over a beautiful Hollywood wannabe and spilling your chai infusion all over your Manolos. Perhaps that was why everyone drove. This guy had a face too—California surfer meets Wall Street broker, with carefully disheveled sun-bleached hair, a permanent tan, hazel eyes, and a square jaw, all topping a lean athletic build that was tastefully wrapped in a tailored suit. Dark chocolate with a caramel shirt. No tie.

After grinding the beans, the assistant asked, "What brings you to Kanasis?"

Oliver would not normally deign to discuss such personal business with an underling, but there was an intensity in the assistant's stare and a confidence in his voice that Oliver found at once compelling and disarming. "Two counts of manslaughter."

The man nodded as though he heard this every day. "What are you looking at?"

"My attorney back in Las Vegas, Tiberius Fitch of Fitch & Mathers, tells me that the best deal he can negotiate is four years."

"Minimum sentences for involuntary manslaughter, consecutively served. That's a very good deal, Mr. Horton. But not good enough, I take it?"

Oliver felt his hopes begin to fade as he nodded. "Concurrent cuts it down to two. I could live with two. I was expressing that sentiment to an old friend the other night over a bottle at the Sportsman's Lounge. He grilled me on the details for twenty minutes and then suggested that I pay you a visit."

"I'm glad he did," the assistant said, handing Oliver his espresso with a twist.

Oliver accepted the cup and saucer with polite thanks. It was delicious and the head rush immediate. "Wendell told me that Mr. Kanasis is something of a miracle worker."

The GQ model nodded graciously. "I appreciate the endorsement. In fact, I only work with referrals. Makes things so much more efficient, more … civilized." He took a slow, deliberate sip of espresso. "As a matter of fact, if I agree to consult on a case, I guarantee my client's satisfaction with the outcome. Why don't you have a seat and we'll see if we have a good fit." He motioned toward the calfskin suite.

The speaker's use of the first person hit Oliver like a slap in the face. This was Mr. Kanasis? Was it possible that the young Adonis who just fixed his drink had once been voted the California Bar Association's Man of the Year? Oliver looked down at the espresso in his hand as he reddened. He wondered what the beverage was worth at Kanasis's hourly rate.

Kanasis stood quietly through Oliver's moment of revelation. Clearly this was not the first time someone had mistaken his identity. Once Oliver had regained his composure, Kanasis held out his hand and said, "Call me Luther."

Chapter 15

Luv

TROY DROVE the coastal highway between George Town and Savannah while Emmy rummaged through the burgundy suitcases in the back seat. "I should have taken the other car," he said. "The couple was old, but at least their clothes would be wearable."

"No, you got it right," Emmy said. "Fat people can diet, but old people can't get younger."

"What are you talking about?"

She turned to meet his eye. "I'm talking about IDs."

"Did you get a look at the couple driving this car? They were enormous. We can't use their identification."

"Sure we can, if they were foolish enough to leave any in their bags. People rarely study ID pictures as long as the skin color is right and there's no glaring discrepancy. Who wants the bother? Not me. Next please. Trust me; I know a thing or two about using fake IDs."

An approaching truck kept Troy's eyes on the road, and it was probably just as well. He did not have the energy to keep up a convincing poker face while pondering Emmy's latest revelation. Struggling to keep his tone neutral, he asked, "How is it you know these things?"

"I'm a grifter," she said, with the casual, almost breezy air of a waitress mentioning the soup of the day.

Troy could hardly believe his ears. This bright, beautiful, courageous woman was a self-proclaimed grifter. Perhaps he had his definitions confused. "Like someone who cheats at cards?" he asked.

"Like an entrepreneurial actress."

"An actress," Troy repeated. That was rich. "And what do entrepreneurial actresses know about fake IDs?"

"We tend to run in the same circles as entrepreneurial artists."

"Oh, I see," he said, not seeing at all. He reminded himself once again that she was the one who awoke holding the murder weapon. He also recalled that the sniper had aimed for her head, not his. Maybe he had been wrong about her. His mental acuity was hardly at its best.

His tone must have betrayed his feelings, because Emmy snapped, "Don't judge me. I've been on my own since I was fourteen, doing what I had to do to survive. Just like you did today." She sat back, folding her arms across her chest.

Troy hated it when people said things like: I did what I had to do. There were always options; choices to be made. She may have lost her home at fourteen, but she still enjoyed fourteen more years than he had … Troy stopped himself. Got down off his horse. He reminded himself that he had been headed for jail rather than college until one kind soul intervened. Sure, he could swap stories with Oliver Twist, and he had worked incredibly hard after getting his one break, but it was that one lucky break that made all the difference. He needed to give Emmy one now.

Troy's thoughts were interrupted by the sound of Emmy rummaging around in the suitcases again. As he dared a look in the rearview mirror, a navy Nike baseball hat flew from the back and landed on the gear shift. A pair of sunglasses followed, then dark socks and black tassel loafers. "Size ten," Emmy said. "I saw that you're ten and a half but those should fit in a pinch."

"Are we in a pinch?" Troy asked, trying to lighten the mood.

"I think this counts."

Emmy continued to pull useful objects from the suitcases like a magician producing fluffy creatures from a hat. She got a white sun visor and Nike tennis shoes and a wraparound bathing suit cover-up that could replace her distinguishing pink shorts.

She made the change behind him and then climbed back into the passenger seat holding a fanny pack. She unzipped it and cooed. "Traveler's checks. Looks like about five-thousand dollars worth."

"Do you know a thing or two about those as well?"

"I do."

Troy was glad it was traveler's checks and not cash. He was feeling bad enough about stealing the suitcases as it was.

"Well, look at this," Emmy said, her excitement in crescendo. "Passports." She opened one and then the other. "You're Jeffrey Gordon. I'm Elizabeth. We're British, luv." She held Mr. Gordon's passport open so he could see the picture. As he looked over to examine it he saw Emmy go pale. She whispered, "Oh my god."

"What is it?"

"The issue date on these passports is July 19, 2005."

There it was, Troy thought. Confirmation. "What's the date on the Cayman Islands stamp?"

Emmy leafed through the pages until she found the right one. "4 September 2008," she said softly. "The day after Evan's petrol purchase."

Troy remained silent while Emmy digested the news. He had more or less accepted the fact that he could not account for the last seven years, that those memories were at least temporarily inaccessible. He had seen and felt his healed abdominal scar. But Emmy had apparently still been harboring hopes of a conspiracy theory.

"There's no way these were forged to fool us," Emmy said. "I really am thirty-two."

Troy reached over instinctively and rested his hand on her firm thigh in an offer of support. "Beats thirty-eight," he said. "And with the three-year gap since the Gordons' pictures were taken, your weight loss story becomes plausible. We can claim that we came to the islands to celebrate losing a hundred pounds."

He felt something wet on his hand and realized that Emmy was crying. He gave her thigh a little squeeze and she placed her hand over his. They entered Bodden Town in silence.

Troy kept his eyes peeled for the right kind of hotel, but did not have any luck. Before he knew it, they were seeing signs for Breakers. He pulled the Camry into a Marriott and started snaking through the parking lot.

"We should pick a smaller hotel," Emmy said. "The management is more likely to be flexible, and there will be fewer people to see us."

"I agree. But I wanted to stop here first." He parked next to another gold Camry. After ensuring that nobody was looking or headed in their direction, he got out and tried his key on the other car's door. It did not work.

"Did you really think it would open?" Emmy asked.

"You would be surprised at how few variants there are within a brand—at least there used to be when I was a kid, and more entrepreneurial. Regardless, the main reason I stopped was to switch license plates. Once the cops find a gold Camry with the license plate they're looking for, they'll call off the search. We'll be safe driving until they figure out they've been hoodwinked."

"So, you weren't always a high and mighty physician?"

"No. My life was once headed down a very different path." As he spoke, Troy used the tip of the ignition key to unscrew the clean Camry's plate and replace it with their tainted one. The procedure was so quick that he decided to take an extra minute to swap plates again with a neighboring Jeep's, adding another layer of confusion. "We'll be off the island by the time they untangle this triple play."

"You seem very sure of yourself."

"You should talk, Miss On your knees!" Troy said, sliding back behind the driver's seat.

As he was pulling out of the Marriott, Troy stopped suddenly and put the car in park. "Hold on a minute," he told Emmy. He got out wearing Jeffrey Gordon's sunglasses and ball cap and approached the driver of a waiting cab. He handed him the two tens he'd earned as a valet and said, "Pop the trunk."

The driver did as asked and Troy transferred the Gordons' suitcases to the taxi. Before closing the trunk he went back to the driver. "You got a pen and paper?"

"Yeah, mon," the driver said, handing him a clear Bic and a Post-it from a local real estate company. Troy went back to the bags and scribbled a note, slipping it inside the carry-on before wiping it and all the bags off with a rag from the trunk. "Please deliver those three bags to The Imperial. Mr. Jeffrey Gordon is expecting them. He's a big tipper."

"Jeffrey Gordon, The Imperial. Okay, mon."

Troy patted the roof of the cab and the driver pulled away.

"That was risky," Emmy said as he slid back into the Camry. "But very nice. What was on the note?"

"I told them that we'd mail their passports back to the hotel before they had to leave. You did say that their return tickets are for the twenty-second, right?"

"Yeah, mon," Emmy said with an appraising look in her eye.

They stopped just outside Bodden Town at a beachfront hotel called the Pirate's Cove. Troy pulled in when he saw the sign advertising private bungalows. "What do you think, Mrs. Gordon?" he asked, affecting a perfect British accent.

"Looks good to me, luv," Emmy replied in kind.

Troy nodded his head toward the CayMart convenience store on the other side of the street. Its windows were flush with bright, hand-painted signs boasting American Cigarettes, Cold Beer, Calling Cards, and Checks Cashed. "What about signing the traveler's checks? Are entrepreneurial actresses good forgers as well?"

Emmy donned Elizabeth Gordon's sunglasses, then pulled a pen from the glove box. "Give me two minutes to practice, luv, and Elizabeth herself wouldn't notice the difference."

Chapter 16

Tricks

AS HE ACCEPTED Luther Kanasis's firm hand, Oliver was struck by the thought that the attorney had encouraged his misperception. Luther had played to Oliver's preconceptions in order to slip behind his defenses and have an unguarded look around. No doubt this tactic served Luther well as an attorney, but Oliver suspected that Luther did it more for the sport.

"Tell me about your case," Luther said, motioning to the suite of chairs.

"What did Wendell tell you?"

Luther cocked his head. "Wendell? Nothing. A few days ago he phoned to say that I might be getting a client from Vegas, but he didn't even mention your name much less the details of your case. In fact, I had to call him while you were in the elevator to ensure that it was you he was vouching for."

Oliver noted that Luther used the word vouch like a Sicilian. He found himself fearing that this suave man might have a very rough side. He would follow up with Wendell on that point. For the time being, however, he was captivated by Luther's promise of guaranteed satisfaction—not to mention intrigued by Kimber's clairvoyance. "But your receptionist, she knew my name?"

"Parlor tricks, Oliver. Simple parlor tricks. Please. Time is money and the clock is now running."

Oliver laid out the details of his case over the next forty-five minutes with little interruption, selling it as best he could. Luther listened intently, using hand gestures rather than speaking if Oliver rambled or wandered to points deemed irrelevant. It was as though the lawyer found the sound of his own voice disruptive. Once Oliver had aired his whole sad story, however, Luther stepped in to summarize. "Given the facts as you present them, the prosecution's case hinges on the testimony of the site foreman, Matthew Lopez?"

"That was Fitch's conclusion as well," Oliver concurred.

"There's no physical evidence? No security video? No tape recording?"

"None." Oliver shook his head vehemently.

"So at worst they've got you for criminal negligence—until Mr. Lopez ups it to manslaughter by testifying that you specifically ordered the use of struts known to be faulty in order to complete the job on time."

"Right."

"In order to earn your bonus."

Oliver felt himself reddening despite the fact that he was talking to a lawyer. "Right. Look, Lopez is just a glorified construction worker. I, on the other hand, was a major contributor to the governor's campaign, and am a friend of the mayor."

Luther let that appeal sail past without a glance. "And this happened in Clark County, Nevada?"

"Yes."

"And the judge assigned to the case is Owen Rodgers?"

"Yes."

"And the prosecutor is George Hue?"

"Yes."

"And assuming that you don't take a plea bargain, your trial is set to start three weeks from tomorrow?"

"Yes."

Luther paused to think, staring into his espresso cup. After a long moment of silence, Oliver could no longer hold back. "Can you do it, Luther? Can you help Fitch get me two years?"

Luther looked up, his hazel eyes afire. "No."

The finality of Luther's verdict hit Oliver like a slap in the face. He suddenly felt dizzy. He had let his hopes rise. Two years was manageable. He had come to accept that. But four years, more than a thousand days: that crossed a line. He would be a different man when he emerged. If he emerged. He would not fare well in prison as a rich white man whose greed for a bigger bonus killed two poor Hispanic kids.

"No," Luther continued, "two years would be virtually impossible to plea-bargain in this political environment. Fitch was right about that. In fact, the four he already negotiated is a hell of a deal—no doubt due largely to your contacts. But if you place your faith in me, if you turn down the prosecutor's offer and go to trial, I can get you off."

Chapter 17

Scars

THE CAYMART CLERK was a skinny white male with a greasy ponytail and teeth that would have embarrassed an old mule. Troy watched him ogle Emmy unabashedly as she approached the counter.

"Good morning," she said, seemingly unfazed by the stare. "I'd like to cash some traveler's checks, Earl."

Earl said, "We charge three percent," and kept right on staring.

Emmy produced a plastic envelope from Mrs. Gordon's fanny pack, counted out four hundred-dollar checks, and then added a fifth as if by afterthought. "Do you have a pen I could use?"

Earl grabbed one from the side of the register and asked, "Do you have ID?"

"Sure," Emmy said, accepting the pen before withdrawing Mrs. Gordon's passport from the fanny pack. She laid it off to the side of the counter and began signing checks. When she finished, she stacked them neatly and handed the pile to Earl with a smile.

Earl accepted the checks with his left hand and scooped up the passport with his right. He opened the passport to the picture page and ripped his eyes from Emmy long enough to study the photo.

Emmy said, "Gotta love that Atkins."

Earl did not comment. He just shifted his attention to the traveler's checks and sorted through to the fifth one Emmy had signed. After another tense moment he said, "To my eye, the signature looks perfect. To my nose ... not so much. And then there's the picture ..."

Emmy reached over the counter and took the passport and checks from Earl's hand. He did not resist. He just gave her a surprisingly penetrating stare and said, "I could ignore my nose and cash all the checks you want, but there would be an additional fee involved."

Emmy stared back at him, her expression noncommittal.

Earl answered without further provocation. "Fifty percent."

Five minutes later, Troy and Emmy left CayMart with six Snickers bars, twenty-five-hundred dollars in cash, and the agreement that Earl would not process the checks until his shift ended at three that afternoon.

"You should check in alone," Emmy said. "They'll be looking for couples, and single women raise more questions than single men."

Troy did, and shortly thereafter he was admiring their bungalow's king-size bed. "You want the left side or the right?" he asked, testing the springs.

"What are you doing?" Emmy asked. "We don't have time to sleep."

"I'm not going to be much good without it," he replied, aware of the reversal in their positions but too tired to care. "Just a thirty-minute catnap to recharge the processor."

Emmy did not yield, and before he knew it Troy was behind a table in a semicircular beachfront cafe called The Grotto. He was looking out at sugary sand and crystalline water while a waitress informed him that, "Stingrays be swimmin' there at the edge of the shelf where the water changes from turquoise to indigo. Morays and octopi too. What will you be having? I recommend the lobster omelet with brie and papaya salsa."

Troy looked over at Emmy who nodded. "We'll take two, along with the bakery basket, orange juice and coffee."

She poured the coffee into waiting white mugs and disappeared. As Troy stirred in cream, he tried to find the best kickoff question for their let's-get-acquainted conversation. He knew a lot about Emmy's character, but little about her biography. Her choice of profession left him halfway between concerned and enthralled, and he could not help wondering if her work had somehow caused their predicament. It was on that sensitive topic that he wanted to start, but Emmy beat him to the punch. "I lied to you earlier—in the garage."

Troy managed to swallow his sip of coffee without choking, but only just. "How so?"

"I ... I ... I really couldn't have changed the tire in five minutes. I've never changed a tire in my life."

Troy exhaled.

Emmy smiled. "Just wanted to jump-start your processor."

"You did that."

"Good. Tell me, what's the last thing you remember?"

Troy added another creamer to his coffee and took another sip. "Afghanistan. I'm—I was—a military surgeon who was stupid enough to volunteer for the Special Forces after my first tour with a forward surgical team. I was tired of seeing corpses that had bled to death on the battlefield. Figured I could save a lot more lives if I was at the scene."

"That sounds almost suicidal," Emmy said, her face a mixture of admiration and concern.

"I convinced myself that it wouldn't be that much more dangerous because the Green Berets are so highly trained. But as time went by and death and injury thinned the ranks, replacements came from deeper and deeper down the barrel. Many weren't what we call tab qualified. Weekend warriors who had been given the beret without all the training. One such reservist, an accountant from Paducah called to active duty, made an amateur mistake and triggered a booby trap. He literally and figuratively kicked a bucket —one that the Taliban had packed with silverware and explosives.

"The accountant and two other soldiers were instantly shredded.

I got a fork in my belly, and four others were similarly lucky. The last scene I remember is looking down at the inch of protruding aluminum handle as it siphoned off my venous blood like a spigot." Troy held up his fork with a piece of lobster omelet speared on the end. "I'll never forget the joy of pulling that baby out and stuffing gauze in its place to staunch the bleeding. I remember giving myself a morphine shot and running to help Captain Chapman, but nothing more.

"I must have passed out.

"When I awoke locked in Evan's trunk, my assumption was that I had been captured by the Taliban. But when I found the healed scar after seeing the dates on Evan's documents and evidence that I was on Grand Cayman, I put the pieces together."

"Incredible. Did you get the scars on your forehead then too?"

"I don't know when I got those, but they're fresher than this." For some mysterious reason, he felt uneasy talking or even thinking about his forehead scars. He wanted to change the subject. "Tell me, what did you think had happened when you first woke up?"

"I thought I had been kidnapped by some South L.A. gang. Waking up in a strange dark car spattered in blood, with a gun in my lap and a jackhammer in my head, it was ... horrible. Let's talk about something else. Do they teach you about memory loss in medical school?"

Troy nodded appreciatively as he worked to swallow the remainder of his croissant. "We studied the brain and the functions assigned to each of its various lobes. After combat I'm also very familiar with the psychological manifestations of cranial trauma. What we have is called episodic amnesia. We don't remember certain experiences—in our cases those from the past six or seven years—but we do remember biographical data and skills, so our semantic and explicit memories are intact."

"Is there a cure?" she asked.

"I don't know for sure. Memory involves billions of neurons

and trillions of neural connections. Much of their function remains a mystery—or at least it was seven years ago. Anyhow, if the neurons themselves are damaged, the memories are likely gone forever. If it's a matter of bad connections, like what Alzheimer's patients suffer, we can get those memories back if we heal those connections or establish new ones."

"Is there a pill for that?"

Troy shook his head. "Unfortunately, it's not that kind of headache."

"I take it we can assume that we don't have Alzheimer's, or some other naturally occurring condition?"

"No, we can't assume that. For all we know, we could both be patients of the same clinic. If I got Alzheimer's or some other similar disease at this age, I would seek out the best clinic on Earth. Perhaps we both did and that's how we came to be together on Grand Cayman—you from L.A., me from Afghanistan or wherever the army had me."

"Do you believe that?" Emmy asked.

"No. Clinics don't dump you in a car with a dead cop ... unless perhaps they've injured you in some failed secret experiment and want to cover it up."

"I could never have afforded a fancy island clinic," Emmy interrupted.

"Drug companies often pay for your treatment during clinical trials, but I agree that scenario is a long shot. Still, it can't hurt to check the phone book for clinics when we get back to our room."

Emmy shrugged. "So you favor the alternative—that someone intentionally did this to us?"

"I think that's the most logical conclusion given the violence that has followed us. But to anticipate your next question, No, I don't know how they did it."

Troy finished off his omelet while Emmy digested his words.

Emmy finally set down her own fork and said, "In the movies

it's always either a whack on the head or brain surgery."

"Every whack on the head is different. That could account for one of us, but not both."

"Well, then it's obvious what we need to do next."

"What's that?" Troy asked.

Emmy tilted her head to the side and flashed him a breathtaking smile. "Check each other for scars."

Chapter 18

Cop Killers

HONEY DISMISSED the last of the eleven couples his colleagues had scooped off the streets with a shallow word of thanks for their cooperation. Eight hours into the chase and he had nothing. The murderers had vanished.

"You get the security photos yet?" he asked, coming up behind the staff secretary.

"Shouldn't you be sleepin', Captain?" Susanna replied, swiveling around in her chair and looking at him over the top of her glasses.

"I'll sleep when they're behind bars. Meanwhile, I'll thank you to answer my questions without editorial."

Susanna's cheery features dimmed. Honey knew he was being a grouch, but didn't care. He would apologize when the job was done. "Oscar just sent them," she said, pulling a grouping of four photos up on her computer screen and proceeding as though he could not see them for himself. "We got three-quarter and profile shots of both the man and woman as they pulled out of the garage, but the resolution is poor. The low lighting and rain-streaked car windows didn't help either."

"I know what the lighting was like. I was there."

"Yes, captain."

"Take this down," he said, stepping around to the front of her desk. "He's mid-thirties, height about a meter eighty-five, weight about eighty kilos. Blue eyes, dark hair cut like a politician's. He's got two v-shaped scars descending just below the hairline above his right eye, and a big old dimple on the middle of his chin like Kirk

Douglas. Last seen wearing running shoes, khaki shorts and an olive shirt. All bloody. Got it?"

"Got it," she said, her French-manicured fingers still tapping keys.

"Good. Now the woman. She's about thirty. Tiny, say a meter and a half high, forty-five kilos. Got bright green eyes and thick dark shoulder-length hair. Last seen wearing tennis shoes, pink shorts, and a white button-down top—also blood-spattered. Both are to be considered armed and dangerous, even though I did recover the guns."

"Got it. What you want me to do with the descriptions?" Susanna asked.

"Paste them beneath the photos and make me wanted posters. I want every law enforcement and customs officer on the island to have a copy within the hour. Put COP KILLERS on the top in big bold letters."

"What about taxis? I can drop off stacks at the cab companies, and they can pass them out to the drivers when they come in."

Honey was impressed. He took his fidgety fingers from his Adam's apple and said, "Good idea. But add a bold note that no civilian should try to apprehend them. They should just call 911 as soon as possible. Do the same for the marinas. And don't forget the charter flights to the Sisters," he added, referring to Little Cayman and Cayman Brac. "For once it will work to our advantage to be an island. If we get a lock on transportation, it's just a matter of time till they're rotting away in my jail."

Chapter 19

SBT

"WHAT'S YOUR FIRST NAME?"

Troy opened his eyes and looked down at the lady shaking his leg. She had roused him from a deep dreamful state, and he found himself struggling to resurface. As she came into focus, he had the strongest feeling that she was the wrong woman. She should be taller and blonde, and her eyes turquoise blue instead of emerald green.

Then, quick as a blink, the disorientation evaporated. Everything came back to him—the trunk, the sniper, the loss of seven years—and Emmy. "We didn't find matching scars, did we?" he asked, referring to their inspection of each other's scalps. He reached up reflexively and ran his fingertips across his forehead. "We've still got no clue as to the cause of our collective amnesia."

"I did find another angry scar on your scalp," Emmy said. "But unlike the forehead scars, you knew where it came from. You told me it was from a bicycle chain, the remnant of one of your weekly rows with Tommy McGuffin. As for me, I don't have any scalp scars at all."

Troy nodded, remembering.

"Then I crashed," Emmy added, "while you, apparently, went shopping." She stood up, held out her arms and twirled, exhibiting the jade Pirate's Cove polo shirt and khaki shorts that he had purchased in the gift shop. "You did a good job guessing my sizes."

"I had a pretty good look at your body."

The expression on her face told him that a change of topic

would be a good strategic move, so he rolled up into a sitting position and said, "What was it you asked me?"

"Your first name. I had assumed Troy was your first name, but I see now that it's your last."

Troy wondered how she could possibly see that. When he hesitated, she mistook the reason and added, "You know my sizes; surely I can know your name."

"Sebastian. My first name is Sebastian."

Emmy nodded. "Not the best name for a skinny kid with mismatched eyes growing up in an orphanage."

"How'd you know I was skinny?"

"Lucky guess," Emmy said with a wink.

"I forgot," Troy said. "That's what you do. But seriously, how did you know Troy was my last name?"

"Your tattoo."

"I don't have a—" Troy stopped himself. He pulled up the sleeves of his Pirate's Cove polo to check his shoulders. Nothing. He checked his calves and ankles. Again nada. Where else could it be? Had she checked his butt while he was sleeping?

Emmy headed off that embarrassing train of thought by saying, "It's on the bottom of your left foot. Pretty strange place for a monogram if you ask me."

He crossed his left leg over his right knee and took a look. There it was, plain as day. Two palm branches arced around the initials SBT. The tattoo was in an unusual place, Emmy had been right about that, but the location was not the strangest part.

"Do you remember getting it?" Emmy asked.

"This is odd."

"That's what I said. Plus you don't strike me as the tattoo type. An officer and a gentleman and all that. Tattoos speak volumes, so I pay a lot of attention to them. It's not just what a person chooses, but where he or she puts it, the color, size, quantity. They're—"

"No," Troy interrupted. "I mean—I don't have a middle name."

Emmy put her hands on her hips. "Come on, it's Bartholomew, isn't it? Sebastian Bartholomew Troy. You can tell me."

"Seriously. No middle name."

"Huh. So you don't remember getting it?" Emmy repeated.

Troy looked back down at his foot. "There's no way that I could. This is a henna tattoo. They don't last more than a month."

"You're up on your body art," Emmy said, more to herself than to him. "That's surprising." She snapped her fingers after a moment of thought. "Henna is all over the place in Asia and the Middle East, including, I presume, Afghanistan. Am I right, doctor?"

"You are."

They both stared at the tattoo in silence for a minute. Then Emmy said, "Perhaps the initials are your wife's?"

"I'm not—" Again Troy cut himself off. Seven lost years ... Was there a Sara Beth Troy out there somewhere, worried sick?

Emmy reached out and took his left hand. She held it up. He was wearing a gold band. How had he failed to notice it earlier? "Oh my ..."

"I know," Emmy said, holding up her own left hand. She was not wearing a ring, but looking closely Troy could see the pale indentation where one had recently resided.

They both sat in silence on the edge of the bed as the implications ran the first lap of what promised to be a long course. Had they been having an affair? Was the dead cop moonlighting as a detective sent by one of their spouses to get incriminating photographs? Were they married? Was it possible that he did not remember his own wife? What if he had kids? The questions were maddening. A man could go crazy just thinking about the possibilities.

He ran his fingers over the tattoo in an effort to refocus his thoughts and another possibility entered his mind. "Is Emerald Green your real name? Or is it a professional name?"

"A professional name?" Emmy asked, her tone bordering on

belligerent.

"Yeah," he added quickly. "Like Norma Baker's Marilyn Monroe."

"Emerald Green is my legal name."

"Oh."

"But it wasn't always," she added with a grin that betrayed her false indignation. "For the first fourteen years of my life I was Carly Jo Andrews."

Troy had wanted to hear her say Samantha Brie Andrews or Sandy Brooke Andrews more than he was comfortable admitting even to himself. To cover his embarrassment he turned his attention back to the tattoo. "Forgetting the discrepancy with the initials for a minute, why in the world would I ..." His speech trailed off as he spoke, leaving his last words barely audible.

"What is it?"

After a moment of silence, Troy looked up at her, excited. "If you knew that someone was going to erase your memory, what would you do?"

"Run. Fight. Hide. Depends on the situation."

Troy shook his head and then reached out to take her hands in his. "I would try to send myself a message. Wouldn't you?"

Emmy's eyes grew wider. "Of course. Like in that Schwarzenegger movie Total Recall."

"Or Christopher Nolan's Memento. That's actually the last movie I remember seeing."

They both turned their gaze to Emmy's left foot. She kicked off her new sandal and crossed her leg. Another henna tattoo stared back at them from her sole, this one a series of twelve digits: 004995625425.

Chapter 20

Impressions

LUTHER LOOKED OVER at his new client, thrilled, but hiding it. Contrary to all appearances, he needed Oliver's money. Desperately. And the greedy contractor's case fit Luther's rules to a T. "Did Wendell mention my fee?"

Oliver still had the glow of a man delivered from the gallows, and he answered accordingly. "Yeah. He led me to expect to pay seven figures. You got it."

"Good. You do understand that the million is just my consultation fee? Fitch will still be your lead council. You will still pay for his services as before. Just tell him that Mr. Lopez's testimony will no longer be a problem—without reference to me."

"I understand."

"Did Wendell mention anything about how you were to pay me?"

"How? No. But cash is no problem."

Luther held up a hand. "The million is payable immediately to an offshore account, and is fully refundable if you do not hear the words, not guilty."

"Fair enough."

"In exchange, I expect, I demand absolute discretion. Is that understood? You are never to mention this payment nor our agreement to anyone. Not Wendell. Not Mr. Fitch. Not your wife. Not your accountant. Not your priest. No one. Ever. Is that clear?"

Oliver nodded.

"Say it, Oliver."

"It's clear. No one is to know of our arrangement. Ever. But how are you going to—"

"Don't ask."

"It's my money, I have the right—"

"And I have the right to refuse your case. You are only here as a favor to Wendell. It's not as if there's a shortage of wealthy individuals needing legal miracles." Just those whose case hinges on witness testimony, and who have no other legal issues or addictions, and who are appearing before a prosecutor and judge I haven't already cheated.

Oliver responded by sitting silently with his head bowed and his fingers tented.

Luther saw the move for the hollow threat it was. Oliver might be one of Las Vegas's top building contractors, but Luther could make him jump on one leg and cluck like a chicken if he chose to do so. He was the only man on the planet selling get-out-of-jail-free cards.

"Are you in, Oliver, or out?"

"I'm in. I'm in. Just tell me this much: it's the judge, isn't it? You've got a relationship with Rodgers; an understanding, don't you?"

"I've never met the man," Luther said with a shake of his head. "Never even heard of him."

"Come on … then why did you ask?"

Luther decided to throw his new client a bone. "I asked because, like any good magician, I never perform my trick twice before the same audience. It is precisely because I don't know Rodgers that I accepted your case."

"So it's some kind of trick?"

"Ask again and you'll never see it."

"Okay, Luther, okay. I just want to be sure it's reliable. A million dollars isn't what it used to be, but it's still a lot of money."

"It's not money, Oliver … It's four years."

The words had their intended effect, and Oliver sagged back into his chair, slack-faced and nodding.

Luther let the sentiment sink in for a moment and then stood to end their meeting. "When you have everything set up on your end, give me a call and I'll give you an account number with strict instructions. Be sure you follow them to the letter, and then forget them—forever."

"Agreed," Oliver said, holding out his hand.

As Luther took it, the macaw said, "It's a deal. It's a deal."

"What's with the bird?" Oliver asked.

"Jury's my secret weapon."

"Jerry?"

"Jury. If he likes my speech, I know the jury will. I practiced all my arguments before him back in the day." Luther pressed the elevator button.

"I just need to know one thing before I go," Oliver said. "How did Kimber know my name?"

Luther bit back his reflexive reproach, deciding that a show of ingenuity would serve him well at this point. "Now that we're in business together, I'll share that little secret with you, Oliver ... if you'll promise to take it to your grave."

Oliver nodded his solemn acceptance of the terms.

Luther held up his hand, fingers spread. "Fingerprints."

"Fingerprints? How did you ... oh, the door! It was the door handle, that brass cylinder, wasn't it?"

"Very good, Oliver. The electromagnetic lock won't release until the cylinder has captured your prints."

Oliver began nodding his appreciation but stopped suddenly. "Bullshit. That's not how you do it. I've never been printed for comparison. Ever. In fact, I've gone to great lengths to avoid it."

Luther shook his head as if to say "Tisk tisk." "Then you've wasted your time, my friend. Believe it or not, the government doesn't tell us everything. With the Patriot Act, they don't have to."

"You talking about some big secret program?"

Luther smiled.

The elevator door opened.

Oliver stepped inside but did not press the button. "How's it work?"

"Quite simply, actually. Ever buy anything with plastic?"

"Who hasn't?"

"Ever use one of those electronic signature pads, the kind with a thick tethered stylus?"

"Sure."

"Did you know that most of them are manufactured by a major defense corporation?"

Oliver raised a skeptical brow. "I don't generally pay attention to things like that."

"Of course you don't. Nobody does," Luther said. "But think about it. The stylus on those signature pads is wired to a computer that has just verified your identity by both your credit card swipe and your signature. It covertly uploads your prints direct from your hot little fingers into a database. Over time, Homeland Security builds a complete set from those partial reads."

"And you have access to it?"

"Everything is for sale, my friend."

"That why those government laptops occasionally disappear?"

Luther smiled. "You just need to know whom to ask. Speaking of which, you owe Wendell a show of thanks. I'd suggest a case of Chateau Margaux '96; clarets are his favorite. Then you can get back to planning the next four years of your life—after you've transferred my money."

Chapter 21

Interpretations

THEY BOTH STARED at Emmy's foot for a moment as though hoping it would speak. Finally, Emmy said, "Looks like an international phone number."

"Yes and no," Troy replied. "Yes, zero-zero is international from Europe and, I assume, from the Caymans. Also, forty-nine is Germany, a big country, and twelve digits makes sense too. But there are no parentheses or dashes. Why leave it ambiguous?"

Emmy shrugged.

Troy continued to think out loud. "I don't know either. Maybe it's nothing. But it seems to me that in a situation like ours, where people are after you and you fear that your memory is about to be erased, that you would tend to be as clear and succinct as possible. You would leave yourself whatever link you needed to reconnect with your life, to pick up wherever you were before your memory got erased. A phone number to a confidant would be perfect for that." Troy felt his excitement mounting. "The owner of that number probably knows what happened to you."

"To us," Emmy said. "I'm guessing that SBT is the owner. And he or she is just as likely to be your friend as mine. Do you think it's safe for us to use the hotel phone?"

It was Troy's turn to shrug. A pay phone or the lobby phone would probably be safer, but the only credit card he had was Detective Sergeant Johnson's and he was not about to touch that. He should have ditched it long ago, but was keeping it for an emergency. "Let's find out."

His hand shook as he reached for the receiver, scaring him more than the sniper shot. Surgeons needed steady hands. He handed the phone to Emmy rather than attempting to dial, and hoped that his infirmity had gone unnoticed.

Emmy dialed 9 for an outside line and then 004995625425. When it started to ring she pressed the speakerphone button. The line picked up and a message came on, first in German, which neither of them understood but both could gist, and then in English: "The number you have dialed is not in service. Please recheck the number and try again." She dialed again as Troy read the numbers off her foot. The same recording repeated.

Troy stood and began to pace the room, his right elbow resting in his left palm, his chin between his forefinger and thumb. Emmy remained on the edge of the bed. "There are two logical possibilities," he said, as much to himself as to her. "One, the number was disconnected after the tattoo, presumably by the same people who wiped our memories. Two, the tattoo is not a phone number."

"What else would it be?"

"I don't know. We've been assuming that the number leads us to SBT. But if you think about it, it's equally logical that SBT leads us to the number."

"Or perhaps SBT is some kind of decryption code for the number?" Emmy ventured.

"Perhaps. But that seems awfully complicated. Why would we do that to ourselves?"

"So nobody else could read it."

Troy shook his head. "We have to assume that anyone clever enough to induce amnesia is also capable of deciphering any code that we can crack. Unless of course you're some kind of mathematical whiz. You never did specify what kind of grifting you do. I gather from your previous reaction that it's not card counting?"

"I'm pretty good with numbers, but not that good. I make my living as a counselor."

"Counselor as in psychic?" Troy asked.

"I'm good at reading people," Emmy said, prevaricating.

"I see. Does that really pay the rent?"

"I get by. Most people will gladly pay to have someone tell them what they want to hear—so long as the source is credible. In your world, credibility comes with shoulder patches, medals and letters after a name. In mine, it comes with getting it right. I'm careful to word things ambiguously enough that I can always claim to be right."

"How do you do that?" Troy was asking partly out of genuine curiosity, and partly to give his subconscious a chance to work the tattoo problem.

Emmy looked up at him, indecision in her eyes.

Troy did not press. He just watched her make up her mind.

She made it up quickly. "I just provide the words. I let the client provide most of the meaning and all of the significance."

"Like a fortune cookie?"

Emmy nodded. "Or a horoscope."

"And there are enough fools with money for you to make a decent living doing that?"

"I don't consult fools, Troy. In fact, counterintuitive though it may seem to skeptics like you, the more logical a person is, the better."

"Come on ..."

"It's true. Logical thinkers are by definition those best at connecting dots. I throw out an array of suggestions, and my clients aptly connect them in the way most meaningful to them— ignoring the incongruities as we all do when hope is involved, I might add."

"But the smarter a person is, the harder he is to fool."

Emmy shook her head. "A person's desire to find meaning in his life is independent of his intelligence."

"I don't buy it."

Emmy grew a crafty smile and crossed her legs before her on the bed. "Come on then, sit. Take my hands." She offered her hands palms up. "Put your money where your mouth is."

Chapter 22

Ava

TROY WAS NOT INCLINED to take time out of the investigation to play psychic games, but on second thought he decided that perhaps a little meditation was just what the doctor ordered. Besides, this kind of trickery had always fascinated him.

"Don't you need tarot cards or tea leaves or a crystal ball?"

Emmy crinkled her nose. "Most people do feel more comfortable if there's some kind of mystical medium involved, enough so that I keep the full spectrum in my office."

"The full spectrum?"

"Everything you mentioned plus runes, incense, the Ouija board and many more in my parlor. I charge differently for each, but the content of the reading is the same as when I go it alone."

"Which is the most expensive?" Troy asked, his curiosity peaked.

"Whichever the client wants most, of course. Come on," she patted the bed. "Have a seat."

He climbed onto the bed and mimicked Emmy's meditation stance. She took his hands and stared into his eyes, her face expressionless, her gaze disarming. Troy focused on the rich green color of her irises. They looked like Monet lily pads sprinkled with little flecks of gold. After a moment she closed her eyelids and began to move her head in circles, whispering "relax" with each revolution. Troy found the atmosphere incongruously soothing and stimulating at the same time.

After a minute, once his shoulders had turned to putty, she stopped and opened her eyes. Staring through him she began to speak, her voice melodic and uplifting. "Some of your aspirations tend to be pretty unrealistic, Troy. It is good for you to have dreams, but you need to be realistic, too." She paused, and took her head through another revolution. "I can see that at times you are extroverted, affable, and sociable, while at other times you are introverted, wary and reserved. You have found it unwise to be too frank when revealing yourself to others, yet sometimes you battle with the temptation to do so."

Another silence found Troy feeling mesmerized as Emmy rubbed her thumbs around the palms of his hands. She continued. "You pride yourself on being an independent thinker and do not accept others' opinions without satisfactory proof. You prefer a certain amount of change and variety, and become dissatisfied when hemmed in by restrictions and limitations. At times you have serious doubts as to whether you have made the right decision or done the right thing, although it usually turns out that you have. While disciplined and controlled on the outside, you tend to be worrisome and insecure on the inside. You must overcome those feelings if you are to grow to your full potential, a potential that I sense is great indeed."

Emmy closed her eyes and withdrew her hands, breaking the spell. Then she rolled her head through two more revolutions and asked, "Well?"

"Well what?" Troy replied, his voice uncharacteristically weak. "We may not have known each other very long, but we have been through a lot together. Of course you know things about me. I know things about you too."

"But was I accurate?"

"I suppose. But not helpful."

"I was just getting started."

"So finish."

"Would you like to hear more?"

"Sure."

"Well, there you have it then: Another fool and his money parted."

"But only because you know me." And because it's so pleasant to hold your warm hands, look into your brilliant eyes and listen to your sweet voice. "I trust you don't run naked through the jungle with all your clients?"

Emmy raised her eyebrows. "No. But I do use those very same words to open with all of them."

Troy could not hide his surprise. "What! Every client?"

"Yep. From doctors to dishwashers. Actually, I would normally modify it a bit, throw in a dozen more stock phrases based upon the client's age, gender, appearance and anything else I happened to know about him or her. But I didn't want to do that with you. I wanted to give you a reading I could have given if you'd walked mute into my parlor while I was blindfolded—although even under those circumstances I still would have modified my reading based upon your footfalls, smell, the way you sat, the feel of your hands, and your physical reactions—twitches and breathing—during the reading."

"So what do you know about me that's not canned?"

"Would you like to know?"

The way she said it, with an intriguing, almost sinister lilt, turned his mouth dry with apprehensive anticipation. "Yes."

"That's how I make my living. I keep them coming back every week."

Troy held his arms wide and bowed his head. "I'm impressed."

"Thanks."

"So, are you going to tell me what you genuinely know about me?"

Emmy surprised him with a sober stare. "Why don't you let me ask you a question instead?"

"Okay," Troy said, feeling inexplicably nervous.

"Tell me about the man who helped you make it from an

orphanage to med school."

"How … how did you—"

"Come now, Troy. Don't make me repeat myself. This is what I do."

"There's more to it than that," Troy insisted.

To his surprise, Emmy said, "You're right. There is. The only reason I'm in good physical and mental health is because I wandered under the wing of a wonderful woman. Most runaways aren't so lucky. Ava Zamora was the queen of the con in L.A. back in the nineties. She's the proverbial person who taught me everything I know."

Troy took a moment to absorb this and then said, "Judge Others. That's his name, really. The third time I passed through his juvenile court, Others saw past my record and rough edges to what lay underneath—an ability you obviously share. He studied my file, gave me the brainteaser questionnaire that I later learned Mensa uses for admission, and then decided I had potential if given a good environment. He put me to work in the courthouse instead of sending me off to juvie."

Emmy nodded. "Was medical school your choice, or his?"

"His. I wanted to be a lawyer like him—as you've obviously already guessed. He knew me better than I knew myself, however, and steered me toward a military medical scholarship. Thank goodness he did. Tell me more about Ava."

"You always change the topic if I scratch beneath the surface," Emmy noted. "But that's okay. As for Ava, telling you about her would take hours."

"Hours we don't have," Troy concurred, feeling strangely disappointed to be getting back to business.

"So what do we do next?" she asked.

And just like that Troy had it. The meditation had worked. Excited, he asked Emmy, "What's odd about the tattoos?"

"What isn't odd. The location for starters."

"No, that's explainable. We just didn't want anyone to spot them
—lest they try to remove them with a cheese grater or blowtorch.
The answer to the question is: palm fronds."

"Palm fronds."

"Why would I have asked the artist to draw them? If I had
wanted to make SBT look like a monogram I would have written
the initials in the shape of a diamond, or put the T in the middle
and drawn it bigger."

"I give. Why?"

"Because SBT is not someone's initials."

"It isn't?"

"No, SBT is a logo."

"Of course!"

"And where do you find logos?"

Emmy looked over at the nightstand. "In the phone book."

Chapter 23

Guests

AFTER LOCKING the elevator to prevent any chance of interruption, Luther removed his suit coat and rolled back the double-buttoned cuff of his right shirtsleeve. He plunged his hand into the cascading waterfall and said, "open sesame." An excited Jury flew from his perch to a rocky outcrop atop the falls, alighting just as Luther's fingers found their mark. The water stopped and the slab of slate backing the waterfall slid aside, revealing the door to Luther's massive safe.

Jury made a wolf whistle.

The safe like the electromagnetic door locks had come with the office, which prior to housing Kanasis had been a jewelry store. The jeweler had the cast-iron monstrosity built into the concrete wall at the time of the building's construction. Since replacing it with a more modern equivalent would have been a major ordeal and drawn unwanted attention, Luther had opted for rock-solid high-tech camouflage instead.

His designer suggested the floor-to-ceiling waterfall, and it was perfect. Luther had soon grown accustomed to the soothing sound (and gotten over the incessant urge to pee) and he now had a duplicate in his study at home, sans safe.

He took satisfaction from dialing in the five-digit combination. Spinning the cold steel between his fingertips felt like foreplay, foreplay that climaxed with the release of the mammoth door.

Today, Luther scored the first time around. He plucked his reward from a velvet-lined shelf. His fingers felt electrified as he flipped through the thick linen pages of the titanium binder to the next available space. This ritual never lost its luster. Entry forty-seven was going to feel every bit as good as the first.

He took a vintage silver Montblanc from its rack on the shelf and filled in the anxious line: Oliver Horton/Matthew Lopez, $1,000,000, September 4, 2008. Luther recapped the pen and twiddled it between his fingers. "Someday, Jury, this journal is going to be in a museum. In the meantime, we're going to have an obscene amount of fun."

"Girls and cigars," Jury replied. "Girls and cigars."

Luther put the binder back on its shelf. He pulled his key ring from his pocket and used a cylindrical vending machine key to unlock the refrigerated safe within a safe. The stainless steel box he withdrew had originally held one hundred and forty-four vials, each cocooned within its own small foam and fiberboard container. Ninety-six remained. Ninety-six. He had shown exceptional self-control in the use of his magic potion. Until now.

Aside from the single backup dose Farkas always kept on hand, Luther had never supplied Formula 456 to his operative without designating the recipient. This first deviation did not constitute the breaking of one of his rules per se, but Luther knew he was crossing a line. Furthermore, as an attorney he knew all too well that crossing lines was what got people caught, or worse. He promised himself that this deviation would also be the last.

He withdrew three vials and applied a label to each, designating them as a popular brand of rapid-acting synthetic human insulin. The ruby-red color might once have raised uncomfortable questions, but marketing knew no bounds these days. He placed the three vials in a padded manila mailer along with a corresponding package insert. He would go home early today in order to hit FedEx by three. Farkas would have his ammunition in the morning.

Luther returned to his desk and tried to work on one of the legitimate cases that provided his cover, but between the new case and Farkas's predicament, he could not concentrate. As a result, the front gate to Luther's Bel Air estate yielded to his Porsche just sixty minutes after he closed his safe. He pulled his convertible onto the circular drive and parked before the main entrance. Looking to his left he saw his gardener's perfect ass peeking out from beneath her kelly-green shorts. It swayed alluringly back and forth as she scrubbed the bottom of his Spanish fountain. Coming home early definitely had its advantages, he thought.

"Good afternoon, Giselle," he said from his car.

Giselle kept scrubbing, her tight ass wriggling away as if guided by a conductor's baton. After another silent moment he noticed the white iPod clipped to the waistband of her shorts. She had not heard his approach. Given the good mood Oliver had put him in, Luther was tempted to take her where she knelt. She had been with him for three weeks now. His anticipation was nearing its peak …

He got out of the Porsche and slammed the door, ending all chance of surprise and forcing his return to discipline. He had waited this long, he could last until the weekend when he would have the time to seduce her properly. Giselle jumped up at the bang and whipped her head around, a startled look on her glistening face. Luther reached out and hit the pause button on her iPod. "Good afternoon."

"Luther. You're home early." They kissed cheeks. Her blouse was unbuttoned halfway to her navel, exposing some world-class cleavage. She seemed to understand the unwritten rules, and appeared most willing to play the game—this far, anyway.

"Yes, I had a good day. Don't let me interrupt you," he said, turning toward the house. "Just wanted to say Hi."

The cook had the afternoon off, so the kitchen was quiet. Luther grabbed a Corona from the special fridge that kept his booze just shy of frozen and headed up the winding staircase to his study. He had a stack of mail to manage, and he wanted to see how the market was doing.

He found the arched double doors to his study closed, making the doorway look like the entrance to a castle keep. That was most unusual and a little disturbing. He wondered if Brandy was snooping around. That was one drawback to his revolving-door system of domestic help; no matter how well the agency tried to screen, you were bound to get people unworthy of trust. He would talk to her and then check the security tapes later to see if they corroborated her story—more out of curiosity than anything else. Brandy's transgressions or lack thereof would make little difference at this point. He was tiring of her. She had been with him for nearly four months, and three was usually his limit.

He flung both doors open wide, eager to catch her in flagrante delicto, but the sight that met his eyes sent his Corona to the sandstone tiles instead.

Jimmy Scapone—"Orca" as he was called by all unfortunate enough to know him—was seated ten feet in front of him. Another man roughly the size and weight of a Frigidaire stood silent guard off to Orca's right by the waterfall. And then there was Brandy. Poor Brandy. Orca had repositioned Luther's favorite leather armchair directly beneath the large domed skylight, center stage so to speak. He was leaning back in it with his hands behind his head, and his legs splayed out in front. Brandy was between them, her head in his lap. She jumped and spun at the sound of the shattering bottle. Luther saw that her left eye was swollen and turning black. She had obviously been crying.

While Luther's mind was still processing the incredible scene, Orca reached out and swatted the back of Brandy's head, displeased by her cessation. As Brandy turned to resume her forced servitude, Luther caught a glimpse of her project and saw that the rumors were true; the nickname was more than the figment of a wishful imagination. Orca really was a whale, a killer whale.

Orca gave him a smug smile. "Luther. Good afternoon. I wasn't sure when you would be getting home. Do lawyers play golf on

Thursdays, or is that just doctors?"

Luther could not conjure up a response fitting to the situation, so he just stood there staring at the vile scene and praying that the WWF poster boy to his left was only there to watch.

"Aw, doesn't matter," Orca continued, speaking as though they were long-lost friends chatting on a chance elevator ride. "Fortunately, Brandy was here to keep me entertained." He patted her on the head. "What does matter is that you're here now. We have to talk."

Chapter 24

Support

WHEN THEY FOUND the Cayman Islands yellow pages to be four hundred pages thick, Troy purloined an extra copy from an adjacent bungalow so they could go at it from both ends. They ordered a whole pot of room-service coffee, but Emmy struck gold before Troy drained his first cup. "Solomon Bank & Trust," she said. "I found it."

Troy left his phone book on the desk and walked over to the bed where Emmy lay prone, reading with her ankles crossed in the air behind her. Sure enough, there it was, SBT surrounded by palm fronds. "A bank," he said. "Of course. Did you ever read The Bourne Identity? The classic Ludlum thriller."

"Afraid I missed that one."

"It's one of my favorites. The hero wakes up having lost all his memory. He doesn't know his name or profession or anything. His only link to his past life is a piece of microfilm implanted under his skin with the name of a Swiss bank and a numbered account. Arriving at the bank, he finds that all he has to do to access his account is write out the number longhand for handwriting analysis. It was perfect, because like us he had no identification. This gains him access to a safety deposit box where he finds passports, disguises, millions in cash, and a gun."

"Do you really think that we're going to be so lucky?"

"Somehow I doubt it. But the point is, I would have recalled that story when trying to figure out how to communicate with myself in the future. I can't believe that I didn't think of it immediately—

probably because I know my identity. Anyhow, I'm sure that's it. There's a safety deposit box waiting for us at Solomon Bank & Trust."

Emmy was nodding along as he spoke, but Troy could tell that she did not seem to share his level of enthusiasm. "What is it?" he asked.

"How did it go for Bourne at the bank?"

Troy reached up to loosen a collar that wasn't buttoned. "Actually, by accessing the account he alerted the people who were after him that he was still alive. They tried to kill him on the spot."

"And let me guess, there was a woman with him who all the while was telling him to run away."

"Marie. Yes. Sort of."

"So maybe that was the message, Troy. Maybe this was your way of telling yourself to run."

Troy shook his head. "Why not just tattoo RUN then?"

"On the bottom of your foot? Lots of ways to interpret that, don't you think? I had a client with ARMY tattooed on his shoulder. Every time I saw it I wanted to look for LEGY on his thigh."

"I've got to go with my instincts on this one, Emmy. And they're telling me that the answers to our questions are at SBT."

Emmy stood and squared off her slender five-foot-two frame against his solid six. "But it's not just your instincts that matter. We put the other half of the puzzle on my foot, so obviously I'm supposed to have equal input."

"Okay, you tell me then. What do we do if not the bank? Mug a Chinese couple, steal their passports and spend the rest of our lives hiding in a rice paddy?"

"At least that way we'll get the rest of our lives! We've lost enough already. I can't stand the thought of us losing anymore."

Emmy's use of us stilled Troy's tongue. Her Freudian slip had spotlighted the elephant in the corner.

Judging by the mollification of her expression, she realized it too.

After a moment of strained silence he reached out and clasped both her hands. "As tempted as I am to run off with you, I can't do it until I know that I wouldn't be leaving someone else behind. I'm sure you can't either."

Emmy met his stare for a minute, her eyes misting over. Although no words passed between them, he knew that they were thinking as one. The foundations had been ripped from their lives, replaced by corpses, snipers, and guns. The only support each now had was the other. What would they do if the secrets within Solomon Bank & Trust somehow stole that too?

But in their hearts they both knew that there was no escaping the bank.

Chapter 25

Leasing

MESMERIZED THOUGH HE WAS by the surreal scene transpiring in his study, Luther still found himself feeling for Brandy. This emotional flare-up surprised him—given his own situation and the fact that he planned to fire her soon anyway. It also bothered him. He had to walk a fine line when talking with the Mafia boss. He had to act tough and superior yet subservient. Compassion had no place on that overcrowded landscape. Looking Orca in the eye, he said, "Our business is man's business. Let's not mix it with pleasure."

Orca gave an appreciative shrug and said, "Brandy, darling, we're going to have to finish this later."

Brandy backed her head away, hesitant, fearing another swat. When none came she stood silently and bolted for the door.

Orca made no attempt to cover himself after she left. Zipping up would be dangerous if not impossible given his engorged condition. He just left his flag waving in the primitive display of manly superiority that Luther suspected was the true objective of Orca's assault.

As Brandy fled, Orca said, "I was just getting ready to explain your domestic situation to Zero, seeing as how we was getting to know Brandy and all. I was telling him that I thought you had discovered a trend for the twenty-first century. Much better that you're here to explain it to him yourself though, don't you think?"

Luther looked over at Orca's steroid-stuffed companion. "Zero?"

"It's from sub-zero," Orca said. "You know, the big freezers?"

"I get it," Luther said, guessing from the dull look on the bodyguard's face that the nickname was a double-entendre.

"So tell him," Orca pushed.

Luther was perversely proud of his unique domestic arrangement, but he did not like to discuss it. He did not like to discuss anything revealing with anyone. Unfortunately, a bottle of Courvoisier had loosened his tongue while he was trying to secure his loan from Orca, and the braggart in him had escaped. Since then he only drank alone. "Let's not go there today."

"He uses domestic help as rent-a-wives," Orca said, ignoring the plea. "He has this employment agency that works with a lot of Hollywood wannabes who can't pay their rent. The agency sends him hotties like Brandy on a regular basis. They clean the house during the day and polish his knob at night. Ain't that right, Luther?"

Luther just nodded and tried to look bored.

"Come on Luther, show some pride. It's a brilliant system. Tell Zero how you came up with it."

Luther turned to Zero, accepting that the fastest way to end the game was to play along. "I got the idea while leasing a car. I only lease cars—never buy—so I can trade them in for a new model as soon as I get bored with my ride. The salesman got a long call from Vin Diesel while I was in his office, so I picked up an exotic car catalog. Looking at the different models astride each vehicle, I found myself wishing that I could get the same deal on the girls that I could on the cars they were advertising. Before the salesman hung up, I decided that there was no reason I couldn't.

"I drove my new Ferrari straight to Fernando's, a talent agency representing wannabe models and actresses and made a deal with the man himself. It's actually a very symbiotic arrangement. The women on my domestic staff get to live in a mansion and make good money doing easy work. I get to cut it off quick and clean whenever I want, with no backtalk, guilt, or alimony. And I don't waste time in pickup bars."

Zero opened his mouth for the first time. "Why not just call hookers?"

Luther gave the enforcer a double take. Despite being crude, it was a reasonably intelligent question. "Two reasons. First of all because hookers are dirty, bitchy crooks and I don't want them in my house. Secondly because there's no challenge in it. No conquest. I like the hunt. These girls don't show up at my door with their legs spread. They come to cook or clean or tend the grounds. I have to seduce them."

Zero nodded like a big dog appreciating a good bone. "So how long you keep 'em?"

"Depends. Usually about three months: One to seduce them, one to try everything out, one to tire of them. I keep three girls, so that makes for a new one every month which is just about right."

Orca slapped his knee and Luther looked back to see that he had managed to zip up. "He got the idea from leasing cars. Cars, can you believe it? Too bad you're not Italian, Luther. With a business mind like that you could be working for me. But then, you are working for me, aren't you?" Orca asked, his tone suddenly serious.

"You are working, right?" he repeated. "I'm asking because you are two weeks behind on this month's payment. Now, in principle, I'm not opposed to late payments 'cause the vig keeps right on giving. But I do need to make sure that there is no fundamental problem." He turned his head toward Zero. "One percent a week don't sound like much when yous borrow it, but when the principal is twenty-five million, that's a mil a month in vig alone." He let his gaze drift back to Luther. "We don't have a problem, do we, Luther?"

"No, we don't have a problem," Luther said, kissing Oliver Horton's fee goodbye. "You'll have your money within forty-eight hours."

Chapter 26

Invisible

THE NEXT MORNING Troy and Emmy watched a big brown UPS truck rattle to a halt in the alley behind Cayman Computing. The game was afoot. They had not broached the subject of their relationship since putting their plan together the previous afternoon. The elephant was back in its corner, but still very much in the room. If all went well these next few minutes, the safety deposit box would be in their grasp, and the elephant would be free to retake center stage. Until then, however, their focus was all business.

As Troy's eyes locked on the driver, he felt the same adrenaline surge that had preceded every combat mission. A familiar sense of calm wrapped him like a shroud. Time slowed.

The UPS driver left the radio blaring the melodic opines of an island talk show host as he disappeared into the back. He emerged from the side doorway a few seconds later with two small boxes and an electronic clipboard. As he disappeared through Cayman Computing's delivery entrance, Troy and Emmy tossed down the cigarettes they had been pretending to smoke, walked casually over to the truck, and hid inside.

No sooner had they taken up their positions in back than the driver reappeared. He started the truck and drove forward about forty feet, stopping again behind the Pet Palace. This time when he entered the rear compartment in search of the appropriate packages, he found himself looking down the barrel of a gun. "Hello Marvin," Emmy said, her tone calm and serious. "I need you to take off your clothes."

Marvin held up his hands, his look as much amused as concerned. Despite the gun, Tinkerbell did not appear overly threatening.

Troy stepped forward and pulled him into the back of the truck. "No worries, friend. We just need to borrow your truck and uniform for a few minutes."

"Tampering with the mail is a federal offense, you—"

"We're not going to touch a single package," Emmy interrupted. "As my colleague said, we just need to borrow your uniform and truck. You behave yourself and you'll be back on your route within the hour. We'll even give you five hundred dollars American for your trouble."

Marvin shifted his gaze from the gun to Troy. "No shit, mon?"

"No shit, mon," Troy replied as Emmy placed the gun in the pocket of her windbreaker. It was just a plastic toy, so she did not want Marvin getting a good look.

Troy was into Marvin's clothes and behind the wheel in no time. He drove the truck on a circuitous route from the Pet Palace to SBT so that Marvin could not track their movements in his head. Without the knowledge of their destination, the only evidence Marvin would have was the green kind, and Troy felt safe in assuming that he would not want to present it.

Troy double-parked the truck directly in front of the bank's door. He looked back at Emmy who nodded but said nothing. He said, "Just borrowing this," to Marvin as he hoisted a random package onto his shoulder to hide one side of his face from passersby. Already spending the evidence in his mind, Marvin said, "Good luck, mon."

The interior of Solomon Bank & Trust was solid but stylish, a gentleman's bank. Only big money need apply. The designer had selected white marble floors and cream-colored walls with a few oil paintings depicting classic island scenes. Troy headed for a central stone pedestal supporting an enormous bouquet of fresh tropical flowers. He recognized the birds of paradise and lilies but the rest were just yellows, oranges and pinks to him. He stopped as if to admire the arrangement while surveying his options. Beyond the lobby, four teller windows split the room off to his right. Centered across from them a clerk's desk stood guard before two glass-walled offices. The focus of the back wall was a very solid-looking door, presumably leading to the vault and the safety deposit boxes.

The clerk, Thomas Delacroix according to the nameplate on his desk, was an impeccably dressed man with a thick mop of blond hair slicked back atop his head. Although Troy suspected that he was only in his late twenties, Thomas already wore the permanent obsequious pucker of a seasoned executive banker. The office immediately behind Thomas's desk belonged to a haughty-looking woman named Agnes Andrews. Agnes wore her black hair up, her reading glasses on a gold chain, and apparently went to great lengths to avoid sun exposure. The corner office housed a thin fortyish gentleman named Gunter Gustafson. Gunter wore what Troy guessed was the only bow tie on the island.

Troy decided to start with Thomas.

As Troy approached his desk, Thomas stood and held out his hands to accept the package. "I'm actually here for personal business," Troy said. "I'm on my lunch break."

"I see. Well then, it would be my pleasure to help you," Thomas said, a little too halfheartedly by Troy's reckoning.

"I need to access my numbered account."

"Very well," Thomas said, a bit more interested. He pulled a white index card from a drawer and slid it across the table. The card was blank except for the SBT logo in the corner and twelve short lines printed across the center in the same golden-brown ink.

Troy's hand trembled as he reached for the pen. That was twice now. The infirmity was beginning to give him serious concerns. He would have to give up surgery if the shaking became chronic. His immediate concern, however, was passing the handwriting test. Praying that it was nerves and not nerve damage, he dropped his arm below the table and shook it out before penning a longhand number in each of the twelve blanks.

Thomas accepted the card with a polite nod, fanned it twice as if to dry the ink, and slid it into a machine reminiscent of a bill changer. "This will only take a minute," he said, but began frowning at his computer screen a few seconds later.

Seeing Thomas's face contort, Troy knew that the smart move would be to run, but he held his ground, met Thomas's eye, and asked, "Problem?"

"Yes, ah no, ah sort of," Thomas replied. "This is a valid account number, but not for a numbered account. It's a traditional bank account."

"A traditional account?" Troy repeated. "Not a safety deposit box?"

"No," Thomas said, his voice growing thin. Dealing with deliverymen who could not keep track of their pennies was obviously beneath him—the mighty clerk of Solomon Bank & Trust. "It's just a checking account," he continued. "That does not mean that the contents are any less secure or your privacy any less sacrosanct, it just means that your name is associated with the account rather than your handwritten account number."

Troy was flabbergasted. Why would he choose to make his lifeline the number of a traditional checking account? He must have sat there with a dumbfounded look for a bit too long because Thomas finally asked, "Is there anything else I can do for you?"

Troy ignored him as the old saw about the best place to hide a grain of sand ran through his mind.

"Anything else?" Thomas repeated.

Finally Troy looked up. "I'm sorry. It's been a while since I accessed this account—obviously. There was a fire and I had to move and ..." He trailed off, shaking his head. "Would you kindly call up an account summary?"

Thomas made "But of course," sound amazingly like "Piss off," but his attitude changed visibly a second after hitting the enter key.

"I have your summary here, sir, and I would be most happy to print you out a copy for your perusal. Perhaps some espresso and scones? We do have private courtesy rooms that you would be more than welcome to use."

"Just the summary report would be fine," Troy said, biting back both his excitement and the urge to leap over the table to study Thomas's computer screen. "It's most kind of you to offer, but I'm on a schedule."

"Of course. Now, I'll just need to see your identification."

Chapter 27

Guess who's coming to dinner?

FARKAS FINISHED sanding his fingertips just as the UPS truck pulled away. He leaned back in the balcony chair, put his feet up on the rail, and began sharpening the edge of his right thumbnail, pleased to have an unobstructed view of the bank's entrance once again.

He checked his watch. Eleven o'clock. Twenty-five hours down, five to go. He did not actually expect Troy and Emmy to appear in his crosshairs. The odds against their clambering back on Luther's trail were a million to one, not to mention that only fools would stick around an island plastered with posters of their wanted faces. These two were not fools.

The tinkling of a bell drifted to his ears through the open doorway to his back. The sound put a deep double crease between his thick eyebrows. He did not have time for George and Ilene right now.

He checked the street as far as he could see in both directions, looking for anyone the height and color of Troy or Emmy. Seeing no contenders, he walked to the bathroom, pulled the wedge from beneath the door and flung it open. "I told you not to ring if it wasn't a dire emergency. You've got your tea, your biscuits, and your toilet. So what is it? Do I need to give you another shot of sedative? Or do you want me to tie you down to the posts of your bed?"

George stood shielding Ilene behind his stooped body. "Yes sir, sorry sir ..." His voice cracked and he had to pause. Ilene put her trembling veined hand on his bony shoulder.

Farkas felt like a heel for terrorizing them, but he had learned long ago that in this world, you had to do what you had to do to take care of yourself and your own. Damn the rest. Besides, any trauma the Wootens were experiencing would soon be forgotten. And, since he was such a nice guy, not much else. He had set his UV-C flasher to its lowest wavelength so the radiation would only effect memories formed within the last thirty days. Given the Wootens' lifestyles, they probably wouldn't even notice the loss. No harm, no foul. Right?

George got his voice back and said, "It's just that, well, my son is going to be coming for dinner at six. I thought I should warn you so there wouldn't be an overreaction."

Farkas narrowed his reptilian eyes. "Overreaction?"

"Yes, you see, Martin is the Deputy Chief of Police."

Chapter 28

Reversal

EMMY LOOKED OVER at Troy as they waited at a stop light. He continued staring straight ahead down Elisabeth Avenue, looking at nothing.

"Well?" she asked, eager to hear what he had learned in the bank.

"I'm completely confused," he blurted, turning to face her. "It's not a numbered account. It's a traditional checking account."

"What about the safety deposit box?"

"There isn't one."

"The light's green."

"What?" His mind was spinning in a rut. He couldn't get past the fact that there was no box.

"The traffic light is green. Drive."

"Oh." Troy pressed the accelerator and continued north along Seven Mile Beach toward West Bay. He did not know where to go next, but wanted to keep them on the move.

"How much is in the account?" Emmy asked.

"I don't know. You need identification to access a regular account. I don't even know what name is on the account. The only good news is that there's a lot of money in it. At least I assume there is. The snotty clerk perked up considerably when he saw the balance."

"You don't even know what name is on the account," Emmy repeated sotto voce. At the next stoplight she said, "Troy, remember when you caught our earlier mistake, when we had been assuming that the number would lead us to the initials, rather than the other way around?"

"I remember."

"Well, maybe we've got it backwards again. Maybe the important thing is not what's in the account, but who owns it."

Troy chewed on Emmy's idea for a moment, liked the taste, and started thinking out loud. "So why not just tattoo his name on your foot, or at least his initials? Why write his bank account number?"

"Isn't it obvious?" she asked, clearly enjoying her moment of power.

"Not to me."

"We didn't know his name, just his bank account number. We came to Grand Cayman to learn his name. That's when we popped up on his radar and he erased our minds."

We came to Grand Cayman, Troy repeated to himself. Obviously Emmy was continuing to assume that they had been together prior to the erasure. Deep inside he wanted to believe that she had placed the ring on his finger. His attraction to her—emotional, intellectual, and chemical—dwarfed any compulsion he could recall. His little voice, however, was expressing big doubts. Until he could figure out why, he knew the prudent move was to keep his feelings locked inside.

Troy forced his mind back to business. Emmy's analysis of the clues was nothing short of brilliant. "You're a genius," he said, and had the pleasure of watching her light up. "As long as you're on a roll," he added, "why don't you hypothesize on why we would have done that."

"Hypothesize, huh ..."

As she teased him, Troy knew that he had walked right into her trap.

"My pleasure. It's the oldest trick in the detective's handbook. We were following the money."

"What money?" he asked.

"I don't know. Is there an amnesia business? In any case, I vote that we keep following it."

That had Troy's vote too, but he decided to push back for the sport. "I might buy your scenario, were it not for one thing."

"And what's that?"

"We're not detectives."

Emmy's eyes telegraphed checkmate. "Are you sure?"

Chapter 29

Vogue

TROY AND EMMY spent the rest of the morning formulating their plan of attack over a basket of conch fritters and a pot of strong coffee. Then they drove to the heart of George Town's shopping district where Emmy disappeared to do her thing while Troy hit an internet café for his. It took him about thirty minutes and ninety dollars in information brokerage fees to get what he needed.

After another errand, Troy returned to their designated meeting spot and sat on the edge of a fountain to wait for Emmy. He was restless by nature, but the setting invited him to a respite long overdue. He enjoyed deep leisurely breaths of the jasmine scented air and listened to the medley of bird calls and cascading water. As he watched a passing woman pry her stiletto heel from the cobbled walk, his mind returned to Emmy's *are you sure we're not detectives* comment. He noted how naturally they were working together to plot what amounted to a covert operation and felt a strong and sudden sense of déjà vu. He knew it was a nonsense feeling, the dividend of reading a thousand thrillers. He would never have given up his scalpel and stethoscope for a cloak and dagger—even for a woman as amazing as Emmy—unless …

Troy rose and began circling the surrounding plaza, massaging his right forearm and thinking the unthinkable. After an indeterminate number of laps he found himself standing before the window of an upscale children's clothing store. They had the cutest pink and white outfit in the window, with a pleated skirt and

white ruffled blouse and tiny matching shoes all decorated with
bows. For some inexplicable reason, the display buoyed him with
enough warmth to lift him out of his funk.

No sooner had he sat back down on the fountain's edge than
Emmy called his name. She gave a twirl as he looked up, shopping
bags sailing out to her sides. Her stunning appearance all but sent
him toppling backwards into the water. She wore a turquoise and
teal suit the likes of which he had only seen on news coverage of
fashion shows. The top exposed her entire beautiful back as it
looped around her neck and down in what was little more than
ribbons over bare breasts to cross again just above her belly button
before fastening in back. The pants started well down her hips
where they clung tightly all the way down to her knees before
flaring out for the remainder of the journey to her ankles. Troy was
vaguely aware that she was wearing matching strappy high heels,
but his attention was riveted higher. She had obviously spent some
time at the makeup counter and now appeared to have blossomed
from the pages of Vogue. "Wow," was all he could manage to say.

"Did you get the video camera?" she asked, holding up a small
matching handbag while ignoring his stupor. "I picked one that will
make the hole difficult to detect. Built the whole outfit around it."

"Not that anyone will be looking," he said, adding "Wow," again
for good measure.

"Thanks. I'm glad you like it, but please don't say that again.
Tactics like this make me feel cheap. Since we don't have a lot of
tools in our bag, I'm not going to be foolish enough to ignore
those that will work based on principle, but I still don't enjoy it."

Troy felt the shame of a chided schoolboy sweep over him, but
just for a second. "Sorry. And thank you. I do appreciate your ...
flexibility."

"Let's go. The bank closes at four. You can tell me what you dug
up on Gustafson while we drive."

Chapter 30

Visible

THEY PARKED on a side street two blocks from Solomon Bank & Trust. Emmy gave her platinum-blonde wig a final inspection in the mirror before getting out. Between the new hairdo and four-inch heels that propelled her up to average height, she would not be easy to recognize. She was hiding in plain sight.

She would have preferred Troy's approach, but that did not fit with her need to be distractingly sexy. He had purchased a sweat suit and padded it with towels and a pillow. Together with a baseball cap and sunglasses, that left his chin dimple as his only tell. She could have disguised that as well with stage makeup, but the bank's four o'clock closing precluded its procurement.

"Yas ready?" he asked, his intonation reminding her of a Bronx gangster.

Emmy crinkled her nose. "First Irish, then the Bronx. What's with the voices?"

"Been doin' 'em ever since I's a kid." He switched back to his normal voice. "I don't want Thomas to recognize my voice if he overhears me talking."

Emmy nodded her approval while digesting the voices news. "So you used humor to compensate for the Waardenburg syndrome?"

Troy stopped dead in his tracks. "How on earth—"

"I can see that you only wear one contact, and that it's tinted cobalt blue to make your right eye match your left. And when I examined your scalp I saw the roots of the shock of white hair starting to show beneath the dye job. The rest is simple deduction.

Kids are cruel. You're obviously very bright and you found a way to compensate."

"No one outside of the medical profession had ever detected my condition before. I don't have the hearing loss that commonly accompanies Waardenburg. My ailments are purely cosmetic, and in this day and age, that means they're easy to assuage. At least for an adult. Everything is harder when you're a kid—and double that for orphans."

"I hope I didn't embarrass you," Emmy said. "It's just what I do. I'm always observing people, compiling and analyzing little bits of data and history like that for use in my work. I need to learn to keep my mouth shut."

"No worries. My skin is far from thin."

"Psychologists do the same thing, you know. I just look for ties to your social desires or career aspirations rather than your mother."

"That's good, because I like talking to you, but I don't have any ties to my mother." He gave her his high-voltage smile. She would have swooned were the effect not diminished by his silly outfit. "I'm going to run on ahead," he added when she did not topple. "Why don't you slow down so that we arrive a couple of minutes apart?"

"Probably safer that way," Emmy replied, pointing to her flamboyant heels.

As he took off, she corrected herself. She had it backwards. The safe move was probably running—in the opposite direction.

Chapter 31

A Bird in the Hand

FARKAS USED his rifle scope to confirm the sighting. His eyesight was tip-top, but he wanted to be absolutely sure before making the call. Satisfied, he used the speed dial without taking his eye off the mark.

"Talk to me," Luther said.

"I've just spotted Troy. He's added fifty pounds to his frame with pillows, is walking with an altered stride, and has his face and forehead hidden with sunglasses and a baseball cap, but it's him."

"You're sure?"

"I'm looking through a rifle scope at his Kirk-Douglas dimple right now. No way to mistake that chin. A feature like that would be tough to camouflage on short notice. Troy obviously decided to ignore it and hope for the best. I'm about to give him the worst—assuming that's still what you want?"

"Where are you?" Luther asked.

"On a private balcony across from Solomon's. He's entering the bank as we speak."

"I can't believe it! How did he do it? How did he find the bank again? Are you sure you wiped his memory?"

"I'm sure. I did them just like the others. After forty-six straight successes, I'm confident in both my skills and the technology."

"And you're sure they're working alone?"

"Well, they were working with Detective Johnson. But as you well know, I've already plugged that hole. I never observed them in extended conversation with anyone else, but even if there was someone, they can't possibly remember him now. They must have left themselves a trail of breadcrumbs—although I can't imagine how. I didn't leave them with so much as a scrap of paper." Farkas kept the Hensoldt scope sighted in on the bank entrance as he spoke.

"Bloody Hansel and Gretel," Luther said. "Wait a minute. You only mentioned Troy. What about Emmy? Is she there?"

"Shit," Farkas said, realizing the obvious. He couldn't risk taking out one without the other. "I'll have to follow him to her."

"Do that. Then do what you have to do to find out what trail they're following before you kill them. I don't want to give anyone else the chance of picking up where they left off."

Farkas was already disassembling his rifle as Luther spoke. When his boss finished, he said, "Agreed," followed a moment later by "Hold on."

"What now?" Luther asked, his irritation showing.

"I just spotted Emmy. She's approaching the bank from the opposite direction, and … incredible."

"What?"

"I would have expected her to wear a dumpy disguise like Troy, maybe even try to sneak past me as a teenage boy. Instead she's dressed for a Milan runway, and let me tell you, the effect is enough to make the Pope himself go dry in the mouth."

Farkas began reversing the disassembly procedure.

"It's going to be a shame to spoil that with an ugly red spot. Do you want me to drop them as they exit, or do you still want to go for an interrogation?"

Luther remained silent for a moment of contemplation, then said, "Better a bird in the hand than two in the bush. Go ahead and take them out."

Chapter 32

Aura

GOOSE BUMPS TINGLED Emmy's arms as the air conditioning blasted her exposed flesh. It seemed that Solomon's management feared their money would melt if the mercury crested sixty degrees. Now, if she could just stop sweating on the inside.

She glanced off to her left where Troy was distracting Ms. Andrews with questions about mortgages. Then she shifted her focus to Gunter Gustafson's office. He was alone. Had he not been, Troy would have headed her off at the door and they would have tried again a few minutes later. She made a beeline for Gustafson's door but Thomas intercepted her halfway, standing behind his desk and offering assistance in a tone that sounded more imploring than obsequious.

"Thanks for the kind offer," she said, flashing her smile, "but I have an appointment with Gunter."

Thomas nodded and returned to his seat, but she could feel his eyes caressing her flesh all the way to Gustafson's door. She gave the glass a light knock and then walked in and closed it without waiting for an invitation. "Good afternoon, Mr. Gustafson. My name is Maya. Maya Lamb. I have some money to put away and was told that you are just the person to help me."

"Really, well ah, quite so, yes. Please, have a seat." His pupils were dilated, his face beginning to flush. Despite some superficial evidence to the contrary, Emmy knew then and there that Gunter was not gay. She could still have worked him if he was, but that would have required a bit more verve. She didn't mind expending verve, but preferred to save it for special occasions.

Emmy took the cushioned chair before Gunter's desk, crossed her legs with her purse in her lap, and gave him her warmest smile.

"Do you already have an account with us, Miss Lamb?"

"No, no. That's why I'm here. I need help in selecting the right kind of account."

"I can surely help you with that. Why don't you tell me exactly what you're looking for."

Emmy rambled on a bit about inheriting some money and wanting to see it put to good use while asking enough questions to ensure that Gunter did most of the talking. After four or five minutes of back and forth during which she frequently crossed and uncrossed her legs, Emmy leaned forward and put her purse on Gunter's desk. "Excuse me for saying so, Gunter, but I can't help but be distracted by the life force you're radiating right now."

"The life force?" he asked, glancing down to assure himself that his force had not sprung free of his pants.

"Yes. Yours is most powerful. It's as though you're a tiger trapped in a man's body." She glanced around the office. "But then I suppose you do spend most of your day in a glass cage."

Gunter had no idea how to react to this, of course, so he just stared at her. Emmy leaned still closer. "Would you mind if I read your aura?"

"Ah, well, I …"

She pushed her purse further back on his desk, adjusting the angle as if to get it out of the way. Then she reached out and took his hands. "Oooh," she gasped, as though they conveyed an electric shock. "Very powerful indeed. Capricorn obviously. You are going to be easy to read."

Gunter just stared at her in lusty disbelief. Apparently this did not happen to him every day.

She looked into his eyes for a good sixty seconds before beginning, allowing her gaze to grow vacuous, possessed. "You are extroverted, affable, and sociable at times, I'm glad to see that. But on other occasions, far too often, you are introverted, wary, and reserved. You also have a great need for other people to like and admire you, but you keep it hidden away."

She massaged the palms of his hands with her thumbs as she spoke, without looking away from his eyes. "I sense a great deal of unused capacity, both personal and professional, which you have not yet turned to your advantage. Perhaps this is because of your tendency to be critical of yourself. Much too critical, Gunter. While you do have some weaknesses, as we all do, you are generally able to compensate for them if you try. But you don't try often enough because, although disciplined and self-controlled outside, you tend to be worrisome and insecure inside." She cocked her head to the side and narrowed her eyes a hair before continuing. "At times you have serious doubts as to whether you have made the right decision or done the right thing but you worry in vain. You need to trust your instincts more.

"It's clear to me that you would prefer more change and variety than you currently have in your life. Monotony is at the core of your dissatisfaction. Sometimes you feel hemmed in by restrictions and limitations. You pride yourself as an independent thinker, but don't get to exercise that talent nearly enough.

"I get a strong affinity for numbers from you. I've got that too. They rule my life. I'm seeing twos, threes and sevens."

She released his hands and shook her head, bringing her eyes back into focus. "I'm sorry if I bored you, but I thank you for the indulgence. When I see an aura like yours I just can't help myself."

"My pleasure. That was ... remarkable. I, I don't know what to say. My sister didn't send you, did she?"

"Your sister? No. Nobody sent me. It's just a gift I've always had. A gift or a curse—depends on how you look at it."

"I see, well, ah, where were we?"

"Oh, I think your Priority A account sounds perfect."

"Excellent. It is our most popular account. I have one myself."

"Tell me something, Gunter. Would it be possible for me to pick my own account number?"

Emmy could sense a surge of reservation, so she added, "Please. It's important to me."

"Well, uh, I suppose it might be possible if it's the right format and the number is not already in use."

"What format do you need?"

"It will start with two zeros and a four. After that the next nine digits can vary."

"If I give them to you will you try to make it work."

"Okay."

Emmy brought her index and middle fingers up to her temples and closed her eyes. "Nine, another nine, five, six, two, five, three— no wait, four, two and five."

She opened her eyes and looked up expectantly as Gunter finished typing.

"I'm sorry," he said, studying the screen. "That number is not available."

"Are you sure? Can you read it back to me?"

Gunter recited the correct number.

"And there's no way to get me that number?"

"I'm afraid not."

"Is it new? Perhaps I could—"

"No, it's an old account. I'm sorry, really. We'll have to pick another."

Emmy stood and extended her hand across the table to shake his. He looked at her in disbelief as he stood to accept it. An encounter like this would be difficult for any normal person to comprehend and impossible to forget, much less a fastidious banker. "Is the exact number really that important?" he asked, no doubt reluctant to end what was likely the only enchanting customer experience of his career.

"It is," she said, giving his hand a final squeeze. She released his hand and picked up her purse, doing her best to give the camera a clear and close-up parting shot at Gunter's screen. "You take care of yourself, Gunter. And try letting that aura of yours get a bit more fresh air before you become dangerous."

Chapter 33

Mist

"THAT'S REALLY THE BEST we can offer," Agnes Andrews rebuffed. "Perhaps you should try the internet." She spoke the name as though it would poison her tongue.

Troy shrugged and nodded along. He had toyed with the haughty banker for fifteen minutes now—the amount of time Emmy predicted it would take her to manipulate Gustafson. Clearly, the moment to retreat had arrived. He stood, said, "T'anks for ya time," and left her fishbowl office without further comment.

Glancing over his shoulder, he thought Emmy appeared to be wrapping up. She had the camera-purse in perfect position and Gunter shaking his head at the computer screen. Troy whipped out his cell phone as he shuffled his padded sweat suit past Thomas. He continued to the far side of the exotic flower arrangement where he spun back toward Gunter's office, said "Yeah?" and pretended to listen.

Emmy was standing now. Gunter's prim face was contorted into an unnatural combination of distraught and perplexed. Troy was so entranced by watching Emmy's smooth moves that he failed to notice the man approaching from his left. "Hey buddy, you mind giving me a hand for a second. This frickin contraption takes two."

Troy turned to find himself confronted by that all-too-familiar uniform. The police officer was struggling to stuff a flyer into the thin crevice of an advertising display. "Bloody thing is too tight," the cop added.

Troy's eyes darted from the COP KILLERS headline to the

grainy headshots beneath without revealing the emotions that erupted within. It was he and Emmy, right there in black and white. His split-second appraisal was that it would take a pro to identify them from just the shadowy security shots, but combined with description of his forehead scars and dimpled chin, it was a no brainer. The question was: had the cop bothered to read it?

Troy turned an appraising eye to his adversary. Officer Jacobs was a handsome man, a ladies' man, the kind of guy who spent a lot of time at the gym and never gave you a chance to forget it. Troy hoped he pressed iron to compensate for a lackluster mind rather than a puny penis—otherwise it all ended right here.

Maintaining the Bronx accent, he said "Hold on," into the phone, and then "Pardon" to Jacobs.

Jacobs pointed to the display. "Just hold this doohickey open so I can slide this wanted poster in on top. Capice?"

"Uh, yeah, sure officer," Troy replied, pushing past the surreal nature of the situation. "Anything I can do to help." He pressed the phone between his ear and shoulder, keeping his dimple covered and scars in the shadow of his baseball hat while he pried the display's plastic lips apart.

Jacobs slid the poster in and stepped back to admire his work. Troy caught him doing a double take just as Emmy came around the corner. Turning toward her, Jacobs' eyes bulged and then bulged again.

He drew his gun.

"You're the two in the poster," Jacobs said, backing toward the door and cutting off their only means of escape. "Get down on your knees. Holy shit! On your knees."

Troy knew that this was the time to do something miraculous like they always did in the movies, but he had seen too many real gunfights to be stupid enough to try. Instead he primed himself to pounce. Despite the fact that Jacobs was holding a gun and sported more muscle than most cows, he was now a bundle of rattled nerves and thus prone to mistakes. Captain Honey must have talked them up as super-villains in order to keep from looking like a putz. Or perhaps, Troy would later reflect, Jacobs somehow sensed what was coming—just not from where. As he shouted "Down!" for the fourth or fifth time his head vanished into a red mist, exploding off his shoulders like a watermelon at a target shoot.

Chapter 34

But for a Nail

FARKAS WATCHED the cop's head disintegrate through the magnified perspective of his sniper scope. He found it more odd than gory, a magician's now-you-see-it, now-you-don't—except for the telltale red mist. Farkas had been expecting the magic, so he had the rifle collapsed and back in its shoulder canister before Troy and Emmy had fully registered their gift from above.

Popping the cap on the end of the canister, Farkas felt his blood pumping with a hunter's fury. He could not kill them where they stood, but there was no way he was going to let his quarry escape again.

As he slung the case over his shoulder and leapt over the balcony rail toward the soft grass twelve-feet below, Farkas never once took his eye off the ball.

He was halfway to the ground when he realized his mistake. It felt like a hollow-point round tumbling through his gut. He had been so focused on dealing with the cop and his quarry, that he had forgotten to flash the Wootens.

It would have taken him less than ten seconds to reach the bathroom door, throw it open with a violent smack, and meet the wide-eyed stares with a programmed UV-C flash.

The crucial mistakes were always just a matter of seconds.

Even before his feet hit the ground he knew that there was no going back. He did not have a key to the Wootens' front door and Troy and Emmy would get away in the time it took him to pick his way in or climb back up. "Govno!"

"What?" Luther asked. "Did you miss? Kill the wrong guy?"

Farkas had also forgotten that his boss was on the phone. He pulled the black helmet over his head before answering into the wireless mike. "I don't miss. The cop's toast and they're going to get the blame. I just twisted my ankle jumping from the balcony," he lied.

He hopped on his scooter and brought it to life.

"Don't let them escape," Luther said, adding the obvious. The man was more nervous than he was.

"No worries. Between Troy's padded clothes and Emmy's high heels they're not setting any land speed records." Farkas watched them disappear around the corner before the first police car arrived.

"What's your plan?" Luther asked.

"I'll follow them to wherever they were hiding out, interrogate them, and then end this whole fiasco such that they get the blame for killing the cop."

"How you gonna do that?"

"Make sure their bodies are never found. I'm leaning toward concrete galoshes."

"I mean the cop part. Won't ballistics prove that it wasn't them?"

"What ballistics? I'm on a tropical island. They've got known cop killers and another dead cop. These bozos aren't going to look further than that."

"What about the bank's security video?"

"Icing on the cake. Solomon's has cameras over the front door and behind each teller, but nothing in the entryway. Troy and Emmy will be identified walking in and running out right after the shot."

"I hope you're right."

"Where did that come from?" Farkas said to himself.

"What are you talking about?"

"They're getting into a car. A gold Camry. I didn't know they had a car. I'm going to have to let you go—"

"No! Keep me on the line. Go ahead and focus on them, but keep me on the line. Update me when you can. I'll keep quiet."

Farkas did not reply.

Luther broke his promise almost immediately. "You still on that scooter?"

"Yeah … Shit."

"What is it?"

"I think Emmy spotted me."

"You said scooters were invisible there. You said—"

"I know what I said, but they weren't looking for tails before, and even the best tailing tactic is going to be far from perfect when it's one on one. The pros use teams, but you won't let me use anyone else."

"Shit."

"Exactly." Farkas sped up as the Camry did the same. There was no sense trying to hide anymore. "I'm not going to get that chance to interrogate them. They won't stop moving until they've lost me. I've got to take them out on the road." He reached for the Glock 36 in his cargo pocket.

"No. That will draw attention, raise questions."

"Do you have a better idea?" Farkas asked, pleased by the opportunity to avoid Luther's Monday morning quarterbacking.

Luther's one word response came after a surprisingly short interval. "Yes."

"I'm all ears."

"Did they see you shoot the cop?"

"Of course not. Nobody did."

"So this is the first time they've spotted you?"

"Absolutely."

"Then don't shoot. Shout. Pretend to be their friend. They don't remember anyone they've met in the past six years. Troy doesn't even remember his wife and daughter. Pretend that you were helping them on the case. Get them someplace alone and give them a soft interrogation. Then make sure no one finds the bodies."

"Luther?"

"Yeah?"

"You're brilliant."

Chapter 35

Second Chance

HONEY AWOKE to the ringing of his mobile phone. "Yeah?"

"Captain, it's Molly. They did it again. The couple. They killed Jacobs. Shot him in broad daylight."

Honey bolted upright on the couch, knocking a bag of chips to the floor. They were still on the island! "When? Where?"

"Just a few minutes ago, at Solomon Bank & Trust on Elizabeth."

"Are they still at the bank?"

"No. They got away."

Honey felt his adrenaline stutter. "In Jacobs' cruiser?"

"No. It's still at the scene."

"Damn."

"As far as we know," Molly continued, "nobody saw where they went. Information is still coming in. I knew you'd want me to call you right away."

"You did good." Honey looked at his watch. Four-fifteen on a Friday afternoon. His mind was churning like an outboard prop. "Okay, here's what we're going to do," Honey said, pressing the phone to his ear with his shoulder as he buckled his utility belt. "Contact the police stations on all the surrounding islands. Let them know that the blue brotherhood needs their help catching a couple of cop killers. Ask them to volunteer their weekend to the cause. We'll fly in everyone who can come tonight on the Coast Guard plane and bunk them at the Ivory Inn—old Morris owes me a favor."

"Okay," Molly said, drawing the word out. "Then what?"

"At dawn we'll launch the biggest manhunt in island history."

Chapter 36

Momentum

"CAN'T YOU GO ANY FASTER?" Emmy shouted. "He's still behind us."

"Faster isn't going to help. On these roads he'll still be able to keep up and we'll just run the risk of attracting cops. We need to go smarter."

"Smarter? What does smarter mean?"

"Getting him caught at a light. Finding a narrow alley where I can jam the car into reverse and back over him. Luring him close and then braking hard so he crashes into us and goes flying. I'm not sure what opportunity will present itself, but I figure that it's kind of like obscenity; I'll know it when I see it. Speaking of which, I don't suppose you recognize him?"

"He's a hundred feet away and wearing a black helmet with a tinted face shield."

"Kind of distinctive, don't you think?"

"You know what I mean."

"I do. I just thought that with your talent for reading people, you might recognize him by some other means."

Emmy was struck by Troy's insight. She made a point of

learning to recognize her regular clients by the sound of their footfalls and the smell of their toiletries. It was always impressive to greet a client by name when he approached from behind. But all she had to go on now was the visual input of a man dressed in black on a scooter. "I don't recognize him."

"That's all right. I just recognized smarter. Hold on."

Emmy turned back to face forward just as Troy jerked the wheel hard to the right. The Camry jumped the curb onto a wide staircase whose yard-long steps connected the sidewalk along an upper business road with the lower beachfront one. He punched the gas and the horn simultaneously, evoking stares and screams from all around. "What are you doing?"

"Being smarter. The scooter may be as quick as the Camry, but it has much smaller tires and only minimal ground clearance. He won't be able to climb the stairs."

"Will we?"

"God, I hope so."

Emmy planted her feet flat against the floorboard and clenched her seat in a death grip. It was a good thing she did. The impact of the first stair would have given her whiplash otherwise. A series of bone-jarring jolts followed as the car bucked from stair to stair like a playground pony. By the time they neared the top their momentum was spent. She thought the car was going to stall out and reverse directions—crushing their pursuer with any luck—but then the rear tires caught and they bounced over the top.

She immediately turned back to see how the scooter was fairing but their trunk blocked her field of vision.

Troy got the car back onto a proper road without killing anybody and before she knew it the staircase and the scooter were both far behind. The whole maneuver had taken less than ten seconds, but fear had made them feel like an hour.

"Well done," she said, her dry mouth capable of only a whisper. "What now?"

"Finally—an easy question," Troy said, sounding considerably more chipper than she felt. "Now we find someplace out of sight to park. We need to have a look at your videotape. We need to find out if that close call was worth it."

The quiet place they selected some thirty minutes and fifteen miles later was the parking lot of Reefer's Dive Shop. Reefer's boat was out for a sunset dive so the place was deserted. An easel on the counter predicted calm waters for the eight AM boat dive to Ten Sails—no reservation required. There was a kid running about, but he was too busy washing out gear and filling up tanks to pay them any heed.

Troy busied himself swapping license plates again while Emmy used the zoom feature on the video recorder's built in three-inch LCD display to transcribe the information on account 004995625425 onto the margin of their map. The angle was a bit too sharp to make reading Gunter's computer screen a piece of cake, but working letter by letter while using the appearance of known words like *account* for reference, she had it pieced together by the time Troy plopped back into the driver's seat, his mission accomplished.

"Are we happy?" he asked, handing her a vending machine Snickers bar.

"We got what we came for. How happy that makes us remains to be seen."

"Do tell."

"It appears to be a personal account, with one Kostas Kanasis as the sole owner. I'm not sure if that's a man or a woman."

"It's a man," Troy said. "A Greek man. I don't suppose you got a meaningful address? Just a PO box in Delaware or Mykonos, right?"

Emmy smiled and it felt good to use those muscles for a change. She pointed to the coastal region of West Bay. "Actually, Kostas lives right here on Grand Cayman."

Chapter 37

Anticipation

"I SHOULD HAVE SHOT THE DAMN TIRES," Farkas cursed to himself. "Instead of struggling to ride, push, carry and toss a two hundred and fifty pound scooter up a staircase, I should have just whipped out the Glock and shot the damn Camry's rear tires. Then I could have walked up, put a bullet in each of their brains, and ridden straight to the airport never to return. Witnesses be damned."

He looked down at the satellite phone in his left hand and then over at the bottle of Tortuga rum in his right. He weighed the two like competing melons at a farmer's market. Then he thought about his sisters and remembered why he was working for Luther in the first place. "Perhaps later, my friend," he told Tortuga, and then turned on the phone.

Farkas expected Luther to start out cursing him for ending their call in the middle of the action. Instead, he simply said, "Tell me."

"I lost them. I fucking lost them. That bastard drove his Camry up a staircase. Up a staircase. The scooter wouldn't follow. I blew it. We're screwed."

"Do you know if they got any information at the bank?" Luther asked, the calmness of his voice surprising Farkas.

"I don't know anything, but I bet they did."

"Why so certain? The Caymanians are like the Swiss, secretive as pedophiles."

"You should have seen Emmy. Dressed the way she was, given her charms and talents, she could have gotten Cheney to confess why he really invaded Iraq. Anyway, do you want me on the next plane to Vegas?"

"No. Obviously we still have business to deal with there."

"Look, I know that my judgment has fallen far short of flawless lately, but we can consider our business here done. Troy and Emmy are far from fools. They've seen the wanted posters and are feeling serious heat. With a second cop killing now attributed to them, they know they'll get burned if they stick around. Either they already got what they came for or they never will. In either case, they'll run now."

"Where do you think they will run?"

"I haven't a clue."

"Well, fortunately I do."

"I can—" Farkas interrupted himself as Luther's words sank in. "What did you say?"

"I said I know exactly where they'll be running to—and it's right there on the island. So do us both a favor: quit your whining and pick up a pen."

Chapter 38

Kostas

"WHAT DID YOU LEARN? What's he like?" Troy shot the questions at Emmy the moment she closed the Camry's door. She had used a large bouquet of flowers and a FedEx envelope full of real estate advertisements to con her way past The Tropical Towers' guards and up to the luxury penthouse condo of Kostas Kanasis himself. This was primarily a reconnaissance mission to prepare for their impending attack, but Troy was dying to know if the owner of bank account 004995625425, the man who had stolen their lives, was more like The Godfather or Doctor Frankenstein.

"Kostas is not the man behind our misfortune. He is a harmless old man living out his golden years alone."

"What! That can't be. If this is a dead end then everything we've done since waking up in the police garage has been in vain. He must have pulled the wool over your eyes." Troy knew that assertion was nonsense even as he spoke the words, but his frustration had a mind of its own.

If Emmy took offense, she did not show it. "I did not detect a hint of deception the whole time we spoke."

Her tone was far too chipper for the news she conveyed.

Troy blinked twice as if to clear his ears and said, "And you saw no flash of recognition when you said the flowers were from Emerald Green and Sebastian Troy?"

"No. I don't think he's ever heard of us. When I handed him the envelope and explained that Troy and Green were with a real estate developer he deflated before my eyes. In my professional opinion,

Kostas Kanasis is just another bored and lonely senior citizen."

"So that's it then," Troy said, his voice trailing off.

"Not necessarily. Just because he doesn't know us, doesn't mean he doesn't know the people who did this to us. We should be able to learn everything we need to know by asking him the right questions the right way."

"What questions? What way?" Troy had asked, his hopes rising. Two hours later, he was about to find out.

Emmy had explained her plan while they shopped for clothes. Yet again. Troy noted that Emmy's plans always seemed to involve buying a new wardrobe, and that was fine with him. By his amateur reckoning, her scheme was as brilliant as her smile.

Looking at the door to the penthouse of Tower A, he asked, "Are you ready for this? You sure look it."

She had her hair pulled back and knotted, and wore sunglasses that robbed her emerald eyes of their fire. Her gray suit, like Troy's, was off-the-rack, and her black pumps had three-inch heels. Unless Kostas had Emmy's talent for reading people, he would not recognize her as the Flowerama delivery girl who had knocked two hours earlier. "Absolutely," she said. Then she reached up, pulled his head down to hers and gave him a breathtaking kiss.

She turned and knocked on the door before he knew what hit him.

Now there was a first kiss he would never forget, Troy thought, even as he struggled to purge it temporarily from his mind.

Emmy cleared her throat and pointed to her lips.

He hastened to wipe the lipstick transfer off in time.

Troy's first thought when he laid eyes on the man who haunted his dreams was that Emmy's "harmless" appraisal had been an understatement. For starters, given the veins and age spots on his hands and neck, Kostas appeared to be well into his seventies. His gray cardigan sweater and thick dark-framed glasses, showed little inclination toward either the evil mastermind or backstage powerbroker stereotypes. Troy detected no hint of malice in his watery grey eyes, nor deepening crease between his long curly brows. The man slated to change their lives looked about as alert and intimidating as an old squirrel.

"Mister Kanasis?" Emmy asked, holding up her false identification.

"Yes."

"I'm Julia Sanders with Interpol. This is my colleague, Agent Harold Singer. May we speak with you for a moment?"

"I suppose. What is this about?"

"Perhaps we could step inside. It's personal in nature."

Kostas took a step back, pulling open the door. "Of course."

"Did you receive an unexpected delivery this afternoon?" Troy asked, noting the flowers on the dining room table off to his left.

"Yes. I got the bouquet of flowers you see over here and an envelope full of advertising materials."

Troy and Emmy gave each other grave nods for Kostas's benefit before turning back to him. "We're going to need to see your driver's license, passport, and latest bank statement, Mr. Kanasis."

"What for? Am I in some kind of trouble?"

"No, sir. You've done nothing wrong. Our purpose here today is to keep you and others from becoming victims of a crime."

"A financial crime," Emmy added. "If you'll show my colleague the documents he requested, I'll be happy to explain everything to you while he makes note of your information."

Kostas looked unsure for a few seconds, but then laid his suspicions aside. Motioning toward a doorway he said, "Why don't you have a seat at the kitchen table. I'll be there in a moment with the documents."

Troy and Emmy nodded appreciatively and headed for the kitchen. The moment they entered Troy understood why Kostas favored this room. The kitchen offered a spectacular view of West Bay and the Caribbean Sea. Looking down he could see four distinct shades of blue in the water, as though the sea was painted by numbers. The hues ranged from the faintest turquoise near the beach to a midnight blue further out. All of it looked inviting, and though it was just there beyond the glass, it seemed a million miles away.

They were still standing at the window when Kostas came back in. "Here you go," he said, handing over his passport and driver's license.

Emmy accepted them with a nod and immediately passed them off to Troy. Then she got busy distracting Kostas so Troy could photograph the documents without his noticing. "As I indicated earlier, it appears that you've been targeted as part of a financial scandal. The group we're after provides legitimate real estate documents to which they have no actual connection, and then they try to get you to invest in them through their organization. It's kind of like selling you the London Bridge if you're familiar with that expression."

"Why the flowers?"

"That's just part of the confidence game. They invest a hundred dollars so that you'll have a warm and fuzzy feeling while you listen to them ask you for a hundred thousand."

"But they did not ask for any money. They just delivered the flowers and an envelope."

"Yes," Emmy said. "That's all part of it. The request to hear them out will come within the next twenty-four hours—unless of course they spotted us and got scared off."

"So what am I to do?"

"Well, that depends. You can either just refuse them outright, and that will be it …"

"Or?"

"Or, if you'd like to help us bring them to justice, you could agree to meet with them and we'll catch them in a sting. It's completely up to you, and I don't want to pressure you in any way."

"I'll need to think about it."

"Yes, of course. In the meantime, we still need to see your banking documents. We're trying to figure out why they targeted you, so we know who to warn in the future."

"I don't have any banking documents."

"You don't have an account at Solomon Bank & Trust?" Troy chimed in.

"No."

Troy felt a chill run up his spine. He wondered if they'd gotten the wrong Kostas Kanasis. Perhaps this was senior and they needed junior? "Well then, if you don't mind my asking, how do you pay your bills?"

Kostas blushed. "I don't pay them. I mean, I do pay them, but not personally. I have an attorney who handles all my banking."

"Your children don't handle that for you?" Emmy asked, her thoughts obviously following the same track as his.

"No. I don't have any children. No family at all, as a matter of fact."

No family at all, Troy repeated to himself.

"Could you get us your attorney's name and number?" Emmy asked.

"Yes, of course. I'm sure I have his card somewhere."

Troy turned toward Emmy and they exchanged perplexed looks as Kostas got up and went in search of the business card.

"How often do you see your attorney, Mr. Kanasis?" Troy asked loudly, so Kostas could hear him from the other room.

"Oh, I never see him."

"What I mean is, how often do you speak?"

"Not very often. In fact, I don't remember ever speaking to him."

"Ever," Emmy repeated. "How is that?"

Kostas walked back into the room with a rumpled old business card. "I don't remember a lot of things. I've developed a problem with my memory."

Chapter 39

Arlen

LUTHER LAID his satellite phone down on his oak desk and let out a long sigh. Between Orca's visit and the Farkas fiasco, these last few days had been unnerving. Life was supposed to be easy when you made the kind of money he did, wasn't it?

The problem, he knew, was that the money just passed through his hands, teasing him. He never got to hold it, fondle it, revel in it. The bulk of his earnings went to Orca. The rest went to pay his mortgages, his social fees and expenses, and his professional and domestic help. At the end of the day, even with annual earnings well into eight figures, he was still living off credit cards.

A light two-toned bell intruded on his thoughts and Kimber's face appeared on his videophone. He could tell by the look in her eyes that she had good news. "You've got a visitor, Luther," she said, holding an embossed business card up to the camera. "Arlen Blythe, CEO of Savas Pharmaceuticals is here to see you." By stating his name that way, Kimber was signaling that she had confirmed Blythe's identity with his fingerprints. "He said to tell you that Bogart sent him."

Bogart, that was good news, Luther thought. "Please make Mr. Blythe comfortable and then send him up in five minutes."

Bogart had been Luther's best paying client. Whereas Luther charged a million dollars to erase a single witness's memory, he doubled his fee for each additional erasure on the same case, keeping the cost in line with the incremental risk. If the prosecution's star witness suddenly could not swear to what he had seen anymore, that was tragic, but not necessarily unusual. It was a different kettle of fish altogether if the prosecution's two star witnesses both "developed amnesia." Then the judge might smell something rotten and decide to take a closer look. Closer looks were exactly what Luther most wanted to avoid.

Rather than refuse multiple erasures outright, however, he had put a risk-reward matrix in place. Bogart had paid Luther a three million dollar fee for a double erasure. Given that Arlen Blythe was the CEO of a pharmaceutical corporation, Luther could imagine myriad scenarios for which he might require a double. Perhaps a couple of clinical investigators had observed regrettable adverse effects, or his security division had identified a couple of whistleblowers about to toot. Hell, it could even be a triple, Luther mused. Three wipes were worth seven million dollars. Four was worth fifteen. Dare he even hope? Luther shook his head. No. He dared not. Although a big job would not break the letter of the inviolable rules he had established in the beginning to keep from getting caught, it would certainly crack their spirit.

Still, to get Orca off his back ...

Luther Googled Savas Pharmaceuticals. Scanning the summary posted on an investment website, he saw that Savas was a one-drug firm—but what a drug it was. Vitorol, their oral insulin, was the world's number-one best selling pharmaceutical, bringing in a staggering twelve-billion dollars last year. Twelve Billion. All from pills that probably cost a penny apiece to manufacture. That was the kind of return he had hoped to be earning when he plunked half his tort earnings into Aridon Biotech six years ago. He had hoped to cash in on the Alzheimer's pie the way Savas was cashing in on the diabetic. He had rolled the dice and taken his chances, and lost. Big time. Never again.

The elevator doors chimed, and Arlen Blythe walked into his office. With his radiant aquiline features and thick crop of gray-tinged hair, the CEO looked like his title: the head hired gun for one of the world's most profitable firms. At forty-six, he was young enough to represent the next-generation image that Savas sought to portray, yet experienced enough to impress the industry analysts and roundtable hosts with his acumen and gravitas.

Luther knew instantly that it would be a mistake to try to pass himself off as the hired help to this guy. Arlen no doubt knew his Shakespeare. According to the rumors Luther now recalled, the founder of Savas had spent eighteen months working with all three of the world's top executive search firms to identify the perfect man to assume the reigns of his company. The man whose identification and recruitment had commanded millions in fees was standing before him now. And he needed Luther's help.

As Luther walked from behind his desk to greet his potential new client, he could not help fantasizing about the fee they might be agreeing to the next time they shook hands—if only Arlen had the right kind of case. "Good afternoon, I'm Luther Kanasis. Please, make yourself comfortable," he said, motioning toward his suite of black calfskin armchairs.

Arlen nodded and complied, but did not offer an opener. Not even his name. Apparently, he wanted Luther to make the first move. His clients tended to do that for some reason, as though they thought it a clever way to test his oratorical skills. Little did they know that despite the nature of his business, oratory had nothing to do with Luther's ongoing success. "It truly is a pleasure to have you here, Mr. Blythe. I've been an admirer of yours for years. Your work at Savas has been little short of miraculous. Twelve billion last year. Now that is impressive."

When Blythe failed to reply or even nod, Luther added, "So, we have a mutual friend in Bogart …"

"Yes," Arlen said. "I was most impressed by the resolution of his case."

Luther nodded.

"We had a long talk about it over a couple of splendid Padron cigars. I don't usually smoke, but given Bogart's affinity I joined him and actually enjoyed it immensely. Even ordered myself a couple of boxes of the same limited edition just to have around when the occasion warrants." Arlen kept his gaze riveted on Luther the whole time he spoke, giving Luther the impression that the words were just filler, packing peanuts around some greater purpose.

"He doesn't have the faintest idea how you helped him," Arlen continued. "His assumption is that you simply used bribes."

Luther kept his best poker face securely pasted throughout this speculation. His clients always wanted to know how he did it, but of course he never told them. He never even hinted.

"That's one of many areas where Bogart and I differ," Arlen added.

Luther waited for more but nothing came. Finally he said, "I don't follow."

Arlen's lips smiled, but his eyes continued with their dissecting stare. "You see, Luther, I have deduced your secret. I know exactly how you've been winning. You've been erasing memories—chemically."

Chapter 40

Cutout

EMMY LOOKED OVER at Troy as they waited for the elevator, trying to gauge his state of mind. She was not pleased with the results of their meeting with Kostas Kanasis, but judging by Troy's expression, his jury was still out.

Not hers.

All that work, all that exposure, all that danger ... Discovering and deciphering the tattoos, hijacking the UPS truck, scamming Gunter, watching a cop's head explode before their eyes, impersonating Interpol officers, for what? For the name of Kostas's accountant, an attorney in Miami. What good was that to them? "I can't believe that after all this, all we have is the name of a lousy attorney."

Troy held up his index finger without turning toward her, indicating that he was deep in thought. When the elevator arrived on eighteen, he took two steps forward to enter but did not turn around. He just stood there, staring intently toward the back wall.

Emmy was about to hit the lobby button, when she thought better of it. She pressed seventeen instead. They descended one floor, the doors opened and closed, and then she hit sixteen, all with Troy barely blinking. And so it went: fifteen, fourteen, thirteen, twelve. On eleven, Troy suddenly turned to her. "It's brilliant. Bloody brilliant." He wore a smile a mile wide.

"What is?"

"The system."

"What system? What are you talking about?" Emmy asked,

frustrated and anxious.

"Kostas Kanasis."

"Kostas Kanasis is just a sweet old man, a victim whose memory has been wiped—just like us."

"No, he's not like us. You were on the right track earlier, but you need to take it one step further. He's a cutout."

"What on earth are you talking about?" she asked, pushing the button for ten.

"Think about it, Emmy. Think about the chain of clues."

"The chain of clues?"

"Yes. Go all the way back to the tattoos. Why did we choose to make that bank account the one thing we told our future amnesic selves about?"

"I don't know. All we've gotten from it, besides a few attempts on our lives, is the name Alexander Tate, Attorney at Law, Miami. That hardly blows my skirt up considering our predicament and what we went through to get it."

"I'll tell you why we chose it," Troy said. "We chose it because that was all we had. Before our memories were stolen from us, we were following a money trail. You had it right."

"It sounded good at the time, but not anymore. What makes you so cocksure?"

"Cocksure?"

Emmy blushed, remembering the kiss. "I'm sorry. I'm just frustrated."

"Don't be. Here's your answer. It's the only sensible explanation that covers everything. As soon as you assume the money trail scenario to be true, then everything else falls into place."

Emmy did not feel everything falling into place, but seeing the conviction in Troy's cobalt eyes, she sensed inspiration coming. She pushed the buttons for floors nine through one to buy some quiet elevator time and said, "Do tell."

Troy began to pace, speaking to himself as much as to her. "For some reason—and I don't know what that was yet—we were following a money trail."

"A trail that we now know leads to a sweet old man whose mind has also been wiped," Emmy interjected.

"That's where we're wrong," Troy said triumphantly.

"It doesn't lead to Kostas?" Emmy asked, incredulity muffling her voice.

Troy shook his head. "It leads through Kostas."

"Through Kostas," Emmy repeated, not understanding yet. "Go on."

"Okay. But let me back up. I'm going to postulate that back when we were following the money trail before our amnesia, our investigation kicked up enough dirt to alert those concerned and make them nervous. At some point—I'm guessing when we showed up here on Grand Cayman—we crossed a line and they decided to make their problem go away."

"By erasing our minds and having us incarcerated for murder," Emmy finished the thought.

"Exactly."

"And Kostas is a cutout on this trail?"

"Right again."

"I'm not sure I know what that means."

Troy nodded his understanding. "Kostas is blindly holding the real criminal's money, perhaps laundering it as well. The money trail looks like it leads to him. And as far as the banks and tax authorities are concerned, it does. But this evening we learned that it really passes through him—without his knowledge."

Despite Troy's explanation, Emmy was not there yet. "You're going to have to explain that."

"Of course. And again, I'm speculating with assumptions that make everything else fall into place. Here goes. Mister X, the guy or guys or organization we're really after, is doing something illegal that makes him a lot of money—money that he has to launder. I don't know what that business is, but I think your earlier assumption that it involves erasing memories is a good one."

Troy paused for Emmy to nod that she was following, and then continued. "Like any smart crook, he's obviously very cautious, perhaps even paranoid about being identified and caught. And of course he's also well aware of rule one in the detective handbook. He knows that anyone coming after him is going to try to follow the money trail. So what does he do?"

"He sets up a blind middleman, a cutout," Emmy answered, seeing the light. "How do you think it works?"

"I think Mister X found a sweet old man with no family living on an island and offered him a deal. I think he offered to set Kostas up in a luxury condo and pay all his bills, in exchange for running his money through the account Kostas has maintained for the last twenty years. He gets Kostas to assign him full power of attorney over the account to him. Then he wipes Kostas's mind so he has no recollection of the arrangement. That's why all Kostas knows now is what Mister X's attorney told him afterwards: that all his bills are taken care of and he doesn't have to worry about money. And that's all Kostas cares to know. Why question it? He lives a good life."

"And Mister X is safe," Emmy added.

"Right."

"Because Kostas is a cutout."

"Right again. Except that we now know about Counselor Alexander Tate in Miami."

"And Tate will know who Mister X is," Emmy said, finishing the chain. "He has to know to manage the arrangement."

Troy shook his head. "Not necessarily. All he needs to know to run normal operations is Kostas's financial information."

"If that's true, then we've got nothing. But you look like the cat who swallowed the canary."

"Things aren't always normal. There have to be contingencies ..."

The elevator opened onto the lobby before Emmy could get Troy to elaborate.

They walked quickly past the concierge's desk so that he would not get another look at their faces. Emmy suspected that it would not matter if he did. She doubted that they would ever return to the Tropical Towers—or Grand Cayman for that matter. Time to head for Miami.

Assuming they could find a way off the island before they got caught.

Back out in the balmy Caribbean air, they were making a silent beeline for the Camry when a bearded man in a Kangol cap stepped out from behind a garden bush onto the sidewalk before them. Emmy felt a shudder of shock as he locked on her with his copper-colored eyes.

"Emmy! Troy! Thank goodness I found you. I've been so worried."

Chapter 41

Something Big

DESPITE ARLEN BLYTHE'S specific language, Luther reacted to the CEO's allegation as he always did when a client claimed to know his secret. He maintained his poker face, assumed that the allegation was just a fishing expedition, and ignored it. "How can I help you, Arlen?"

"We'll get to that," Arlen said with a slow, confident nod. "We're not there yet."

Luther sat quietly and waited. He knew every trick in the interview game and was not about to fall for something as amateur as filling the awkward silence. Sixty seconds later he was feeling pretty good about his ability to project a relaxed, confident air when Arlen opened his mouth and took Luther's breath away.

"Jeff Landis came to me first."

Luther did his best not to react to the mention of his deceased former colleague.

"Looking for money that is," Arlen continued. "I was tempted to have Savas take the same minority ownership position in Aridon Biotech that you eventually did. A cure for Alzheimer's would be a blockbuster of Vitorol's magnitude, so even with the odds of a thousand to one against their taking the compound all the way to market, the financials were right. But I turned it down because I was committed to the strategy of maintaining Savas's laser focus.

"You know, ours really is an incredibly powerful strategy, for one so simple. When you've only got one product, there's no ambiguity or confusion about where everyone in the entire organization is to pour their best efforts. The efficiencies gained by cutting out all the superfluous crap and distractions and honing in on doing one thing better than anyone else in the world are staggering. Still, there are those on my board who worry about the risk of having all our eggs in one basket. But I digress …

"I'll be honest with you, Luther. When Aridon's facility exploded, taking out Landis and his entire research and development team, my first thought was: Thank goodness I walked away. Of course, by then word had already leaked within the biotech community that his compound had fizzled, that it destroyed neurons along with the plaque.

"Tell me, how much did you have invested, Luther?"

"Why don't you tell me, Arlen."

Arlen nodded his approval of the challenge. "Twenty million dollars. That gave you what, twenty percent?"

"And a seat on the board."

"Yes, the only outside seat," Arlen said, casually crossing his legs.

He knew. Luther could feel it. Arlen actually knew. Everything... Impossible. "Are you going somewhere with this? I do pretty well with my law practice, but four years later I can still feel that bite, so I would appreciate it if we could stop picking at the scab."

"Your law practice … yes. I see the office—" Arlen said, holding out his hands palms up and looking around. "And like most leading members of the California business community, I know the name. But my researchers haven't discovered any substantial legal activity coming out of your law practice since you lost that Optiplase tort at trial—also four years back. Talk about a bad year."

Luther wanted to throw this guy out, toss him out on his ear. But something had him hooked. He knew what it was and the knowing made it bitter. Greed.

"You know," Arlen continued, in his increasingly annoying lilt, "I spoke to a tort attorney friend of mine who told me that for national medical torts like that, the lead attorney can expect to shell

out ten to twenty thousand dollars per plaintiff in recruiting costs
—given all the advertising and testing required to sort the
diamonds from the rough. Ten to twenty thousand per. And my
researchers tell me that you had three thousand plaintiffs. That
means the not-guilty verdict cost you in the neighborhood of forty-
five million out of pocket—versus what, the seven hundred million
you would have won with guilty? Now that must have hurt. And
that was what, two months before the twenty million you had
invested in Aridon went up with Landis's team and their facility in a
big ball of fire? I pity your accountant that year. Sixty-five million
in the red. Sixty-five."

Luther did not take the bait. He left the ugly numbers sitting on
the table like candied Brussels sprouts.

Arlen pushed on without missing a beat. "According to the GQ
article Luther Kanasis, the California Bar Association's flamboyant
Man of the Year, you only cleared forty million on the Iprophine
tort that made your name. By my calculations that left you with a
twenty-five million dollar hole.

A hole like that can put a lot of pressure on a man. Could force
him to take steps that he might never otherwise consider ... drastic
steps."

Luther felt his stomach turn somersaults as Arlen dissected his
past with the cold surgical precision of a veteran coroner. Arlen
had pulled everything from the air. He had no proof, could not
convict, but he was spot on. Luther did not like where this was
going. That was exactly the point, of course. Arlen wanted him to
feel helpless and afraid. Arlen wanted Luther to tip his hand.
"Forgive me, Arlen. But if you have a point, I would prefer that
you get to it."

"Or what? You'll brush me off to get back to your thriving law
practice? To servicing your clients? According to my sources—and
I have impeccable sources—the fresh UCLA grads you have slaving
away downstairs do all the work, and then it's only enough to make

Kanasis look legitimate to the IRS. You asked about my point. My point is this: I know that you make all your money using Aridon's technology to rescue people like Bogart from impending crises. I know that you took a goose egg, added a dash of desperation, and turned it golden. And you know what?"

Luther could not resist biting. "What?"

"I think that's brilliant. I think that makes you exactly the kind of guy I want to do business with."

Luther tried to keep his face impassive as a granite bust, but he could not help cracking. Ever since he blew up the Aridon complex with all staff inside to secure exclusive alternative use of the failed Alzheimer's compound, blackmail scenarios like the one Arlen was surely about to propose had been among his worst recurring nightmares. A second whale was about to hop on his already overburdened back, and there was nothing he could do about it. "If you're so sure of your preposterous claims, why the dog and pony show? Why all the speculation? Why not just come out and tell me what you want?" Luther strained to convey casual indifference in every word, if not each facial expression.

"It's called courtship, Luther. I thought it appropriate, perhaps even necessary. You see, I'm not here for blackmail. Nor am I here to propose a penny-ante job like the one you did for Bogart. I'm interested in something big."

Chapter 42

Fritz

TROY STEPPED REFLEXIVELY between Emmy and the stranger, shielding her, even as the thrill of hearing his name coursed through his body. The man who confronted them by name wore a dark brown Kangol cap that matched his stylishly scruffy beard. Both the cap and the beard looked out of place, given the warm weather, and the thought that they were probably worn to hide a balding head crossed his mind. Perhaps Emmy's talents were rubbing off on him.

Kangol was a couple of inches shorter than Troy at about five-ten, but much broader. He projected the solid meat-on-bones look of a rugby player. Kangol's most notable feature, however, was his reptilian irises. They were the strangest coppery color and shimmered with an almost metallic sheen. Troy empathized with the stranger's ocular plight, but did not drop his guard.

"Whoa," the stranger continued, holding up his hands in surrender and offering what seemed to be a genuine smile. "Didn't mean to startle you. But I did, didn't I?"

Troy did not answer.

"Look, you guys came to me, remember?"

"No," Emmy said. "We don't."

Kangol's face took on a concerned expression. "Oh my god, it really happened. Didn't it? You lost your memories, just as you feared?"

Emmy nodded while Troy just studied the man.

"Wow. That changes things. Where do I begin?"

The question was rhetorical, but Troy answered anyway. "How about giving us your name and telling us what you're doing here."

"Yeah, sure. My name is Fritz. Fritz Morgan. I'm a reporter with the Miami Herald. We ran into each other a few times while doing similar research. Familiarity led to chitchat and eventually we became friends. These last few weeks we've had a contest going over who could find the best rum drink. Each night we hit a different bar. Last time we met you asked me to come find you if you ever dropped off the grid."

Troy thought about that for a minute. "So you think we're fellow reporters?"

Fritz weighed his words. "More like private detectives."

"How did you know where to find us?" Emmy asked.

"That's a longer story. I'll be happy to give you all the details and answer your other questions, but not here. I think someone has been following me. Why don't we go down to the West Bay marina? I've got a small yacht docked there. We can take her out where no one can overhear us and talk till dawn. You guys must have loads of questions."

Troy looked at Emmy. He wanted her read of this guy. She beckoned off to the side with her head. "Give us a minute, Fritz," he said.

"Yeah, sure. Whatever. I'll be right over there," Fritz said, pointing to a bench at the center of a nearby garden alcove.

Troy put his arm around Emmy's shoulder and they turned to walk in the opposite direction.

"What do you think?" he asked, as soon as they were out of earshot.

"I don't know. He's nervous and is definitely holding something back. That may be explained away by the situation, but there's one other thing."

"What's that?"

"I don't like rum."

"I'm not a fan either, or at least I wasn't last time I remember. I guess it all boils down to one question: Can we trust him?"

"Do we have a choice? His story sounded plausible enough within the context of our situation. In any case, it's great to meet someone who knows our names and isn't shooting at us. I'm dying to hear what he has to say."

"Yeah, me too."

They rejoined Fritz and Troy said, "Sorry about that. We're a bit jumpy these days. We'd love to talk."

"And we appreciate your doing as we asked. Finding us, I mean," Emmy added.

"No problem. Do you have your own car, or do you want to ride with me?"

Troy was about to confirm that they had their own car when Emmy said, "We do have a car but we'll ride with you. I just need a minute to get a few things." She thrust her hand into Troy's pocket, withdrew the car keys, and was off.

Troy looked over at Fritz as they turned toward his car, searching for the hints of nervousness that Emmy had found so apparent. All he saw was a mask of concern.

"So what's the last thing you remember?" Fritz asked.

Troy saw no harm in answering truthfully. "Afghanistan. 2001."

Fritz sucked in breath. "Seven years. That must have been one rude awakening."

"You have no idea," Troy said, wondering if Fritz actually did. Troy did not elaborate. He did not want to relive the joys of waking up locked in a dark trunk with a corpse. Fritz seemed to understand this.

They completed the walk to his Citroen in silence. Emmy showed up a minute later carrying the two beach bags that held their clothes.

"So how did you find us?" Emmy asked, once they were headed for the marina.

Fritz did not answer for a good thirty seconds, so Emmy repeated the question.

"I think we're being followed," Fritz finally replied, his voice low, his eyes on the mirror.

"Is it a man on a black scooter?" Troy asked, turning with Emmy to look out the back window into the night. No sooner had Fritz said, "Yes," than a side window blew out, sending glass everywhere.

"Duck down!" Fritz yelled. "He's got a gun!"

Troy pushed Emmy into the foot-well and lay down over her as Fritz accelerated and began weaving in and out of traffic.

"Stay down. I think I can lose him."

They complied, winding up face to face on the floor as Fritz continued to bob and weave. Emmy had a splotch of blood on her cheek. When Troy wiped it away and found no scratch, he realized that his own face was dripping blood. Emmy put her lips to his ear. "I don't trust him. I'm not sure why; it's just instinct. But on the other hand a yacht is exactly what we need—especially if he's heading for Miami."

"I was thinking the same thing—about the yacht," Troy whispered back. "There's no way we can go through the airport with our faces on wanted posters."

"Do you think it's safe?" Emmy asked.

"Getting on a boat with Fritz? I think so. I was skeptical before someone shot at us, but that erased most of my doubts. Besides, he could have shot us the moment he had us in the car if he wanted to."

"I hope you're right, but I have the nagging feeling that you're wrong."

"Why did you want to leave our car?"

"I wanted the chance to study him further before we got on the boat. That's a point of no return, so to speak."

Fritz brought the Citroen to a screeching halt. "I've lost him for now," he said. "But it probably won't take him long to spot the car. Let's make sure we're on the Lady Jane before he does."

Troy gave Emmy an inquisitive look as he straightened up. She just shrugged an I-don't-know.

Chapter 43

USSC

"BEFORE WE GET TO THE SPECIFICS of my proposition," Arlen said, "let me give you some background."

"All right," Luther said, pleased to shift the topic from his own woes to someone else's.

"Vitorol, Savas's blockbuster oral insulin and only product, is set to go off patent in December 2012. Vitorol's original patent actually expires next year, but thanks to a Hatch-Waxman extension, we've got another three years."

"A Hatch-Waxman extension?"

"Yes. Back in 1984 Senators Orrin Hatch and Henry Waxman sponsored what has become the defining patent legislation for the pharmaceutical industry. It includes provisions for granting patent extensions to corporations who perform the costly clinical trials required to safely extend a compound's approved indications to classes that would not otherwise be served. In Vitorol's case, we got a three-year extension for obtaining both a pediatric indication, and for proving Vitorol's safety and efficacy in a form of diabetes prevalent only among Native Americans."

"So without Hatch-Waxman, Vitorol would go off patent next year?"

"Eleven months from now."

"And since you are telling me this, I presume that your extension has come under scrutiny?"

"That's correct. It has been challenged by Braxton, the generic manufacturer who holds the patent on the buffering agent we use to get the insulin past the stomach to where it can be absorbed in a pH neutral environment."

Luther was not interested in the chemistry. He needed to know who the key players were, and how much money was involved. "How big a deal is this?"

"Do you have any idea what happens to a drug when it goes off patent?"

"I assume the generics move in to steal market share."

"When it's a blockbuster like Vitorol, they swoop in like rabid vultures. We will lose between sixty and eighty percent of our sales in the first year off patent. By the end of the second year, Vitorol's sales will be less than ten percent of their patent-protected level."

"So basically, once you go off patent, it's all over? Savas is kaput?"

Arlen nodded. "There are a few games we can play to squeeze more out of the lemon, but you're essentially right. That's it."

Luther did the math in his head. It was not tough. At twelve billion a year, every additional month of patent protection was worth a billion bucks. Three commas. Nine zeros. The three years Hatch-Waxman got them were worth a staggering thirty-six billion in sales, virtually all of it pure profit, no doubt.

Luther would have liked nothing more than to take a thick slice of that pie. In fact, this was exactly the kind of opportunity he had been waiting for. But alas, he could not solve patent problems with 456. Laws did not have memories. "I'm not confirming any of your earlier rampant speculation by telling you that my specialty is criminal law, particularly those rare instances where witness testimony is the lynchpin of the prosecutorial case. Your case is about as far from my center of competence as they come. I'm sorry, Arlen, but I really can't help you."

Rather than rising, Arlen leaned further back into the couch and spread his arms out along the top as if he owned the place. "You know, I spent a lot of time thinking about what I would have done if I were you, if I had complete control of 456. I think I would have adopted a strategy very similar to yours. I would have made secrecy my absolute first and highest priority. After all, there may be a lot of wiggle room for the rich in this great country of ours, but overly greedy or careless millionaires can still wind up in jail.

"As far as I can tell, you have managed to conduct your nefarious business for over three years now without a whiff of scandal by operating like a micro-mafia. You work only with known entities, and only by strict bona-fide referral. Your clients are people of means who have no bigger legal challenges hanging over their heads. And you only work with people whom you're sure you can get off, so they won't later point the finger your way in exchange for a reduced sentence. Nonetheless, you keep your clients completely in the dark as to your methods. And it works.

"Bogart did not have a clue that you were using a drug. As with everyone, I suppose, the notion did not cross his mind because he assumed that if a memory-erasing drug had been invented, he would have heard of it. Rumor would have gotten out. Yet it has not. Not a peep."

"Again, I have to ask you if this is going somewhere," Luther said.

Arlen smiled. He appeared to appreciate directness. "My point is this. Your adoption of an ultra-conservative business model has caused you to overlook what we in the pharmaceutical industry would call a major line extension." Arlen crossed his legs, giving pause to emphasize what came next. "Shall I tell you what I have in mind?"

Luther found himself staring at a fork in the road. He could either walk away now and end their meeting with his façade intact, pretending that Arlen's conclusions were nothing but wild speculation. Or, he could tacitly acknowledge that the pharmaceutical executive was batting a thousand, and learn more. Arlen had obviously put a lot of thought into this, just as he had said. Furthermore, his insight was little short of miraculous—judging by the clients, attorneys and judges Luther had worked with who had not a clue. Among outsiders, only Sebastian Troy had suspected the truth, and Luther had neutralized him before he got within three thousand miles.

Arlen might only be here because he was familiar with Jeff Landis's research, but he was here, and that meant he had serious needs. One way or the other, Luther had to deal with him.

Luther also thought of Orca, and what a relief it would be to have the killer whale off his back at last. That image was the clincher. He nodded. "Tell me."

Arlen's eyes flashed with the satisfaction of a chess master whose opponent made a long anticipated move. He got straight to the point, to the line extension. "You have focused exclusively on the witness stand. I want you to turn your attention to the bench."

Luther's jaw dropped and he gave up all pretense of control. "You want what?"

Arlen remained silent, allowing him to process.

Luther thought out loud. "If the judge loses all memory of evidence and testimony presented, all you get is a mistrial."

"Keep going," Arlen urged.

"A mistrial buys you time, perhaps months ... months at a billion per."

"You're getting there."

"The exact outcome seems unpredictable. Is there any precedent for this?" Luther asked, certain that Arlen had checked.

"There is some. Judges have died, had strokes, or otherwise become disabled in the middle of trials. In a few cases a replacement judge has simply stepped in. But in the vast majority, a mistrial had to be declared and the whole proceedings restarted."

"How much time are you expecting to buy?" Luther asked, trying to gauge his fee for this new line of work.

Arlen shook his head. "You need to back up, Luther. You still haven't asked the critical question."

"Critical question?"

"By switching from the witness stand to the bench, you're only halfway there. You need to make one more leap."

Luther squirmed uneasily in his chair. He did not like having his intellect put on the spot like this. After a minute of drawing blanks, he got up and stared into his waterfall, determined not to give in. Arlen sat quietly while Luther tried to let his mind run free before the cascading wall of water. It took two minutes, a full hundred and twenty seconds, but the right question came. He turned around slowly. "Is your case already on appeal?" he asked, not bothering to hide the trepidation in his voice.

"Bravo, Luther. Bravo. Savas versus Braxton is about to go before the United States Supreme Court."

Chapter 44

Why

PEERING OUT from adjacent portholes in search of signs of pursuit, Troy and Emmy watched the West Bay marina fade behind them. All appeared peaceful and quiet, as indeed it was supposed to be in paradise, but whoever had shot out the window of Fritz's car minutes before was still out there. Had they lost him? Or was he watching them right now through binoculars, making plans to capture them at sea?

"Care for a drink?" Fritz asked. "I've got the autopilot set to take us to Jamaica. It's a hundred and eighty miles. We won't be there until morning."

Troy had been so intent on the view that he had not heard Fritz descend from the bridge. Judging by her jolt, Emmy had not either. He turned to see Fritz holding up a chilled bottle of Pinot Grigio in one hand and an Appleton Dark Jamaican Rum in the other. Troy was not much of a drinker, but given the circumstances … "A cool glass of wine sounds great."

"Make that two," Emmy said.

"You guys have more control than I do," Fritz replied with a shake of his head before turning back towards the kitchen.

The forty-foot Lady Jane had a simple floor plan. Up top there was just the bridge with some extra seating and a large sundeck. Below there were two bedroom suites separated by a central lounge area and a kitchenette. You did not get a lot of room for half-a-million bucks, but then Troy supposed that the guys who bought these floating motels were not counting their pennies. "How does a reporter afford a ride like this?" Troy asked.

"Believe me, he doesn't," Fritz called back from the sunken kitchenette. "It's the publisher's, but he doesn't pay for it either. He writes it off as a business expense. My trip is just part of the justification. I'm doing a feature series on financial crime in the Caribbean. Nice work if you can get it."

"Is that how we overlapped?" Emmy asked. "You said earlier that we had run into each other a few times while working on the same story."

"That's right," Fritz said, unloading two wine glasses, two bottles, and two tumblers full of ice from a platter. After filling Emmy's wine glass he turned to Troy and said, "You sure you want to go with the soft stuff?"

"I'm sure. Rum gives me a headache."

"Fair enough," Fritz said, and poured accordingly. "Cheers."

"Why are you taking us to Jamaica?" Emmy asked.

"Because your pictures are on wanted posters all over Grand Cayman. Because someone is shooting at you. Because according to the news you've killed two members of the Royal Cayman Islands Police in the last forty-eight hours. Because—"

"We didn't kill anyone," Troy interrupted.

"I know, I know. That's why I'm putting my own neck on the line to help you. That said, I do need to know what's going on. Why were you at the Tropical Towers?"

"Did we tell you what we were investigating?" Emmy asked, throwing the question back at him.

Fritz cocked his head to the side such that his coppery irises reflected the glow of a candle, and Troy realized that he was wearing contacts. That observation struck a cord—why would anyone wear lenses that made his eyes look so reptilian?—but it was forgotten with his new friend's next words. "Not specifically. You implied that you were here because of a private grievance."

Troy felt his throat go dry as his heart skipped a beat. He

brought the glass to his lips and took a long sip of the crisp white wine. Fritz was about to read them the latest chapter of their lives, the chapter that would link their past, their present, and their missing seven years. They were about to learn why someone wanted them dead, and what it was they had lost.

"Are we married, Emmy and I?" Troy asked, surprising no one more than himself as the words leapt from his mouth unfiltered by his conscious mind.

Adding to Troy's surprise, Emmy reached over beneath the oval table and took supportive hold of his thigh while Fritz shifted his gaze back and forth between the two as though he were watching a tennis game. "Ah, no. No you're not."

The proclamation hit Troy like a bucket of frosty water. As the chill reverberated, he wanted to look over at Emmy, to see if her features registered a pain akin to his own, but fear stilled his head. He was not willing to risk another crushing emotional blow at that moment.

As her hand slid limply off his thigh, Fritz added, "But then, you are both single."

Troy and Emmy turned to look at each other, and he saw hope nudging the pain from her eyes. He turned back to Fritz and held up his left hand. "What about this?" he asked, pointing to his wedding ring.

Fritz grimaced. "That's why you're here."

Chapter 45

Nine

"THE SUPREME COURT!" Luther shouted as Arlen confirmed his suspicion. "Are you crazy? The justices are guarded like the president."

Arlen remained on the couch, silent and apparently content to let his host vent his frustration by shouting and pacing before the waterfall. Luther took advantage of the opportunity to pull his thoughts together. After a full minute of pacing brought his blood pressure under control, he realized that despite Arlen's supernatural insightfulness in other areas, the otherwise clairvoyant CEO assumed the use of a traditional delivery system. He did not understand that erasing minds was not as simple as slipping someone a pill. "My work ... it requires physical contact."

"I appreciate that," Arlen said, breaking his silence in a calm, even monotone. "But you're wrong."

Luther stopped pacing and stared at his prospective client. "With all due respect for your deductive powers, I think I know my methods better than you do."

"Calm down, Luther. Listen to your waterfall. I'm not referring to your methods. I'll take your word for those. I'm talking about the supreme court justices. They're not guarded like the president."

"They're not?"

"No. In fact, they're not guarded at all—although I too had assumed they were. It's a common misconception. The truth is, if they're not looking at abortion, the supreme court justices receive fewer threats than your average federal employee. Makes sense if you think about it. Only a complete idiot would provoke a judge."

That did make sense, Luther thought as he sat back down across from Arlen. Why was he so tense anyway? He knew the answer, of course. Orca had him all riled up. The bastard kept him under both tremendous financial pressure and the threat of physical danger. Arlen would potentially be offering him a means of getting out from under the whale—but the risk would no doubt be commensurate with the reward. Luther hated risk. He took a deep breath, and said, "Tell me more."

A thin smile cracked Arlen's face. "Despite the extraordinary power they wield, the lives of supreme court justices are not that different from yours or mine. Believe it or not, Justice Goldstein actually had her purse snatched while walking near the Kennedy Center. And Justice Stoffer was mugged while jogging the city streets. Both perpetrators got away. Getting to the justices is not going to be that big a problem."

"Then why not just shoot them?"

Arlen shook his head. Perish the thought. "You'd have to hit all nine at once, and that would be virtually impossible to orchestrate since the only time they're together is at the court or an occasional state function, and they are well guarded at those. Plus bullets and bombs are unambiguous, whereas mass amnesia opens up all kinds of doors to speculation and debate. Was it something in the water? Speculation and debate buy me time—months, at a billion per."

Luther began to relax as various scenarios danced through his head. Given Arlen's wealth and the profile of the target, Luther could probably ask for five million dollars, maybe even ten. Hell, with billions at stake, why not ask for twenty-five. Twenty-five million and he would be free of Orca.

That was it, he decided, drawing a mental line in the sand. Twenty-five million was his price. But wait a minute, he thought, recrossing his legs. Arlen had used the plural. He had said getting to the justices. Did he need two neutralized to sway the opinion his

way? Three? No way. No way was Luther going to risk attracting
that kind of heat. If more than one justice drew a blank, the cause
was going to get some serious scrutiny. Just one on the other hand,
and the court would probably try to cover it up. Hell, the justice
might not even confess to having lost his or her memory—so long
as it wasn't the chief. "Which justice do you have in mind?"

"Have you got any Scotch?" Arlen asked.

It was the chief, Luther thought. Otherwise Arlen would have
come right out with it. That would make it easier to request twenty-
five million with a straight face, but still ... "I've got a twenty-year-
old Macallan. How will you take it?"

"Straight up."

Luther forswore drinking during business after his slip-up with
Orca, although at the moment he was mildly tempted. If ever a
situation needed a bit of lubrication, this was it. But he would not
yield. Not until he was out of the woods.

He poured two fingers of Macallan into a Baccarat crystal
tumbler for Mr. Arlen Blythe, and then gave himself an equal
serving of similarly colored apple juice, adding a couple of rocks.
He often did this with drinking clients. He would confess if the
topic came up, but found that this minor deception made his guests
more comfortable.

After handing Arlen his Scotch, Luther resumed his seat and sat
in silence thinking, Please, not the chief.

"So, where were we?" Arlen teased, holding his tumbler
appreciatively to the light after enjoying the first sip.

"You were going to tell me which justice, which member of the
United States Supreme Court, you need neutralized."

"Oh yes, right. Actually, Luther, I need you to erase the
memories of all nine."

Despite all his training, despite Julliard, despite gliding gracefully
through countless courtroom surprises, Luther choked. He literally
choked on his drink and began to cough uncontrollably. "All nine!"

< Out Receipt

sville Branch
387-1234
ocpl.info

sday, August 20, 2020 11:01:09 AM
)

: 31183198126036
e: Flash
no.: Fiction TIG
09/30/2020

l items: 1

just saved $16.99 by using your
ary today.

ibrarian:

intments for personalized assistance
apps eBooks job searches writing resumes
l setup & more.

a staff member or visit
ocpl.info for details.

he screamed through a juicy mist. "You are crazy, Arlen. I'd like to help you, but really, there's no way." He stood and walked back to the bar for a towel.

"Of course there's a way, Luther. All we need is a will."

Luther stopped in his tracks. He knew code when he heard it. "It would take one hell of a will."

"I'm well aware of that."

I bet you are, Luther thought. But if you were fully aware, you wouldn't be here. Luther had calculated his fees for three, four and even five wipes during one particularly boring afternoon in court. By doubling his fee for each additional wipe, three wipes got him seven million. Four wipes netted fifteen. And five wipes earned him a cool thirty-one million dollars. For nine … it would take him a while to do numbers like that in his head. And it was pure fantasy, so why bother. He set his tumbler down on the coffee table, knocking the daydream from his mind. It was time to stop flirting with disaster, time to be done with Arlen Blythe. He would find another way to rid himself of the killer whale. "Did Bogart explain my fees?"

That chess-master gleam flashed across Arlen's eyes again. "Indeed he did. He explained that your fee doubles with each additional case. I believe he paid you three million for his double."

"That's right. It's to keep the reward commensurate with the risk. I'm sure you understand."

"Indeed I do. In fact, I did the math."

"You did?" Luther asked, certain that Arlen had gotten the equation wrong.

"For nine erasures, you get five hundred and eleven million dollars. I've brought you a check."

Chapter 46

Balinorm

TROY DID A DOUBLE TAKE, trying to fully comprehend Fritz's last words. "What do you mean, the ring is why I'm here?"

Fritz did not answer immediately, taking an eternity to refill their glasses first. Finally he said, "As I understand it from bits of your conversation, you both woke up on the island with no idea where you were or what you were doing here?"

"That's right," Troy said. "I was in the trunk of a car with one of the dead cops you heard about. Emmy was in the front."

"And how did you get from the trunk of a cop car to the Tropical Towers?"

"It's a long story."

Fritz motioned toward the kitchenette with his head. "There's a couple of more bottles in the fridge, and we've got all night ..."

"We were—" Troy felt Emmy kick him below the table. "—tracking down the man whose business card was in my shoe."

"Why would you do that?" Fritz asked, his tone skeptical. "The card could have belonged to the man who attacked you. You could have been walking into the lion's den."

"Where else were we to turn?" Troy retorted. "We had no idea what was going on, why the cop was dead, or why we were on Grand Cayman. We didn't even know what year it was."

"Tropical Towers is a residential complex," Fritz said. "Did this man have his home address on his business card?"

"No," Emmy said. "But he gave it to us after we called his cell phone."

"The kind of discussion we required was hardly suited for the telephone," Troy added.

Fritz shook his head and pushed away his rum. "Look, I'm a reporter. I interview people for a living. I can tell when people are lying."

"I'm not lying," Emmy said.

"So why did you go to Solomon Bank & Trust?"

"How did you know we went there?" she asked.

"That's where they say you killed the second cop."

"That was the other card in my shoe," Troy offered.

"Show them to me," Fritz said, his skepticism on his sleeve. "Show me the cards."

"We don't have to show you anything." Troy said, wondering why Emmy had chosen to deceive their only friend, but willing to follow her instincts.

"And I don't have to take you to Jamaica. I can drop you right back on Grand Cayman. Look, I don't mean to be pushy, but I'm taking a big risk by helping you guys. I'm becoming an accomplice. In return, I think it's only fair to ask for all the details. Furthermore, I have to think about the story that's going to justify this to my boss." He motioned around the yacht. "Now be honest with me, or get off my boat."

Troy looked over at Emmy. She shrugged and said, "I'm sorry. I guess everything we've been through has us wound a bit too tight. Go ahead, Troy, tell him everything. I'm going to the bathroom— feeling a bit queasy." She stood and disappeared into the aft cabin.

Troy turned back to Fritz. "This is where it all started," he said, taking off his left shoe and sock.

By the time Emmy returned, Troy had laid it all out: the sniper at the Seagull's Nest, the discovery of the tattoo, Emmy's trick at Solomon Bank & Trust, the man on the motor scooter, and the meeting with Kostas. The only thing he left out was mention of Kostas's attorney, Alexander Tate.

Emmy returned as he was finishing up. Troy noted that the sparkle was back in her eyes.

"So what's your plan now?" Fritz asked.

"I don't know. I guess that depends on what you tell us."

"I'll be happy to tell you everything I know. Ironically, all that amounts to is what you told me before your amnesia. I've no new information for you, so I'm not sure how much it's going to help." Fritz took a long pull on his drink. "To be honest, I think it's going to hurt. If I were you, I think I'd rather live in ignorance."

Fritz set his tumbler down and it immediately slid across the table as the Lady Jane rolled over a large wave. He stood. "Tell you what. You think about my advice for a minute. I'm going to take my motion sickness medication. When I get back, tell me what you've decided." Fritz began walking to the aft cabin, but stopped after two steps. "Say, I've got extra medication, if either of you would like a shot. Could make the difference between twelve hours in the bathroom and a good night's sleep."

"Sounds good to me," Emmy said, placing a hand on her stomach.

"A shot?" Troy asked. "Not a pill or a patch? What is it?"

"The trade name is Balinorm. It's only been out for a year or so, but it works like a charm. Keizer is making a killing. I couldn't sail without it."

Fritz disappeared into the aft stateroom and came out a minute later with a black syringe pen resembling what diabetics use to inject their insulin. He pulled up his shirt, plunged the whisker-thin needle into his abdomen, and hit the button. Troy heard a click.

Fritz swapped needles and ruby-red cartridges, recocked the pen injector, and passed it to Troy. "Any fatty tissue is fine," Fritz instructed.

Accepting the injector, Troy felt a twinge of doubt even though he had just seen Fritz inject himself. A second later, however, that twinge was supplanted by a wave of nausea, and he pressed the button.

Emmy followed suit.

Fritz said, "I'm feeling better already."

Chapter 47

Bo

FARKAS COULD NOT HELP basking in the glow of his own cleverness as Emmy cleared the dishes from the table. Not only had he tricked his guests into injecting themselves with 456, but he had even managed to cover his tracks by lacing their dessert pudding with crushed Dramamine.

On the downside, he had used up his stash of 456 and was once again left with only a single dose in reserve. And he too now had the miracle drug shellacking his dendrites. But without the subsequent UV-C exposure, his system would flush it within forty-eight hours. No harm, no foul.

Now he just had to pump enough booze into them to dull their edge.

Fortunately, he had just the ticket.

Once Emmy retook her seat, Farkas asked, "Did you make up your mind? Do you want me to tell you what I know about your tragic backgrounds, or would you rather let sleeping dogs lie?"

"Tell us," Emmy said. "The good, the bad, and the ugly."

"As you wish. But first I'm going to freshen up our drinks. Trust me, you're going to need them."

After pouring healthy measures of rum and wine, Farkas said, "Ladies first," and began the unlikely task of telling Emmy her own story. There was no percentage in lying to her, no need to spice things up. He just told it like it was. "Back in 2005, having worked for years as an upscale psychic in L.A., you moved into the Beverly Hills estate of one of your former customers, a man named Bo Beaulieu, with whom you were in love.

"Bo was much older than you, and very wealthy. Needless to say, his relatives were displeased to see anyone without her own money coming between them and their inheritance. To make a long story short—your words, not mine—they pressured him not to marry you and he never did. That did not bother you because you were happy just to be with Bo, much happier than you had ever been before. You were a good 'wife.' That situation lasted for a year and a half, until Bo was killed while jogging in a hit and run.

"Adding insult to injury, Bo's family moved into his estate and kicked you out before the body was cold, claiming that you were just domestic help on par with the maid and gardener."

"Shall I continue?" Farkas asked, wanting to appear empathetic.

Emmy nodded as he knew she would.

"You did the only thing you could, not having any money of your own. You went back to working as a psychic. It was hard going. You had gotten used to living the good life and felt that your discontent affected the quality of your readings. Furthermore, all your old, hard won clientele had moved on during your eighteen-month hiatus, and so it was pretty rough going.

"You brought a civil suit against the man who was allegedly behind the wheel of the killer Porsche Cayenne, but you lost when the only witness to the crime developed amnesia and could not testify.

"After that you were back on the streets."

Farkas watched Troy reach over and pull Emmy toward him

with both arms, using one to hold her tight, the other to stroke her hair. She looked limp as a rag doll, staring forward, her cheeks dry but expressionless.

One down, one to go.

Farkas turned toward Troy and said, "That's Emmy's story. Are you ready for yours?"

Chapter 48

Leapfrog

HONEY RETURNED to his office after four long hours at the bank. Getting nowhere was exhausting. He was hungry too.

"Any luck?" Molly asked.

"Luck? What's that?"

"Are they bank robbers? A new Bonnie and Clyde?"

"No," he said, wondering if she had peanut butter crackers in her big beige handbag today. "Their intentions remain a mystery. She spent fifteen minutes talking to one of the account managers, but then didn't open an account when the number she wanted wasn't available."

"That's weird."

"It gets weirder. She spent five of those minutes reading the account manager's aura. Did a hell of a job too, he said."

"What was her partner doing?"

"He was chatting up the other senior banker about mortgage rates. I'm guessing that they were waiting for Jacobs to arrive."

"You think maybe it was personal? Johnson and Jacobs both?"

"I don't know what else to think. Maybe they're just complete psychopaths. But then there's that anonymous tip ..." Honey shook his head. "How we doing with the blue brotherhood?" he asked, changing the subject.

"Got over fifty confirmations with more coming in all the time. Coast Guard will have them here around midnight."

"Great. I want them in place when the air and sea ports open. With the ports manned, our guys will be free to sweep the interior en masse."

"How can I help?"

"Oscar is getting us new mug shots off the bank's security cameras. They're much sharper than the old ones and in color. I'll need you to make up new wanted posters and several thousand flyers. Then I need you to get on the phone with channel 9 and the radio stations. I want them all broadcasting the description I gave you."

"Okay. I take it you're going to be leading the chase?"

"No."

"No?"

"No. I'm done chasing. This time ... I'm going to get out in front of them."

Chapter 49

Agent Simms

TROY STUDIED FRITZ for a long minute, trying to decide if he wanted this to be the man who narrated his life. Despite all appearances and what they had been through, he did not trust their reporter friend. In the end, however, he simply had to know.

"I'm ready. Give it to me straight."

Fritz nodded and took another sip of his drink. "I know quite a bit more about you than Ms. Green. I was planning to make you the subject of a separate human interest story."

"Just give me the highlights," Troy said, knowing that exposing his past would be like ripping a Band-aid off his heart—a very big and sticky Band-aid. Best to be quick.

"Very well. Three-and-a-half years ago you married an international correspondent for CNN. Her name was Sabrina Trevino. The two of you had met on several occasions in Afghanistan and then dated throughout two years of coincidental service in Iraq. When she got a job with CNN's Washington bureau, you resigned your commission, married her, and went to work at Bethesda Medical Center as a civilian.

"You sure you want to hear this?" Fritz asked.

"I am," Troy replied.

"As you wish.

"Sabrina got pregnant on your Hawaiian honeymoon. She gave birth to Alisandra nine months later. That was about two-and-a-half years ago." Fritz paused to let Troy digest this while he drained his tumbler of rum.

"Nine months ago," Fritz continued, "you were driving home from dinner when you were clipped by a drunk going sixty in a Hummer. The road was icy and your 3-series BMW spun out of control. It flipped over a railing and fell down into a ravine where it landed upside down on some boulders. The roof of the car caved in, killing your wife and daughter. The steering column shielded you from the brunt of the impact, and you walked away with a couple of gashes on your forehead and a smashed up arm.

"The drunk, Russell Rankin, never even slowed down."

Troy felt the room begin to spin. This could not be happening. He looked over at Emmy and saw tears rolling down her cheeks. She reached over and put her hand atop his.

Mercifully, Fritz kept talking, not allowing Troy to dwell. "You were pulled out of the car by an FBI Agent on his way home from work. Agent Simms witnessed the accident and saw the driver clearly, but did not get the license number. He lost his memory the day before the trial and could not testify, forcing the prosecution to drop the case."

"They dropped the case?" Emmy said. "What about the physical evidence, the drunk's Hummer?"

"It turns out that Rankin's wife had a matching black Hummer. When the police showed up the next morning and asked to see his vehicle, Rankin produced his wife's. Before the police figured out that they had been duped, Rankin reported his own stolen. He also had a group of friends willing to provide him with an alibi."

"And the man who killed my boyfriend?" Emmy asked. "What happened to him?"

"Similar story, I gathered. You didn't give me the details."

"Yet no one connected the dots?" Emmy pressed.

"Drunk drivers kill over ten thousand people a year in the US. You would have to be looking pretty hard to distinguish those two dots."

Troy slumped forward with his elbows on his knees and his

palms on the back of his head. If more were coming, he did not want to see it telegraphed by slanted eye or crinkled brow. He wanted a blindfold for the execution.

Apparently Fritz was out of ammunition, because Emmy asked, "How did Troy and I meet?"

There was a long pause, during which Troy guessed that Fritz and Emmy were passing silent signals. Then Fritz cleared his throat, reloading so to speak, and took the next shot. "Troy lost more than his family in the accident. The nerve damage to his right arm cost him his ability to operate. With no job to pour himself into as he worked through the stages of grief, he devoted himself to obtaining justice. His first stop was Agent Simms, whom he assumed Rankin had bribed. But after a thorough interrogation and a month of follow-up detective work, Troy became convinced that Simms' amnesia was real.

"His next move was to look for similar instances."

"He connected the dots," Emmy interjected.

Troy looked up to see Fritz nodding. "He dug up an article on your case that made the society pages. He flew out to L.A. and the two of you clicked. While your situation was not as dire as Troy's, you were also very motivated to get to the bottom of what happened and eager for a break from L.A. So you joined forces.

"I don't know the specifics of how you ended up on Grand Cayman, other than that you were following the trail of payments made by the unconvicted murderers. I got the impression that you were using illegal means—stealing financial records, hacking into banking networks, things like that—because you avoided revealing your methods. That's about all I know."

"I see," Troy heard Emmy say. "Well, I think that's enough for one sitting. I'm going to put our friend here to bed."

Chapter 50

Recipe

LUTHER STARED at Arlen with his mouth agape as the number replayed in his mind. Five-hundred-and-eleven million dollars. Half-a-billion. Talk about life changing on a dime. After repeating the musical number five or six times to himself, however, the lawyer in him regained control and he settled back into the plush armchair. "What's the catch?"

Arlen spread his hands, palms up. "There's no catch, Luther. Just a few conditions."

"I see … Do tell; I'm all ears."

"Is that an espresso machine I see over there?" Arlen asked.

Luther stood, more pleased to have an excuse to walk off some tension than irritated by the delay. "Single or a double?"

"I'd love a double," Arlen said, standing as well.

They walked over to the granite bar where Arlen leaned with one elbow on the countertop. After Luther ground the beans, Arlen began. "There's one thing we need to agree on up front. It will help everything else fall into place."

"Go ahead."

"Given the amount of attention that your history-making performance will garner, and the corresponding size of your payout, I trust you can see that it would be in everyone's best interests for this to be your swan song. After successfully wiping the entire United States Supreme Court, you, the compound and your five hundred and eleven million dollars are to retire permanently. Hell, let's make it an even five fifty, agreed?"

Luther's knee-jerk reaction was *no way*. He was not going to let a client dictate his life. But after a moment's thought, he realized that retirement was the only sensible move. After this job, the FBI would forever be on the lookout for new occurrences of wiped minds. Meanwhile, with Who shot JFK? getting old, conspiracy buffs would look at the amnesic Supreme Court as tigers do red meat. Thousands of closet nerds would begin digging through past cases, sifting the minutia for clues. Yes, Luther thought, he would be well advised to be living on a distant island when that happened —his own private island.

And it wasn't as though he enjoyed his work.

Feeling a profound if unexpected sense of relief, he said, "Agreed."

"Excellent, my friend. I'm glad we're of like mind. Now, let's discuss tactics."

"I work alone. Always have, always will," Luther replied. He was a proud man, the California Bar Association's Man of the Year for chrissake. He had to show some spine. He drew a line, and vowed not to let Arlen cross it.

To Luther's chagrin, Arlen's expression remained as cordial as could be. "Have you ever wiped anyone as high profile as a US Supreme Court justice?"

"My client list is confidential."

Arlen took a sip of his espresso and then set the cup back down on the saucer. "I'll take that as a no. Tell me this then; have you ever done more than two wipes for a single case?"

"No. Multiple wipes are just too dangerous. Despite the higher pay, I prefer sticking to singles."

"I see. So now that we've determined that the size and scope of your experience are both but a fraction of the task at hand, do you still find it reasonable to ask me to part with half-a-billion dollars without some kind of oversight?"

Luther recognized Arlen's tactic as one of his own courtroom favorites: framing. Luther had reduced the world of possibilities to a yes or no based upon an overly simple set of parameters. Luther also realized that Arlen had just run him through a subroutine. Luther had routinely prepared dozens of similar argumentative loops before his courtroom appearances. If the prosecutor says A, get the jury back on track with subroutine X, if he says B, use Y. Luther hated being on the receiving end of such tactics. Their use implied that Arlen was currently holding him in intellectual contempt. He resolved not to end up there again, and tossed out a framing question of his own. "Do you really want to involve yourself so deeply in something so risky?"

Arlen smiled as if to say touché, then changed his tack. "When I was negotiating with Landis, Aridon was on their 243rd compound. How much further did he get?"

Luther decided to play along. "All the way to 456."

Arlen raised his brows at the implied progress. "I trust that the compound still requires UV-C activation after implantation?"

"That's right."

"Is the amount of memory erasure constant?"

Luther could think of no reason to hold back that detail. "No. We can vary it from a minimum of around four weeks up to about the last twenty percent of a person's total episodic memory."

Arlen looked off into space for a minute, then nodded and asked, "Do you know why twenty percent is the limit?"

The pharmacology of 456 was a testy topic for Luther. He was embarrassed not to understand it. Landis had been Luther's only source for such information, but he flaunted his PhDs in Biochemistry and Molecular Biology every time he opened his mouth. No doubt that was part of the reason he had trouble getting financing. Initially, Luther had not given a crap about the science—he was in it for the money—so he had let Landis's explanations fly over his head with little more than a contemplative nod. Now that Compound 456 was the sun in his universe, however, Luther was very curious indeed. He sensed an opportunity, swallowed his pride, and said, "No."

Arlen gave an understanding nod and said, "Landis wanted to cure Alzheimer's. While the biochemistry of the disease remains largely mysterious, we know that the formation of plaque clusters in the neuron forest is key. The plaque clusters strangle nerve cells —like weeds in a garden. Landis's strategy was to devise a compound that destroyed the plaque.

"He had a patent on an enzyme that fluoresced with heat when exposed to ultraviolet-C radiation. So his tactic was to develop a carrier for that enzyme that would bind uniquely to plaque—a guided missile to deliver his heat bomb, so to speak. Once in place, he planned to expose the enzyme to UV-C via the optic nerve, and destroy the plaque. With the plaque gone, the progression of Alzheimer's should be halted if not reversed.

"Incidentally, this is exactly the kind of treatment the pharmaceutical industry loves, because you have to keep coming back at regular intervals to have the weeds pulled.

"Landis's problem was finding a carrier that would bind only to plaque—a very smart missile. Unfortunately, the plaque in question, beta amyloid, is a peptide comprised of the same amino acids that are the building blocks of the nerve cells storing memories. Thus after 456 attempts, he still had nothing that attached to plaque and only plaque."

Luther knew that last point all too well. An announcement to that effect had marked the second worst day of his life. He said, "Landis thought he had it with 456. It worked in monkeys—but not in humans. When 456 destroyed the memory of the first volunteer, he threw in the towel."

"Hard to get more volunteers after that," Arlen agreed. "Now, you said that you can wipe memories from a minimum of about four weeks up to around the last twenty-percent of a person's life, right?"

"Right."

"Do you regulate that interval based on the quantity of 456 injected, or the exposure to UV-C?"

"The exposure to UV-C."

Arlen nodded as though this was the answer he expected. "And the higher the frequency, the longer the erasure, right?"

"Right. So how does it erase memory?" Luther asked.

"Memory is another gray area—pardon the pun. We still know surprisingly little about how memories are created and stored. The building blocks of memory are neurons, and you have billions of them. Each neuron has myriad branches, called dendrites, which conduct the flow of information. Over time, the dendrites become more stable, like the branches on a tree growing thicker. You follow?"

"Sure."

"Good. Now, there are also different types of dendrites, and again they are not fully understood. But nonetheless, given your explanation, it's obvious to me that in addition to attaching to beta-amyloid plaque, 456 attaches to dendrites associated with episodic memory. When activated with UV-C, it heats up. The heat fries the more fragile dendrites, the thinner branches so to speak."

"And at the most powerful setting, the heat is high enough to fry the most fragile twenty percent of branches," Luther said. "Got it."

"Good."

"I'm surprised that the heating doesn't damage the rest of the brain."

Arlen nodded. "That's one of those things you never know until you try. Since no one has caught on to you, apparently not. But I do have to believe that it causes one hell of a headache."

"So I've heard," Luther said. "Thanks."

Arlen drained his cup. "Now, with that arsenal in mind, let's get back to the battle plan."

Chapter 51

Alisandra

EMMY SHUT the stateroom door behind them and turned the lock as Troy flopped onto one of the twin beds. She should have felt numb from Fritz's revelations about her own past, but pity for Troy consumed her instead. She had lost the man that she loved. That was tragic ... and probably true. But at the end of the day he was just her boyfriend, not even her fiancé. Troy had lost his wife, his daughter, and his career.

Although Troy had neither expressed nor voiced his feelings, she knew that he was attracted to her—spiritually and romantically. She also knew that those emotions were now fueling fires of guilt. She should probably be feeling guilty too, but she was not. Bo Beaulieu was gone forever. Troy was there with her. He was the only man she knew. And she loved him.

She wanted to lie down next to Troy, to put her arms around him and hold him until he cried himself to sleep. No, she corrected herself, that wasn't exactly true. In fact, she wanted to rip off their clothes and make love to him all night.

Neither was in the cards.

They had work to do.

Which meant she had to bring her partner around. "I'm so sorry, Troy. I can't even imagine what you're feeling."

He looked up at her with tears in his eyes. "Alisandra. My daughter's name ... was Alisandra. It's a beautiful name. I'd always wondered if I'd have boys or girls and what I would name them. Now I know."

Emmy did not want to risk the potential fallout from a supportive squeeze, so she offered a reassuring nod.

"Now that name is all I have," Troy continued. "I have no idea what she looked like, so I can't even mourn a picture. Was she a pony-tailed brunette or a pig-tailed blonde? Big blue eyes? Hazel? Brown? Did she inherit my condition? Was she an angel or a mischief-maker? Did her voice sound like little bells? Did she call me Papa, or Daddy, or some variant that was easier for her to pronounce? Will I ever know? She's not just gone from this Earth, you see, she's also wiped from my mind. So is her mother. So is … my wife."

Troy made eye contact once again, his eyes suffused with pain.

"May I make a suggestion?" Emmy asked.

Troy nodded.

She took his hands and pulled him up into a sitting position. Without releasing them, she said, "If I were Sabrina, if I had died in the terrible accident that somehow spared your life, I would want you looking forward, not back. I would tell you it's a blessing that you don't remember and I would urge you to treat it as such."

Troy blinked a few times but did not speak.

Staring into his eyes, trying to lend him strength, Emmy swore she could actually see Troy pulling his act together. She could almost hear the drill sergeant screaming Pull yourself together, soldier! in his mind.

And then the pain passed like a summer storm and the old Troy began to shine. "You're right, of course. And I'm being selfish. You lost someone too."

"That's not the same and we both know it."

Troy kept going as though she had not spoken. "I need to start thinking big picture. Someone out there can wipe peoples' minds at will. The sanctity of memory is at stake—and no one is truly safe. Right now he seems to be using his diabolic power to win court cases, but what if he decides to branch out? What if he begins selling his potion or whatever it is to terrorists? What if the presidential aide carrying the nuclear football suddenly forgets his job and thinks it's just another briefcase? What if he slips the Kool-Aid to the crew of a nuclear sub? The damage this guy could do is limitless. God, I've been so self-centered."

"No," Emmy said. "You've made tremendous sacrifices in an attempt to bring this guy to justice. The fact that you've been doing it for personal reasons is irrelevant. If you boil it down, everything everyone does is for personal reasons."

Troy did not look convinced. "We've got to get to Miami immediately. We need to track this guy down right away. Who knows what violations he has planned for tomorrow, and the day after. There's no time to waste."

"Well, I've got good news in that regard," Emmy said, amazed by the speed of Troy's recovery, but knowing that this was just a break in his psychological storm. "You're not going to have to wait until tomorrow to start tracking this guy down."

"How so?"

"It's time I let you in on a little discovery of my own...."

Chapter 52

Sharks

FARKAS WATCHED the second hand on his stateroom clock make the sweep that would turn two fifty-nine to three AM. He had tried to sleep for a couple of hours after sending Troy and Emmy to bed, but it was a lost cause. The knowledge that he would be feeding his guests to the sharks come sunrise, kept the sandman from calling.

He was glad that he had gone the extra mile to learn how Troy and Emmy had gotten back on Luther's trail. Tattoos. A couple of lousy henna tattoos. It was a clever and insightful insurance policy —but one that would disappear when their feet did.

As an added bonus, Farkas now knew Luther's bank account number. He had memorized it when Emmy showed him the bottom of her foot. One step closer …

As the second-hand hit twelve, Farkas rose from his queen-size bed, his eyes fully adjusted to the dim recessed light that bathed the entire yacht. He grabbed his special camera and crept toward Troy and Emmy's sleeping quarters. Given the gusting wind, sloshing waves, and ever-present hum of the dual Mercury inboard motors, Farkas found it easier to creep unnoticed about a moving yacht than any home. He would keep that in mind when planning future wipes.

Farkas paused outside the forward stateroom for a moment to listen. He pictured the stateroom's triangular layout in his mind. It consisted of little more than two twin beds and some storage, all arranged in a V-shape along the curvature of the ship's prow.

He heard no sound.

Farkas donned his custom sunglasses, gripped the doorknob, and began to turn. Troy and Emmy's heads would both be about seven feet in front of him when he entered. He would step in and shut the door loudly behind him in order to wake them with the noise and get them looking in his direction. Then he would hit them with the UV-C flash.

This time, they would awake on a reef infested with sharks.

This time, there would be no miracle escape.

The knob stopped turning. He took a deep breath, and threw open the door. He stepped in and slammed the door behind him. The blankets neither moved nor rustled. For a second he worried that his plan to inebriate them had backfired. Then he felt the cord bite into his neck.

Attempting to whirl about, Farkas felt the noose constrict. He dropped the camera and brought both hands to his neck, only to feel something hard crash into the back of his head.

~ ~ ~

When Farkas awoke, his head was pounding and his neck was on fire. He was seated in an aluminum chair, his forearms bound to the armrests with duct tape. The noose Troy had snared him with still encircled his neck. As he tested his bonds, the cord began to tighten.

"Stop moving your legs. You're only choking yourself," he heard Troy say.

Understanding at once that they had tied the end of the noose to his ankles—a tactic he and his brothers had often used to interrogate Serbs—Farkas pushed his feet back under the chair. The cord slackened, but his neck still burned. "What the hell are you doing to me?" he asked. "Is this how you treat all your rescuers?"

"You can cut the act, Rokus," Emmy said, stepping into view. "We found your passport. Rokus Farkas of the Republic of

Croatia."

"And the sniper rifle," Troy added from behind Farkas's back. "And the flasher concealed in your camera."

Like any good field operative, Farkas had a cover story prepared. "Call me Farkas," he said. "Everyone does. I'm with Interpol. What gave me away?"

Emmy shifted her gaze away from him to look at Troy and said, "He's lying." Then, turning back to him she said, "We had our suspicions confirmed hours ago when I feigned motion sickness and searched your room. And just to be accurate, what gave you away was what I did not find, namely the tools of the journalist trade: a notebook, voice recorder, and laptop computer."

"Let me show you—"

"Save it," Emmy said, cutting him off. "I found this a few minutes ago." She held up her left hand as if giving him the finger. She was wearing her engagement ring. A three-carat brilliant cut set in platinum. Farkas figured he could sell it on eBay for at least thirty grand.

"You rigged the window in the car, didn't you?" Troy asked. "You blew it out yourself with a remote-detonated charge. It was a clever move. Made me a believer. Unfortunately for you, Emmy here wrote the book on cons. She saw right through it."

Farkas needed time to think of plausible explanations. Given their memory loss, there had to be a formula that would work, if only for a few seconds. That was all it would take to snap their necks. He churned the waters of his mind. Nothing surfaced. He could hardly pretend to be infiltrating them for Interpol after having told them their own sad stories. The ring was a real kicker. And to top it all off, Emmy appeared to be a human lie detector.

Realizing that he was out of time, he decided to stick near the truth, but minimize his own involvement. They weren't going to hurt him, after all. Were they? No. They weren't killers. And they couldn't take him to the police. All he had to do was cooperate until they made a mistake. They had a long way to go and it would only take one slip-up.

An idea bubbled up from his problem-solving center. A delightfully wonderfully simple plan. He knew how to escape.

"Yes, I rigged the car's window. What else do you want to know?"

Chapter 53

Revelations

TROY LOOKED UP from the greasy pair of pliers and ball-peen hammer he'd found in the yacht's toolbox. Farkas had given what sounded like an honest answer. As ironic as it sounded, Troy was not sure that an honest answer was what he wanted at that moment.

He had waited in the dark for five hours, steaming and scheming, waiting to see if Emmy's conclusion proved correct. When it had, when Farkas stormed into their room holding the camera that Troy now knew not to be a camera at all, Troy had boiled over. Now that Farkas was awake, the hickory shank of that hammer was itching his hand.

"What else do you want to know?" Farkas repeated.

Troy looked over at Emmy, hoping she would shake her head and tell him Farkas was trying to play them for fools.

She nodded instead. Farkas was not holding back.

Still thumping the hammer head against his open palm, Troy walked around to face his foe, then sat down to watch his secret weapon work.

"What were you planning to do with us?" she asked.

Farkas shrugged. "I was going to erase your memories again."

"With the Balinorm," Troy asked, stressing the phony name.

"You figured that out, huh?" Farkas said, sounding amused.

Looking into his captive's eyes, Troy realized that Farkas was the real deal. His bravado was not dependent upon superior firepower. Troy knew the type. They were rare. He'd probably be wearing a green beret or a SEAL's Trident if he'd been born beneath an American flag. As it was, the Croatian really was an army of one.

"And then what?" Emmy pressed.

"And then drop you off while you were still unconscious."

"Unconscious?"

"Yes, the erasure overloads the mind, knocking you out for about three hours. Gives you a hell of a headache, too. But I guess you already know that."

"Drop us off where?" Troy asked.

"Jamaica. As agreed."

"He's lying," Emmy said.

"On the island, or in the surf?" Troy asked.

Farkas grew a faint smile and looked Troy in the eye. "I know a reef—lots of sharks."

Emmy shook visibly as Troy felt a shiver run down his spine. He had not thought it was possible, but there actually was an experience worse than waking up in a trunk with a dead cop—and Farkas had planned to give it to them. The admission gave new meaning to the words brutally honest.

Troy changed the subject. "Who are you working with?"

Farkas's expression became uncomfortable for the first time. "I honestly don't know."

"Not good enough," Troy said, standing. "You've been doing this for years. Of course you know." He gave the hammer another thump. "The only question is how many toes we're going to pulp before you remember."

Farkas did not blanch as any normal person would. He seemed completely indifferent, and that sent a second chill up Troy's spine. What had this guy been through that the ball-peen prospect was not worth a rise?

"Think about it," Farkas said. "Everything you know. The big picture. This guy gets his hands on a drug that can erase memories. He's sitting on a vein of pure gold, and he decides that the best way to mine it is to use it to win court cases. What's his biggest challenge?"

"Sleeping at night?" Emmy suggested.

"Keeping things secret," Troy said.

"Bingo."

"So how did he find you?" Emmy asked.

"Another clever move. I lost my license to practice medicine while still in my residency. He called me the day after the notification was posted on an AMA database."

"He wanted a desperate doctor," Troy said, nodding.

"How'd you lose your license?" Emmy asked.

Troy could not care less about this scumbag's personal history, but he decided that letting Emmy probe for details might not be a bad idea. Perhaps she would trip him up.

"I went to medical school at SUNY-Brooklyn. It was a big deal for a Croatian. My family pooled all their money to send me, to get me out of the civil wars—where most of my family eventually died. They gave me everything they had, but it still barely covered tuition. Since foreign nationals are not eligible for student loans, I had to work nights. Full-time. Even then I couldn't afford so much as a dorm room. I rented an armchair to sleep on from a fellow Croat living in a one-room apartment in Queens. Long story short, I took a lot of speed to keep going. I had been up for thirty-two hours when I screwed up a diagnosis, mistaking congestive heart failure for an asthma attack. The kid died. A fellow intern—a man after my girlfriend—tipped the administration off to the fact that I was high at the time. They tested my blood, and I lost my license."

"You're lucky that's all that happened," Emmy said.

"The hospital wanted to keep things quiet."

"That kind of thing happens more often than you think," Troy added. "Just check the phone book for medical malpractice attorneys."

"I didn't know what to do," Farkas continued. "I went from

hero to zero overnight. Nonetheless, my sisters were still counting on me for financial support. I was distraught and desperate. Then the phone rang. A man who called himself Luther offered ten thousand dollars cash for secretly administering a special treatment, just a simple two-step procedure. That was nearly four years ago, four years and forty-six procedures."

"Including ours?" Emmy asked.

"No. You weren't cases. You were cleanup. Forty-six witnesses. Although you, Ms. Green, were one of those too. You have the honor of being the only person ever flashed twice."

"Almost three times," Emmy added. "But we digress. Are you telling me that through forty-six jobs you never once met your employer?"

"Never. We just talk via satellite phone. I don't even know for sure what country he lives in, although I assume it's the US."

"What else do you assume?" Troy asked.

"I assume that he's an attorney, since he chose to use the drug toward legal ends, and people tend to stick with what they know."

"What's his last name?"

"I don't know. I'm not even sure if Luther is his real first name or not. I get the feeling that it is. It comes naturally to him."

"How old is Luther, judging by his voice," Emmy asked.

"Late thirties, early forties."

"Caucasian voice?"

"Yes."

"American accent?"

"Yes."

"What's the area code on his phone?" Troy asked.

"312. Chicago."

"You ever hear the El running in the background, or station announcements, like on The Fugitive?" Emmy asked.

"No. I don't think he lives there. He's too relaxed. Never mentions the cold either."

Emmy looked at Troy and nodded. She believed him.

"Tell me how the drug works," Troy said. "I want the details."

Farkas met Troy's eye, and nodded. Former doctor to former doctor. "It's a two-stage procedure. First the victim must be injected with a biopharmaceutical compound Luther calls 456. Within fifteen minutes of injection, 456 bonds to fresh dendrites. It —"

Troy held up his hand, cutting Farkas off and turning to Emmy. "Memories are stored in neurons. You have billions of neurons which interact through trillions of connections. Those connections have physical, electrical, and chemical components. Dendrites are the physical portion, the wiring so to speak. They're like the roots to the neuron plant."

Emmy said, "Thanks," and Farkas continued. "Once bonded to your fresh dendrites, a process requiring just fifteen minutes from injection, 456 is activated by Ultraviolet-C radiation. Depending on the wavelength used, I can erase anything from around four weeks' worth of memories to about the last twenty percent of a person's life."

"Is that range related to dendrite maturation?" Troy asked.

"Right. Dendrites, like roots, grow thicker with age and thus less vulnerable. Perhaps that's why Alzheimer's patients tend to lose their earliest memories last."

With a sinking feeling in his gut, Troy asked, "What, exactly, happens when 456 is activated?"

"The UV-C fluoresces the 456, causing it to emit heat that cooks the dendrites. The higher the wavelength, the greater the heat, the thicker the dendrites it destroys."

Hearing those words, Troy collapsed backwards onto the couch.

Emmy looked over at him, panic in her eyes. "What is it?"

Troy shook his head. "If what he says is true—and I have no doubt that it is, from a medical perspective it makes too much sense —then there is almost no chance of ever getting our memories back. All links to them have been physically destroyed.

"My family is gone forever."

Chapter 54

Half

"BACK TO THE BATTLE PLAN," Arlen said, apparently having explored the biochemistry of 456 to his satisfaction. "Tell me more about the mechanics of memory wiping."

"It's a two-phase process," Luther replied, holding up one hand and then the other. "First, we inject the 456. Then we flash the target with UV-C."

"Tell me about the injection," Arlen said. "How much is needed?"

"Like cyanide, a little goes a long way. One milliliter is enough."

Arlen arched his aristocratic brows. "Great. So darts work, and you can use the old Cold War devices like injector rings and umbrella tips?"

"We've used all of the above."

"Any special conditions? Does 456 have to be refrigerated?"

"For storage, but not for use. It's like insulin in that regard."

"Got it. How about timing? Any limits there?"

"On both ends. It takes fifteen minutes to activate—to bind to the beta-amyloid-like peptide as I now understand. You have forty-eight hours from injection to expose the 456 to UV-C. After forty-eight hours, its bioavailability drops rapidly, depending on a person's metabolism."

"Got it. Tell me, since the UV-C travels directly to the brain through the optic nerve, am I right in assuming that they have to be looking at the flasher when it happens?"

"You are."

"How do you manage that?"

"Simple. We usually imbed it in a camera flash. People tend to look at a camera when it's pointed in their direction—it's a subconscious reflex, if not a conscious one. And a camera provides perfect camouflage. The whole process looks as natural as can be—until the victim drops unconscious."

Arlen smiled. "Excellent. So once you've got the subject injected, it's all downhill from there."

"You got it."

"And for how long does the procedure render the victim unconscious?"

"Again it varies with metabolism. About three hours."

"Is there any way to tell if a person has been primed with 456?"

"There is. If you look at him through lenses that filter out all light above and below the 300 nanometer range, his eyes will appear to glow with a violet tinge."

"Excellent," Arlen said, sliding forward in his chair. "Okay, here's my proposal, the good stuff, the moment you have been waiting for … I will pay you half your fee once you present me with an acceptable plan to flash all nine Supreme Court Justices. Then I will —"

"Hold on!" Luther interrupted. "You said earlier that you brought me a check."

"A figure of speech," Arlen said, splaying his hands. "As I was saying, I will pay you two hundred and fifty million dollars upon approving your detailed plan, and then the balance—we'll make that an even three hundred million after I verify that you have injected all nine justices with 456. That way you can be ready to disappear the moment you flash them."

Luther considered the proposal. He could try to insist on immediate payment of the first half, but what would be the point? It shouldn't take him more than a week or two to come up with an acceptable plan—assuming the task was possible. The only reason for insisting upon payment now would be to run off with the down payment if it wasn't possible, and Arlen had no doubt thought of that.

What if it wasn't possible? Luther wondered, beginning to worry. Now that he had half-a-billion dollars dangling before him, the thought of losing them was unbearable. He could not let that happen. He would find a way. "Your terms are acceptable," he said, holding out his hand.

"I'm glad to hear it," Arlen said. "But I'm not finished yet."

Luther felt his face going red and used his extended hand to reach for his espresso. "What else?"

"Just one more thing, and I'm afraid that it is a deal breaker. Non-negotiable."

Luther nodded as his throat went dry, then took a sip of his drink.

"Given the size and intensity of the investigation that we both expect, I am going to have to insist that you flash everyone involved in this and all your previous operations. The day after the justices go amnesic, you and I are to be the only two people on the planet who have a clue as to how it was done."

Finished and obviously pleased with himself, Arlen held out his hand to seal the deal.

Luther tried to look taken aback, as though the thought of betraying his colleagues offended him. In truth, Farkas was the only person Luther had ever worked with, and it had always been Luther's plan to flash him when all was done.

With visions of private beaches and Playboy Bunnies and Jury screeching "It's a deal" in the background, Luther took Arlen's hand.

Chapter 55

Unhealthy Returns

"SO WHO'S YOUR NEXT VICTIM?" Troy asked, resuming the interrogation without the benefit of having a human lie detector by his side.

"I don't know," Farkas said.

"Do I need the hammer?"

Farkas's expression remained calm, almost detached. "I'm supposed to fly to Boston when I'm done with you. Check into the Hyatt Regency and wait for an envelope. That's how it always works. Usually a different city. Always a different hotel. Never any details in advance."

Troy was not happy with that response, but it sounded reasonable given what he knew of Luther's operating style. He decided to stir the waters a bit to keep Farkas talking in the hope that something would slip out. "Don't you ever stop to consider the big picture?"

Farkas raised his bushy brows. "Big picture?"

"You're creating a world where one man can rob another of his mind."

Farkas shook his head and chuffed. "Samuel Colt created that world long ago."

"No. A bullet to the brain only keep's a man from moving forward. 456 reaches back in time to steal his past. You're opening up a whole new dimension of destruction."

Emmy shouted down from the bridge before Farkas could retort. "Farkas lied. We aren't en route to Jamaica. We're headed back to Grand Cayman. He took us in a big circle."

Troy shouted, "I'll be there in a minute" without taking his eyes off Farkas.

"I already admitted that my real destination was a reef," Farkas said. "You'll forgive me if I didn't point it out as we passed. I didn't think that would be to my advantage."

It was Troy's turn to chuff. He might well have been tempted to toss Farkas overboard if he'd seen a school of dorsal fins off the prow.

Troy decided he had all the information he was likely to get, and in retrospect there was no sense discussing ethics with a man who had no soul.

He reached forward to recheck Farkas's bonds. The duct tape had bunched up a bit around the ends overnight, but it had yielded little to the Croatian's best efforts at escape. Farkas may as well be in chains. "We're going to leave you now."

"Just like that?"

"Not quite." Troy reached into a drawer and withdrew Farkas's modified camera and special UV-C filtering sunglasses. "I figured out how your neuron-frying system works. Now you're going to learn how it feels. Got anything you want to get off your chest? Any message you'd like to leave for yourself?"

Farkas eyed the camera for a long moment, and then looked up at Troy. "I had expected the sharks," he said, his voice cool as glacial ice.

Troy donned the sunglasses. "You deserve the sharks. As does your employer, and for that matter all the lawyers who pull tricks to set guilty clients free. But I'm not starting down that slippery slope. I'm not going to become like you." He brought the camera to his eye and added, "That said, I will feed you to the sharks if you blink."

Farkas nodded his understanding, his approval.

Troy paused with his finger on the button, and then lowered the camera. He confirmed for the third time that he had set the wavelength to erase four years according to the chart taped inside the back cover. "When you awake, you will have no recollection of compound 456, or Luther, or the lives you have ruined."

Farkas nodded stoically. "I suppose you think I should thank you."

Troy pressed the button.

Farkas's head jolted back as though shocked when the UV-C bathed his face. Then his eyes rolled back and closed and his body went limp as a wet noodle.

"You're damn right you should. Four destructive years. Dozens of damaged lives. And instead of paying for your crimes, you're getting a clean conscience and a second chance. Make the most of it, you bastard."

Troy ran up the stairs without looking back.

As soon as Emmy saw him she pointed to the navigational display. Troy saw the elf's shoe silhouette of Grand Cayman dead ahead. They were actually coming at it from the northwest, whereas Jamaica was on the other side of the island, one hundred and eighty miles to the southeast.

"So we lose half a day," he said. "It could be worse."

"It is worse. We're low on gas. We have no choice but to stop at Grand Cayman."

"You worried about the wanted posters?"

"It's more than that," Emmy said. "I listened to the radio while you were below dealing with our friend. The whole island is looking for the Cop-Killing Couple. That's what they're calling us. No doubt they have our pictures—fresh color ones from the bank's security cameras—decorating every gas pump on the island."

"Maybe we could siphon off another yacht's gas."

"No good. They're intercepting and searching all outgoing vessels. Once we enter port, that's it."

"Can't we make Little Cayman or Cayman Brac?"

"They're both ninety miles away. Out of range."

"So you're suggesting that we dock and abandon the yacht?"

"I don't think we have a viable alternative."

"So be it."

"But what then?" Emmy asked. "How do we get to Miami with the whole island looking for us? I might be able to slip through the gauntlet disguised as a teenage boy, but not you. Those scars of yours are like bullseyes on your head—and I absolutely refuse to lose you."

Troy wrapped his arms around her. "So what's new? Personally, I'm glad to be back in the game—so long as I've got you by my side. Besides, I'm sure you'll think of something."

Chapter 56

Drama

"DUDE, YOU'RE BURNING."

"It's an experiment," Troy replied without looking up. "Coppertone pays me to do this. You should talk to them. Easy money."

"No thanks, man. But you have yourself a ball."

With the whole island looking for his famous dimple and scars, Troy was hiding in plain site like an ostrich with his head in the sand. Emmy had left him on Seven-Mile and told him to burn.

As the teenagers walked off down the beach, laughing among themselves, the sea breeze brought a familiar scent to his nose. A second later he heard, "This is going to hurt." Then he felt an icy blade slip between his shoulder blades.

Troy whipped his head around to see Emmy standing over him holding an inverted bottle of aloe vera. "I wasn't finished," she said. He saw her face crinkle and knew that she had winked behind her imitation Cartier sunglasses. He flipped back over and checked Ironman while she rubbed the freezing lotion into his scorched skin. She had been gone for over three hours.

"How did it go at Tropical Towers? Did you get the car?"

"I did," Emmy said, finishing with his back. "I also picked up some children's sunscreen for your face. It's thick and white and will camouflage your scars." She popped the top off a small tube and began dabbing lotion on his forehead as though she were finger painting. Satisfied, she moved on to his nose and ears. "It might look like a disguise if I only do your forehead. This way, you look more like a careless tourist." She finished and said, "Those ripe shoulders of yours complete the picture nicely, so long as you have your shirt off."

"Aren't you going to put any on my chin?"

"Too conspicuous. But I picked you up this lovely cognac cigar." She pulled a glass tube from her beach bag. The cigar inside was long and fat, and looked like it would burn for hours. Liberating the cigar, she popped it in his mouth and then stepped back to admire her creation. "Way too goofy to fit the cop-killer mold."

"Thanks. But this isn't going to get me past the kind of serious check they're bound to have at the airport."

"Sea port," she corrected. "I picked us up a couple of cruise ship IDs. And probably not. My sunglasses won't cut it either. That's why our next stop is the Cayman Drama Society."

"Cruise ship IDs?"

"They're like electronic hotel keys, except that they have your name and cabin number printed on them. You use them for identification when embarking and disembarking."

"And you just picked them up?"

"From a beach bag emblazoned with the Neptune cruise line logo. Now, get in the car."

Troy made the connection between the Cayman Drama Society and disguises as he hunkered down in the back seat. He closed his eyes as they drove, focusing on the hum of the Camry's tires and shifting as necessary to keep his back out of the sun.

Emmy turned on the radio and station surfed until she found news. The announcer was midway through a story about the impact of increased cruise ship traffic. Apparently, the island's 9,200-person cap on cruise passengers was routinely exceeded, sometimes by as much as two hundred and fifty percent. The bumper crops of tourists were a boon to George Town's working residents and business owners, but a bane to everyone else.

"Back to the day's top story. Sixty-two law enforcement officers from neighboring islands arrived on Grand Cayman this morning, volunteering their weekends to join in the hunt for the couple that brutally murdered two of their own. We advise all our listeners to be on the lookout for the unidentified pair, but not to approach them under any circumstances as they are considered extremely dangerous. He is Caucasian, approximately one hundred and eighty-five centimeters and ninety kilos, with dark hair, blue eyes, two v-shaped scars above his right eye, and a Kirk-Douglas dimple on his chin. She is around one hundred and sixty centimeters, forty-five kilos, with dark hair, fair skin and bright green eyes. Anyone—"

Emmy turned off the radio. "We're here. Just in time from the sound of things."

"Is it safe for me and my distinctively dimpled chin to emerge?" Troy asked, pulling Farkas's Kangol cap low on his forehead.

"Looks that way; I only see one other car, an old green pickup. The theater is sandwiched between a forest and a school, and it's Saturday afternoon."

He got out and asked, "What exactly are you hoping to purloin?"

"Heavy makeup, facial hair, tinted contact lenses. I figure that this is the best place on the island to get everything we need with minimal exposure."

"What technique do you have in mind?"

"You'll see." She knocked on the right half of the double door. No answer. As she began a second round the left door swung out and a tall black man of some sixty years asked, "May I hep ya?" He had a mouth bursting with white teeth, friendly eyes, and wore navy coveralls that had seen no fewer than a thousand washings.

"Hi. I'm Josephine Jamison. I'm a makeup artist at Universal Studios, Hollywood. I'm on vacation—here on a cruise—and I was hoping to talk some kind soul into showing me around your fine theater, particularly backstage." She flashed a heart-stopping smile.

"Well, I dunno how our li'l the-ater compares to what you got in

Hollywood, but we's mighty proud of it. Come on in, Miss Jamison." He looked up at Troy. "Mista Jamison. Welcome. I'm William."

They stepped inside and the janitor secured the door. The theater was dark but for the light emanating from someplace backstage. The air smelled of freshly cut wood.

"I's been here since we opened back in eighty-seven. Know every inch of her, so I don't really need the lights 'cept where I's workin'. I can turn them on for you though if you'd like?"

"It's really the backstage we're interested in," Emmy said. "Particularly your costume and wardrobe facilities. That's my specialty."

"Right this way, ma'am. Right this way."

Troy had an uneasy feeling as he followed William back toward the source of the light. Emmy was good, but this struck him as too easy. Then again, he had not gone through life with a centerfold figure and a smile that opened doors.

William led them down a passage to the right of the stage which turned into a wide hallway that ran behind it. The hallway was as tall as the stage itself, and full of tethered ropes and electrical switches and miscellaneous props. Several doors lined the wall off to the right. "This is the room you're looking fa'," William said, opening a door marked Makeup. Troy held back as William ushered Emmy through.

Troy heard Emmy gasp as she entered and knew what she had seen even before he peeked around the doorframe. Officer Honey stood there with satisfaction beaming from his eyes. This time he was the one holding the Colt.

Chapter 57

Sketch

FARKAS WATCHED THE CLOCK, waiting for ten long minutes after hearing Troy and Emmy leave the yacht before moving. His plan had worked perfectly, but the jig would be up if Troy returned for something forgotten and found him awake.

Then the ball-peen hammer would come back out and stay out until Farkas revealed his secret.

Then Troy really would flash his memory away.

The upside of the whole bungled episode was that his custom contact lenses had been battle-tested. Now he could go forward without the nagging fear that some UV-C might still slip through. When Luther decided to terminate and erase their relationship—an end Farkas saw as inevitable—he would find the tables turned.

The downside of Troy and Emmy's escape was that it made him look like an idiot. Luther might now decide to end their relationship with a bullet rather than a flash, especially when Troy and Emmy showed up at his door. That too was inevitable—unless Farkas killed them first. To do that, he had to escape.

Troy had used duct tape to bind the entire length of Farkas's forearms to an aluminum deck chair. Farkas was going crazy trying to sever the thick gray coils. They were tough as steel gauntlets and Troy had removed every blade from the kitchen. Farkas tried everything from snagging the tape on shelf corners to puncturing it with drawer handles. Meanwhile, his quarry was slipping further and further away. Nothing worked. The legendary tape was just too resilient.

Since his only means of movement was hopping on two bound legs, and he could only do that while bent at an L-shaped angle, he was inadvertently giving himself a real beating. At a quarter past noon, Farkas finally conceded the inevitable. He would break his neck before breaking free.

He needed help.

He decided to scream.

Aware that he was more likely to break his neck than make it to the top of the stairs and through the door, Farkas positioned himself at the base of the stairs. Keeping his eyes on the wall clock, he began screaming "Help!" once every sixty seconds. After an hour, with his throat dry and sore, he switched to every two minutes. Then to every three. Four hours after his first scream, nearly six hours after Troy and Emmy had fled, he finally felt movement on the boat. "I'm down here! Please, help!"

Farkas heard cautious footsteps, and then a black face poked around the doorway at the top of the stairs, followed immediately by a gun. "Thank goodness you heard me," Farkas said. "I've been robbed."

"Are you alone?" the officer asked.

"Yes. The couple who did this to me left hours ago."

The officer did not holster his weapon as he and his partner came down. After a brief visual inspection of his bonds, they searched the two staterooms in a manner much more professional than Farkas would have expected from paradise cops. Satisfied with their search, they began conversing in a language Farkas could not understand.

Farkas read their name tags. The senior officer was a sergeant named Brandell. Junior's name was Mertins. They seemed to be studying him while they spoke, and were paying particular attention to his eyes. Farkas frequently received double-take glances since the reflective nature of the custom lenses gave his eyes an unusual metallic sheen. They were kinda cool, he had always thought. They meshed nicely with his scruffy beard and Kangol cap to complete a tough-guy image. He half expected to start a Hollywood trend. But admiration was not written on the officers' faces, and an uneasy feeling overtook him. "Would you guys mind cutting me free?" he asked. "I'm getting pretty tired of this chair."

Brandell nodded to Mertins, who went to the kitchen in search of a knife Farkas knew he would not find. He brought back a pizza cutter instead. Eventually, Mertins cut through the tape on the inside of Farkas's right arm. The instant the final strand gave, Farkas ripped his arm free with a motion that would have made a veteran bikini waxer faint.

Farkas said, "Thanks," and had begun to rub his bloody forearm against his shorts when Brandell stepped forward and slapped a handcuff around his wrist. Then the sergeant linked it to his left wrist before slicing through one side of the tape and signaling for Farkas to repeat the depilatory procedure. Farkas looked Brandell in the eye, gauged his intentions to be serious, and complied without breaking eye contact.

"What's the problem?" Farkas asked. "Why the cuffs?"

Neither officer replied. They just pulled him to his feet and escorted him back to their squad car.

Perhaps Troy and Emmy had been captured and broken. He could think of no other explanation for this cruel twist of fate.

As they pulled away from the West Bay marina, he pressed his luck. "I deserve to know what this is all about."

Neither officer spoke, but Sergeant Brandell held his clipboard up to the Plexiglas partition without looking back. It displayed a police artist's sketch—of his face.

Chapter 58

Tango

STARING DOWN the barrel of Officer Honey's Colt, Emmy felt like her air supply had been cut off.

Then the lights went out.

In the blink of an eye the theater became dark as a cave. Before she could react, someone grabbed her arm and yanked her violently backwards. She careened into someone else and they both tumbled to the wooden floor. The makeup room door slammed as she fell, blowing wind across her face.

Lying there in the dark, Emmy pictured the circuit box they had passed in the hall. Troy must have flipped the big gray switch. His reflexes were amazing.

She waited through a moment of stunned silence for Troy to place a hand on her shoulder or whisper in her ear. Neither came. Had the slamming door drowned out a gunshot? Was Troy wounded? She reached out tentatively toward the figure beside her. She felt the soft fabric of old coveralls. William.

He groaned in response to her touch, his tone more winded than wounded. He was not shot, just stunned.

If William was with her, then Troy must be on the other side of the door. He had used the momentum of swinging her out to sling himself in. He had gone after Honey.

She braced for the gunshot that would change her life while picturing the two combatants blindly circling one another on the other side of the door. William stirred, breaking her trance with, "Oh Lordy." As he began rising to his feet, she knew instinctively that he was going for the circuit box. She had to stop him before he found the lever.

At five foot two and a hundred pounds, Emmy was not born into the warrior class. But she had come of age on predatory streets. She sprang up, wedging herself between William and the wall. Her left shoulder knocked his probing arm aside as she rose while her hands grappled for his neck. As William staggered backwards to slip her grip, she moved with him, getting her legs into position. When he brought his hands up to claw at hers, she brought her right knee up with full force. It found the soft target.

William let out an agonized, "Ooph," and doubled over, whacking his forehead against the top of hers. The wallop dazed Emmy, but she remained standing. William crumpled to the floor, where he began to rock and moan.

A gunshot boomed through the dark like a cannon as scuffling sounds erupted from the makeup room. Emmy froze and strained her ears. The noise peaked with a loud smack followed by a crash.

Silence ensued.

She got a splinter groping for the circuit box, but found it and pulled the central lever.

William lay off to her left, still rolling around much as she had envisioned. If only he had waited a few seconds ... As she reached for the knob of the dressing room door, it opened. Troy stood there, his face a mask of concern.

"Are you okay?" he asked.

"I'm fine." She poked her head into the room to see Officer Honey on the floor.

"He'll be okay," Troy said. "I just knocked him out."

"With your bare hands?"

"It's not that hard, medically speaking, if you know what to do. The tough part was doing it in the dark. I had to direct my blow by touch which meant grabbing before I struck. That was when he got the shot off. But enough history, let's get the hell out of here."

"Not yet," Emmy said. "We still need disguises. Pull William in here while I search for what we need. Then change into Honey's uniform. When you're done with that, tie them up together, back to back."

"You want me to impersonate a police officer?"

"It's the only way, Troy. You heard the broadcast. I'll explain as we get dressed."

Chapter 59

End of the Line

FARKAS UNDERSTOOD what had happened the moment he saw his composite picture. The old couple from Elisabeth Avenue had given his description to the police. He felt like kicking himself. If only he had remembered them a few hours earlier...

Lifting his gaze from his handcuffs to the patrol car window, he spotted the pier where Troy had dumped the detective's body. He only had a few minutes to escape. The first order of business at the police station—after calling the Wootens in for a lineup—would be to print him. Once they found his fingerprints sanded, they would know they had their man.

He had to attack while they still harbored doubt.

Using the sharp nail of his right thumbnail, he began slicing the skin of his left wrist just above the calloused lump. He had imagined this moment a thousand times since placing the implant, but found it much more difficult in real life. His skin did not yield so easily, and warm blood turned his fingers so slick that they could not wrench the key free. He clawed on in desperation, ignoring the pain as he dug into the scarred tissue. He had only seconds, only one chance, and it was slipping from his grasp.

He looked back up as they hit the curb to the garage where it all began. His eyes scanned the garage for other occupants while his fingers continued working.

"Let's see if we can't get this straightened out," Mertins said, getting out and opening the rear door.

Farkas stayed put.

"Come on, buddy," Mertins pushed. "It's time for the moment of truth."

"Where are we?" Farkas asked. "How do I know you're really cops?" It was weak, but the only disarming stall tactic that sprang to mind.

The question was surprising enough to buy Farkas another second of delay. That second proved enough to wrest the key from its encapsulation.

"We're at police headquarters," Mertins said. "Look at the other cars in the garage."

Farkas made a show of looking around from the back seat while mating key with lock out of sight. He continued to study one car in particular as he emerged. His puzzled stare prompted Mertins to follow his gaze.

That was all it took.

Farkas whipped the empty cuffs around like a flail, catching Mertins square in the temple. As Mertins fell, Farkas bounded off the doorsill, banked off the open door and lunged over the roof at the shocked sergeant. Brandell made the mistake of going for his gun rather than getting out of the way. Farkas slammed into him before he could raise his weapon. As the sergeant tottered, Farkas whipped around, windmilling the handcuffs into the back of Brandell's head. As Brandell slumped, Farkas saw that he had not been as lucky as his junior partner. The handcuff spur had impaled his neck around the second cervical disk. He would likely be paralyzed if he lived.

Farkas picked Brandell's hat up off the bloody concrete and placed it on his own head. Then, for the second time that week, he heaved two bodies into a patrol car trunk. Again, he had to arrange the unconscious forms like spoons in a drawer so they would fit. He slammed the trunk, got into the driver's seat, and uncuffed his right wrist. Time to fly.

Emerging from the dim and dreary garage into the freedom of

the bright Cayman sunlight, Farkas felt like he was being born again. He drove straight for Owen Roberts International Airport with dark lights and a silent siren. It was only a few miles. He found a place in the corner of the lot where a good thirty meters separated him from the nearest other car. He needed the buffer. Mertins would soon awake and start making noise.

He stuffed the composite drawing of his face into his pocket for later study and got out. His first impulse was to lock the keys in the car to add further delay to the chase. Realizing, however, that this would limit his escape options if the shit hit the fan, he stuffed them into the exhaust pipe instead.

He walked to the terminal and scanned the departure board for the first flight out. He found one headed for Orlando leaving in just thirty minutes. With luck, he would be aboard. If not, the next departure was not for an hour and ten minutes, and it was headed for Mexico City.

Farkas made it to the gate with enough time to grab a cup of Blue Mountain Jamaican coffee. Boarding was just starting as the barista passed him his steaming beverage, so he decided to get the call over with.

Picking up a payphone receiver, he half expected to see Emmy and Troy walk past disguised as a nun and priest. He knew the odds of that were infinitely small given the manhunt, but kept his eyes peeled nonetheless. What was that quote about luck being at the intersection of preparation and opportunity?

"Hello Luther? It's me."

"You're not calling from your satellite phone," Luther said. It was a statement, not a question.

Farkas did not want to explain that the phone was now on a yacht, and that it would likely end up in police custody. So he just said, "That's right. The battery died."

"So let's have it."

"You want the good news, or the bad?"

"Start with the good."

"I figured out how they got back on your trail. Emmy tattooed your bank account number on the sole of her foot."

"Wiley sons-of-bitches. Well, at least once the foot is gone, the clue will be too. I suppose that's your bad news—that the foot has escaped with Emmy still attached?"

Farkas could hardly believe his ears. Luther's tone was calm and cordial. What had gotten into him? He was usually a prick even without cause. Now that Farkas had genuine bad news, he seemed unfazed. Perhaps he had finally gotten laid. Perhaps he was in love. "Yeah, I'm afraid so."

"And I suppose you have no idea where they are, or where they're headed?"

"Nope."

There was a long, painful silence ending with, "Get your ass on a plane to Las Vegas. You've got a job to do, and just forty-eight hours to do it. Instructions will be waiting for you tomorrow morning at the Bellagio."

"Okay. You got it. What's the rush?"

"I've got another project for you after Vegas, a big one."

"Sounds good. Where?"

"I'll tell you that when we meet," Luther said.

"Meet?"

"Yeah. Meet. In LA. Forty-eight hours from now. Call me when you know your flight details. I'll send a car for you."

Luther hung up the phone before Farkas could respond. It was just as well. Farkas was in shock. They were finally going to meet. That could only mean one thing: His gravy train was approaching the end of the tracks.

Chapter 60

Officer Jones

TROY—or Officer Jones as he would call himself for the next hour—dropped Emmy off a block from the cruise terminal and then backtracked in order to leave the patrol car halfway to the airport. It was worth a mile's walk to keep the clues ambiguous.

He moved like a man on a mission—which he was—having reverted to his military bearing the moment the cap hit his head. He spotted Emmy where she said she'd be, doing some convincing window-shopping, and made a swift approach. She was wearing brown contact lenses, stage glasses with silver frames, and a curly blonde wig that ended at her shoulders.

"Don't you look dapper," she said as he walked up beside her. "I've always been drawn to men in uniform. Not so sure about the mustache and goatee, though. Makes you look a bit too Pancho Villa for my tastes.

He touched the shiny black bill of his hat and then grabbed her beneath the elbow like a formal escort.

Turning toward the terminal he said, "Three ships, that's a blessing."

"I was hoping for more," Emmy said. "And where are all the people? Judging by what we heard on the radio, I had expected this place to be a virtual anthill."

"Don't worry about it. Everyone will assume that you can't be a fugitive if you're already with the police. Trust me, I've worn a uniform enough to know how people react to one."

Just then a pink and yellow courtesy trolley pulled into the terminal cul-de-sac. Before it had finished disgorging its jolly crowd, a second trolley pulled in.

"Ask and ye shall receive," Troy said.

"I wish."

They blended into the herd of beach bag-toting cruisers. Emmy flashed her stolen cruise ship ID at the terminal checkpoint, but the guard paid more attention to Troy. It was as if he expected Troy to point at her and mouth "prostitute" with a wink. Troy maintained his no nonsense expression.

As they approached the Neptune III, a pair of uniformed officers with binoculars rose from a table and began walking their way. Troy asked Emmy a question, using conversation to augment their camouflage. "So how do you think Honey found us?"

Emmy's cool and reasoned reply reflected her battle-ready state of mind. "He just put himself in our shoes and set an intercept course. I'm sure he orchestrated the media blitz just to make sure we were thinking about disguise."

"My thoughts exactly. I'm just embarrassed that I didn't play a better game of chess."

"You did okay," Emmy said. "Why do you think he came alone?"

"That's an easy one. Pride."

The officers were almost upon them now, and they looked serious. Troy could not see their eyes for their mirrored shades, but he felt their gaze boring into him. So close …

And then they walked past. He heard, "Would you two please come with us?"

"What's this about, officer?" a male voice behind them responded.

"Step this way, please. This will only take a minute."

Troy listened without looking back as the couple was toted off through the murmuring crowd. Fifteen steps later he and Emmy reached the Neptune's gangplank. A sailor seated behind a podium eyed Troy and then said, "May I see your Neptune ID, ma'am."

Emmy handed him her stolen credential and the sailor ran it through a reader. He smiled when he got the green light and handed it back.

Emmy turned to Troy. "Thank you so much for seeing me safely back. It means a lot."

"My pleasure," Troy said.

"You always hear about how scary such situations are, but you never really understand until it happens to you."

"Mrs. Beaumont was mugged," Troy said, addressing the sailor.

The sailor's eyebrows shot up. "So sorry to hear that, ma'am. Are you okay? Is there anything I can do for you?"

"No, thank you. Officer Jones has been most kind. Made me feel safe again."

"Can I buy you a drink," She said, turning back to Troy. "There's a beautiful lounge up on the, the ..."

"Promenade deck," the sailor supplied. "You're thinking of the Atlantis Lounge on the promenade deck."

"When do you weigh anchor?" Troy asked the sailor.

"You've got ninety minutes till the whistle," the sailor said. "Plenty of time for a drink."

Chapter 61

Mix-up

HONEY OPENED his eyes to see big white teeth attached to an old black face. William, the theater janitor.

He sat up to rub the back of his head only to note that they had stolen his clothes. Rage and shame battled within him for emotional dominance—but pride was the real culprit. He had blown his perfect plan by attempting to bring them in alone.

"What time is it?" he asked, grasping at straws. "How long ago did they leave?"

"'Bout fifteen, maybe twenty minutes ago. They done tied us up back ta back, an' it took me a while to wrangle free."

Twenty minutes was too big a gap for Honey to overtake them, but he might still catch them if he could guess where they were going. He had no doubt that the theater was their last stop before leaving the island because that's what he would do. The only question in his mind was: By air or by sea?

"Have you got another set of coveralls?" he asked William.

"No, sir. These here is all I got."

Honey thought of making the old man give him his clothes, but he wanted to take him along. Another set of eyes was another set of eyes. After weighing the alternatives for a brief moment, the obvious struck him. "Where do you keep the costumes?"

Five minutes later Honey was racing William's old Chevy pickup toward Owen Roberts International Airport with the janitor by his side. He was dressed in the blue chalk-stripe suit coat and pants worn by the actor playing Willy Loman in Death of a Salesman. It was six inches too short and sixty pounds too fat for his frame. He felt ridiculous.

As he pulled into the airport's long drop-off drive, he saw a police car parked off to his left in the far corner of the parking lot. He made a snap decision and cranked the wheel left, taking the old pickup over the curb and grass toward the parking lot.

"What you doin', Captain?" William asked.

"Getting reinforcements," he said. If he was going to walk through the terminal in that ridiculous suit, he was going to do it with a shotgun over his shoulder like Elliot Ness.

He expected to find a couple of his men napping in their car. That seemed the only explanation for their remote choice of parking spots. To his chagrin, however, the patrol car was both empty and locked. As he whirled about cursing the precious seconds he had lost, he heard "Help!" coming from the trunk.

Honey felt his hopes surge.

He had guessed correctly.

They had come to the airport.

"Hold on!" Honey yelled back. "You got a tire iron?" he asked William.

"I got my tool chest. There's a hamma'"

William handed him the tool without delay. Honey took it and proceeded to wedge the claw beneath the trunk lock.

"Wai' Captain," William said, reaching for the instrument. "Betta' ta just break the window an' pop the boot."

Christ, Honey thought, even the janitor was outsmarting him today. He gave William back the hammer so he could do the honors. William did, and Honey popped the trunk.

Mertins scrambled out as soon as the latch released. Honey saw that his right side was covered in blood and asked, "Are you shot?"

"Not my blood. It's Brandell's."

Honey moved around to where he could see into the trunk. The man he had known for close to a decade, ever since he joined the force from the Royal Navy, was dead. "That makes three," he said. "First Johnson, then Jacobs, now Brandell. Unlock the shotgun and let's go get the bastards."

"Bastards?" Mertins repeated. "Captain, it was just one guy."

"Christ, Mertins. Haven't you been paying attention? He's got an accomplice. Pretty little she-devil. She must have been waiting out of sight."

"Captain, no Captain. This wasn't the couple that killed Johnson and Jacobs. This was the man who kidnapped the Wootens."

"The Wootens?"

"Yes, sir, Deputy Chief Wootens' parents. He held them hostage in their condo for two days—over on Elisabeth Avenue."

Honey felt his hopes dash. Not only did this make it less likely that he'd catch the pair who had twice humiliated him, but now he had another killer on his hands. The island was going to pot. "Shit."

"We'll get him though, Captain. Don't you worry. His prints are bound to be all over the car."

Chapter 62

Alexander Tate

TWO DAYS AFTER entering Miami as Jeffrey and Elizabeth Gordon, Emmy wheeled Troy toward the law office of Alexander Tate. The con was on.

"Twelve o'clock sharp," she said, looking at her watch. "Here we go."

"How can you be so sure he's going to walk through that door?" Troy asked. "We only have one data point."

"He's punctilious. You'll see."

"Punctilious?"

"You doctors have your vocabulary, we psychics have ours. Are you excited?"

"I feel like I'm going into combat."

"We are," Emmy said. "Really makes you feel alive, doesn't it?"

Troy looked back over his shoulder at his partner. "You know, you're right. I never would have guessed it, but I think I'm getting hooked."

On more than just the job I hope, Emmy thought, looking up at the building before them. Tate's office was not the penthouse floor of a majestic downtown high-rise as they had hypothesized while stowaways aboard the Neptune. Rather it occupied a few modest rooms on the third floor of a suburban office park, wedged between a podiatrist and medical billing firm.

The sliding glass door opened to their approach just as Tate stepped off the elevator.

Troy mumbled "Punctilious" just loud enough for Emmy to

hear but did not look back to see her smile.

Tate was a handsome man for a back-office attorney, with a full head of chocolate hair and one of those semi-firm physiques that screamed club membership. She dropped her purse as their eyes met, sending pills across the pavement around Tate's feet. "I'm so sorry," she said, bumping into him once and then again as they both bent over to retrieve the spilled medication. "So clumsy of me."

"No problem," Tate said, giving her an appreciative once-over. "It happens to the best of us."

They worked together to reassemble Emmy's purse while Troy looked on from the wheelchair. Then she said, "Thank you so much," stood, and pushed Troy into the lobby. Tate said "My pleasure," and made for his car.

"How'd you do?" Troy asked, once the elevator door closed behind them. Emmy turned to him and produced Tate's cell phone in her hand as if by magic. Then she turned it off.

"Very impressive," Troy said.

"That was the easy part. Now, get into character. Remember, you're old-money rich and accustomed to getting your way. Your body may no longer be what it used to, but your mind is still sharp as a whip."

"Just who do you think you're talking to, young lady? I've been dealing with situations like these since before you were born."

"Perfect," Emmy said as the elevator doors opened. She assumed the fawning air of a pretty young nurse caring for a rich old man and began pushing him toward suite 3B.

During their two partial days of surveillance, Troy and Emmy had determined that The Law Offices of Alexander Tate and Associates employed just three people, including Tate himself and two women. Judging by their cars and carriage, Emmy speculated that the younger woman was a fellow attorney working for Tate, while the older one was a secretary—or legal assistant in the vernacular. Alice, the secretary, seemed mildly surprised to find that they had unscheduled visitors. "May I help you?" she asked.

"I certainly hope so," Troy said, in his best septuagenarian voice. "We're here to see Alex."

"I'm afraid Mr. Tate is not in right now. He has a working lunch."

"Not anymore he doesn't," Troy said, raising his voice. "Get him on the phone. Tell him Kostas Kanasis is here, and I don't have time to wait."

"Yes, sir. I'll see what I can do."

"Please do," Troy said, looking back over his shoulder at Emmy and shaking his head at Tate's audacity.

"I'm afraid his phone is going straight to voice mail. He must have it off. Would you like me to leave a message?"

Troy shook his head and raised his voice. "I need a person, not a message, and I need him now."

"Is everything okay out here," a woman asked, appearing from the back much to Alice's relief.

"Mr. Kanasis here has urgent business with Mr. Tate," Alice said.

"He should be back any minute," the woman said. "I can recommend a good restaurant nearby if you would like to get some lunch."

Emmy did not like the words back any minute—it would be a disaster if Tate returned before they left—but she sensed that Tate's coworker was just being diplomatic.

Troy said, "Look, Miss ..."

"Sylvia," she said. "Sylvia Dashell."

"Well, Sylvia, any minute is not good enough. Can you guarantee me that it will be one of the next ten minutes?"

"No sir, I'm afraid I can't."

"Because that's all the time I have, I—" He held up a hand, cutting himself off and deflating a bit of pressure from the room.

"The problem, Sylvia, is that I have to be back on my plane very shortly. I'm hosting an important dinner this evening on Grand Cayman. The banking commissioner and three ambassadors will be there. Besides, I'm not really here for Alex's legal advice. I just need to review my records. Perhaps you could help me?"

"Mr. Tate doesn't like—"

"Mr. Tate doesn't like losing his best customers," Troy interjected decisively. "I'm sure we can agree on that."

Sylvia looked over at Alice who shrugged. Emmy sensed that they were about to hit a wall and chimed in. "We just need to make a copy of Mr. Kanasis's bank records. We don't need to make any transactions," she said, proffering a Cayman Islands driver's license with a picture of Troy made up to look like Kostas Kanasis. "It should just take you a minute. I'm sure Mr. Tate has the file in order."

After a tense moment, Sylvia reached out and accepted the license. She gave it a quick, cursory glance, and then said, "Please hold on a minute."

Emmy used the occasion to slip Tate's cell phone onto the corner of Alice's desk.

Sylvia returned three minutes later, wearing a smile. "Why don't you come back to my office."

Once they were resituated, Sylvia asked, "Which records, exactly, do you need copied?"

Deviating from the script they had rehearsed, Troy beckoned her over toward him so that he could whisper in her ear. Whatever he said, his improvisation worked. Sylvia backed away when he was done and said, "That should be simple enough. Just give me a minute."

Troy avoided Emmy's eye while they waited, trying to stay in character no doubt.

It did not take Sylvia long. When she returned she slid an envelope into Troy's hand.

Troy said, "Thank you" in his most sincere voice and then he added the phrase that Emmy had him memorize. "I'm a pretty good judge of character, Sylvia, and I get the feeling I can confide in you. Can I confide in you, Sylvia?"

"Why yes, yes of course."

"I have the strong suspicion that something funny is going on. No hard facts, mind you, it's more of a feeling. Given your tender young age, I don't suppose you know what I mean …?"

"I think I understand, Mr. Kanasis."

"Please, call me Kostas."

"What can I do for you, Kostas?" Sylvia asked.

"I'd like you to keep an eye on my account for the next few weeks."

"Keep an eye on it?"

"Yes, I'd like you to be my eyes. I'd like you to monitor my account and call me at this number," he held out a thick, embossed card, "and only this number any time funds come in, or go out. Just till the end of the month. Could you do that for me, Sylvia? I'd be most grateful."

"Well, sure, I'd be happy to. But perhaps Mr. Tate—"

Troy held up his hand. "Checks and balances, Sylvia. Checks and balances. Let's just keep this between us."

Chapter 63

Redirect

"THE BALLISTICS REPORT IS BACK, CAPTAIN."

Honey could tell by the tone of Susanna's voice that he was not going to like what she had to say. The cop killers had somehow slipped through his massive dragnet and their trail was now seventy-two hours cold. More bad news would be a perfect cap to the worst five days of his professional life. "Give it to me."

Susanna held out the piece of paper, obviously not wanting to be the bearer.

"Why don't you just tell me what it says."

Susanna looked down at the floor for a moment, then looked back up and said, "It says that the couple in question could not have killed Jacobs. He was killed by a high velocity rifle round. The shooter had to be on the other side of the avenue at the very least."

What the hell was going on, Honey wondered. "Is that it?"

"The rest is technical." She proffered the printout again. "Perhaps you better read it."

Honey took the paper and gave it a quick glance. Ballistics wasn't his bailiwick and he was not in the mood to pretend. As he handed the report back to Susanna to file, his eyes landed on the address in the header. Solomon Bank & Trust was located at number nine Elisabeth Avenue.

He felt a warm glow fill his chest as clarity dawned.

He knew where he had seen that address before.

Chapter 64

Contingency Planning

AS SHE PUSHED Troy's wheelchair from Tate's office back to their rental car, Emmy could sense his excitement. The mysterious document he had procured with a secretive whisper was obviously both a major clue and the confirmation of some theory. She had no idea what either was. Despite her burning desire to know, however, she vowed not to ask. She wanted to figure it out on her own.

"You did great," Emmy said, sliding into the driver's seat. "I think you're a natural."

Troy said, "Thanks," in his normal voice after removing his wig and nose prosthesis. Then he flipped down the sun visor to expose the mirror, and began attacking his makeup with handy wipes. "I'm glad I don't have to do this every evening. What a pain."

She put the car into drive and started fishing, "To the airport?"

Troy looked over at her with a mischievous smile. "Yep."

"Where are we flying?"

"I'm not sure yet. Kind of exciting, isn't it?"

"Because you haven't opened the envelope."

"That's right."

Now that Troy knew she was playing the game, Emmy was doubly determined not to ask. She considered what she knew. Kostas Kanasis was a cutout. He was laundering Luther's money without knowing it and shielding him from his crimes. An attorney in Miami was their middle man, but he was half blind. Tate only knew Kostas's identity. He couldn't know Luther's identity because then there would be a chain instead of a cutout. So what document could Tate have that would help them? Emmy was stumped.

She tried another tack. Troy had figured it out. He had figured it out right after making the cryptic observation that Luther had to have contingencies. Contingencies for what? Tate did not know his name and Kostas was a feeble old man. What was an old man going to do …?

And then she had it. Just as simple as that. She knew what was in the envelope.

She looked over at Troy. All remnants of his Kostas disguise were now gone, but the mischievous grin was still there. "Why don't you go ahead and read Kostas's will. I'd like to know where we're going."

Troy's eyes bulged. "Don't tell me you can read through envelopes. Wait a minute, did you read my lips?"

"I can read lips, but no, I didn't read yours. Like you, I realized that Luther needs a contingency in case Kostas dies. He can't have his life savings going to Kostas's cousin."

"More like the state," Troy said, unfolding the last will and testament. "I'm sure Luther picked someone without any relatives."

Emmy took the turnoff to Miami International Airport as Troy began to read. "This thing would easily fit on one page were it not for all the legalese. It's just what I expected, a single beneficiary for all assets of the estate. And there's a nice little twist," he said.

"What?" Emmy asked.

"Luther and Kostas do have one thing in common. I was wondering how he picked his mark."

"What's that?"

"A last name. Kostas's sole beneficiary is Luther Kanasis."

Emmy let out a long breath. "You think they're related?"

"If so, I'm sure it's distant. Makes sense though. Pick the same last name, especially an unusual one like Kanasis, and the inheritance seems natural enough to any casual observer or bureaucrat. But at the same time, you would never locate Kostas by studying Luther's family tree."

"Does it list Luther's address?"

"Oh yes, it certainly does."

"Well ...?"

"You're going home, my dear. Luther Kanasis lives in Bel Air."

Chapter 65

New Light

LUTHER POUNDED the leather-wrapped wheel of his black Porsche 911 Carrera. "Damn! Damn! Damn!" he shouted into the breeze. "It just can't be done." He pounded the wheel again. He wanted the private island and lifetime supply of Playboy Bunnies.

From the minute Arlen left his office a week earlier, Luther had been scouring the internet and racking his brains, searching for inspiration. He was desperate to find a creative way of wiping the entire Supreme Court of the United States. If there were such a way, it eluded him. So he was going to pound out his frustrations on the heavy bag in his home gym.

As he drove down Wilshire, the feeling that he was overlooking something simple began nagging at him. After turning onto Beverly Glen, he lowered the Porsche's steering wheel so that he could grip it between his knees and began rubbing both his temples, trying to slip his mind through the loophole in his thinking.

Flashing was not the problem. He had found the perfect opportunity for Farkas to do that. The opening ceremony for the court's new term was just three weeks away.

The rub was the injections.

Farkas would need to inject all nine justices within the preceding forty-eight hours. It was a weekend devoid of any functions that might bring the whole bench together. That meant Farkas would need to inject each individually, and forty-eight hours simply wasn't enough time. With luck and meticulous planning he figured Farkas could do two in one day, maybe even five in one weekend. But not nine. Not undetected.

What was he missing?

A second operative? No. There was also no way Luther was going to bring someone new into his operation. Not at this stage. Not when the stakes were this high. Likewise, there was no way he was going to get dirty himself. Half a billion dollars was an awfully sweet prize, but no amount of money in the world was worth spending the next ten years of his life in prison. He would not survive one year of owing Orca twenty-five double-large.

He shook his head and repeated himself as he turned into his estate's circular drive, "It just can't be done."

As he pulled the 911 to a skidding halt on the drive's crushed stones, Luther resolved to call Arlen and tell him as much. Best to get it over with. Best to get temptation out of the way.

Giselle waved to him from across the yard and began walking his way. He had been too distracted by Arlen's offer to seduce her over the weekend as planned. And despite the enticing bounce beneath her tight white shirt, he did not see his ardor returning anytime soon.

The agency had not sent an automatic replacement for Brandy yet, as was their norm. Either she had told them about the forced fellatio, and Fernando's had blacklisted him, or she had not told them anything at all, and they did not know that a replacement housekeeper was needed. He assumed the latter, since the agency got too much business from him to cut him off over a blowjob. He thought about giving Fernando a call, but decided to put it off in case he was wrong. One unpleasant call a day was enough.

"Good afternoon, Mr. Kanasis," Giselle said, approaching with enthusiasm. She stopped just two feet away holding a trowel in her gloved hands and flashed him a big smile. Luther felt a stir and reconsidered his previous conclusion. Perhaps Giselle was exactly what he needed. Arlen could wait.

"How many times do I have to tell you to call me Luther?"

"I know. It's just that, well, my brother's name is also Luther. And I just can't think of you as my brother."

Luther took that as a good sign. "Well then, why don't you just call me Mr. K? Or better yet, just K."

"K. Yeah, I like that."

This was the time, Luther thought. "Giselle, as you know, Brandy's not with us any more. Would you mind coming inside to give me a hand? The yard already looks perfect."

Giselle's smile faded. "Maybe later, after your guests leave."

"Guests?"

"Yeah. That's what I was coming to tell you. You've got a couple of visitors. Big guys. The ones who were here a week or so ago. They said you were old friends and they just barged right in."

Luther felt the passion drain from his body and ice water begin to flow in its place. Two visits from Orca in as many weeks—that could not be good.

He turned toward the house without another word to Giselle.

"There you are, Luther. Zero and I were beginning to worry about you."

"I'm touched," Luther said, resolving to end this meeting as soon as possible and go beat the stuffing out of his heavy bag. "To what do I owe the pleasure?"

"An opportunity has arisen ..."

"Opportunity?" Luther did not like the sound of that.

"Yeah. Opportunity. You ever hear of Jimmy Choke?"

Luther blinked. Every cop and criminal attorney in L.A. knew about Jimmy. He was Orca's primary rival, and the only person Luther knew who made Orca the Killer Whale look like a catfish by comparison. Jimmy Cortese got his nickname by slicing off men's penises and stuffing them into their mouths where, unwilling to chew, they usually tried to swallow it whole and choked. "I've heard of him," Luther replied, his voice wavering.

"That's too bad. Zero here was looking forward to telling you about him. Anyhow, Jimmy has gone and pissed off a mutual friend of ours back in Chicago. That transgression has given me the opportunity to take over Jimmy's territory, consolidate our operations so to speak."

"Congratulations. You need me to draw up a contract? Some new articles of incorporation?"

Orca turned to Zero. "You hear that, Z? Articles of incorporation. Now that's a lawyer for you." Turning back to Luther he said, "No. We don't operate that way. All I need to do is pay Chicago for Jimmy's franchise and it's mine. Well, almost all," he added, winking at Zero who nodded back. "So, as much as it pains me to say, I'm going to need to call in the principal on your loan. I'm going to need the full twenty-five mil. Plus the outstanding vig, of course."

Luther stared at the Mafia boss, unwilling to believe his ears.

Orca stared back.

The sound of grinding walnuts filled the silent void.

Finally Luther said, "That's impossible. I don't have—"

Orca held up his hand, cutting Luther off. "Believe me, I'm enjoying my fifty-two percent interest. If there was any other way, I wouldn't be asking. But don't worry, I don't need the money now."

"Well, that's good because I haven't—"

"I can give you a week."

As Luther stood there dumbfounded with thoughts of life in Mexico pecking around the edges of his mind, Zero held up the fist containing the walnuts and squeezed. The nuts cracked loudly in his paw. Zero worked his fingers until he had pulped them and then opened his fist to let the dust slip through his fingers and onto the tiled floor.

Luther felt his testicles give an involuntary tug. "Is there anything else?" he asked.

"Yeah, as a matter of fact there is. Do me a favor and go fetch me that pretty little gardener of yours."

Chapter 66

Timeless and Reliable

"I'VE GOT A FEELING this could be our break," Emmy said, looking over at Troy after the beautiful young gardener crashed through Luther Kanasis's front door and made a beeline for her scooter with tear-filled eyes. "Let's follow her."

Troy pulled the Honda Odyssey they had been using as their observation base out into traffic a hundred yards behind the girl's red Vespa. "What are you thinking?" he asked.

"I'm thinking she looks like someone who needs a friend."

"Don't you think she has a few of those already?"

"You'd be surprised, Troy. So many pretty young girls like her come out here to take their shot at a Hollywood dream only to meet with an endless stream of rejection. They end up living reclusive lives among people they don't like because that's the only place they can afford to be. Television becomes their only friend. I used to do readings for a lot of them when I was getting started."

"That sounds morally precarious. What did you tell them?"

"Morally precarious, eh? Are you a doctor or a priest?"

Troy shrugged, and she saw pain in his eyes.

"I'm sorry. It's a sensitive topic for me. To answer your question, I tried to help them. I would encourage them without making promises, trying to keep their spirits up, knowing that a good attitude could give them that vital edge. Most didn't make it, but a couple of them did—not to the A list, but far enough to be happy."

As they turned right off West Sunset onto San Vicente Boulevard, Emmy said, "She's headed for the beach." A few blocks later the gardener parked her Vespa before a liquor store. Troy stopped the car before the air hose of a neighboring gas station and stepped out for reconnaissance. He returned a few seconds later and said, "A bottle of Merlot and a single plastic cup."

"What brand?"

"Kendall-Jackson."

Emmy said, "I've got a good feeling about this."

The Vespa continued down San Vicente to Pacific Coast Highway where it turned left toward Venice Beach. A few blocks later it pulled into a beachfront parking lot and took the last spot in the motorcycle section. "There's nowhere for me to park," Troy said, frustration evident in his voice.

"There's no need," Emmy said, opening the passenger door. "Just go back to Luther's before she gets a good look at the car. I'll meet you there later."

As Troy pulled away, Emmy watched the gardener head across the sand with her purchase.

Confident that she would be easy to find, Emmy walked over to the Vespa and crouched down to adjust her sandal. After making sure that no eyes were upon her, she drained the air from the Vespa's front tire.

Next on her mental to-do list was obtaining the supplies needed for what psychics called mirroring. In order to help establish immediate rapport, she would replicate the gardener's actions and appearance. Fortunately, she already had the dress right: shorts, sandals, and a polo shirt. Mirroring body position, gestures, and even breathing patterns was second nature for Emmy. All she needed was the Kendall-Jackson.

Emmy found The Wine Cask just half-a-block away after asking a meter maid for directions. When she headed out across the warm sand, Emmy was just ten minutes behind her quarry.

She spotted the gardener near the base of the pier, sitting cross-legged in the sand just inches from the surf. She was staring out toward the setting sun with a cup of wine in her hand and a blank look on her face.

Emmy angled her approach to hit the surf line beyond the gardener's peripheral vision. She took off her sandals at the water's edge and walked through the swishing surf in the gardener's direction, her eyes staring out into space, the uncorked Merlot bottle hanging dejectedly from her left hand.

She trudged slowly past the girl, just inches in front of her, but stopped a few feet after passing as though struck by a random thought. Certain that the gardener's eyes were on her, Emmy backed up and turned to make eye contact.

They looked at each other in silence for a moment, and then Emmy let her eyes drift to the gardener's own Merlot bottle. "You having that kind of day too?" she asked, plopping down into the sand beside her new friend. "I just lost my job. It wasn't a great job or anything, but it was the only job I had."

Emmy filled her plastic cup with Merlot and then poured half the contents down her throat. Turning toward her new friend with her cup raised, she said, "I used to do this all the time, back when I was dating Kevin. We'd get into the worst fights." She shook her head slowly and smiled. "But when we weren't fighting ... it was the best."

She set her cup down in the sand and waited for the girl to comment.

She didn't.

After a long minute of silence, Emmy said, "I haven't been back here much since he moved on. Ironically, I kind of miss it. The sea, the setting sun, and a good bottle of wine. All timeless. All reliable."

Emmy picked her cup back up and took another sip. The gardener had yet to utter a single word. After more awkward silence passed and a group of teenagers walked by, she asked, "How about you: guy problems, or work problems?"

The gardener turned to look at her and said, "Guy at work problems."

Emmy knew she had her.

Chapter 67

Tails

IT WAS ONE-O-FIVE AM when Troy hit the button that automatically opened the Odyssey's left sliding door. Even before Emmy flopped into the seat beside him, Troy knew that she was drunk. She was moving with far less poise than usual and he could smell the wine on her breath. She did look happy though. "I got it all," Emmy said, her speech slightly slurred.

Troy poured her a cup of coffee from his thermos. Handing it to her he said, "Do tell."

"According to Giselle—that's her name—Luther Kanasis is using an employment agency to find himself a wife."

"What?"

"Yeah. He has a revolving door of cooks, maids, and gardeners cycling through. How's that for a novel approach. Apparently the potential-wife part is a badly kept secret. The agency just hints that that's his intention, indicating that he wants a genuine, all-American wife rather than one of the princesses that run in his social circles."

"A Mary Ann rather than a Ginger," Troy said.

"Huh?" Emmy asked.

"From Gilligan's Island. Before our time, I know, but it's still a classic comparison."

Emmy rolled her glazed eyes.

"So what happened?" Troy asked. "Did Giselle find out that she's not the one?"

"She sure did, but not directly. She was forced to pleasure Luther's guest, that mafia-looking toad of a man we saw entering with a bodyguard."

"Did she comply?"

"She did what she had to do until she got the chance to escape."

"So I take it she's not going back, even though it wasn't Luther who attacked her?"

"No, but she hates to walk away. She loved the job. Light work doing what she loves and she pockets triple what she'd get elsewhere. Can you believe Luther pays his domestic help ten grand a month? Plus she lives there, rent free, in a room over the garage."

"It doesn't sound rent free to me," Troy said.

"I agree. But I'm still going to give it a try."

"You're what?"

"Luther's maid quit a week or two ago for the same reason. The agency hasn't replaced her yet."

"So you're just going to show up, say the agency sent you, and begin dusting?"

"Why not?"

"Lots of reasons, the first being that he'll recognize you."

"I'm not so sure about that. Given what Farkas told us about Luther's operation, I figure there's a fifty-percent chance that the only thing he knows about me is my name. Remember, Farkas has never met the guy, and he's been working for him for almost four years. In any case, there's only one way to find out."

"What if your 50:50 bet comes up tails?"

Emmy's eyes suddenly sobered. "Then you'll have to rescue me."

Chapter 68

Brute Force

NUBILE NUDE BEAUTIES gyrated above Luther within gilded, glass-floored cages while a large-breasted caramel-eyed Asian frolicked before him on the stage. As he made his way across the floor toward the back, Luther felt a newfound appreciation for his creditor. While Orca's place of business could not be more different from Luther's own, they did share a commonality: both were best in class.

Although Luther knew for a fact that Orca kept no less than half-a-dozen knuckle-breakers on hand during busy hours, besides the paying customers there was not a pair of testicles around. Even the entryway cash register was manned by one of the gorgeous off-shift strippers. No doubt the muscle was all packed into a Vegas-style security room. Luther could picture them there, dressed head to toe in black and ready to react with decisive discretion as required. He was about to find out just how accurate that image was.

Approaching the camouflaged door to the left of the stage, Luther asked himself if he really wanted to go through with this. He could still back out. He could drive to LAX and fly off to a new life. Once he knocked on that door, however, once he let the Killer Whale into his world, there would be no turning back. Like a shark smelling blood, Orca's primitive instincts would take over the instant he sensed a possible kill.

Before Luther's knuckles even tapped the door, a steroid-stuffed security guard opened it and said, "This area is private." The black-clad teenager appeared to be nearly as wide as he was tall. Looking over fireplug's shoulder, Luther caught sight of Zero and looked into his lifeless eyes.

"It's okay," Zero said to Fireplug. "Mr. Kanasis here is a friend of the boss." Then, addressing Luther he said, "You're in luck; the boss is in."

Luther would not necessarily have called that luck, but it was efficient. "Lead the way."

"I'm going to have to search you first," Zero said.

Luther held out his arms once the door closed behind him. Sixty seconds later, he entered Orca's office. He had been there before, but the stark contrast to the rest of Lisa's Place still caught his eye. Rather than being dim and plush, Orca's environment was bright and harsh—kind of like a shark tank, Luther mused. Halogen lights beamed down onto glass shelves, while a black granite desk with matching coffee table and bar stood like oases on the thick, sand-colored carpet. Orca looked up, surprise registering on his face. "Luther, I half expected you to be in Rio by now. Glad to see that you're not so stupid. Did you bring my money?"

Luther ignored the question. He wanted to take control of the conversation, and going on the defensive right off the bat was not going to help him accomplish that. "Lisa's Place. You never did tell me where you got the name."

"The clientele we target don't want Pussy Palace appearing on their AmEx bills."

"Good point, but who is Lisa?"

Orca smiled. "There is no Lisa. The original owner was from Moscow. Before he died, he told me that Lisa means fox in Russian. He thought it was a nice pun. I don't care about puns, but I saw no reason to mess with a good thing."

Orca looked down at his watch. "You still got seventy-two hours to come up with my money, so that can't be why you're here. What is it, now that the maid and gardener are gone, you looking to get laid? I thought you still had the cook. What's her name, by the way? Great legs."

"I came here because I want to pay you what I owe you."

"I'm glad to hear that. Just don't be asking me for an extension. My offer from Chicago is going to expire, and I'd rather put my balls in a blender than miss that deadline." Orca paused to scratch his sack. "Well, maybe not my balls, but certainly your balls."

"You won't have to bother with anyone's balls."

"Good."

"All you have to do is provide me with a little bit of help."

Orca shook his head. "All I have to do is point Zero in your direction."

"I may be a lawyer, but I don't bleed money."

"That remains to be seen. In any case, I bet he can extract the deeds to your house and yacht in less time than it takes to say twenty-six million."

"I'm sure he could. But they won't help you with Chicago. They're mortgaged for all that they're worth. Don't you think I'd have sold them already if that was an option, rather than paying you fifty-two percent?"

"I thought maybe you was emotionally attached. People get that way. So tell me, counselor, what was this little bit of help you had in mind?"

"I need you to connect me—or rather a colleague of mine—with nine soldiers on the East Coast. I need top guys, ex-CIA or Special Forces, James Bond types. Guys who can do a sophisticated job with absolute discretion."

Orca nodded appreciatively. "And this is going to get me my money?"

"As long as they're the right kind of guys."

"What's the job?"

Luther shook his head. "All you need to know is that with their help, you get your money. You get Jimmy Choke's franchise.

Without them, you don't."

"How long you need them for?"

"About two weeks."

"Starting when?"

"In forty-eight hours."

"What you going to pay them?"

"Enough."

"I need to be able to tell them what to expect."

"Tell them that they'll be well paid."

Orca cracked his neck, first on the right, then on the left. "And when do I get my money?"

"You get me the names today, I get you your money as requested."

Orca moved on to his knuckles. "Anything else?" he asked.

"Yes, one thing. No one besides you and I are to know of my involvement. No one besides you and I are to know that nine people are involved. Each man is to think that he's working alone." Luther handed Orca nine slips of paper. "Those are the times and places for nine meetings on Sunday. Have one man show up at each. That's all they need to know. Each man will get ten grand just for showing up—and taking a vow of silence."

"Very interesting, counselor."

"Do we have an agreement, then?"

"Yes," Orca said, his eyes alight with the glow of greed, "we do."

Chapter 69

The Extra Mile

EMMY LOOKED OVER her shoulder at Troy as she approached Luther's gate. "Wish me luck."

"You sure you want to do this?"

"With all we've been through, do you really need to ask?"

"Well, I—"

"You just keep your ears open and your eyes on the screen so you can come to my rescue if anything happens."

"Of course, but—"

"Don't worry; I'm going to run like hell the moment I sense that he's suspicious."

"With all due respect to your senses, we know they failed us at least once before."

Emmy crossed her arms across her chest. "Do we now?"

"Farkas caught us."

"Huh. Well, I guess that just makes your role all the more important."

"I guess it does," Troy said, climbing over the Odyssey's third row bench seat. Once settled in on the carpeted floor, he popped an earbud in his right ear and checked the screen on his Blackberry as Emmy whispered, "Testing. Testing."

"Loud and clear."

"How's the picture?" Emmy asked, placing a large sun hat on her head.

"With the phone clipped to your belt, all I see is the underside of the steering wheel, but the image is clear." They had rigged a cell phone to send streaming video clandestinely so Troy could see and hear everything Emmy did.

Emmy pulled the Honda into Luther's driveway and pressed the intercom button. Luther's voice came on a couple of minutes later. "Yes."

"Mr. Kanasis?"

"Yes."

"This is Vicky Dixon. The employment agency sent me over to fill the maid position." She looked ahead rather than into the camera. It was important that she be able to look into Luther's eyes the instant he got his first good look at her face.

"It's about time," Luther said, buzzing her in.

Emmy pulled in as the gate swung open and parked so that the minivan was facing the gate, just in case she needed to make a quick exit. To that end, she had decided to leave the keys with Troy as well.

"Good luck," Troy whispered as she tossed the keys over the back seat.

Stepping out, she removed her sun hat and placed it behind the driver's seat. It had done its job. She hoped the rest of her outfit would perform as well. Emmy had chosen to wear white shorts and a green shirt that offered a peek at cleavage and added flare to her eyes.

Luther answered the door just seconds after her knock. "Hello Vicky, I'm Luther Kanasis. It's a pleasure to meet you."

Emmy studied Luther's face for the slightest flash of recognition —flaring irises, contracting lids, increased blood flow to the cheeks. Nothing pinged her radar. The only suppressed emotion she detected was a hint of lust. "Likewise."

"Please, come in," he said, stepping back and pulling the arched door open wide.

"Your home is beautiful," she said, thinking, "so are you." Luther had a charismatic presence that gripped you right away—a powerful aura, people in her business would say. If she did not hate the man with every fiber in her being, she might well have been attracted to him. As it was, she found it hard not to spit.

"Thank you. Let me show you around. What did Fernando tell you about the position?"

"He said you needed live-in housekeeping for an unspecified duration."

"That's right. Anything else?"

"He said it was the best deal in town, and I was lucky to have qualified. Judging by the numbers he quoted, I'm inclined to agree."

Leading her up the sweeping semicircular staircase, Luther asked, "And did he tell you what those qualifications were?"

Giselle had primed Emmy to expect this question. "Of course there was the standard reference to diligence and hard work, but the real emphasis was on discretion. He told me that you demanded absolute discretion and rewarded blind loyalty."

"That's right. Does it bother you?"

"That depends on why it's an issue. Are you involved in anything illegal?"

Luther forced a chuckle that sent a chill up Emmy's spine. "Well, I suppose that depends on your definition of involved."

Emmy stopped walking and turned to face Luther. "How so?"

"I'm a criminal defense attorney. On rare occasion, the people I represent are convicted of illegal acts."

"I'm okay with that. But why the great need for secrecy?"

"Lives depend upon my discretion, and I must pass that requirement on to all around me. You are never to mention a word about your work here to anyone, nothing you see, nothing you hear. Is that understood?"

"Yes."

"No griping to friends, not even an I-love-my-job. Are we clear?"

"Yes, sir."

Luther's serious visage vanished in a millisecond and he was all charm again. "No need for sir. Please, call me Luther. Any questions?"

"Just one."

Luther nodded.

"What happened to the last girl? I mean, if I may be blunt, I can't imagine anyone giving up a job like this."

Luther shrugged. "I had to let her go. She was good at the day-to-day routine, but in a crunch, she wasn't willing to go the extra mile. Her devotion was not absolute, not congruent with the paycheck. You would be wise to keep that in mind, Vicky. We've only just met, but I already have high expectations for you ..."

Chapter 70

Accounting Adjustments

"YOU FIGURED IT OUT," Arlen said, stepping off the elevator into Luther's office. "I knew you would."

"Good morning to you too," Luther said, just finishing up behind the espresso machine. He motioned his guest toward the suite of chairs before picking up the two piping-hot beverages. "You bring your checkbook?"

Arlen nodded in appreciation of Luther's directness. "As promised. Let's hope I'm impressed enough to open it."

As the two titans took their seats, Arlen looked around the room as if searching for something. Luther understood immediately, but chose to enjoy his first sip of espresso before commenting. When Arlen returned his gaze to his host, Luther said, "Expecting PowerPoint or flip charts?"

Arlen nodded. "Corporate habit."

"In my businesses—both my legal practice and my ancillary services—I'm well advised to commit as little as possible to paper. I have also found that juries are more likely to believe an attorney who speaks extemporaneously than one who constantly refers to notes." This was a ploy, of course, and a fairly clever one Luther thought. He had concocted it to help ensure that the bluff he was about to attempt would fly. Studying the skeptical reaction on Arlen's face, he felt a rumble of doubt.

"In my business, I'm well advised to always get promises on paper." Arlen paused, inviting Luther's comment.

Luther made none.

Finally Arlen said, "But I see your point." He settled back into the leather and added, "Do be advised that my checkbook and I will walk out of here at the first sign of smoke and mirrors."

"Fair enough," Luther said, resisting the urge to stand as he began his performance. Placing far more certainty in his voice than he currently felt, he said, "The wiping will occur Monday morning, September twenty-ninth, at the press conference preceding the annual opening conference. I trust you agree that the timing is ideally suited to create maximum chaos?"

"It's perfect," Arlen said, sliding forward in his chair. "And less than three weeks away." He was trying to play the role of the cool senior executive but he couldn't hide his excitement. Luther's news was worth tens of billions of dollars. "It will take months for congress even to figure out where to start when the entire court is found to be mentally unstable. By the time the president nominates replacements and congress approves them, they'll almost certainly lose the entire court year. Once sound minds are eventually in place on the bench, they'll have an additional year's backlog to deal with. My experts concur that our case will slip at least one additional year back in the queue if it isn't removed all together." Arlen rubbed his hands together subconsciously. "How, exactly, are you going to do it?"

"The activation itself is the easy part. That's how I can be so confident about the date. I'll get a man into the press conference with the necessary equipment. It's the implantation that will take real guile. To accomplish that, I've assigned a top man to each of the nine justices. They have spent the last few days studying their assigned target's routines, and have mapped out an implantation strategy accordingly."

"It only took a few days?" Arlen asked.

Luther nodded confidently as he spoke. "My men are pros at infiltration. It wasn't hard for them to get their hands on the justices calendars. All of them are men of habit, creatures of routine. The older ones are all pretty domestic, but each has regular outings. The younger guys, the ones in their fifties, both jog on a regular basis. They will be particularly easy pickings.

"Let me tell you what I've learned about the routines of each justice," Luther continued, preparing to let loose a long list of memorized bullshit. "We've got primary and backup plans for each, taking all foreseeable contingencies into account."

"Please," Arlen prompted.

And so Luther rattled off detailed plans of attack that resembled what he expected Farkas and Orca's men to compile in the coming days. He did it all without notes, drawing on skills developed during his courtroom days. Studying Arlen's features, he could tell by the time he got to the second name that the CEO was sold. Nonetheless, Luther continued with the same confident enthusiasm and attention to detail through all nine.

Arlen remained silent once Luther had finished, giving the appearance of one who was deliberating on the words he had just heard. Luther remained calm, trusting in his instincts and minding the old maxim to shut up once a person was sold.

Finally, without a word, Arlen reached into his pocket, withdrew his cell phone, and speed-dialed a number. "Make the transfer."

Luther waited in silence, very aware of the beat of his own heart.

Arlen smiled, closed his phone, and said, "It's done. Two hundred and fifty million dollars has been transferred to your account."

Luther found himself unable to speak. A quarter of a billion dollars. He held out his hand.

Arlen grabbed it and pulled Luther close. He whispered in Luther's ear, his voice cold as death. "I've got ten times this amount in my war chest, Luther. If you run, I will track you down."

Luther backed away as Arlen released his grip, acutely aware that he was exchanging one mafia boss for another. Orca was old school, Arlen new, but they were equally deadly. After a long silence, Luther found his voice. "I'm doing this exactly because I want to live the rest of my life in peace, rather than looking over my shoulder. You have nothing to worry about, Arlen. Our interests are aligned."

Arlen nodded, his cordial mask back in place. "I trust you haven't forgotten our agreement that all your colleagues are to share the justices' fate?"

"I'm a details man, Arlen. I haven't forgotten a thing." Actually, it was not the thought of additional wipings that was grating across Luther's mind. It was the impending murder.

With just one more deposit on the horizon, it would soon be time to close Kostas Kanasis's account.

Chapter 71

Oops

USING A MIRROR to keep an eye on the estate's front gate, Troy tried to get inside his enemy's head. Now that he had seen Luther's face, house, car, clothes, office and servants, he had a good framework from which to extrapolate.

While this exercise might pay dividends later on, he was really just killing time. Crouched behind the third row of seats in the Honda Odyssey Emmy had parked in Luther's drive, his options were limited. Meanwhile his need for distraction was severe. Emmy's video cell phone had run out of juice four hours earlier, leaving him in the dark. She had a regular cell phone as backup in her purse, but had yet to call.

As he checked his Nokia's battery level and signal strength for the tenth time, it finally began to vibrate. "Are you okay?" he asked.

"I'm fine," Emmy said, her voice free of duress. "Sorry to be incommunicado for so long. It's the cook, Desiree. She's been finding excuses to follow me wherever I go."

"Is it possible that she suspects something?" Troy asked. "Maybe you used to know her but don't remember."

"That's not my read. I think she's bought into the bullshit about Luther looking for a wife and is trying to find a way to eliminate me as competition."

"So where are you now?"

"In the basement. Kind of hard for a cook to justify popping down here. Wasn't easy for me either. I had to dust the rest of the house first so as not to look suspicious."

Troy could tell by Emmy's tone that she was excited about something. "You uncover anything interesting?"

"A lot of high quality reproductions—both artwork and furniture. If I weren't trained to spot a fake I never would have known that they weren't genuine."

"That skill come from another of your entrepreneurial acquaintances?"

"That one came from Ava herself. One of her favorite confidence games involved a switcheroo."

"Any conclusions?"

"Luther is not as wealthy as he wants to appear."

"Who is? Did you inspect the guest house?"

"No. I'll do that tomorrow."

"How about safes or hidden rooms?"

"I haven't found either yet. I used the laser tape measure just like you showed me. Got every room. We can study the results later, but I'm pretty sure that all space is accounted for."

"Anything interesting in Luther's study?"

"I spent a lot of time there, dusting every crevice. It's obviously the center of his universe. In addition to the normal desk and bookcases covered with pristine legal tomes, he's got a huge waterfall along one wall, an enormous fireplace on the other, a big domed skylight over the center, and sandstone tiled floors—all four elements converging."

"All four what?" Troy asked.

"The original elements. Water, fire, air, and earth."

"That tell you anything?"

"His subconscious is screaming for stability and balance."

"We'll have it screaming for something else soon enough. Did you search his desk?"

"I did. Picked my way in. Nothing unusual."

"How about the basement? Anything there?"

"I hope so. I've been working the lock to a closet for these last few minutes."

There was the source of her excitement, Troy thought. "How big a closet?"

"I'm guessing it's about five foot by eight."

"What makes you think there's anything more special than old knickknacks inside?"

"First of all, those are in the attic. Secondly, Luther installed a seven-tumbler lock on the door. That's exceptional. The vast majority of locks have only five. He's definitely hiding something here. Oh, hold on …"

Troy waited through a long silence before Emmy said, "Got it, I'm in."

He refrained from asking the obvious questions. She would tell him what she saw.

"It's a computer room. The air is a lot warmer than in the rest of the house and it has that computer smell."

"Ozone," Troy said.

"Right. There's a narrow table running the length of the eight-foot side, and a single-wheeled armchair, a Herman Miller."

"So Luther spends a lot of time there."

"Or at least he did at one time. The room's fairly dusty, although that could just be because the maid doesn't come here."

"Except you."

"Except me."

"What do you see?"

"There are computer monitors all along the wall above the table, two rows of them, eight long. They're numbered one through sixteen. So are sixteen black boxes stacked at the far end."

"What kind of boxes?"

"They look like small DVD recorders. There's also a big computer with its own monitor and keyboard. All the DVD recorders are connected to it."

"Is there anything on the monitors?"

"No. Wait, one of them is coming to life. Number fourteen. It's a beautiful woman in an ornate elevator."

"Is DVD player fourteen doing anything?" Troy asked.

"All the DVD players have a green diode lit up, but fourteen has a red one too. Okay, the elevator door just opened. The woman is exiting. Now I see her on monitor fifteen. She's in a room with a waterfall like the one in Luther's study. There's also a granite bar in the background. She's walking toward the camera. Now she's on sixteen. So is Luther. He's seated behind a big oak desk. That must be his Rodeo Drive office."

"So the security system is motion activated," Troy said. "And everything that moves is recorded."

"Oh my god," Emmy said. "Monitor seven just came to life. It's Desiree. She just entered the kitchen from the pantry."

Troy understood the problem immediately. It was a monster. Everything Emmy had done that day, from searching Luther's desk to picking her way into his security room, everything had been recorded.

Chapter 72

Promotion

FARKAS REMOVED the safety cap from his injector ring and inspected the weapon. Three tiny needles glistened in the elevator light. The ring was ready; was he? He had no choice.

The doors parted to reveal an enormous office, complete with a granite bar, slate waterfall and one Luther Kanasis. Luther's appearance surprised Farkas—much more Hugh Jackman than Gene Hackman.

Crossing toward Luther's desk, Farkas tried to exude an image that would fit an iron grip. He knew that was not a stretch. He was much more Van Damme than DeVito.

"We meet at last," Luther said, coming around his desk and extending his hand.

Farkas did not reply at once. He looked Luther in the eye while catching his hand such that Luther's knuckles aligned. Then he smiled and squeezed like a vice, knowing the pain he inflicted would drown out any pin prick. "The pleasure is all mine."

Farkas saw a shadow flicker across Luther's eyes, but as predicted, he continued to smile. Men hated to appear weak.

The injection ring did its work in less than a second, so Farkas only pumped twice before releasing. He broke eye contact for a second to diffuse the tension and used his left hand for a diversionary pat on Luther's right shoulder. "Nice place you have here. Hardly the discreet hideaway I had envisioned."

"Sometimes the best place to hide is in plain sight. Please, have a seat. Tell me how it went in Vegas."

"After you," Farkas said, not wanting to give his boss the opportunity to inspect his injured hand.

Farkas had expected Luther to start out exactly thus, with a cordial question about Vegas. Best to be sure his affairs were in order before terminating Farkas's services with a bullet or a flash. For his part, Farkas was more than happy to play along. He needed to buy fifteen minutes—time for the 456 to activate. Then at the first sign of trouble, he would squeeze the remote concealed in his left hand and the UV-C strobe hidden in his Kangol cap would flash.

"Is that an espresso machine I see up there?" Farkas asked, glancing toward the bar.

"Yes. But it's nearly five o'clock. Perhaps you'd prefer a Scotch?"

"Naw, you know how Vegas is. This is breakfast time."

Luther nodded and made the drink, gobbling up enough time that Farkas figured he was safe. "So how is Mr. Rodriguez?"

"I'm pleased to report that he has no memory of the last twelve months of his life."

"Excellent. Does that mean you got your groove back?"

Farkas met his boss's eye. "After Grand Cayman, you mean?"

"Yes."

"I did."

"Good. You never did tell me exactly what happened there."

There it was, Farkas thought, the lead-up to the end. He had decided days ago to play it straight, no excuses, but with a bit of panache. "I was bested by a clever surgeon and an evil pixie."

"Evil pixie?" Luther asked, his tone more curious than condemning.

"It's from a Croatian fairytale. Emmy looks like a pixie, all petite and fiery with bright emerald eyes that can see into a man's soul."

Luther nodded appreciatively. "Yes, combined with a clever surgeon they do make a formidable team. I should have taken the time to learn more about them. They were, after all, the first and only people to ever suspect my existence. Some day you'll have to fill me in on the details. At the moment, however, we have more pressing matters."

Farkas raised his brows in genuine query. This was not at all what he had expected. He reminded himself that Luther's stock-in-trade was that you never saw him coming. He would remain wary despite his boss's cordial demeanor and collegial attitude. "So what's next?"

"What's next, my friend, is your bonanza."

"My bonanza?" Farkas repeated, finding the remote with his thumb. "What does that mean?"

"It means that you're about to become rich. Fifteen days from now I'm going to pay you ten million dollars. Eight figures. Tax free."

Farkas knew that was four hundred wiping's worth, having done the calculation many a time in his head. Keeping his tone neutral and his thumb poised, he asked, "And just what do I have to do to earn this bonanza?"

"Actually, you've already done most of it," Luther said. "By working dependably for me these past few years. I'm moving you into management."

"Management? Management of what?"

"A big job. A huge job. A job that will make history."

Luther's excitement appeared genuine. Farkas was actually starting to believe. "You have my undivided attention. Who is it, the president? One of the major party nominees?"

When Luther did not contradict him right away, Farkas knew that was it. A suicide mission. That made perfect sense.

"No," Luther eventually said. "Just the nine justices of the United States Supreme Court."

Same difference. "I see. Is that all? Just nine of the most closely guarded men on the planet?"

"Actually, they're not guarded at all. At least not when they're outside the courthouse."

"So you think that I can just walk up to them like anyone else?" Farkas said, not bothering to disguise his incredulity.

"You're not listening, Farkas. I told you, you're in management now. You're going to have help. Nine men as a matter of fact."

Nine men, Farkas thought. One apiece. That sounded good. Too good. "So what is it you aren't telling me?"

Chapter 73

Cleanup

THE PHONE SLIPPED from Emmy's grasp and clattered across the tabletop. As her nervous fingers fumbled to bring it back to her ear, she heard Troy asking, "Are you okay? Emmy, are you okay?"

"No, I'm not okay. I'm totally screwed. As soon as Luther checks the tapes, he's going to see that I spent the day snooping around. I'll have to quit. Run. And I still haven't found anything. All this has been a waste."

"Calm down," Troy said. "We'll think of something."

Troy's words did not reach her, but something in his tone did. If he was confident, she could be confident too. "Do you think there's some way to edit the tape? Take out the suspicious parts?"

Troy took his time answering her. She pictured him lying on the floor of their rented minivan, looking toward the ceiling with that contemplative thousand-yard stare she had grown to love. "I don't think you're going to have time to review and edit sixteen tapes before Luther returns. Even if you could, we probably wouldn't fool him. Security systems have a built-in time stamp."

Emmy glanced at an active screen. Desiree was rubbing spices into the skin of a duck. "You're right, the time and date are in the corner of every active monitor. Maybe we should cut our losses. I'll keep searching the house until Luther returns. Then I'll run. Maybe we'll get lucky."

"Hold on," Troy said. "I've got another call." He clicked off before she could ask who it was. She could not think of anyone who might be calling him. Probably a wrong number.

Turning her attention back to pressing matters, Emmy looked around for other discs. She found a box of fresh DVD-9s on the floor beneath the table, but none that were used. Either Luther stored the recorded disks in another location, or the system was set up to reuse the same disks. Perhaps she could just copy yesterday's video and paste it on top of today? Who really paid attention to a date stamp anyway? She discarded that idea immediately. She was not in yesterday's tapes, and Luther would specifically be looking for her.

"I'm back," Troy said. "You're not going to believe—"

"Oh my god!" Emmy said, cutting him off.

"What?"

"It's Farkas. Farkas just walked into Luther's office."

"How on earth?"

"I don't know. But that does it. Now I have no choice but to run. Can you imagine if I hadn't gotten into this room? If Luther had brought Farkas home while I was here? Should I bring all the DVD's with me?"

"No! You can't leave." Troy said, his voice emphatic. "That phone call. I've just learned something big. I don't want to go into the details over the phone, but now it's more important than ever that we stop Luther."

"But Farkas can identify me."

"Not necessarily. We don't know that he didn't lose his memory. All we know is that he found his way to Luther's. Remember our own experience."

"He told us he'd never been to Luther's. Never met the man. Obviously his whole spiel was a lie. I don't know how he fooled me so completely, but he did."

"Maybe, maybe not. Maybe he had the equivalent of a tattoo on his foot." Troy trailed off. His silence seemed to last forever.

Emmy knew he was thinking, but eventually could not take it anymore. "Troy?"

"I got it!" Troy said. "I know what we can do. I can fix this thing, but you're going to have to hang in there. I need an hour. Does it look like Luther and Farkas are going to be there for a while? Are they getting comfortable?"

Emmy could not imagine what solution Troy had found, but experience had given her faith in his genius and she found herself willing to make that blind leap. "It's hard to tell. They are sitting down, but they're talking with a lot of passion so it might be over quick. I don't have sound."

"Can you read their lips?" Troy asked.

"Not under these conditions."

"Did Luther give you any idea when he planned to be home?"

"No. Who called? What's your plan? Don't leave me hanging, Troy."

"I'll tell you everything when I get there. We don't have time to waste now. Just trust me. Forget about the cameras and get busy cleaning. You've got a whole day's legitimate work to do."

Chapter 74

Anticipation

LUTHER CLOSED the titanium notebook with a great sense of satisfaction. Two hundred and fifty million dollars. A quarter billion. He was tempted to take the money and run. True, Arlen would send an army after him—but would he send more men than the FBI and Secret Service combined? Actually, Luther decided, he might. And, unlike them, Arlen's mercenaries would know who they were looking for.

Then there was Arlen's point about the ambiguity of mass amnesia.

Deciding once and for all to move ahead, Luther began placing 456 ampoules into mailing boxes. He packed eighteen in total: nine for the Supreme Court Justices, nine for Orca's thugs.

Returning to his desk, he picked up his scrambled phone. Anyone tapping Orca's line would hear gobbledygook and think Luther's call originated in Iceland.

"Talk to me," the killer whale said.

"Did you arrange those meetings for me?" Luther asked.

"I did. All nine."

"You do know these guys personally, right? You can guarantee me that they're James Bonds, not Jack the Rippers?"

"They're on the East Coast, so I can't say that I know them all personally. But I'm told that they're primo. What else can I say? I did what you asked. Now get me my money." Orca ended the call before Luther could comment.

Luther sat there in silence, his stomach shriveling further with each breath. There was a reason he had never attempted to expand his operation before, and this was it. With the involvement of each additional person, the variables multiplied exponentially. His two-man operation had just expanded to twelve. Thank goodness this was the last hurrah, otherwise he'd be in prison within a year. And in any case, it was Farkas's problem now. The risk, hereafter, was all his.

Weaving his Porsche impatiently through Saturday evening traffic, Luther sought another train of thought and remembered that he had a new girl. She was a hottie. Fernando had come through once again, and just in time. With Brandy and Giselle both gone and Desiree too eager to please, he desperately needed a new source of release.

With his departure imminent, his normal rules no longer applied. He could begin to seduce her immediately. Hell, if she had snooped around as much as most first-day girls do, he could go straight to blackmail—tonight. Wouldn't that be grand. He just needed a little something for which she would want to make atonement.

Naughty fantasies began running through his head as he gave his Carrera the gas. He pictured her pouty lips, her fiery eyes, and that hot little body of hers. She could not weigh more than a hundred pounds. He could bounce her around like a gymnast on a beam. She was almost ... pixie-like ...

Chapter 75

Rocky

FIFTY-THREE MINUTES after coming up with his plan, Troy crept into Luther's security room. After returning from his errand, Emmy had guided him past the watchful cook and down the basement stairs. Then she had pounced and begun squeezing the stuffing out of him.

It felt wonderful.

So did seeing the monitor showing Luther behind his office desk. And alone. "Did Farkas leave?"

"About forty-five minutes ago."

"So if he was headed this way, he would already have shown up?"

"Probably ..." Emmy's voice trailed off and she took a sudden step back. "What's in the box? I thought I heard something move."

"That, my dear, was the sound of salvation."

"It sounded more like a rat."

Troy patted the box, eliciting more scratching. "Salvation can take many forms. Rocky here is going to explain to Luther why his computer shut down in the middle of the night."

Emmy took another step back. "It really is a rat?"

Troy nodded and waited for her to get it. Emmy did not take long, and once she did, she switched gears almost immediately. "So who called you?"

"Sylvia Dashell."

"The attorney from Alexander Tate's office? The woman you bribed to keep you secretly appraised of activity in your account?"

"Kostas received a deposit today. Two hundred and fifty million dollars."

Emmy's eyes bulged like a mating frog's. "You sure you heard that right?"

"I'm sure. I had her repeat it. Twenty-five with a seven zero tail."

"The records we saw indicated that he only got one million for a job. Do you think he's going to flash two hundred and fifty people all at once?"

"I was thinking more along the lines of one very important person."

Emmy gasped. "Like the president?"

"Either him or one of the major-party nominees. Now you see why we can't run?"

"Of course."

"Good. Now, you get back to your cleaning. I'm going to erase all the DVDs back to the time when our nocturnal friend here supposedly stepped on Ctrl-Alt-Delete. I'll call you when I'm done so that you can distract Desiree long enough for me to get back to the Honda. Then you find an excuse to run an errand."

"I can't believe that we might be working to save the president," Emmy said. "My whole life I've been operating in a moral gray zone, just trying to get by. Now for the first time I'm working in the white, and it's for the president. It feels different. It feels good."

"Let's hope it's the start of a new trend," Troy said, giving her hand a squeeze. "Now get to it. We're probably short on time."

Troy had just finished erasing the twelfth DVD back to 2:43 AM when Luther rose from behind his desk and crossed the room to stand before his slate waterfall. A big blue Macaw watched him attentively from its perch off to the right. Why were rich people always so flamboyantly eccentric?

As Troy watched, Luther removed his jacket and scrunched up his right shirtsleeve, sending the Macaw to a new perch atop the waterfall. Then Luther plunged his hand into the water.

The flow stopped almost immediately and the slate backing slid aside. Troy found himself looking at the black iron door of a mammoth safe. No wonder Emmy had found nothing upstairs. Luther's office safe was large enough to hold Hoover's secret files.

He watched Luther work the combination with practiced ease. Troy could see the dial, but the camera was too far from the door for him to read the numbers. He found himself expecting to see bars of gold stacked inside, but when Luther hauled the heavy door open Troy saw only empty shelves.

Luther pulled out a metallic binder that his body had hidden from view. He opened it and made a careful entry using a thick silver pen. When he finished writing, he stared at the page as though it were the picture of a long-lost lover or firstborn child. When he finally closed the notebook, he laid it back down lovingly. Next, Luther pulled a key ring from his pocket and crouched down to reveal what appeared to be a mini refrigerator. This he unlocked with a short, round key like the ones typically used on vending machines and bicycle locks. As he swung the insulated door open, a light went on inside, confirming Troy's initial hypothesis as to its nature.

Luther used both hands to extract a box made of the same metal as the binder. He laid it gingerly atop the refrigerator, opened the lid, and began removing small ruby-red ampoules. "There it is," Troy said. "That's what we've been looking for.

"Now all we have to do is get it."

Luther proceeded to place the extracted ampoules into a book-sized cardboard box lined with thick foam padding. Troy counted nine ampoules total. Then Luther repeated the procedure with a second box. Once both boxes were full and sealed, he reversed the procedure to close the safe and restore the waterfall.

When Luther took the package back to his desk rather than the elevator, Troy seized the opportunity to rewind the tape with the hope of deciphering the combination using digital zoom. He paused with the cursor over the rewind button. Perhaps it would be better to just make a copy of Luther's entire visit to the safe and interpret it later.

Using the software's convenient drag-and-drop procedure, he burned the ten minutes from 17:42 through 17:51 off camera 15 onto a fresh DVD. Sliding that backup into his breast pocket, Troy felt a sense of accomplishment. Now even if the shit hit the fan he would not leave empty handed.

Checking the monitor, Troy saw that Luther was still at his desk. He decided to attempt to decipher the combination while all the equipment he needed was at hand.

Troy had the first four digits of the combination scrawled on a notepad when he looked up to see that screens 15 and 16 were both dark. Luther had left his office.

That was when he remembered that he still had four DVDs to erase.

Praying that the DVD in his pocket contained the same high-definition video as the original, Troy forgot about the tape he was watching and began furiously erasing the remaining hard drives back to 2:43 that morning. Questions cascaded through his mind as he worked, but his surgical fingers did not fumble. How long ago had Luther left? Was he coming straight home? Did he carry a gun? Troy knew he should call Emmy to warn her, but he could not risk the time. Besides, she was just cleaning. There was no harm in Luther catching her doing that. Troy was the one out on a limb.

It took him seven minutes to erase the remaining four DVDs back to 2:43 AM. Then he simply turned off the computer. The DVD recorders' green diodes extinguished along with the computer monitor. The wall monitors showing Emmy and Desiree remained lit. Apparently they were part of a separate system.

"Now for the finishing touch," he said, slipping a peanut butter cookie into Rocky's box. With the rat's mouth gainfully engaged, Troy pulled Rocky out and set him on the table. Then he inverted the box and shook it over the keyboard. Several rat pellets dropped out. Two landed on the desk and the third wedged between the F and R keys. This simple ruse probably wouldn't fool Sherlock Holmes, but Troy did not expect Luther to bring in a forensic consultant. As the lawyer himself would put it, this was enough for reasonable doubt.

Reassuring himself that the safe-cracking DVD was in his pocket, he stood just as monitor one lit up and Luther's black Porsche approached the gate. Talk about cutting it close. He tossed Rocky another cracker to keep him distracted, and slid out the door. He used Emmy's tension wrench to re-secure the bolt and then picked up his phone to give her a call. Now, all he had to do was make it out the back door and into the Honda unobserved.

Chapter 76

Tips

EMMY'S CELL PHONE finally began to vibrate. Troy had taken much longer than she'd expected. She moved out of Desiree's earshot and brought the phone to her ear.

"I'm ready," Troy said. "And I've got what we need." He sounded excited.

"You can't come up yet. Desiree is rearranging the pantry near the top of the stairs. It's almost as though she knows you're down there."

"Luther just pulled through the gate. Think of something." Troy hung up.

Emmy walked back toward the pantry, thinking fast. Inspiration tended to strike her on the fly, and her muse did not let her down today. "Have you got a minute, Desiree? I'd love to get your opinion on something."

Desiree looked silently down on her from a step stool. It was a gaze meant to intimidate.

Emmy was unaffected. She was used to talking up to people who tried to use their relative height to tactical advantage. And as a psychic she was accustomed to dealing with skeptics. The trick in both cases was to alter the antagonist's perspective. Right now Desiree saw her as competition for Luther's affection. "It will just take a minute. While dusting I noted that Mr. Kanasis has a nice collection of Swiss chronographs. One of them is the same model Breitling that I was planning to get my fiancé for his birthday. I'd love a second opinion."

The effect on Desiree was instantaneous. She brightened up and said, "Sure." But as her first foot hit the floor she paused and asked, "You're getting him a Breitling, and he hasn't gotten you a ring?"

"Oh, I got the ring. Two carats. But I'm not about to wear it here. I learned in my waitressing days that men treat you much better when they think you're available."

Desiree's smile returned and she finished her descent. "They still don't treat you all that well."

"You're right about that."

They had just reached the top of the sweeping semicircular staircase when the front door opened. Emmy felt as though an icy hand had gripped her heart. Had Troy made it out in time? "Maybe tomorrow," she whispered to Desiree as they both turned to greet their master.

"What are you two ladies up to?" Luther asked, depositing his keys in a vase on a knickknack shelf to the left of the door. Although his tone telegraphed lighthearted banter, Emmy detected suspicion in his eyes.

"Desiree has just been giving me some tips on your preferences," Emmy said. "She's been very helpful."

"Glad to hear it," Luther replied, a penetrating look in his eyes. "Why don't you join me for a drink, Vicky. You can tell me about your first day and I can give you all the tips you need."

Chapter 77

Accommodation

FARKAS PUSHED OPEN the stairwell door with a little too much vigor. It slammed into the cinderblock wall and ricocheted back at him, but he stepped through in time to avoid its ire. His first day in "management" was not going well. Time to bring Luther into the loop.

Luther answered on the second ring. "How's it going?"

"Neanderthals. Your business associate sent us Neanderthals."

"All of them?"

"I've seen eight so far. You wouldn't trust any of these guys with your dry cleaning, much less 456."

Luther paused as though winded, confirming Farkas's suspicion that this was bad news on several levels. "What did you tell them?"

"Not a word about the plan, that's for sure. As soon as it became clear that I'd eaten meals with more brainpower, I pretended to receive a call telling me that the job had been called off. I acted all pissed and gave each guy ten grand for his time and his tongue as agreed. But hey, for what it's worth, your plan of alternating the meetings between the sixth and seventh floors worked like a charm. No one suspected that this would have been more than a two-man op."

"Swell."

"I take it you went this route due to a lack of alternatives?" Farkas asked.

Luther prevaricated with a collegial, "How about you? Know any talent?"

"Farkas means wolf in Hungarian. Like my namesake, I work alone."

"Maybe number nine will work out. Maybe he'll have friends."

"Maybe monkeys will fly out of my ass and do the job for us, Luther, but I wouldn't count on it."

"You sure you went to med school?"

"You sure you're an officer of the court?"

After another long pause, Luther said, "Tell me something. How many people do you really need to do the job?"

"Nine people, one city, forty-eight hours ... If I had four people, each could do one a day and I could pick up the ninth."

"What if it was just you and two others?"

"Three apiece ... yeah, that should be possible with enough planning."

"Two weeks good enough?"

"If they're good people."

"You're being awfully accommodating."

"I want my ten million bucks."

"Glad to hear it. I want to give it to you. In the meantime, go ahead with your last meeting. Maybe we'll get lucky. In either case, I want you to come back to LA when you're done. We'll finish the recruiting here."

"You sound like you have someone in mind."

"As a matter of fact, I do."

Chapter 78

Craps

"SO THIS IS THE FAMOUS RODEO DRIVE," Troy said. "I'd expected Chanel No 5, but this smells more like Eau de Armpit."

"This isn't Rodeo Drive," Emmy said. "This is the alley behind Rodeo Drive. Now, do you want to let me know why you're interested in the fashion boutique three doors down from Kanasis rather than Kanasis itself?"

Troy turned from his appraisal of the back wall toward his co-conspirator. Boy did she look good in black. "According to the sticker in their front window, Balthazar uses the same security company as Kanasis. I figure it's perfect for a dry run."

"Uh-huh. And that mysterious black box I saw you slip into your backpack; you going to tell me what that's all about?"

"The Y400? According to Pedro-the-Procurer, it blocks the full commercial spectrum of cell phone transmissions within a two hundred foot radius."

"And you think that's going to keep the armed response away when we key into Kanasis?"

"Pedro wasn't sure if the full commercial spectrum included the frequencies used by security companies. That's why we're going to try it out here first, just to be sure."

"Well, be quick about it. Luther expects me to be on hand to greet his guests when they arrive at ten."

"Is that all he expects—the sight of your pretty face and a few welcoming words?" Troy had been so busy preparing for tonight that they had hardly spoken since the close call in Luther's security room.

"That's what he said. He is very image conscious, and a pretty maid answering his door exemplifies his preferred persona."

"Well, if the next few minutes go as planned, then the only people opening Luther's door from now on will be foul-breathed federal employees with sadistic streaks and penchants for sodomy." Of course, if the next few minutes went badly, Troy and Emmy would be the ones going to prison, but he left that caveat unsaid.

Highly motivated by both carrot and stick, he used a dumpster and then a drainpipe to climb quickly atop the two-story building. Troy wanted to put the Y400 beside the alarm's antenna to maximize its jamming effect, but he found only air-conditioning equipment. Aware that the clock was ticking, he planted the jammer atop the air handler's fuse box and climbed back down.

"My cell phone is drawing a blank," Emmy said. "That's a good sign."

Troy shook his head. "The only good sign is no sign of Atlas Security."

"How are you planning to test the alarm—put a brick through the window?"

"Something a bit more surgical. Come see for yourself."

All the businesses on North Rodeo Drive were closed at this hour, leaving the street relatively deserted. A group of young tourists meandered loudly about, drinks in hand, but at the moment they were clustered across the street, taking pictures before the entrance to Ralph Lauren.

"Keep a discreet eye on them," Troy said, checking to ensure that his cell phone was still searching as they approached Balthazar's front door. He pulled a long thin white clown's balloon from his pocket, secured the neck to a manual pump and gave it just enough wind to make it rigid. Then he pushed the balloon through the brass mail slot and finished the inflation. Fixing his eyes on the motion detector's green diode he released the neck of the balloon, sending it in a spiraling flight around the store until at last it came to rest on the shoulder of a black-clad mannequin.

The diode turned red.

Pleased with the result he said, "Whoever finds that in the morning is going to wonder what goes on after hours at Balthazar."

"Not here," Emmy replied. "This is Hollywood."

Troy linked his arm through hers. "Let's walk toward Santa Monica Boulevard to wait for the response that we hope won't come."

They did—and it did.

In just five minutes.

"That was quick," Emmy said.

"Yeah. So much for the Y400 and that thousand bucks. Pedro doesn't have a return policy." In Miami they had pocketed a pretty penny by pawning Emmy's engagement ring, but that money was running short. Troy still remembered the number from the AmEx card he had always used, but was keeping it as an emergency reserve. Credit cards put you on the grid.

He watched over Emmy's shoulder as a security car screeched to a halt before Balthazar and three armed men burst out. Two of the guards drew their guns and converged on Balthazar's entrance while the third sprinted for the smelly alley. "They're using the same tactics my Special Forces unit did when clearing buildings in Afghanistan. Must be ex-military."

"Judging by the way they move," Emmy said, "one has to wonder if they sit on the edge of their chairs all night, drinking Red Bull and waiting for the horn." Once they disappeared inside, she added, "What's plan B?"

"You'll see," Troy said, extracting a handkerchief and two small atomizers from his backpack. "Once they leave."

She gave his tools the once over and then said, "I can't wait more than fifteen minutes. If we haven't opened Luther's safe by then, I'm going to have to go back. If I'm not there when Luther's guests arrive, he might get suspicious, look around, and notice that his keys are missing."

"That reminds me," Troy said. "Did you manage to turn the contrast to black on Luther's security monitors?"

"Numbers fourteen through sixteen."

"Great. And don't worry. It shouldn't take them long to clear a small fashion boutique."

The three guards emerged a few seconds later, no doubt having already reported a false alarm. Troy and Emmy began walking toward Kanasis as soon as the Atlas Security Jeep pulled away.

Emmy unlocked the door with Luther's key and Troy pulled the handle. "It's still locked," he said, checking the crack between frame and door for bolts. "Are you sure you turned the key all the way."

As Emmy said, "I'm sure," the door yielded to Troy's tug. "There's some kind of an electromagnetic lock in place. I'm not sure what that means, but it can't be good."

The alarm keypad began to beep and glow yellow. Troy went to work with the handkerchief and spray bottles. "First we give it a cleaning with some good old Windex ... then once it's clean and dry ... we give it a thorough misting with bottle number two."

"What does bottle number two do?" Emmy asked.

"It's a micro-granulated tacky powder that fluoresces under black light."

"You don't say."

Mid-way through the misting the beeping turned frantic and then flatlined. The keypad began to flash red. "Sixty-seconds," Troy said. "Not bad. I was afraid we might only get thirty. Let's go."

Troy led her back across the street. They concealed themselves behind a potted azalea bush halfway down the block.

The Atlas men arrived in just three minutes this time, no doubt because they had already been on the road, but they spent much longer inside than they had at Balthazar.

"I can't wait any longer," Emmy said. "I have to get back to

Luther's."

Troy looked at his watch: Quarter to ten. "I'll call you as soon as I've got it and you can run." He bent his head to kiss her. "Good luck."

"You too."

The Atlas men left shortly after Emmy. Now that the time pressure was off, he waited fifteen minutes to be sure they were back at base with their boots off before going back in.

He spent the time mentally rehearsing his next steps in order to maximize their speed. The first key the guard had pressed would show a clean fingerprint under his black light, because it was touched by a clean finger. The second key pressed would display the outline of the first number on it, because the numbers themselves were recessed within the buttons and thus would not transfer powder. The third number in the code would have the second number outlined strongly over a weaker first, and so on.

Troy had practiced the deciphering exercise a hundred times back in his hotel room on a similar keypad. He knew he was safe as long as the code was just four digits in length. Five was still possible, but six was the next likely length after four and that was too much. If it was six or more, or if the guard had used multiple fingers, he was SOL.

Sometimes you just had to roll the dice.

Checking to ensure that he was not being watched, Troy crossed the street and keyed back into Kanasis. Again, the alarm console began its sixty-second countdown. He turned on the black light and bathed the keypad. Given all his practice, he could tell immediately that the guard had pressed the three, four, five and seven once apiece. That would have been fine, except the guard had also pressed the eight, twice.

Sometimes you crapped out.

Chapter 79

Green Light

LUTHER'S GUESTS WERE LATE, but not late enough. They arrived before Troy called. Emmy could not skip out.

Luther had not told Emmy who was coming for cocktails, but when the two monsters emerged from the black Mercedes S600 she recognized them from Giselle's descriptions. Orca and Zero—the killer whale and his refrigerator-sized bodyguard.

At Troy's suggestion, Emmy had unlocked windows at various strategic locations throughout the house in case she ever needed to bolt. As she walked toward the front entrance, she went over the escape routes in her head like a paranoid preparing for a hotel fire. When she reached the door she paused to take a deep breath. Things could be worse; it could be Farkas. Where was that weasel?

She slipped into character and opened the door before the bell's echo had died. "Good evening, gentlemen. Mr. Kanasis is waiting for you in his study, if you'll please follow me."

"So you're Luther's new girl," Orca said, giving her a slow inspection from head to toe. "I'd be happy to follow you, dear. What's your name?"

"Vicky," she said, turning toward the stairs.

"Vicky as in Victoria, or just Vicky?"

"As in Victoria," she said, without pausing or looking back.

"I'm glad to hear that. These days, parents have a tendency to be cute—at their kid's expense. I figure you gotta give a person a choice, you know. After all, what if ya'd wanted to be a lawyer, or run for president."

Emmy knew she should remain silent, but could not resist the tempting barb. "I'm so glad you approve, Orca."

"Cute and feisty too. I bet Luther keeps you around for more than the normal couple of months. Still, when he does let you go, stop by Lisa's Place if you want to make some real money. Ask for James, that's my Christian name."

Emmy did not so much as turn to acknowledge the offer. She just knocked on the arched double doors to Luther's office and announced, "Your guests have arrived."

Orca pushed past her without waiting for a response. As he walked in with Zero following the requisite four paces behind, Luther rose from his armchair and said, "So glad you were able to come, my friend. Please, have a seat. We have a lot to talk about. A lot to talk about."

Emmy heard two hundred and fifty million dollars' worth of excitement in Luther's voice, so she made the split-second decision to advance rather than retreat. Walking to the corner bar she asked, "May I pour you gentlemen a drink?"

"Don't worry about it, Vicky. I'll pour the Scotch," Luther said. "You just make sure the door is closed. We don't want to be disturbed. Feel free to go out or to bed if you wish. We won't be needing you anymore this evening."

Emmy nodded and left without comment. This was it. Her chance to foil an evil act worth a quarter-billion dollars. She stepped to the side of the study doors and perked her ears. She could hear muffled voices, but the thick oak garbled individual words. Thinking fast, she ran down the hall to snatch a glass from the bathroom. While pulling it from the gilded holder, however, an even better idea popped into her head.

The ceiling of the closet off Luther's study had a trapdoor accessing an unfinished portion of the attic. She had peeked up there her first day on the job while searching for a safe. What's more, the closet door was louvered. She would be able to see and hear everything Luther and Orca said—if she could get inside.

She had to hurry.

Emmy raced down the hall and up the attic stairs. She yanked the chain that switched on the bare bulb and wove her way through the piles of dusty boxes. The finished part of the attic ended where the angle of the roof brought it close to the floor. She ducked under the low beams and found herself disoriented in a dark jungle of wooden rafters and blown fiberglass insulation.

Maybe she should have stuck with the glass.

Emmy worked her way in what she thought was the direction of the study, stepping rafter-to-rafter, ducking beams and avoiding nails. She had hoped that boisterous voices would guide her, but heard only the wind whistling through the tiles above. While glancing back toward the light of the finished section, trying to orient herself and judge distance, a familiar rat scurried over her foot. Emmy reared back in shock and punctured her scalp on the tip of an exposed roofing nail. She let out an involuntary scream before slapping her own hand over her mouth. Now she had to add a tetanus shot to her to-do list. With her luck she would survive all the trauma of the Kanasis investigation only to succumb to lockjaw. Then she wouldn't be able to kiss the very man she was fighting for.

Emmy continued her quest for what seemed like hours even though she knew it was barely minutes. It was maddening, knowing that she might miss the big payoff by seconds. Her skin began to itch from some kind of allergic reaction. She finally found the trapdoor on the far side of a ventilation duct. She brushed the insulation back from the edges so no telltale crumbs would drop inside and hauled it open.

The voices drifting up from below were muffled. Distinct, but indecipherable. "In for a penny, in for a pound," she whispered, and lowered herself through the hole. She dropped to the ground knowing that the shelving would serve as an escape ladder.

Once inside the closet, she pressed her ear to the door and tried to peer through the slats.

"… kill the president?" Emmy recognized Orca's voice.

"Fifty million dollars. Not a penny less," Luther replied.

"That's a bit steep, don't you think? I mean, I got friends who would give it a try for ten and would throw in the Pope for free."

"Enough of this," Luther said. "I see that our guest has finally joined us."

Emmy strained to see who else had joined the meeting, but the slats in the door were too narrowly spaced. She was attempting to widen the angle with her pinkie when the door flew open beneath her fingers. Two gorilla paws reached in, grabbed her beneath the armpits, and hoisted her off the ground as though she were weightless.

Zero carried her over to the suite of chairs where Luther and Orca were sitting and held her out like a cat. Unwilling to look Luther in the eye, she looked down and saw that her toes were a good two feet off the ground.

"Miss Green," Luther said. "My little pixie. So glad you could join us."

They knew her real name, Emmy thought, still trying to comprehend the sudden twist of fate.

Orca stood and did a full circle around her and Zero.

She felt like a slave being appraised at auction.

"I'm a bit concerned," he said to Luther. "She's so tiny. I don't think it's going to fit."

Emmy tried to wriggle free as Orca unzipped his pants, but she was wrestling with iron. For the moment at least, it was up to Troy to save her. She thought of the horror story Giselle had relayed, and prayed that he would hurry.

Chapter 80

Fade to Black

THE TEMPO of Troy's heart increased with the alarm's warning beep as the implications of a six-digit security code sank in. He could attempt to read the keys and hope to get lucky, but he had another avenue to try first. He had used a mnemonic device to make a few likely codes available for quick mental access. Converted to numbers, LAWYER had two 9s, MEMORY two 7s, and another likely candidate the two 8s the Atlas guard had pressed. Troy keyed in L-U-T-H-E-R, 5-8-8-4-3-7, and the beeping stopped.

Troy heard the waterfall before the elevator doors opened and he smiled. He knew why Luther chose to keep it working even at night. Regardless of the reason, the cascade was beautiful. It shimmered like a silver veil in the dim light filtering through the far window. Troy was not there for the aesthetics, however; he had come for the ledger and ampoules on the other side.

He removed his backpack and withdrew a camping lantern that he had cloaked on one side. He angled it so that no light would shine toward the window and turned it on. The moment he did, the macaw began to rustle in its sheet-covered cage. Troy felt similarly excited. It was time for the moment of truth.

Standing where Luther had stood, Troy pulled up his right sleeve and plunged his hand into the waterfall just as Luther had done. As spray misted his face, he explored the slate backing beneath with his hand. No matter where he pressed, nothing happened.

Feeling around more carefully, Troy thought he detected the outline of what could be a button, but it would not depress. He began to worry that the waterfall was on some kind of a timer, that it could not be opened when the office was closed. What a shame it would be to have come this far yet be able to go no further. "Not a chance," he mumbled. One way or the other, he was moving that mountain.

Returning to his backpack, Troy pulled out a portable DVD player and booted up the video of Luther opening the safe. During the second playing, he realized that he had fallen for a classic magician's trick. He had focused on the hand that appeared to be working all the magic, the hand reaching through the waterfall. He had failed to pay any attention to Luther's left hand, which rested on the structure's rocky left edge.

Troy set the player down and then mimicked Luther's moves with both hands. He felt the rock hinge in a quarter inch beneath his left hand, but still got nowhere with the button beneath his right.

Again he watched the video.

This time he figured it out on the first pass. The bird. A three-point trigger. Very clever indeed.

Troy removed the sheet from the macaw's cage and opened the door. The bird climbed down to the doorway, but went no further.

Troy walked over to the waterfall and reached for the buttons. The bird did not move. "Fly, bird, fly." He pointed to the perch atop the falls.

The bird just scratched his beak and began to preen.

Again Troy watched the tape. Luther made no special movements that Troy could detect. He must have said something, but the recording had no sound and his back was to the camera. Troy had never owned a bird. What was the avian equivalent of fetch? How did you get a bird to help you open a safe? How did you bring Mohammad to the mountain?

And then he had it.

Reassuming his stance, Troy said, "Open Sesame."

The bird flew.

The water stopped.

The slate backing slid aside.

Troy wiped his right hand off on his jeans and then rubbed both hands together vigorously before attempting to work the combination. Fourteen, ninety-two, seventeen, seventy-six, sixty-four. He got it open on the first try. Studying a digital magnification of the video, Troy had not been entirely certain of the numbers he thought he saw Luther dialing until he recognized the pattern. 1492, 1776, (19)64: three great dates in American history, the last being the year of Luther's birth.

The massive black door surely weighed more than he did, but the hinges were balanced so perfectly that it moved with little effort. The view that the swinging door revealed was identical to the one on the tape. They were in time.

Troy pulled the titanium binder off the black velvet shelf and flipped it open. Jeffrey Randal/Lionel Esposito, $1,000,000, June 16, 2005. Wendell Branson/Gregory Harris & Paul Culleton, $3,000,000, July 2, 2005. Archibald Martin/Wendy Caffrey, $1,000,000, July 26, 2005. He ran his finger down the list until he came to Isaac Goldfarb/Emerald Green, $1,000,000, November 27, 2007. That confirmed it. A warm pulsing glow suffused his body from head to toe. This was the end of the journey, the payoff for all the risk, the damning evidence for which he had traded the memories of his wife and daughter.

Flipping the page with sweaty hands, he found another familiar name three entries down. Russell Rankin/Charles Simms, $1,000,000, February 15, 2008. Charles Simms was the FBI Agent who had witnessed Russell Rankin claiming the lives of his wife and daughter and robbing him of his ability to operate. Charles was the fourth victim of that wealthy drunk. Troy and Emmy had decided that they would take whatever evidence they found to Agent Simms, retired or not. "We've done it, Emmy," he said.

With a heart that was at once victorious and sad, Troy tucked the ledger into his backpack. Turning back to the safe, he crouched and used the circular key on Luther's ring to unlock the refrigerator. Opening it, he found just one item: the metal box he knew to house ruby-red vials. Peering inside, Troy found the box divided into a twelve-by-twelve grid, one hundred and forty-four chambers. About half of them were empty. So many stolen memories. Troy pulled one of the remaining vials out and held it to the light. "Liquid amnesia."

Troy considered the option of smashing the whole lot then and there on the rocks of the waterfall, but realized that this would be destroying evidence, evidence that he would need. Besides, for all he knew, Luther had gallons of the potion stored away in some underground bunker. Deciding that the sensible move was to take them all, he pocketed the ampoule in his hand and slipped the box into his backpack.

As he secured the box, another thought struck him and Troy pulled the binder back out. Flipping it open to the last page with entries, he found a surprise. Instead of seeing the name of the president or one of the major party nominees, he found a list of nine names he did not recognize following the contractor's. Arranged in alphabetical order, he read, "Alverado, Brewer, Goldstein, Lincoln, Reynolds, Secada, Stoffer, Stevenson, and Thompson."

The dollar amount also knocked him for a loop. Instead of the two hundred and fifty he had expected, the ledger listed five hundred and fifty million.

He was still staring at the enormous number when another thought hit him and he reread the names. A few struck bells this time through and he found himself supplying their first names as well. "Anthony Secada, Daniel Stoffer, Charles Thompson." Some of them were completely unfamiliar, but then he would not recognize any name from the last seven years. He counted them again to be sure. Nine. "The Supreme Court Justices," he said aloud.

"That's right," a familiar voice boomed behind him.

Troy whirled about to find Farkas glaring at him over a shifty smile. First Troy focused on the beaming, metallic eyes, and then his eyes drifted down to the instrument in his nemesis's hand. Before he could react further, a crackling sound broke the silence and a burst of blinding pain invaded his chest, turning his world white before it faded to black.

Chapter 81

Choke

"PUT THAT AWAY, you're scaring the girl," Luther said.

"But I like it when they're all aquiver," Orca replied, rubbing his rising manhood between his fingers.

"I need her."

Orca rolled his eyes. "Wait your turn. There will probably be something left."

"For the job. I need her for the job."

Orca rolled his eyes, stopped rubbing, and asked, "How so?"

"It's a surprise."

"She looks surprised enough already. But hey, now that you mention it, I've got a surprise for you, too. You owe me nine hundred grand on top of the twenty-six mil."

Luther had seen this coming, but he wanted to make Orca work for it. "How do you figure?"

"I got you nine guys. The fact that you chose not to use them is not my problem."

"Your men were unacceptable. I asked for James Bonds, you sent me buffoons."

"Make it an even million, or I just might let them know you said so." Orca walked over and stood toe-to-toe with Luther.

He was good at playing tough with Zero around, Luther thought. But then, who wouldn't be. For the last couple of minutes the giant had been holding Emmy up with such relaxed ease that you would think her weight was on par with a glass of beer. Take Zero out of the equation, however, and Luther could wipe the floor with the fat, balding thug. "Even if they were acceptable, a hundred grand is a bit steep for a referral fee, don't you think."

"I'm not renting apartments. I'm a banker. We work on percentages. If you paid me twenty-six double large without breaking a sweat, I figure the operation's got to be worth at least three or four times that, say an even hundred mil. At one percent, I'm letting you off easy."

Luther nodded as if in defeat and walked over to his desk. "Tell you what, James, let's make it an even two."

"Now you're talking. I knew you could be reasonab—"

Luther whipped a Beretta from his desk and put a round in each of Zero's eyes.

The giant collapsed without a sound—or so Luther guessed. It was hard to tell over Emmy's screams. He had the gun leveled at Orca's chest before the mafia boss fully comprehended the amazing turn of events.

Keeping his eyes on Orca, Luther said, "Shut up, Emerald!"

She did.

Beckoning toward the heavy wooden armchair he had brought to his office in anticipation, he told Orca, "Sit down."

"So you do have a pair," Orca said. "I'm glad to see it. I was beginning to get worried. You know, now that my territory is expanding, I'm going to need a legal advisor with balls, a true consigliere."

"Sit down and shut up."

"You ever read the Godfather?" Orca asked, ignoring the command to shut up as he took the seat.

Luther brushed off the question and addressed Emmy instead. "You'll find some thick black zip ties over there on the bookcase. I want you to use them to bind my guest's wrists and ankles to the chair."

Luther had expected Orca to make a bolt for the door at this point, but he remained seated. Now he realized that Orca probably interpreted the bindings as a sign that he was not going to be killed. It was a reasonable hypothesis, but it was wrong.

When Emmy had all four zip ties in place, Luther put the Beretta in his pocket and gave each of the bindings an extra tug to be sure they were tight. Not one had an extra ratchet left. Emmy had done a good job. "Sit down and cross your ankles," he told her, motioning to the floor.

Emmy complied.

Luther bent down and bound her ankles together with another zip tie. "Can't have you running off on me while I'm busy."

"Busy with what?" Orca asked. "Don't you go doing anything stupid, anything you're going to regret. Zero, we can forget about. Water under the bridge. I was planning to get rid of him soon anyway. He knew too much. Besides, as I said, I can use you by my side."

Satisfied that Emmy would not be able to slip free and relatively certain that she was too traumatized to try, Luther turned his full attention back to Orca. He found the look of panic seated there to be immensely satisfying. After three-and-a-half years of sweating his monthly vig payment, he had a lot of hard feelings built up inside. The Killer Whale's latest extortion attempt had put him over the edge.

"You shouldn't have gotten greedy, Orca. You should have left well enough alone. I was just about to give you twenty-six million dollars. Twenty-six million on top of the forty-two I've dished out these last three-and-a-half years."

"Hey, Luther, it's my nature. You ever hear that anecdote about the scorpion and the frog?"

Luther ignored the pitiful attempt to lighten the atmosphere. "I've got good news for you, James, and I've got bad. The good news is: I'm not going to shoot you."

Orca let out a big sigh and Luther actually saw a tear trickle down his cheek. "You're making the right choice, Luther. If for no other reason than that you wouldn't last a day if you did."

"My thinking exactly," Luther said. Then he stopped talking and waited for Orca to ask.

The grandfather clock along the west wall ticked off a good thirty seconds before Orca could not take the waiting any longer. "So what's the bad news?"

Luther walked over to Zero's corpse and pulled the racquetball from his pocket. He knew that Zero always kept one there for practicing his favorite walnut-crushing trick. Standing, he put the ball in Orca's lap so it would be handy for shoving into the pig's mouth the minute he began to scream. Then he reached into his pocket and pulled out a switchblade. He flipped it open and tested the edge with his thumb. It sliced off the outer layer of dermis without drawing blood. You couldn't get a blade any sharper than that. Looking up from the mirrored finish to Orca's eyes, he said, "The bad news is that Jimmy Choke is going to get the rap for your murder."

Chapter 82

New Shoes

TROY DRIFTED BACK toward consciousness feeling woozy. His first jolting thought was that Farkas had erased his memory again, but he dismissed it with a quick sigh of short-lived relief. If his memory had been erased, he would recall neither Farkas nor the erasing procedure. Then his chest protested to the accompanying deep breath and he remembered the Taser.

When the floor did not stop moving as his grip on consciousness improved, Troy realized that his wooziness was seasickness. He was on a boat.

Opening his eyes, he found himself seated in the dark cabin of what he guessed was a thirty-foot boat. Farkas had bound his hands securely behind his back and his feet … What had happened to his feet? They were cold and he couldn't move them at all. He was weighing the medical likelihood of a Taser blast to the chest doing nerve damage to the feet when the hum of the engine changed. A moment later a door opened behind him and moonlight streamed in, casting his shadow over a grungy wooden floor. The door closed as quickly as it had opened and a florescent bulb flickered to life overhead.

Troy blinked twice, looked down at his feet, and felt his heart drop through the floor. Unfortunately, the cold numb sensation was not the result of nerve damage.

As reality sank in, Troy actually pined for the time he had woken up back on Grand Cayman, locked in a dark trunk with a cop's bloody corpse. A quote from Dean Acheson leapt forth from the abysses of his mind: "The manner in which one endures what must be endured is more important than the thing that must be endured." He suspected that the former Secretary of State would recant his famous bromide if he found himself in Troy's shoes, but nonetheless Troy vowed not to give Farkas the satisfaction of sensing the fear that gripped his heart. "Concrete galoshes. That's hardly original."

The coppery-eyed perpetrator of all Troy's woes walked around him in silence until they were face to face. "True, but then I'm an old fashioned kind of guy. And there's nothing more reliable. I decided that reliable was high on my list of priorities this time around. I'm sure you understand."

Troy did understand. And Farkas was right. He was helpless as a newborn kitten. In a strange kind of way, he found that thought comforting. It took the tension out of the situation to know that there was absolutely nothing he could do to change things—short of getting Farkas to change his mind... There. He had gone and done it. The tension was back. And for what? The slimmest thread of hope? Better to go out calm than flailing. At least he would look like a man. Drowning wasn't supposed to be such a bad death, was it? After all, you did spend your first nine months floating in a bag of water. And your body was ninety percent water. So how bad could it be?

"It's your contact lenses, isn't it?" Troy asked. "That's how you retained your memory."

Farkas raised his wiry brows. "Very good. I'm impressed. Even Luther hasn't figured that one out."

"You sure about that? I mean, if he did figure it out, would he tell you?"

"Why wouldn't he?" Farkas asked.

"Oh, I don't know. Maybe because you're wearing them for him. I mean, I was thinking, why would you be wearing protective lenses? Yours is the only game in town. But then it occurred to me.

You figure that once Luther has his mattress stuffed to capacity, he's going to erase your memory and walk off into the sunset, knowing that all evidence linking him to his crimes has been destroyed."

"As I said, you're very good."

Farkas walked back behind Troy, grabbed the top of his chair and tilted it back on two legs. This put the full weight of the concrete bucket on the back of Troy's calves at the point where they hit the steel crossbar. Nerves Troy did not know he had screamed in agonized protest, but pride kept him from crying out. Once Farkas had dragged him clear of the cabin door and out onto the deck, however, he forgot about the pain. This was it. The last stop. The end of the line. Go forth and feel no more.

Troy looked up at the heavens. Out on the water far from the lights of L.A., the night sky reminded him of Afghanistan. In the category of last-thing-you'll-ever-see, the pearls-on-black-satin shroud of the Milky Way would be near the top of his wish list. Emmy, he realized, was number one. At least she wasn't there with him. He prayed that she had gotten out. Praying was all he could do. He was powerless to help her now.

The deck of the old wooden craft stunk with the odor of rotting fish. Just as they had flailed about here, drowning by the thousands, so he too was about to perish in the depths below. That was what Farkas had reduced him to, a fish.

He scanned the peeling decking as a desperate thought surfaced, searching for a stray scaling knife or pair of wire-cutting pliers. His eyes found nothing but a scrap of old netting—and a sledgehammer. The gleaming twelve-pounder stood propped against the cabin wall, near the doorway Farkas had just dragged him through. The price tag was still attached.

"That's in case you decide to get too lippy," Farkas said, following his gaze. "Works much better than stuffing a sock in your mouth."

"Charming place you've got here. Is this the boat from the original Jaws?"

"No, I think the shark ate that one."

Farkas had stopped the boat near a buoy that was taller than the boat itself. Troy pictured himself clinging to it for dear life and wondered if there was a radio beacon aboard that he could rewire to send out an SOS. "You stop here to ask directions?" he asked, motioning toward the buoy with his head.

"I just wanted to make sure that when you go down, you stay down."

"Huh?"

"Trawling is not permitted within a hundred yards of a buoy," Farkas said, sliding open the prow gate to reveal the black water below.

Troy realized that he only had seconds left. If he was going to act, this was his last chance. "After you zapped me with that little toy of yours, did you take a look at your boss's accounting ledger? Did you see how much he's making? I mean, Wow!"

"It's a good business."

"Yeah, but that's not my point."

"What is your point?"

"My point is this: You think you're his partner, but partners make fifty-fifty." He shrugged. "Maybe sixty-forty or even seventy-thirty. But I'll bet you're not even making ten percent. You're just a tool. But then you already knew that, as your special lenses suggest."

"I am well paid," Farkas said. "Sometimes I even enjoy my work. I'm not falling into the American trap of comparing what I earn to others. I make enough."

"Nice speech. Who you trying to convince?"

"Did I mention the sledgehammer?" Farkas asked, moving toward the gruesome tool.

"You can't get a refund if it's been used."

As Farkas drew in a breath to retort, his satellite phone rang. He pulled it from the pocket of his dark slacks and brought it to his right ear, covering the left against the wind. "Yes ... Are you sure?" He hung up without saying anything else.

"God calling?" Troy asked.

"Change of plans," Farkas said, putting the phone back in his pocket. He picked up the sledgehammer before Troy's preoccupied mind could churn out another wise crack.

Hoisting the sledgehammer over his shoulder with both hands, Farkas said, "This is going to hurt."

Chapter 83

In the Bag

EMMY SAT in the corner of Luther's study, ankles bound together with a zip tie that felt like it was made of steel, trying to make sense of her world. The giant who had effortlessly held her aloft for what seemed like ages was now lying dead a few feet away in a pool of blood.

Luther and Orca were arguing loudly just a few feet away, but their words reached her ears like a television coming from another room. She was in shock. The bullets that entered Zero's skull through his eyes had flown just inches above her head. And Luther had fired twice. Had he intended one of those bullets for her, and just not gotten around to fixing his mistake? No, she decided, if that were the case he would not have bound her ankles. Still, why did he fire twice? It wasn't as though anyone could survive one bullet through the eye.

Orca's voice crescendoed, drawing her out of her dazed stupor. She looked up to see Luther shove a racquetball into the mafia boss's mouth. While that struck her as a dangerous thing to do, Luther's next move left her flabbergasted. She stared in morbid fascination as Luther unzipped Orca's fly, reached inside, and pulled out an organ the size of a tennis ball can. Then he picked an open switchblade off the floor and proceeded to … She couldn't watch. Clenching her eyes as tight as they would go, she put an index finger in each ear.

When she opened her eyes again, Orca was thrashing about in the chair like a man who … well … exactly. After a minute his movements got sluggish, and then he passed out. That was when Emmy noticed the waterfall of blood cascading off the edge of his chair onto the tiled floor. The crazy thought actually shot through her mind that as Luther's maid, it was her job to clean up the spreading mess. When she pulled her eyes off the morbid pool, she saw that Orca's face was a deathly pale. She also saw the bloody stump sticking out of his mouth. That was when she passed out.

When Emmy drifted back into consciousness, Luther was not in the room. The clock on the wall registered two AM; she had been out for a full five hours. Either her body had finally yielded to the accumulated stress, or Luther had injected her with a tranquilizing agent. Somewhere deep inside Emmy knew that this was her chance to escape, but she still felt spent. The ordeal on Grand Cayman had been the worst she had ever heard of, much less experienced, but even that was tame compared to tonight's experience. Her senses were fried. Her adrenal glands wrung out like the season's last lemons. But then she thought of Troy, and that gave her strength.

The image of Luther's switchblade danced through her mind. If he had left it behind she could free her legs. Then escape would be easy. Emmy worked herself onto her knees and then her feet using the back of Orca's chair. Because of the way Luther had bound her feet, with her ankles crossed, it would be difficult if not impossible for her to hop around. She did not even think that she could stand for more than a few seconds unsupported. But she did have a better view. The switchblade, however, was nowhere to be seen. Luther must have taken it with him.

Inspiration struck when her eyes fell on Luther's desk. Desks had scissors. She even knew where Luther kept them. She tried hopping toward the desk, but the zip ties bit painfully into her ankles and cost Emmy her balance. She caught herself on the edge of the desk as she fell. She pulled herself up onto the desk so that her ankles dangled freely over the side, and opened the center drawer. The scissors had been removed. Of course they had, she told herself. Luther had taken them when he left her alone in the room. The man was a lot of things, but carefree and foolish were not two of them.

Sitting there like a shipwreck survivor on a deserted island, looking across a scene of carnage that belonged only in a gangster movie, Emmy enjoyed another flash of inspiration. Maybe it didn't matter that she couldn't escape. If Troy now had Luther's journal and supply of ampoules, he would bargain them for her release. Luther would do anything to get them back, she was sure of that. But was it worth the price? Was her freedom, her life, worth the price of letting Luther continue with his business? Could she allow him to continue with a quarter-billion dollars' worth of destruction?

She did not have the time to process that question before Luther burst back into the room with a bag full of paper towel rolls, a package of heavy-duty trash bags, and a pair of handcuffs. Seeing the latter, Emmy wondered momentarily if Luther was working with a crooked cop, but then she realized that the cuffs were probably from his box of sex toys.

After setting down his load, Luther picked her up off the desk and carried her over toward the closet Zero had snatched her from. Emmy assumed that he was going to lock her in the dark, but he set her down outside the door and cuffed her right wrist to the doorknob instead. "I take it you're not going to make me shove that racquetball in your mouth," he said. It was not a question, but she shook her head anyway.

Emmy clenched her eyes as Luther went to work with the bags and tape. She forced her mind to go elsewhere, and focused on the memory of breakfast in The Grotto with Troy. She tried to taste the conch and brie omelet and hear the swishing surf. She succeeded in blocking out the grotesque noises coming from a few feet away until a new sound registered from below. Someone was coming up the stairs, and judging by the thumping sound, he was dragging something heavy.

She opened her eyes to see that Luther now had both bodies in thick black trash bags. He had placed one bag over the top of each corpse and another over the bottom, joining them in the middle with duct tape. A fifth bag, this one full of blood-sopped paper towels, stood off to Emmy's side.

Luther had obviously heard the noise too, but he did not seem concerned. The thumping moved closer until the door to the study flew open—and Farkas walked in. He was pulling a rope as though dragging a sleigh, although this rope connected two ankles. Emmy felt all hope drain from her body when the shoes came into focus and she knew that those ankles belonged to Troy.

Chapter 84

Live Another Day

TROY'S HEAD was pounding like a small nuclear war after Farkas dragged him feet first up Luther's marble staircase, but that was nothing compared to the pain that erupted in his heart when he saw Emmy handcuffed to the closet door.

Luther said "Welcome" as Farkas let go of the rope. Troy's feet dropped to smack against the parquet floor, prompting a reflexive "Aargh" instead of his customary "Hi." While having one's feet sledgehammered out of a bucket of hardened concrete beats the hell out of the alternative, it was not how Troy would recommend spending one's Sunday night.

To Troy's surprise, Luther looked over at Farkas and said, "I told you not to hurt him."

"Nothing is broken. He's only bruised."

That was true, Troy thought. Farkas had been somewhat less than reckless when wielding the twelve-pound mallet of steel. Still, that trip up the stairs had felt like a bout with Muhammad Ali. Didn't they have the fireman's carry in Croatia or wherever the hell that bastard was from?

Troy made eye contact with Emmy and mouthed the words, "Are you okay?"

She nodded and mouthed back, "And you?"

Troy said, "Never better," and then turned to his host.

Luther said to Farkas, "Help yourself to a drink. I need to have a word with our guests." Turning back to Troy and Emmy he said,

"Do you two have any idea how lucky you are?"

Troy was not sure if it was the post-traumatic stress talking or if he was just too slaphappy to give a damn, but his mouth just sprung open and words started tumbling out. "You know, that's just what I was thinking. A quiet Sunday evening, four old friends, and your beautiful home. But if I could make a tiny suggestion: have the trash carted off before inviting company in."

Luther did not bother attempting to camouflage his amused expression, and Troy took minor comfort in having caught him by surprise. It did not last.

"You make my point for me," Luther said.

"Why are we lucky?" Emmy asked.

"Were I any other person, or were this any other moment in history, there would be four sets of trash bags on my floor now, instead of just two."

"Because you can erase our memories," Emmy said. "With chemicals instead of bullets."

Luther spread his hands in a magnanimous gesture. "Not to mention the fact that the memories you'll be losing can hardly be your best. Of course, if you prove to be more trouble than you're worth your luck will change." Luther pulled a Beretta from his pocket. Then, turning back to Troy he said, "She's a lot quicker than you are. I see why you chose to make her your partner."

Troy was thinking that actually the memories of his time with Emmy were the most precious in his head. But he did not want to give Luther a glimpse through that window into his soul, especially given the scenario that he expected was about to unfold. "I get the feeling that there's more to it than that. Perhaps you need our help with something first?"

Luther smiled and Troy knew that he was right. "Well, this is a quid-pro-quo world we live in. Tell me, now that you've been to my office, do you have any idea what that help might entail?"

Troy looked at Emmy. "He's planning to erase the memories of all nine justices of the United States Supreme Court. No doubt that's a bit too tall an order for our friend Farkas here. So he figured, why not involve the clever pair who already know what he's up to. Nothing to lose ..." Troy shifted his gaze back toward Luther. "Half-a-billion dollars to gain. That sound about right, old friend?"

"I'm glad to see that we're on the same page," Luther said.

"I'm not going to help you make anybody an amnesiac," Emmy said.

"Don't be silly," Luther said, his voice honey but his eyes ice. "Of course you are—although perhaps not in the way you think. And besides, it's no big deal. Even Shakespeare wanted to kill all the lawyers."

Troy said, "First of all, Shakespeare was defending lawyers by suggesting that killing them was the first step toward tyranny. Although to be honest with you, Luther, I can think of one lawyer worth killing. Secondly, the United States Supreme Court is a cornerstone of the greatest democracy the world has ever known. Weakening that foundation could have disastrous consequences, consequences that will be far reaching and impossible to predict. I'm with Emmy. Go fuck yourself."

Ignoring the last of Troy's remarks, Luther said, "Well then, I guess I'll just have to leave the country when we're done." He walked over and held the Beretta to Emmy's right temple. "But that's then. Let's talk about now. Now you and Farkas are going to go to Washington to begin stalking your prey. Meanwhile, Emmy and I are going to take a little vacation, a retreat so to speak. During which it's not myself I'll be fucking."

Troy resisted the bait and remained silent.

"Once you wipe all nine justices," Luther continued, "I'll set her free—less any recollection of these past few weeks, of course. If you're really nice, I'll even set her free in the same place we flash you. It will be just like old times all over again—except there won't be any tattoo on your foot, and by then it wouldn't even matter if there were."

Emmy said, "Don't do it, Troy."

Luther pulled back the slide on the Beretta and said, "Your choice. I can always get someone else. You've seen the ledger, you can do the math. This is going to happen."

Now that he thought of the possibility of having all memory of her erased, Troy could not bear the thought of losing her.

He decided to seek comfort and guidance from those who had endured even worse. Those who had persevered through the Holocaust, those who had lived to tell their heart-wrenching tales, had done so by holding on to life through any means available. They had done whatever it took to live another day. Only by clinging to life with an iron fist, no matter how shameful, no matter how selfish, had they made it to Nuremberg. To justice. If he took the high road now, they would both be dead but nothing else would change. If he complied, they still had a chance.

He looked over at Emmy who was shaking her head. As tears ran down her cheeks, he said, "I'll do it. I'll help you flash the justices."

The contemptuous look that crossed Emmy's face scorched his heart. Then Farkas grabbed the rope between his feet and began dragging him out of the room. He prayed that would not be the last he saw of his beloved's face. Luther had obviously seen Emmy's venomous glance, because he said, "You should be kinder to your colleague, Emmy. After all, your life is now in his hands."

Chapter 85

House Call

"THE REPUBLIC ENDURES, and this is the symbol of its faith. Those words were spoken by Chief Justice Charles Evans Hughes on October 13, 1932, during the laying of the cornerstone you see before you." The elegantly dressed African-American tour guide spoke with more reverence than Troy would have thought possible, considering that she repeated her spiel twenty times a day. Troy continued past the group following the red umbrella. He already knew too much about the "symbol of faith" he was about to destroy.

He caught sight of Farkas, who was still talking on the phone with Luther. Farkas had to check in every eight hours with updates, and Troy made sure he never forgot. Luther had warned him that if Farkas missed a call, Emmy got a bullet.

The first words Troy made out as he approached were, "... forged credentials worked out fine. They didn't give us a second glance." Farkas paused while Luther spoke. Then he replied, "Only Stevenson's is left. The man's eighty-eight, so his social life is minimal. We're probably going to have to inject him in his house. We're still finalizing the details of that plan." Again Farkas listened. "Okay, I'll tell him."

Farkas ended the call, opened a text message and then the attached photo. "Here's today's eye candy," he said, holding out his BlackBerry. The screen showed Emmy sitting cross-legged before a white wall. She held a printout of the current USA Today out before her as though reading a proclamation. She looked tan and radiant and wore her breathtaking smile. Troy knew that her smile was almost certainly forced and intended to cheer him up—but it worked anyway. "Thanks. What did Luther say?"

"He said that you weren't going to be getting any more pictures until we figure out how to implant Stevenson."

Troy shook his head. He had racked his brains for a way to get to the eldest justice, and he had come up blank. The other eight justices all had habits that took them outdoors where Farkas could either get close enough to hit them with a dart while they were moving, or bump them with a needle that he swore most people would never feel if they were moving. "Even if they do notice it, they'll assume that it's just a bug bite if you don't act suspicious," Farkas asserted.

Unfortunately, Stevenson spent virtually all of his time at home. "The trouble isn't so much getting to him, as making the injection indoors without his noticing," Troy replied.

Farkas shook his head. "That's not entirely correct. It's all right if he is aware of the injection, so long as he doesn't report it."

Troy understood the power of Farkas's insight the moment he heard it. Although it pained him to admit it, Farkas had impressed him over the course of these past nine days. Of the eight plans they had finalized thus far, Farkas had developed seven. He brought the trademark deductive reasoning of a doctor to his new profession. He approached his operations with the same callous precision as a brain surgeon, focusing entirely on the mechanics of the physical task he was performing without allowing himself to be distracted by emotional factors.

Troy, meanwhile, had spent the bulk of his waking hours trying to devise a way out of this mess. So far, he had nothing concrete, and time was running short.

Switching his processor to the task at hand, Troy deduced that Farkas's latest so-long-as-he-doesn't-report-it insight opened up two new potential avenues of attack. They could look for a way to prevent Stevenson from reporting the injection, or they could look for a way to make him not think to report it. To accomplish the former, some sort of coercion would be the most likely tack. Troy guessed that the Secret Service, even though they did not protect the justices on a day-to-day basis, would have devised the means to immunize them, and thus the Republic, from such threats. So he focused on the second angle: figuring out how to make Stevenson not want to report the injection. "Are you thinking of trying to swap out one of his regular injections for 456?"

"No. That leaves too much to chance. I'm thinking that one of us physicians needs to play doctor."

"To do that we would have to get around Stevenson's regular nurse, McGrady. And if we tried to substitute her, they'd put him through every modern diagnostic available the moment the skullduggery was discovered."

Farkas got the sly look in his eyes that Troy had seen a few times before. "True, but suppose McGrady were to invite one of us for consultation."

Troy had studied Justice Stevenson's personal life backwards and forwards, but did not see where this was headed, unless ... "Did you happen to go to medical school with Mary McGrady?"

"No. Nothing like that. Tell me, how old is Nurse Mary?"

"Thirty-two."

"And she's a looker, right? Safe to assume that Stevenson finds it pleasant to have her around."

"Sure, I guess."

"And how long has this pretty young nurse been working for Stevenson?"

"Eight months."

"Pretty good gig, don't you think? Days off, good pay, prestige ..."

"Sure."

"So suppose Nurse Mary were to wake up with no memory of

the events of the last month. Do you think she would report it right away? Or do you think she would try to cover it up, you know, hope it was just a temporary glitch that went away?"

Troy did not like where this was going. On the other hand, he did not have a better suggestion. "I suppose most people would do whatever they thought was necessary to protect their job, if they saw no harm in it. But how would that help us?"

"Suppose you showed up at Stevenson's the first day of Mary's memory loss, pretending to have an appointment—an appointment Mary won't want to admit she has forgotten?"

Even though he already knew the answer, Troy asked, "What kind of appointment?"

Farkas held out his hand, mimicking a shake. "Hello Mary, I'm Dr. Davis from Georgetown University Hospital, here for that consultation you requested ..."

Chapter 86

An Old Friend

"THAT'S IT THEN," Troy said, looking up from a desk blanketed in hotel stationery and Post-it notes. "We've got all nine implants planned down to the last detail. We're done until Friday."

Farkas brought his hand up to stroke the beard he kept forgetting was no longer there. "You don't sound pleased. You should be. You're saving your girlfriend's life."

"She's not my girlfriend. She's my ..." Troy paused. What was his relationship with Emmy? Thanks to the mind wiping, she was his only friend. She was also his partner, his confidant, and, he suspected, the love of his new life. "I don't know what she is, but obviously she does mean a lot to me. I'm going to go crazy waiting around for two days with nothing to do but speculate on what Luther might be doing to her."

Despite the fact that Farkas had flashed away his memory of his wife and child, and that they were now working together only because Troy was under the cruel heel of coercion, a semblance of camaraderie had developed between them. They were both doctors, soldiers, men of the world, and participants in what would likely become the most famous caper since the Rosenberg kidnapping. As much as he hated to admit it, he could understand Farkas's arms-length point of view—even if he didn't respect it.

"Don't you remember anything from Afghanistan?" Farkas asked.

"What does any of this have to do with Afghanistan?"

Farkas leaned back in the hotel armchair and laced his fingers behind his head. "You've seen war, right? You've seen men rape breastfeeding mothers before shooting them through the heart? You've seen prepubescent boys hacked to death with machetes to keep them from growing into vengeful men? You've witnessed—"

"Okay, okay, I get the gruesome picture. Yes, I have seen war. What is your point?"

"My point is that whatever Luther may be doing to Emmy, it's insignificant. She's a grown woman. And besides, four days from now she won't remember a thing."

Troy bit back a sharp retort in favor of a more subtle thrust. "I was wondering how a man with the intelligence to get through medical school could do what you do—voluntarily. Now I understand. Civil war lobotomized you, robbed you of your ability to feel. You've become little more than a crocodile with a brain."

Troy thought that would either shut Farkas up or bring him to his feet. Truth be told, Troy welcomed a fistfight with the bastard, although it was anyone's call who would win.

Farkas surprised him again. "Like most creatures on this planet, humans included, I do what I have to do to survive. And like the best of those, I do it more for my family than for myself."

"You have a family?" Troy asked, incredulous.

"I have sisters. Their husbands are worthless, the leftovers of a generation that lost its best to war, so they count on me. With the money I make from this job, they will be free to pursue happiness, as you Americans like to say, and I will be able to start my own practice, settle down."

"How much are you getting for this job? What's the collapse of the US judicial system worth to you?"

"The US system did not bring me justice. It robbed me of my career. So as far as I'm concerned, it's not worth a penny. Luther, however, is paying me ten million."

"Of the half-billion he's pocketing?" Troy chided. "That's what, two percent? Not even a bad tip. And you're doing all the work."

"It's as Karl Marx warned a century ago: The man who owns the means of production reaps the lion's share of the rewards." Farkas shrugged. "But when the production is as big as this one, the crumbs are big enough. I'm happy with my ten million."

Troy was still digesting that when Farkas began to squirm in his seat. "Speak of the devil and he appears," Farkas said, pulling the vibrating BlackBerry from his pocket. "Yeah."

As Farkas listened, Troy studied his face for any indication of the news. But as always, the hired gun was a blank slate. Farkas said, "We're confident that we've got all nine nailed. We've even developed backup plans for most." After another pause, Farkas said, "No, he's cooperating. In fact, he's anxious to get this over with. I'm not sure what I'm going to do with him for the next two days. Run up the pay-per-view bill I guess." Troy thought he saw a look of mild surprise flash across Farkas's face after Luther's next question, but it could have been gas. The Croatian doused everything in Tabasco sauce. After a minute, Farkas simply said, "Okay," and then he held out the phone. "He wants to talk to you."

Troy snatched the phone and said, "Let me talk to Emmy."

"Soon," Luther replied, not missing a beat. "In the meantime, I understand that you're bored, that you've got two days to kill?"

Rather than take the bait, Troy waited for Luther to get to the point.

Luther did. "I've got an assignment for you to complete before this weekend's finale. I'd like to say that it will keep you out of trouble, but that's not entirely accurate."

"We've already got our deal. I'm not doing another thing for you, unless you have something else to offer."

"You'll do whatever I tell you to do, or—"

"Or what? You're not going to do anything, so don't make idle threats. You need me to complete this mission. In fact, it's safe to say that at this point in the operation, or more precisely at this date on the calendar, you need me more than I need you." The words just flew from Troy's mouth without forethought. He knew that it was foolish to challenge a top courtroom attorney to a verbal joust, but the frustration pent up inside him demanded release.

"I'm only getting money out of this, Troy. You are getting two lives; your own, and Miss Green's here. Shall I let her know how little you think she's worth?"

"Why don't you just get to the point, and tell me what you want?" Troy said, trying to sound aggressive as he retreated.

"That's more like it. I want you to take a trip—back to Grand Cayman. Have you been missing it?"

"That depends, are you going to send Emmy to join me? It just wouldn't be the same without her."

"I'm afraid not. I need Emmy here, with me. But you are going to get to see an old friend."

"And who would that be?" Troy asked, now genuinely curious.

"Kostas Kanasis. If he doesn't die of natural causes within forty-eight hours, Emmy will."

Chapter 87

Dinner Arrangements

"PHONE FOR YOU, HONEY," Susanna yelled across the bullpen.

Honey looked up from the report he was perusing with Mertins. "Who is it?"

"I don't know, but he's obviously Irish."

Honey felt his heart skip a beat. Could it be? The manhunt had dropped to passive status ten days ago, and he had all but given up hope of redemption.

"You okay, Honey?" Susanna asked, reading his face.

"Fine. Just give me the phone," Honey said, crossing the room. He snatched the receiver, took a deep breath and said, "Captain Honey."

"Have ye put it together yet, Captain?" asked the voice he would never forget.

"I still have a few questions. Why don't we meet for lunch to discuss them?"

"Actually, I did breakfast on yeer fine island. But I'll be lunching here on mine. I will, however, be arranging for you to dine with another person of interest."

Honey's throat went dry. He took a sip from Susanna's cold coffee cup before replying. "The shooter?"

"Precisely, the man who assassinated Jacobs. May the saints bless that quick mind of yours. Of course, after ye anticipated our escape strategy, I expected no less. Tell me now, have ye tied him to the Johnson murder as well? I suspect that took more than simple ballistics. He sands his fingertips, you know."

Honey had surmised as much after finding Brandell's car clean despite Mertins' insistence that the perp was not wearing gloves. "He wore a helmet throughout that operation, but I managed all the same—used a computer to uniquely identify his skeletal measurements. We've got him for the whole trifecta, Johnson, Jacobs, and Brandell."

Irish paused, leading Honey to infer that he did not know about Brandell, then said, "Good. So, if I get him to you, will that get my friend and me off the hook?"

Honey's impulse was to lie, but intuition told him to play it straight. "I've still got about twenty charges with your names set squarely beside them. Everything from assault with a deadly weapon to desecrating a corpse."

"I regret that those actions were necessary. The shooter put my friend and me into a bind we couldn't escape without violence. So I guess this is where quid pro quo comes into play?"

Honey thought about the proposition. He could legally promise anything and renege. No doubt Irish was aware of that. Irish wanted a gentleman's agreement, implying that he was gambling on Honey's need to restore his dignity. A fair wager. Again, Honey asked himself the question he had been mulling over these past two weeks: Would he have done what they had done, if he were in their shoes? The answer had not changed since the last time he asked: Of course. "When can I expect this dinner?"

"Monday. Perhaps you'd like to meet him at the airport? He'll be arriving on a private flight."

Chapter 88

Call Forwarding

FOR HIS RETURN from Grand Cayman, Troy booked the flight that maximized his layover in Miami. Four hours on the ground—less the ten minutes he used to call Honey and the ninety it had taken him to procure a Miami cell phone—left him about half an hour to conduct his business with Tate.

"You mind waiting?" he asked the taxi driver as they pulled to the curb. "There's an extra hundred in it for you. My flight is at two."

The Russian driver just nodded and cranked the volume on his ABBA CD.

Troy recognized Alice from his first visit, but since he had been a wheelchair-bound seventy-year-old then, she did not recognize him. "I'm Arthur Adams," he said, holding out his hand. "I've got a twelve o'clock appointment with Mr. Tate."

"Yes, I know he's expecting you. I'll just let him know that you're here."

"Thanks. Tell me, Alice, is Sylvia here?"

"Sylvia, no, she's out to lunch. Is that a problem?"

"No, no, nothing like that," Troy said, closing the subject.

Just then a man entered whom Troy had last seen picking up pills off the downstairs floor. He said, "I thought I heard someone arrive. He held out his hand, "I'm Alexander Tate. You must be Arthur Adams."

"A pleasure to meet you, Mr. Tate. I've heard good things."

"Please, come on back to my office," Tate said, gesturing.

"Sure, but first, I was hoping that I might be able to impose on your charming assistant to pick me up a sandwich? Say corned beef on rye, or even better a Reuben? I've got a lot to go over with you, and a crazy schedule the rest of the afternoon."

Troy was no Emmy, but he knew voices, and he definitely detected a strain of embarrassment in Tate's when he asked Alice, "Would you mind running down to Lenny's for a couple of Reubens?"

To her credit, Alice said, "Not at all." She opened the filing drawer on her desk, pulled out her Sak purse, and walked out quickly enough that Troy suspected she was hiding either a scowl or tears.

Turning back to Tate, Troy said, "Lead the way."

When Tate opened his door, Troy was delighted to see a long couch residing beneath an oil painting of what he recognized as Miami's South Beach. "Lovely painting."

Tate looked over at him and said, "Yes, when I told my realtor what my budget was and expressed my desire for a view of the beach, this was what she suggested." He winked and then settled down into his high-backed burgundy chair as they both chuckled perfunctorily. Sitting across the cherry desk in a similar chair with a lower back, Troy scooted forward so that the lip of the desk hid his lap from view. That would make things easier.

"Now, Arthur, what is it I can do for you? On the phone you mentioned the need to establish a number of offshore accounts?"

Listening with practiced ears, Troy began to dissect the lawyer's syntax, tone and cadence. Tate was obviously of British origin, and had made no attempt to lose his accent. No doubt that was at least in part due to the fact that Americans were subconsciously more trusting of a British voice. This was good news for Troy, since they also tended to identify a voice by that foreign accent without much regard for its subtler features. "Yes, I've just come into a substantial inheritance," Troy said, using words he wanted to hear repeated.

"An inheritance? So you made your money the really old fashioned way," Tate commented with a chuckle.

"Yes. My uncle's estate on Grand Cayman." He paused, ostensibly for a reaction, but really in order to focus on palming the syringe tucked beneath a rubber band up his sleeve.

"We do a lot of work on the Caymans. And for that matter, a lot of work with rich uncles." Another chuckle.

"That's wonderful. Say, Alex, would you mind showing me to the restroom before we get into the details?" Troy asked. "That will give you a couple of minutes to come up with some specific recommendations."

"Yes, of course," Tate said standing. "Can you give me an idea as to the size of the opening deposit?"

"I don't know for sure yet, since some of the assets have yet to be liquidated, but it will be well into seven figures, perhaps eight."

"I see. I happen to have several outstanding opportunities in that range. But I'm getting ahead of myself. Please, follow me."

Troy slipped the syringe into Tate's left buttock as the lawyer held open his office door. The sedative worked instantly, and Troy had to whirl about to catch the lawyer before he crashed to the floor.

Holding Tate under his arms, Troy dragged him over to his couch and laid him out as though he were taking a nap. Hopefully, that was not an uncommon position for the lawyer. He toyed with the idea of taking off Tate's shoes for effect, but decided not to push it.

Pressed for time both because of the plane and because he did not know how long it would take Alice to return from Lenny's, Troy recited a few practice phrases to get Tate's voice right, and then picked up his phone. He dialed the number he had memorized weeks ago.

"Luther Kanasis." The lilt in Luther's voice betrayed his subscription to caller ID.

"Yes, Mr. Kanasis, this is Alexander Tate calling from Miami. I'm afraid to be the bearer of bad news. Your uncle Kostas Kanasis has passed away."

"Oh, no. So suddenly? Did he have an accident? He didn't fall off that beloved balcony of his I hope."

"No, nothing like that. It appears that your uncle died of natural causes. The coroner will know for certain early next week."

"I see."

"Yes, well, my sincerest condolences."

"Thank you."

"Now, as the executor of your uncle's will, I am pleased to inform you that he has named you as the sole beneficiary of his estate. In addition to his condominium on Grand Cayman, this includes an account at Solomon Bank & Trust worth approximately two hundred and forty-eight million dollars.

"I would be happy to help you—"

Luther cut him off with, "I thank you, but the only assistance I will be needing is for you to open a numbered account for me in Switzerland. I would like the entire balance transferred by close of business today. Less your fee, of course."

"I see, well, the Swiss account will be no problem, but I'm afraid you will have to wait a few days for the transfer. Your uncle's assets are frozen as per legal requirements until the coroner gives the all-clear. I should be able to have your money in Switzerland by close of business Tuesday."

"Are you certain?"

"Well, no. We can't be one-hundred percent sure until the fat lady sings, but you can be certain that I will be on top of it. I'm planning on going to Grand Cayman personally to ensure that this and a few other affairs are handled properly. I'll call you if it looks like there's going to be any delay. Meanwhile, since I won't be reachable here at the office, let me leave you the number of my mobile phone."

Chapter 89

Dog Day

TROY DIALED a number from memory and then cradled the payphone receiver between shoulder and chin while Farkas watched from ten yards to his left. Pretending to make a call at this time on this phone was part of the plan he and Farkas had concocted for injecting Justice Brewer. Still, Farkas was eyeing him suspiciously. Was it the nature of the Croatian beast? Or was Troy's deception easy to spot?

He pushed his fears aside and continued to follow the script, unscrewing the cap from his mineral water and emptying it over an indentation in the sidewalk to create a puddle.

"Seaborn's. Sean Seaborn speaking."

"It's Sebastian Troy calling, Sean. Is my order ready to go?"

Troy kept Farkas in his peripheral vision as he spoke. The Croatian sat on a park bench with three French Bulldogs tethered at his feet, watching him over the top of his newspaper. He had been dissecting Troy with his eyes nonstop since Troy's return from Grand Cayman an hour ago. The logical conclusion was that Farkas thought he was now looking at a bona fide assassin, but Troy's little voice was screaming that Farkas somehow knew his secrets.

"It's four-thirty on Friday, right?" Sean Seaborn said, his squeaky voice conjuring up the image of a thin man in protective goggles and a white lab coat. "I promised you it would be ready by Friday afternoon and it is Friday afternoon, so yes, it's ready."

"And the FedEx—"

"The FedEx guy is due here in a few minutes—also as promised.

I do still need the shipping address however, and of course your credit card number for the balance of the payment.

Troy dictated the AmEx number he had memorized years ago and the address of the Italian restaurant next to their hotel. He and Farkas had eaten late dinners at Benvenutos half-a-dozen nights during the past couple of weeks, not because it was particularly good, but rather because it was convenient. Their marathon of surveillance had them up early and out late, so they were always tired when the job was done. As a result, Troy knew their usual waiter well enough to make an arrangement. "Make sure you specify Saturday morning delivery, care of Benny Azara. If you just do regular priority overnight, I won't get it until Monday, and they're useless to me then."

"I am filling out the form as we speak," Sean squeaked, "and will place it in the courier's hands personally. Thank you for your business."

Troy severed the connection while continuing his pretense of talking on the phone. Amazing the service you could get by offering a ten-fold price premium, he thought. Still he was cutting it close.

Glancing casually back to his left, Troy saw Farkas pull his sunglasses down from atop his head to cover his eyes. That was the sign that a two-year-old mittelschnauzer named Dory had entered the far side of the park—with Justice Stanley Brewer in tow. They knew from prior stakeouts that it would only take Dory sixty to ninety seconds to drag her master to this end. Troy felt the familiar adrenaline rush. It was showtime. Kickoff. The start of a nine-game season.

He moved his paper grocery bag a pace to the left so the corner rested in the puddle his mineral water had created. As the water wicked up the side, his mind drifted to the gamble they were taking with the science.

According to the bioavailability calculations of scientists

murdered four years ago, Friday afternoon was too early to implant a dose that would not be activated until Monday morning. The drug's doomed inventors had estimated forty-eight hours to be the outer limit of its bioavailability. MDs Troy and Farkas had revisited that conclusion after determining that they could not fit nine risky implants into just two days. Knowing that medical treatment in general and drug profiles in particular were required to be conservative, and given the slowed metabolism of a man in his seventieth year, they agreed to risk an eighteen-hour extension. Brewer might not lose as many years' memory as the other eight, but even one year would be more than enough.

Troy cradled the payphone receiver as Dory and her owner strolled into sight from behind a bushy mound. He stooped to gently lift the brown bag by its handles and set off on an intercept course.

The small city park was fairly crowded, this being a sunny fall afternoon and D.C. being a walking town. To Troy's chagrin, Dory was proving to be one popular bitch. Every dog has her day. As she stopped to exchange sniffs with one purebred after another, Justice Brewer exchanged reserved pleasantries with their owners. Meanwhile, Troy was literally left standing there holding the bag.

He glanced around casually, careful not to shake the bag while acting like a vacationer soaking up the view. Soon Dory resumed her quest for fresh scents and pulled Justice Brewer toward ground zero. As Dory passed Farkas, the Croatian kept his French bulldogs heeled by stepping on their leashes. Once they were midway to Troy, however, he stood and followed. The three slobbering hounds strained at their leashes, eager to get a snout full of Dory's scent. Farkas was still about fifteen feet behind Brewer when Troy, closing on them from the opposite direction, tugged sharply at the handles of his brown bag.

The two-pound package of ground beef broke through the paper and split open on the ground, just as it had during his practice sessions in the hotel. This time, however, it was only inches from a schnauzer's nose. Dory's tail began whirling like a propeller and she dove at the feast from heaven before Brewer could rein her in. As Troy bent to reassemble his other rolling groceries, Farkas's three French Bulldogs leapt into the mix.

The startled justice bent over the writhing mound in a frantic attempt to extract his feasting pooch from the sixteen-legged tangle. He failed to notice the mosquito-like prick on his rump amidst the torrent of flying spittle, flapping leashes, and disappearing meat.

Chapter 90

Brinksmanship

LUTHER HAD SLIPPED a needle into Emmy's shoulder as she watched Farkas drag Troy from the room. With her heart breaking, she had not felt the prick.

When Emmy awoke, she was already imprisoned.

Twelve days later, nothing had changed.

The *Brinkman* was sixty-eight feet of floating luxury, a gleaming pearl gliding gracefully through an azure ocean. Emmy felt like a princess locked in a tower while black and white knights battled for her in a land far far away.

She hated it.

She wanted to pick up a sword and fight her own battles.

Brinkman's opulent atmosphere felt hauntingly familiar. She had no memory of ever setting foot on a yacht, or showering in a head, or having a private chef to cook whatever she wanted for breakfast, lunch, and dinner. Yet she had slipped into the lifestyle like a well-worn slipper. This was her first sighting of the ghost of Bo Beaulieu. Oddly enough, it did not spook her. She didn't feel a sense of loss or longing or remorse. The only emotion she had experienced aplenty these past twelve days was guilt.

Seated before her lacquered burl-wood vanity in burgundy shorts and a sleeveless honey-colored top, preparing her makeup for today's photograph, Emmy would rather have been in San Quentin. She tried to imagine what Troy was doing at that very moment. Was he lying in wait with a dart gun beneath a cold wet bush? Passing himself off as a DC cop? Rappelling off a roof?

Whatever it was, she knew Troy was doing it for her. He was performing acts he would rather die than commit, all in the hope of saving her life. And there was painfully little she could do about it.

Emmy was attempting to assist Troy through her daily proof-of-life photos, but feared this was like passing him a garden hose and expecting him to squelch a volcano. Still, she felt better for the trying. For starters, she did everything she could to appear optimistic and happy in the photos, hoping to bolster Troy's mood. Luther, of course, encouraged this, as it played into his hand. But she was also telegraphing clues to her whereabouts. Every day she sunbathed on the *Brinkman's* long bow, so that Troy would come to realize that she was being held in a tropical climate, with access to the outdoors. Luther may have figured this out, but he didn't seem to care. Either he figured that "sunny climate" wasn't much of a clue, or he decided that it was worth the risk to watch her lie about in a bikini.

Luther had been surprisingly gentlemanly with her. Despite Giselle's mention that Luther liked the hunt more than the conquest, Emmy had fully expected him to come to her cabin the first night and take her anyway he liked. On the ocean there was no one to hear her scream. She had lain awake until dawn, a steak knife poised to thrust, but Luther had kept to himself.

The one clue to Troy that Luther would surely have stopped had he noticed, was her use of sign language. Unfortunately, the odds of Troy figuring it out were not good either. On her first day aboard the yacht, Luther had photographed her holding a computer printout of the LA Times article on Mafia Boss James "Orca" Scapone's brutal death. The author led with the suspicion that rival boss Jimmy "Choke" Cortese was behind the execution, given the signature method of asphyxiation. That night she had come up with a plan. The following day and every day thereafter, Emmy held the daily newspaper headline with her left hand positioned so that her fingers spelled out one letter of SS-BRINKMAN in sign language. There was no detectable pattern in any one picture, but she figured that Troy might study them en masse—hopefully every night before bed.

Today she would dangle the printout from her fist with her thumb clenched between her ring and middle fingers, signaling N, the final entry in her code. Her hope was that Troy had devised the means to escape Farkas and would do so the moment he knew where to find her. Luther had implemented the system of thrice-daily checkups as a countermeasure, but Troy had the voice talent to get around that.

Setting down her tube of lip gloss, Emmy rose from her vanity and walked upstairs to the main deck. Luther sat lounging on a semicircular couch, reading the latest issue of Caribbean Lifestyles. He set the magazine down as she approached, and said, "My, you do look lovely."

"It's for Troy," she said, immediately regretting her words. Distasteful as it was, she wanted to keep on Luther's good side. There was no telling when the opportunity to escape might arise, and she wanted the split-second advantage that a cordial relationship would give. Changing her tone to one more friendly, she said, "I've been meaning to ask you a question."

"Yes."

"Why did you choose to use 456 the way you have? Why erase the memories of witnesses. I'd think you could market such a drug legitimately to trauma victims, women who have been raped and soldiers returning from battle. Then none of this would have been necessary."

Luther gave her a look that she interpreted as half suspicion, half admiration. "I owed twenty-five million dollars to the mob. The interest, the vigorish as Orca called it, was a million a month. Given all the delays that a controversial new product like that could expect from wedge-issue politicians, evangelical Christians, and

Scientologists, just to name a few, I'd have been worm food before I saw a dime."

Emmy nodded, trying to show understanding, sympathy.

"And then there's the fact that I had to kill everyone at the company who invented it," Luther added. "That inclined me toward avoiding the public eye. Shall we take that picture now?"

Emmy tried to keep her face impassive as she said, "Yes."

She took her seat on the other end of the semicircle, and raised the fresh printout as prescribed. Luther raised his digital camera and was just about to snap the photo when a call came in on his satellite phone. Emmy checked her own watch and saw that it was four hours too early to be Farkas. When Luther answered, however, she heard the Croatian's distinctive voice ringing from the phone. She strained to hear his side of the conversation.

"We've done it!" Farkas said. "We've implanted all nine."

Luther's face burst wide open as a childish smile welled up from within. "That's fantastic. Did all the implants go as planned?"

"More or less. We had to use our backup plan on Goldstein since she came down with a cold. We caught her at her hairdresser rather than synagogue."

"With priorities like that, she doesn't deserve the bench."

"Speaking of deserve ..." Farkas prompted.

"Don't worry, my friend. Your seven zeros are but a flash away."

Clapping his phone shut, Luther thrust his right fist up into the air and shook it three times in victory.

"You're that happy about disabling the country's judicial branch?" she asked.

Luther shook his head. "I couldn't care less about those nine old farts. Did you know that former Chief Justice Rehnquist spent a decade on the bench as a drug addict? Millions of Americans were incarcerated for using drugs while the chief justice was popping fifteen hundred milligrams of Placidyl a day." He waved a hand dismissively. "What I do care about is this." He flipped his phone back open, pressed seven on his speed dial and then engaged the speaker for her benefit.

"I just got the word," said a voice Emmy did not recognize. "My man has seen the whites of their eyes. Is everything else set for tomorrow morning?"

"Absolutely everything."

"Excellent. Well then, congratulations are in order. As agreed, I'll order the transfer as soon as we're off the phone. You'll have the remainder of your fee within an hour of banks opening in Europe."

"Three hundred million," Luther prompted.

"Three hundred million. Don't forget to tidy up."

"I won't."

"Good. And Luther ..."

"Yes?"

"Have a nice life."

Luther sprang from the couch as he closed the phone and sashayed over to the galley. He opened the cabinet on the far end and pulled an emerald-cut burgundy box off the top shelf. Tucking it lovingly under his arm, he grabbed two tumblers from the bar and brought his loot over to the table before her. He sat down with his hips abutting hers and laid the treasure down before them. Scrawled atop it in gold lettering were the words: LOUIS XIII by Remy Martin. After giving her a moment to digest the words, he drew back the lid with both hands, exposing the famous Baccarat crystal decanter that housed the world's finest cognac. "It's time to celebrate."

Looking over at the lust radiating from her keeper's eyes, Emmy felt a paralyzing chill creep up her spine. Her free pass had finally expired.

Chapter 91

Fireball

"I HOPE your plan for getting us out of here will work as smoothly as your ploy for getting us in," Troy whispered, fishing for information once they were far enough down the Supreme Court's Grand Hall to be out of the guards' earshot.

Farkas ignored him. The payout of a lifetime was just a few steps away, and he was not going to say or do anything that might jeopardize his fortune.

They walked in silence behind the small crowd of reporters to the West Conference Room. Once they had reached their destination, however, Troy leaned toward him and whispered, "Don't you think it's time to brief me on the details of our escape plan? I mean, within seconds of the justices all fainting, security is going to come down like an iron curtain. I don't want to be locked inside while they investigate."

Farkas had kept out of jail by keeping his mouth shut. If somebody did not need to know something, he did not tell them. Period. Troy did not need to know that Farkas had simple smoke bombs hidden in the cuffs of his trousers. When the smoke erupted, he would still run for the doors like everyone else. Likewise, Troy did not need to know about the dozen tiny blasting caps secreted outside, the "gunshots" that would send the evacuating crowd running in all directions. At the same time, however, Farkas did not want to alienate his co-conspirator. They had nine sets of pupils to focus their flashes on. His chances of success improved markedly if he could go at them from two angles.

He needed Troy's unflinching participation.

"Did I ever tell you how I got us press credentials?" Farkas asked.

"No. You ignored my questions on that as well," Troy replied, still avoiding his eye. Farkas had found him uncharacteristically diffident all morning. Even after taking out Kostas, Troy still lived in a world of ideals—a world where survival-of-the-fittest was not the presiding rule. His amnesia was going to be a blessing. It would allow him to look in the mirror after this morning without flinching. It would let him forget what he had done.

Farkas needed no such balm.

"It couldn't have been easier," Farkas whispered. "Wearing a black suit and earpiece, I approached a group of reporters waiting to gain access to the Capital and flashed forged Homeland Security credentials. I asked to see all of their credentials, and one-by-one ran each through a portable scanner which I described as "the latest advance in counter-terrorism technology." Then I pressed a button that made the scanner beep and pronounced each to be legitimate. I gave the scanned files along with our pictures to the same lady who made my Homeland Security creds, and voila, we were golden."

Troy shook his head. "That's the problem with conditioning people to follow procedures, to bowing to authority; you train them not to think."

"And you reduce everyone's operating performance to that of the weakest link," Farkas added, "making loopholes easier for us to exploit. Speaking of which, you go set up toward the right edge of the press area. I'll stay here on the left. Between our two angles, we should catch the gazes of all nine justices simultaneously."

"How about you take the right, and I stay here on the left," Troy countered. "Closer to the exit."

Farkas smiled. He didn't do that very often, but knowing that an overflowing bank account was just minutes away, he was feeling giddy around the edges. "All right. But no comebacks if you get trampled in the rush to leave."

Farkas had trouble keeping his smile down as he set up his camera and pretended to calibrate it for the distance and lighting. This was the most-serious, highest-risk assignment he had ever undertaken, but all he could think about was his triumphant return to Croatia, flush with ten million bucks. He would set up each of his sisters with enough cash for them to leave their deadbeat husbands. Then he would buy the country estate he had always dreamed of, and set up his own medical practice. It would be as though he never lost his license, better even, for he was years ahead of his original schedule. "Whoever said there were no second chances?" he mumbled.

The press conference prior to the Supreme Court's opening conference was far less organized than Farkas had envisioned. People were just milling about the hallowed room waiting for the justices to appear. It was almost like a cocktail party, but for the casual dress and absence of booze. There were also fewer photographers than Farkas had expected, only about twenty in all, including C-SPAN's videographer. In retrospect, he figured that was more than enough. Elderly people wearing baggy black robes were hardly a feast for the eyes—unless they were the victims of a tragic attack.

A camera flash to his left alerted Farkas to the arrival of the first Justice. It was Jack Reynolds, the Chief. Troy had implanted him during his habitual Sunday morning jog around the ellipse. The others followed behind in procession.

Farkas used a camera fitted with a special viewfinder to check their eyes. All nine pairs glowed with a violet tinge.

Farkas switched to the UV-C flashing camera and waited with a hungry finger poised patiently on the button. Eight figures were just a flash away. He and Troy had agreed to wait until all nine justices had taken their seats behind the long mahogany table. They couldn't have anyone fainting too early and triggering an evacuation procedure. He dared a glance to his left to ensure that Troy was in position, and then it was time.

He pulled the string that ran up his pant leg and looped around his belt, releasing the smoke bombs and activating their sixty-second timer. As they rolled in different directions across the floor, he aimed his camera at Justice Reynolds. A tremendous spike of adrenaline hit his bloodstream as he pressed the button that sent three pulses of UV-C per second flashing toward attentive pupils. He swept first to Reynolds' left and then back across the table to the far end, nailing each justice one by one.

None of the Justices reacted.

They just sat there, smiling for the cameras like seasoned politicians. Ideas began to flood his mind about what had gone wrong. Had Troy somehow replaced the 456 with a harmless fluorescing chemical? What about his UV-C flasher? Perhaps the security scanner had somehow disabled it? If so, then Troy's had to be malfunctioning too.

Turning toward his coconspirator, Farkas saw Troy staring back at him. Pointing his camera back at him. Then Farkas felt a fireball consuming his brain, and everything went black.

Chapter 92

Visual Aid

"HE'S DIABETIC," Troy said to the neighboring reporters as he gave Farkas a shot of epinephrine disguised as insulin. "Don't worry, he'll be fine."

Troy had tried to reach Farkas before he collapsed to the floor, but too many tripods had blocked his path. Fortunately, he had the stimulant ready as backup. Now he had to get Farkas out of there before someone called an ambulance.

Farkas's eyes fluttered and then opened without focus.

Troy slipped an arm under his shoulders and pulled him into a sitting position. "Come on, buddy, let's walk it off." He exerted more upward pressure and Farkas rose to his feet.

"What happened?" Farkas asked, his voice weak and uncertain.

"You forgot to take your insulin, again. Come on, let's get you home." Troy needed to get Farkas out of there before someone overheard Farkas ask the inevitable question: "Who are you?" And it was inevitable. There was no doubt in Troy's mind that this time Farkas was not faking it. 456 had literally fried Farkas's mind. His memories of Troy and Emmy and Luther and even his eight-figure payday were all up in cranial smoke.

What wasn't smoking was Farkas's bombs. Troy had disabled them in the middle of the night, along with Farkas's flasher.

Farkas moved as though he was sleepwalking, his legs supporting his weight but his mind relying on Troy for all guidance. Troy piloted him out the visitor's entrance into the back seat of a limo waiting on Maryland Avenue. "Hyde Field," he told the driver, referring to Washington's executive airport.

"That will only take us about thirty minutes. You got me for the whole morning."

"The airport is just the first stop. My friend has a plane to catch."

"Is he all right?" the driver asked, pulling out.

Farkas had slipped back into unconsciousness the moment the weight came off his legs.

"He's a diabetic. Gets this way when his insulin level is off." Troy would have to give him another epinephrine shot when they got to the airport. Officials tended not to scrutinize those who flew private very closely, but there were limits.

The limo driver shrugged and pulled out into traffic.

He had done it! He had taken Farkas out of the picture and saved the United States Supreme Court. Sitting there on the cool black Naugahyde with Farkas slumped against his left shoulder, Troy felt mildly relieved but was not all a tingle with the thrill of victory. He was still a long way from converting his epic tragedy into a romance.

One hour later, after watching Farkas fly off on a charter jet to Grand Cayman and faxing the flight details to Captain Honey, Troy took the first step toward achieving his primary goals. Using Farkas's satellite phone and mimicking Farkas's voice, he made a call.

"Give me the good news," Luther said right off the bat.

"It's done."

"Fantastic. Congratulations. It hasn't hit the news yet."

"And it won't. Not for forty-eight hours. They swore everyone to silence for national security reasons."

"And nobody is going to risk angering the entire Supreme Court," Luther added, half to himself.

"I want my ten million wired immediately."

"Not until it hits the news. I need proof," Luther insisted.

"I've got proof. A video."

"They didn't confiscate it?"

"They kept my camera. Even made me show them my pictures so they could see that I hadn't swapped out memory disks. But they didn't know that it has a video feature that writes to a separate memory disk. I got that disk out."

"That will do. When will you be here?"

"Are you at home?"

"We just arrived."

"We?"

"Emmy's with me, remember?"

"Right. Well, I've decided that it's in my best interests for us to never meet again. So I'm just sending Troy with the video. You watch it and transfer my money this afternoon, understood?"

"Are you sure you—"

"I'm sure. You just transfer my money. Ten million. Today."

After a long pause, Luther said, "Okay."

"And Luther?"

"Yes?"

"If we do have to see each other again, it's not going to go well for you."

Chapter 93

Dirty

BENEATH PORTENTOUS CLOUDS and a blustery wind, Troy pulled his rented Chevy into a BP station a half-mile from Luther's estate. He did not need gas, but he wanted to hide Farkas's effects where Luther would not discover them if the next hour did not go entirely as planned.

Glancing down at the wallet, satellite phone, and remaining 456 vials as he slipped them beneath the spare tire, Troy realized that Farkas would be in custody now—his situation virtually identical to the one he had arranged for Troy four weeks earlier. Whatever followed next, Troy could at least feel good about that.

Settling back into the car, he rechecked the seals on the double-bagged portable DVD player occupying the passenger seat. He found that particular detail squared away, but knew there were countless others that might not be. Emmy would be lost to him forever if he failed to deal with a single one.

He could still call the police, he realized, and report a hostage situation. But the odds were that Luther had Emmy primed and ready to flash at the first sign of trouble. Dialing 911 would likely lobotomize her and land Troy in the cage next to Farkas.

He spit a surge of bile out through the window, and punched the gas.

Arriving at Luther's gate, Troy slipped one of Farkas's covert injector rings onto his right middle finger. This was it. An hour from now the world was going to seem like a very different place— either for Luther, or for Emmy and him. He crossed the fingers of his unloaded hand and punched the intercom buzzer.

The gate opened without a word from within, and Troy pulled the Chevy onto the crushed stone drive. He parked directly between the front entrance and the Spanish fountain and threw open the car door like a man meaning business. While turning toward the door, he reached over his head and slipped the DVD player atop the fountain's third tier where it could not be seen by anyone shorter than a Laker.

He marched up to the massive front door, and rather than using the bell or oversized brass knocker, pounded on the oak with the heel of his left fist. This was where it got tricky, he knew. He fully expected Luther to answer with a gun in his hand, but was committed to pushing ahead regardless.

"Troy, long time no see. Please, come—"

Troy pushed open the door before Luther could finish. Squaring off with the man toe-to-toe he pushed Luther back with a challenging open-palmed double-blow to the chest. Luther was a hard body, his chest all muscle, but the force of Troy's shove still landed him on his butt. "Where is she?" Troy asked, glowering down.

Luther locked Troy's eyes as he rose slowly to his feet. "She's the same place you are: at my mercy." Luther rubbed his left pectoral muscle subconsciously. "You would be wise not to forget it."

"Answer my question," Troy persisted without blinking. "Where is she?"

"I'll take you to her."

"Good."

"Once you show me the proof Farkas promised."

"You see the proof once I see the girl."

Luther shook his head. "Remember the details of our agreement. You don't just get to walk away."

"I'm not asking to leave. I'm asking to see her."

"Very well," Luther said. "Wait here. I'll be right back."

The instant Luther disappeared down the hallway at the top of the semicircular stairs, Troy pulled the injector ring off his finger to confirm that it had delivered its contents. Empty. Smiling to himself, he plunged the ring into the potted palm to the left of the doorway. The soil was still moist from a recent watering, so it left dirt on his fingers. With no other option at his immediate disposal, Troy licked off the evidence.

Luther reappeared almost instantly, dangling a pair of handcuffs from his right index finger. "Turn around and put your wrists together," he commanded. "Then I'll take you to her."

Troy complied, reckoning that the score was now tied at one apiece. Still anybody's match.

Luther walked around to face Troy once his hands were cuffed. "That's better," he said. Then he punched Troy fast and hard in the solar plexus.

Troy doubled over in agony, his lungs craving air.

"Well, come on then," Luther said, heading for the door to the backyard. "Time's a wasting."

After forcing himself into a pose that was more exclamation point than question mark, Troy followed along a cobblestone path through a manicured garden to a guesthouse that was nicer than anything he had ever lived in. Like the Spanish-style master estate, the guesthouse boasted numerous white stucco arches and black-railed balconies and a red-tiled roof. Troy gauged it to be about eighteen hundred square feet, spread over two floors.

Luther pushed open the front door like a cowboy entering a bar and then bounded up the tile stairs two at a time. Troy wanted to keep on Luther's heels, but he needed to run out the clock. 456 required fifteen minutes of activation time. So he took the stairs deliberately, one by one, his hands still cuffed behind.

Luther had the door to a secondary bedroom unlocked and held open by the time Troy reached the top stair. Troy looked in and felt his heart melt. Emmy was spread eagle on a twin bed with a gag in her mouth. She was clothed only in lacy red underwear. Luther had secured her wrists and ankles to the bedposts with padlocked chains.

"I thought you'd like her this way," Luther said with a crocodile smile.

Locking eyes with Emmy and seeing the glow of recognition, Troy felt a warm surge of relief. "Take the gag out of her mouth." he said, struggling to keep his tone civil.

"As you wish."

As Luther pulled the gag from her mouth, Troy saw that it was a pair of pantyhose, secured in her mouth by tying the legs. The moment Luther backed away, Troy bent over and kissed her hard, full on the mouth. He didn't stop until Luther pulled him backwards by his handcuffs.

"You taste like dirt," Emmy said, an inquisitive glimmer in her eye.

"You taste great."

"You've seen her," Luther said. "Obviously, she's fine. Now, back to business."

"It's in your fountain," Troy said, maintaining eye contact with Emmy. "The DVD player Farkas instructed me to give you is in your fountain."

Troy heard the door shut behind him and a key turning in the lock. "Don't get too comfortable," Luther shouted. "I'll be right back."

"Farkas told me to remind you to transfer his ten million immediately," Troy shouted back. "He told me to warn you that Rambo has nothing on him. Having watched him in action these last few weeks, I would have to agree. You don't want him coming for you."

Chapter 94

Backfire

"YOU HAVE TO GET OUT OF HERE, NOW," Emmy said, as soon as Luther was gone. "For both our sakes."

"Luther knows I'm not going to leave without you," Troy replied. "That's the only reason he left us here alone. Besides, the door is bolted, the window is barred, and my hands are cuffed behind my back."

"Kick the door down and run," Emmy pleaded, tears streaming unbidden down her cheeks. "Find me later. Remind me that I love you. If I know that you'll do that, then I can take it. Go now. You've only got seconds before he comes back from the fountain."

Rather than doing as she asked, Troy just stood there staring back at her through misty eyes. She wanted to yell at him again to go, but his face beamed with such a loving glow that she could not do it. Finally, he said, "I think he's going to be gone a lot longer than that."

"Don't be a fool, he's—" She cut herself off. "What do you know that I don't?"

"There is no video of the wiping of the Supreme Court Justices. We didn't do it. Well, we did, but I sabotaged Farkas's camera. I also rigged the DVD player to flash Luther with UV-C. As we speak, he's losing his mind."

Emmy could not believe what she was hearing, and for a moment she thought this was another of her dreams. But Troy was there, using his foot to open the door to the closet. "And Kostas? Luther told me what he had ordered you to do ..."

"Kostas is fine. We had a long talk and then he went to Greece for a month."

Emmy felt a huge weight lift from her heart. She still had lots of questions, but Troy had allayed her chief concerns. "How did you manage to inject Luther? When?"

"I picked a fight minutes ago when I first arrived and injected him then. Farkas had custom built a lot of clever mechanisms for delivering 456. I inherited them. Can you pick handcuffs with a wire? There's a coat hanger here from a dry cleaner."

"I can pick them with the right wire, but that's too thick. Did you know that all handcuff keys are the same?"

"No. Really?"

"Pretty much. How about a bobby pin? I don't suppose you have one of those?" Emmy asked, trying to ease her own tension. Despite what Troy had told her, she expected to hear Luther's footfalls any second. After spending two weeks with the man, she knew not to underestimate him. Luther was the sharpest tool in the shed.

"I'm fresh out. But this obviously used to be a woman's room. Maybe we'll get lucky. I hear Luther's maid leaves something to be desired."

As Troy scrounged, the implications of his earlier statement finally registered. Emmy asked, "What did you mean about inheriting Farkas's tools? Is he dead?"

"No, he's alive."

"You're confusing me, and I'm mixed up enough already. Where is he? Do you know? Luther was furious that he wasn't coming back with you. He tried to hide his anger from me, but I could tell."

"I zapped him too and sent him back to Honey. I'm sure they're having a lovely chat as we speak."

Emmy could hardly believe her ears. How had Troy managed to do all that? "You're a wonder."

"Will this do?" Troy mumbled, picking up a miniature gold

paperclip with his lips.

"That's probably too weak to work as a pick, but it just might do as a shim if the cuffs are a knockoff brand. I'll give it a try."

Troy dropped the paperclip into her hand.

"How on earth did you manage to flash Farkas?" she asked, while working the paperclip into a straight wire. "Before Farkas flashed you."

"I found a specialty optical shop on the internet while supposedly researching the justices. I e-mailed them a rush order for two sets of custom contact lenses."

"Two sets?"

"A blue UV-C filtering pair for myself, and a metallic-brown non-filtering pair for Farkas. Saturday night while Farkas was sleeping contently with the knowledge that five of the nine justices were already in the bag, I swapped his lenses."

"I hope they were in a case at the time, rather than his eyes."

"Of course."

"But how did you inject him? I mean, he must have been wary about that."

"I let him inject himself. I mixed 456 in with his anti-insulin last Thursday. He's been giving himself tainted injections ever since."

"Didn't he notice?" Emmy asked, satisfied at last that the paperclip was sufficiently straight. "I'd think he'd feel different without his medication?"

"Oh, he was still getting two-thirds of his usual dose. And blood sugar levels are always in flux anyway. I'm sure he wrote any unusual feeling off to stress."

Emmy maneuvered the handcuffs around Troy's wrists so that she could access the tiny gap between the teeth and the housing. "Hold very still now," she said. Then she began pushing the wire into the gap. The wire was just thin enough to fit. She worked slowly, careful to keep it straight and parallel to the swinging arm. She hit resistance when it was about a quarter of an inch in.

"Perfect."

"What's that?"

"Don't move. I'm at the junction between the teeth and the ratchet. Now, if I can find the seam … and the wire's stiff enough …" She felt the ratchet give, and it was all over. The handcuffs swung open.

"That was amazing. You are amazing," Troy said, turning around and giving her another big kiss. She kissed back, hungrily.

Luther had not returned.

"It's your turn," Emmy said, when they came up for air. "You think you can break this bed apart?" Catching the look on his face she added, "Not that way."

The bed was an antique, made of sturdy oak, but it was no match for Troy's pent up frustrations. Within five minutes, he had both her hands freed. They were still in chains, but no longer attached to the bed. When he moved toward the foot of the bed to start working to free her feet, Emmy said, "Go to work on the door. Now that my hands are free I can use the paperclip to work the padlocks."

"Okay," Troy said, picking up a bedpost and testing it on the air like a bat.

"What's our next move?" she asked. "Assuming you can get the better of that door."

"Oh, I'll get the better of the door. And then you're going to be the busy one."

"How so?"

"You've got some important calls to make," he said, his eyes all a twinkle. "As Luther Kanasis's personal assistant."

Chapter 95

Rewriting History

LUTHER FOUGHT his return to consciousness. In stark contrast to the monster headache throbbing between his temples, the soft mattress and warm sheets seemed to be sucking him in for a warm embrace.

"Good morning, sir," came a soft sweet voice just inches from his face. The tone was so soothing that it took Luther a moment to realize that he had no idea to whom it belonged. He flashed back to college, where he had often awoken with girls of whom he had no recollection. Usually after a night of partying. Usually with a hangover. He had virtually stopped drinking when he started practicing law, but nonetheless his headache was of that unforgettable variety. Last night's Fourth of July party had obviously gotten out of hand. He hoped she was worth it. Grudgingly he opened his eyes.

Standing beside his bed—dressed, dammit—in a peacock Chanel suit was a gorgeous sprightly nymph of a woman. Her body screamed sex, his kind of sex, but her beautiful face was all business. Her enchanting emerald eyes seemed to study his—a bit too intently for the hour, he thought—as she shot him a smile. "I'm sorry to wake you," she said. "But we've got another big day ahead of us. The media will be here in an hour for the press conference."

"And I wanted to go over the latest poll numbers with you first," came another unfamiliar voice from the other side of his bed. An unfamiliar male voice. Startled, Luther whipped his head around only to be rewarded with a volcanic throb. He clenched his eyes for a second, and then opened them to see a thirty-something man in a conservative suit. He had penetrating cobalt eyes and a pronounced dimple on his chin. Luther had never seen him before either. Yet here he was, in his—Luther interrupted his own thought to scan his bedroom. It too was unfamiliar, although opulently furnished to his taste. "Are you okay, sir?" the man asked before Luther could process the situation.

"I've got one whale of a headache."

"Another one?" the woman stated. "You really should start taking something for the stress, as Dr. Martin has repeatedly suggested. Is this one worse than yesterday's?"

Luther had no idea, but it must be. He'd take just about anything to get rid of this headache, and apparently he had resisted medication thus far. At least it wasn't from booze ... or a tumor. But stress? What stress? The man had said something about poll numbers. Perhaps they would shed light on the source of his stress. Ignoring the woman's question he said, "Give me the numbers."

The man cleared his throat. "Our latest poll pegs your name recognition within two points of the Lieutenant Governor's, thanks no doubt to coverage of the Rigby case. You are also neck-and-neck with Kramer on favorables." The man handed him a printout with several numbers circled in red pen, and +10 to 20 written beside them in the right margin.

Luther still had no clear idea what was going on. The whole situation resembled a dream. But given that he was a bullshit artist by nature, he decided to play along until something clicked. Pointing to the handwritten numbers, he asked, "Where do we get the bumps?"

The man and woman exchanged pleased glances, and then she said, "The press conference, of course. Speaking of which, you really have to get ready. I've selected a suit and tie that will play particularly well on camera. I've laid them out in your dressing room. You choose the shirt, so long as it's white. I'll see that your breakfast is waiting by the time you're out of the shower."

"And here's the final copy of your speech," the man said, handing him another several sheets of paper. "Along with your answers to the most likely questions. Memorize everything over breakfast. We need to make sure this comes off as sincere rather than conniving, so you won't want to carry notes."

"Fortunately, your record over these past couple of years should make that a relatively easy sell," the woman added.

"And regardless, this will generate a ton of publicity. I have every confidence, sir, that just forty days from now, you'll be waking up as California's Governor Elect."

"No doubt, sir," the woman Luther now presumed to be his personal assistant reverberated. "This will end the debate once and for all. Luther Kanasis wants to be governor so he can help improve people's lives. It's not about the power, prestige, or money. You've already got enough of those to burn."

Luther looked down at the paper, his aching brain grasping the fringes of a remarkable situation—or rather, nested situations. He was days away from achieving his life's dream, from becoming Governor of California, but the stress had finally overwhelmed him. He had once successfully sued UCLA for exposing a Mathematics PhD student to so much stress over his thesis defense that he suffered a staggering loss of memory. The poor guy basically forgot that he was a doctoral student and everything associated therewith, including where he lived and who his friends were. Luther's expert witness had called this episodic amnesia a natural defensive mechanism, and compared it to a house blowing a fuse. As he told the jury, the UCLA mathematics department had obviously tried to run an unhealthy amount of current through his client, and his body had responded accordingly.

Studying the two faces hovering over his bed, Luther had to wonder if he had been subjected to enough psychological current during his gubernatorial bid that he had blown a fuse. Was there any other explanation for the fact that he did not recognize his staff, his house, his— "Where's the paper?" he asked.

The woman whose name Luther craved to remember exchanged another brief look with his aide before turning to retrieve the Los Angeles Times from the writing desk behind her.

Luther accepted the paper with a nervous hand, his eye darting immediately to the date: Tuesday, September 30. His mind had blanked out three whole months. It was hard to process. He recalled that in addition to PhD students, combat soldiers were the most common victims of stress amnesia. Perhaps it happened to campaigning politicians as well, but they just covered it up. As he had to do.

Three months seemed at once to be too long a period of time to black out, and too short a period for so much to have changed. Impossibly short. He let his eyes drift back to the date, this time focusing on the year. The last digit was not the 3 he had expected, but an 8. He had blacked out five whole years.

"Are you all right, Luther?" the woman asked. "You're looking a little pale."

Analyzing dates for the first time, he realized that he must have had five amazingly successful years if he was already at the doorstep of the governor's mansion. He had been doing well as an attorney, but not that well. Perhaps he had caught the next O. J. Simpson case. No wonder he had blown a fuse. Regardless, he was not about to throw his life's dream away now. He would play along —bullshit, deduce, and investigate—until he connected enough dots to function appropriately, or his memory returned.

Calling on the nimble ability to compartmentalize his thoughts that served him so well in the courtroom, Luther donned a smile, looked up at his secretary, and said, "I'm just hungry."

Chapter 96

Philanthropy

"YOU REALLY PEGGED HIM," Emmy said, studying Troy with admiration. "I'm supposed to be the people person."

"It wasn't much of a stretch," Troy replied. "What successful, charismatic, ambitious attorney doesn't dream of using Capitol Hill or the governor's mansion as a stepping-stone to the White House —especially here in Hollywood? Let's just hope that the rest of the morning proves to be as predictable." Troy trailed off his speech and then snapped his fingers. "Oh shit. What if he turns on the TV? I say we get back in there and manage the situation."

Emmy's instincts told her that Luther would find it suspicious if they appeared too clingy, and it was key that they keep him in a trusting mood. But to Troy's point, if she were Luther, she'd reach for the remote the first chance she got. "Why don't you go downstairs and wait for the press, help them get set up. I'll manage Luther."

Emmy was a bit nervous that Troy might lash out at her suggestion. Neither of them had slept much during the past forty-eight hours, and the weight on their shoulders was gargantuan. But Troy just leaned forward and gave her a warm soft kiss. Then, without a word, he turned and headed downstairs.

She was going to marry him, someday.

Emmy knocked on the door to the master bedroom suite, said "Luther," and then entered without waiting for a reply. Since Luther did not know what their relationship was, she might as well let him assume that they were intimate. That would deepen his level of trust. She found Luther dressed in the blue suit and red tie she had laid out. He was seated at the secretary, studying his prepared remarks.

When he looked up, she said, "You look perfect. Very gubernatorial."

He nodded and returned his focus to the remarks Troy had given him. Something about the intensity of his gaze piqued Emmy's fears. She wondered if they had gone too far. They had discussed the option of handing him the speech at the last minute, but ruled that out as appearing unprofessional. Well, she decided, it was too late to take it back now. All she could do was press ahead as planned.

The plan was for her to plant a couple of key thoughts in Luther's mind before the press arrived. She cleared her throat and said, "We've got fifteen minutes before we need to go downstairs. I thought you might want to use them to practice for the Q&A?"

"Does this look right to you?" Luther asked, ignoring her question. He held out his copy of the remarks without pointing to any sentence in particular.

Emmy instantly recognized Luther's query as general and open-ended. She used such questions all the time when she needed to obtain guidance from her client without losing her authoritative air. She pretended to study the sheet for a minute, and then said, "It looks perfect." she added. "This is it, Luther. This press conference is what pundits will call the tipping-point moment. And you're going to do great."

"You're sure about the figures?" he asked.

Emmy glanced down for a split second. "The five hundred million? Yes, we've run the tests. The additional press and wow factor you would get by taking it up to a full billion are marginal. As long as the word billion is in there, be it one or a half, most people's reaction is virtually identical. And at ten percent of your personal net worth, a half-billion will play well with churchgoers. They'll see that as your proper tithe. We have definitely got the right number."

She smiled and handed the paper back to him with a reassuring nod. Luther did not meet her eye. His mind was obviously riveted on the glorious revelation that he was worth five billion dollars. By her calculation, he would stop questioning things at that point. If the dream was that good, you did not want to wake up.

And she still had the icing to layer on ...

"Remind me why we chose UNICEF?" he asked.

"That question is addressed on the second page, in the Q&A prep."

"Yeah, I saw that bit about the shrinking world and the neediest among us. But what's the real reason?"

Emmy shrugged. "Well, for starters, you tug at absolutely everyone's heart strings by reaching out to children. It's the only universal demographic. Had you donated it to a children's group here in California—as the old saw: All politics is local might dictate —you would raise questions and perhaps even animus because of who you did not choose. Other politicians have fallen victim to that trap. By donating to the United Nations Children's Fund, however, you avoid all that while showing yourself to be appropriately worldly." Studying Luther's eyes, Emmy saw that he endorsed her calculations. She decided to move in for the kill with the two words that would make him a puppet. "That worldliness image will be invaluable four years from now, when we're looking on upgrading the governor's mansion to the White House."

Chapter 97

Headline News

ALONE AND BEFUDDLED, Luther wandered about his enormous estate, exploring rooms, looking for familiar objects. With each step, the events of the morning replayed uncomfortably in his mind. The press conference had lacked the pizzazz he would have expected, given the dollar amount and political stakes. When he mentioned to his executive assistant—he really had to learn her name post haste—she had assured him that this was normal for anything short of a presidential campaign, and that in this electronic age, a little went a long way. "Newspapers habitually pick the majority of their stories off the wire," she added. "And television networks routinely show pool video clips."

Not wanting to parade the very ignorance he was struggling so desperately to hide, he had let the subject drop. Then she and his aide had excused themselves to "go ensure maximal coverage" while suggesting that he "rest up."

Resting up was, of course, exactly what he needed given his mental condition. Obviously they had sensed as much but had the tact not to mention it. He would not be able to rest, however, until he got a grip on his situation. His search of the house had yielded enough familiar objects to convince him that he wasn't completely bonkers. Space aliens had not beamed his soul into someone else's body. But most of his surroundings still looked unfamiliar, even if they didn't feel foreign. And on the bright side, it would not take long to get used to calling such luxurious surrounds home. Of course, he might be moving to the governor's mansion before he got the chance.

Completing his tour of the main house, he returned to his study, the room with the most familiar objects, and turned on the television. Perhaps, he thought, current events would jog something loose. One of the local network affiliates showed his picture and made mention of a prominent L.A. lawyer's half-billion dollar gift to UNICEF. There was no mention of his campaign to succeed Schwarzenegger. He supposed that this might be intentional. His team had hoped to keep the politics out of the news coverage so that it would play like a pure act, and to that end there was no mention of the gubernatorial race in his speech. Perhaps that linkage would come with the evening news, once the political editors and pundits had time to digest his momentous philanthropic act. Still, he thought they should at least have mentioned his candidacy.

Luther's concern grew when he got all the way through a cycle of CNN's Headline News without hearing mention of his phenomenally generous gift. Was the population at large really more interested in some B-list celebrity's racial slurs, or just CNN's news director? "Hello, people. It's half-a-billion dollars. Wake up."

A crashing sound downstairs brought Luther out of his doldrums. Leaping out of his armchair he ran out onto the hallway and looked over the rail. Two police officers the size of linebackers were running up the stairs at him, weapons drawn. Luther froze, rooted to the spot by confusion and fear. The policeman on the right, the first to the top of the stairs, pointed his weapon at Luther's chest and fired without word or hesitation.

Luther felt his chest erupt in flames as white heat blinded his eyes. As his whole body began to spasm, the understanding that he was being Tasered jolted through his besieged mind. Then everything went black.

Chapter 98

Bad Robot

LUTHER AWOKE to find himself strapped naked to a bed beneath a blinding spotlight that was focused on his bare belly. No, not a bed, he realized, a table, an operating table. The skin on his stomach felt as parched as a rotisserie chicken's, while his hands and feet were frozen. He began to shiver, although whether from cold or nerves he was not sure. Had he gone into cardiac arrest when the trigger-happy cop zapped him? He looked around the room but saw only darkness in every direction. No walls. No people.

Two jointed stainless steel constructions rose around him like robotic arms. The right arm terminated in a menacing set of pincers. The left arm supported a video screen, which although less sinister than the neighboring pincers was no less disturbing. Dark and lifeless, it mocked him. A link to the outside world was just inches away, but given the grip of his restraints, it may as well have been miles.

Shaking like a rehabilitating addict and feeling desperately alone, he strained against his wrist and ankle shackles with all the strength he could muster. Drawing blood or even breaking bones were of little concern to Luther. The physical pain this caused was negligible compared to the torment in his head.

He needed to be free.

But the broad straps of thick leather running tautly across his chest and hips robbed him of all leverage. He called out like a madman howling at the moon and received a hollow echo in return. An echo. The sound sobered him. Wherever he was, it was much more expansive than your typical operating theater.

Luther cried out for what seemed like days. Perhaps it was just hours, but it was definitely longer than minutes, for his voice faded to a gravelly whisper and he began to suffer from thirst. Lying there, immobile, with nothing but the spotlight for company, he began to wonder if the Taser had killed him. This place certainly felt like purgatory. If not for the overwhelming sense that he was waiting for something, it would qualify as Hell.

Somewhere in the swirling haze of passing hours, he figured out what had happened. Someone had seen the news story on his charitable contribution and figured that he was literally worth a king's ransom. He was being held until the ransom was negotiated and paid, kept under maximal stress so that he would readily agree to any demand when the screen finally came to life.

Yes, that was it. He would be asked to authorize a transfer via videophone, and then the robotic arm would release his bonds. With no human contact, the crime was virtually perfect.

As if in answer to his speculation, a dark voice echoed forth from the void, "Hello Luther."

Luther craned his neck and tried again to pierce the blackness, but it was useless. The spotlight spoiled his vision. He strained his ears, searching for a footfall, the rustle of clothes, breathing. They found only silence.

"Who's there!" he shouted, his mind too garbled to manage anything but the cliché.

After the echo of his own cry faded without hint of another noise, Luther began to fear that he was hallucinating. He was so lonely. Food, water, yes he wanted those, needed those, but there in the sterile blackness of that vast space, companionship was what he most craved. He did not want to die alone, a naked chicken roasting on a cold iron spit.

Mocking laughter erupted from silence as the video screen before him sprang to life. When his eyes came into focus, he found himself face to face with a mid-forties male. "Remember me?" the talking head asked.

Luther strained his brain for any trace of recollection, any hint of a memory of the handsome aquiline features that were contorted into a vengeful mask. Never before had Luther wanted anything so much, needed anything so desperately. He felt as though his very sanity depended on his ability to make that single connection, but he was betrayed by his own mind. It offered nothing, a complete blank.

Almost as bad as the cognitive failure was the realization that he would never be able to explain his condition to his captor, at least not convincingly. Stress-induced episodic amnesia. Yeah, right. He hardly believed it himself. Staring into the eyes he now feared would be the last he'd ever see, Luther found a glimmer of hope and latched onto it: The eyes were intelligent, the face dignified, and the skin white.

"You don't remember me, do you?" The intelligent eyes narrowed.

"No." Luther said, his voice hoarse and shallow. "I don't remember a lot of things."

The head nodded slowly as the lips thinned. "My name is Arlen Blythe. I'm the Chairman of Savas Pharmaceuticals."

"Pleased to meet you."

Arlen inclined his head perfunctorily, acknowledging the sentiment. "You do remember giving five hundred million dollars to charity though, right?"

Luther simply said, "Yes." He wanted to say more, but did not know where to start.

Arlen's face hardened as though instantly turned to granite. "It was mine."

Despite Arlen's sinister expression, Luther felt a surge of hope. If this was only about money, he could deal with it painlessly enough. He was a wealthy man. A billionaire. With power. "I'm sorry. There was an accident. I, I just don't remember. I will pay you back though, of course. With whatever interest is appropriate."

"I really wish you did remember, Luther. That would make this so much more satisfying. But alas ..." he shrugged.

"What? Make what more satisfying?"

"The news."

"What news?"

"You're broke, Luther. Wiped out. You owe far more than you own."

"No, no. That's not true. I have five billion. Well, four billion five hundred. And I am about to become the Governor of California. I'm sure we can work this out."

Arlen sprouted an amused look and nodded three times. Seeing this, Luther let out a sigh of relief. Everything was going to be okay.

"So that's how they did it," Arlen said. "I was wondering."

"How who did what?" Luther asked, the knots recapturing his stomach.

"Got you to give my money away, irrevocably."

"It was a scam?" Luther asked, even as the implications sank in. "I really am broke?"

Arlen nodded. "And you know what that means?"

Luther slowly shook his head, dreadfully confused and utterly terrified.

The robotic pincers above Luther whirred to life. They disappeared beneath the table only to reappear a second later clenching a scalpel.

"It means I'm going to have to extract half-a-billion dollars from your flesh."

Chapter 99

Teamwork

TROY LOOKED OVER the sweating silver bucket toward the strawberry sky, and smiled. Aruba's famous green flash had been beautiful, but it had nothing on Emmy's eyes. Had he ever been so happy? He'd never know. And he was okay with that.

As the couples without beachfront bungalows turned to walk back to their rooms, Troy picked the cordless phone off the rattan table and looked over at his breathtaking companion. "You sure this is the way to go?"

Emmy set down her champagne flute and accepted the receiver. "Absolutely. Especially now that Luther's dead." She grimaced while speaking the last word, and Troy knew she was picturing the grotesque scene that had made tabloid covers all over the world. The world's first robotic homicide.

"I mean the part about keeping it anonymous," Troy clarified. "Perhaps it would be better if they knew where the money came from? Perhaps knowing about Luther and his fate would give them closure?"

Emmy shook her head. "It will only raise painful questions, reopen wounds, and make the gift feel like blood money. Best to just let a little good fortune rain on those who have endured so much bad."

Troy raised his flute in a toast to her wisdom as Emmy dialed the first number.

"Hello."

"Good morning. Mrs. Jane Michaels, please," Emmy said,

affecting a British accent.

"Speaking."

"Born January ninth, nineteen sixty-six?"

Hesitation. "Yes, who's asking please?"

"Mrs. Michaels, I'm calling from the All Saints Bank in Geneva, Switzerland to inform you that an anonymous benefactor has opened an account in your interest."

"Come again? Geneva? Anonymous benefactor? I'm afraid I don't follow."

"Yes, I understand your confusion," Emmy continued. "It's to be expected. Do you have a pen and paper handy?"

"Is this some kind of trick?"

"No, ma'am. I'm not going to ask you for a thing. I'm just giving. Do you have that pen?"

"All right," Jane Michaels said after a pause, her voice markedly suspicious.

Emmy read off a twelve-digit number, and then added, "The password is WALTER64. With that information you can access your account in person or over the phone, so don't share it with anyone you do not trust completely. In fact, I would strongly suggest that you keep everything I've told you strictly to yourself. There are a lot of vultures out there, with beaks tuned to sniff out money. Best to be discreet."

"What account is this again?"

"Your new account. The gift of an anonymous benefactor. The balance is one million dollars, American."

Emmy's revelation was greeted at first with silence, and then, "Come again?"

"That's right, a one followed by six zeroes. A gift, all yours, tax free, to do with as you wish. Enjoy yourself, Jane. You won't be hearing from me or anyone else about the money ever again."

"Thank you, I think …"

"You are very welcome. Please, enjoy yourself. You deserve it,"

Emmy said, and severed the connection.

"That seemed to go well," Troy said. "And only forty-four to go —plus Kostas Kanasis."

"You going to call him tomorrow?"

"He's scheduled to arrive home from Greece at noon. I'll call him shortly thereafter." Troy took another swallow, happy to have lived up to the promise he'd made the old man. Then he looked back at Emmy to find that her face was rife with a different kind of emotion. She looked nervous.

"Is something wrong?"

Emmy stood and ran her polished toes through the sand. "When are we going to sit down and figure out what we'll do with our share?"

Troy was about to say "No time like the present" and suggest ordering another bottle of Taittinger when his instincts kicked in. He wasn't as quick as Emmy yet, but he was learning. "Tell me what you're thinking."

"Combined, we've got two million dollars. That gives us a lot of options."

Emmy's use of "combined" and "we" was worth far more to Troy than the money. For the past four weeks, while they used Luther's titanium ledger to backtrack to all his victims, they had managed to avoid any talk of the future. He had hoped all along that they would want to remain together after their last duty was done, but all the same he had worried that the bonds forged under fire would slacken once the heat was off. Hearing her confirm his unstated desire, he couldn't believe that he had ever harbored doubt.

"I've already got it all figured out," he said, standing and taking her chin in his hand.

"Oh you do, do you?"

Troy nodded sheepishly.

"Out with it," she said, poking at his belly with both index fingers.

He stepped back and shook his head.

She held up a fist and looked at him sideways. "How about a hint?"

He dropped to one knee. "We are a pretty good team, you and I."

ABOUT THE AUTHOR

Tim began his career in Soviet Counterintelligence with the US Army Special Forces, the Green Berets. With the fall of the Berlin Wall, Tim switched from espionage to arbitrage and moved to Moscow in the midst of Perestroika. In Russia, he led prominent multinational medical companies, worked with cosmonauts on the MIR Space Station (from Earth, alas), and chaired the Association of International Pharmaceutical Manufacturers.

Moving to Brussels during the formation of the EU, Tim ran Europe, Middle East, and Africa for a Johnson & Johnson company and traveled like a character in a Robert Ludlum novel. He eventually landed in Silicon Valley, where he launched new medical technologies as a startup CEO.

Tim began writing thrillers in 1996 from an apartment overlooking Moscow's Gorky Park. Decades later, he's still writing. His home office now overlooks a vineyard in Northern California, where he lives with his wife Elena and their two daughters.

Tim grew up in the Midwest. He earned a BA in Philosophy and Mathematics from Hanover College, and then an MBA in Finance and a MA in International Studies from the University of Pennsylvania's Wharton School and Lauder Institute.

AUTHOR'S NOTE

Dear Reader,

Although the characters in FLASH do not yet appear in any of my other novels, I do have thoughts regarding their futures. If you email me at Flash@timtigner.com, I will be happy to forward you my unpublished thoughts on what happens to them next, and keep you informed on my new releases.

If you enjoyed FLASH, I think you'll find the characters and plots in my other novels to be similarly engaging. I hope you'll give them a try.

Thanks for your kind attention,

ALSO BY TIM TIGNER

Standalone Novels
COERCION, BETRAYAL. THE PRICE OF TIME,

Kyle Achilles Series
PUSHING BRILLIANCE, THE LIES OF SPIES,
CHASING IVAN, FALLING STARS, TWIST AND TURN,
BOUNDLESS AMBITION

Turn the page for a preview of PUSHING BRILLIANCE,
book #1 in the Kyle Achilles series.

Pushing Brilliance

Chapter 1

The Kremlin

HOW DO YOU PITCH an audacious plan to the most powerful man in the world? Grigori Barsukov was about to find out.

Technically, the President of Russia was an old friend—although the last time they'd met, his old friend had punched him in the face. That was thirty years ago, but the memory remained fresh, and Grigori's nose still skewed to the right.

Back then, he and President Vladimir Korovin wore KGB lieutenant stars. Now both were clothed in the finest Italian suits. But his former roommate also sported the confidence of one who wielded unrivaled power, and the temper of a man ruthless enough to obtain it.

The world had spun on a different axis when they'd worked together, an east-west axis, running from Moscow to Washington. Now everything revolved around the West. America was the sole superpower.

Grigori could change that.

He could lever Russia back into a pole position.

But only if his old rival would risk joining him—way out on a limb.

As Grigori's footfalls fell into cadence with the boots of his escorts, he coughed twice, attempting to relax the lump in his throat. It didn't work. When the hardwood turned to red carpet, he willed his palms to stop sweating. They didn't listen. Then the big double doors rose before him and it was too late to do anything but take a deep breath, and hope for the best.

The presidential guards each took a single step to the side, then opened their doors with crisp efficiency and a click of their heels. Across the office, a gilded double-headed eagle peered down from atop the dark wood paneling, but the lone living occupant of the Kremlin's inner sanctum did not look up.

President Vladimir Korovin was studying photographs.

Grigori stopped three steps in as the doors were closed behind him, unsure of the proper next move. He wondered if everyone felt this way the first time. Should he stand at attention until acknowledged? Take a seat by the wall?

He strolled to the nearest window, leaned his left shoulder up against the frame, and looked out at the Moscow River. Thirty seconds ticked by with nothing but the sound of shifting photos behind him. *Was it possible that Korovin still held a grudge?*

Desperate to break the ice without looking like a complete fool, he said, "This is much nicer than the view from our academy dorm room."

Korovin said nothing.

Grigori felt his forehead tickle. Drops of sweat were forming, getting ready to roll. As the first broke free, he heard the stack of photos being squared, and then at long last, the familiar voice. It posed a very unfamiliar question: "Ever see a crocodile catch a rabbit?"

Grigori whirled about to meet the Russian President's gaze. "What?"

Korovin waved the stack of photos. His eyes were the same cornflower blue Grigori remembered, but their youthful verve had yielded to something darker. "I recently returned from Venezuela. Nicolas took me crocodile hunting. Of course, we didn't have all day to spend on sport, so our guides cheated. They put rabbits on the riverbank, on the wide strip of dried mud between the water and the tall grass. Kind of like teeing up golf balls. Spaced them out so the critters couldn't see each other and gave each its own pile of alfalfa while we watched in silence from an electric boat." Korovin was clearly enjoying the telling of his intriguing tale. He gestured with broad sweeps as he spoke, but kept his eyes locked on Grigori.

"Nicolas told me these rabbits were brought in special from the hill country, where they'd survived a thousand generations amidst foxes and coyotes. When you put them on the riverbank, however, they're completely clueless. It's not their turf, so they stay where they're dropped, noses quivering, ears scanning, eating alfalfa and watching the wall of vegetation in front of them while crocodiles swim up silently from behind.

"The crocodiles were being fooled like the rabbits, of course. Eyes front, focused on food. Oblivious." Korovin shook his head as though bewildered. "Evolution somehow turned a cold-blooded reptile into a warm white furball, but kept both of the creature's brains the same. Hard to fathom. Anyway, the capture was quite a sight.

"Thing about a crocodile is, it's a log one moment and a set of snapping jaws the next, with nothing but a furious blur in between. One second the rabbit is chewing alfalfa, the next second the rabbit *is* alfalfa. Not because it's too slow or too stupid ... but because it's out of its element."

Grigori resisted the urge to swallow.

"When it comes to eating," Korovin continued, "crocs are like storybook monsters. They swallow their food whole. Unlike their legless cousins, however, they want it dead first. So once they've trapped dinner in their maw, they drag it underwater to drown it.

This means the rabbit is usually alive and uninjured in the croc's mouth for a while—unsure what the hell just happened, but pretty damn certain it's not good."

The president leaned back in his chair, placing his feet on the desk and his hands behind his head. He was having fun.

Grigori felt like the rabbit.

"That's when Nicolas had us shoot the crocs. After they clamped down around the rabbits, but before they dragged 'em under. That became the goal, to get the rabbit back alive."

Grigori nodded appreciatively. "Gives a new meaning to the phrase, *catch and release.*"

Korovin continued as if Grigori hadn't spoken. "The trick was putting a bullet directly into the croc's tiny brain, preferably the medulla oblongata, right there where the spine meets the skull. Otherwise the croc would thrash around or go under before you could get off the kill shot, and the rabbit was toast.

"It was good sport, and an experience worth replicating. But we don't have crocodiles anywhere near Moscow, so I've been trying to come up with an equally engaging distraction for my honored guests. Any ideas?"

Grigori felt like he'd been brought in from the hills. The story hadn't helped the lump in his throat either. He managed to say, "Let me give it some thought."

Korovin just looked at him expectantly.

Comprehension struck after an uncomfortable silence. "What happened to the rabbits?"

Korovin returned his feet to the floor, and leaned forward in his chair. "Good question. I was curious to see that myself. I put my first survivor back on the riverbank beside a fresh pile of alfalfa. It ran for the tall grass as if I'd lit its tail on fire. That rabbit had learned life's most important lesson."

Grigori bit. "What's that?"

"Doesn't matter where you are. Doesn't matter if you're a

crocodile or a rabbit. You best look around, because you're never safe.

"Now, what have you brought me, Grigori?"

Grigori breathed deeply, forcing the reptiles from his mind. He pictured his future atop a corporate tower, an oligarch on a golden throne. Then he spoke with all the gravitas of a wedding vow. "I brought you a plan, Mister President."

Chapter 2

Brillyanc

PRESIDENT KOROVIN REPEATED Grigori's assertion aloud. "You brought me a plan." He paused for a long second, as though tasting the words.

Grigori felt like he was looking up from the Colosseum floor after a gladiator fight. Would the emperor's thumb point up, or down?

Korovin was savoring the power. Finally, the president gestured toward the chess table abutting his desk, and Grigori's heart resumed beating.

The magnificent antique before which Grigori took a seat was handcrafted of the same highly polished hardwood as Korovin's desk, probably by a French craftsman now centuries dead. Korovin took the opposing chair and pulled a chess clock from his drawer. Setting it on the table, he pressed the button that activated Grigori's timer. "Give me the three-minute version."

Grigori wasn't a competitive chess player, but like any Russian who had risen through government ranks, he was familiar with the sport.

Chess clocks have two timers controlled by seesawing buttons. When one's up, the other's down, and vice versa. After each move, a player slaps his button, stopping his timer and setting his opponent's in motion. If a timer runs out, a little red plastic flag drops, and that player loses. Game over. There's the door. Thank you for playing.

Grigori planted his elbows on the table, leaned forward, and made his opening move. "While my business is oil and gas, my hobby is investing in startups. The heads of Russia's major research centers all know I'm a so-called *angel investor*, so they send me their best early-stage projects. I get everything from social media software, to solar power projects, to electric cars.

"A few years ago, I met a couple of brilliant biomedical researchers out of Kazan State Medical University. They had applied modern analytical tools to the data collected during tens of thousands of medical experiments performed on political prisoners during Stalin's reign. They were looking for factors that accelerated the human metabolism—and they found them. Long story short, a hundred million rubles later I've got a drug compound whose strategic potential I think you'll appreciate."

Grigori slapped his button, pausing his timer and setting the president's clock in motion. It was a risky move. If Korovin wasn't intrigued, Grigori wouldn't get to finish his pitch. But Grigori was confident that his old roommate was hooked. Now he would have to admit as much if he wanted to hear the rest.

The right side of the president's mouth contracted back a couple millimeters. A crocodile smile. He slapped the clock. "Go on."

"The human metabolism converts food and drink into the fuel and building blocks our bodies require. It's an exceptionally complex process that varies greatly from individual to individual, and within individuals over time. Metabolic differences mean some people naturally burn more fat, build more muscle, enjoy more energy, and think more clearly than others. This is obvious from the locker room to the boardroom to the battlefield. The doctors in Kazan focused on the mental aspects of metabolism, on factors that improved clarity of thought—"

Korovin interrupted, "Are you implying that my metabolism impacts my IQ?"

"Sounds a little funny at first, I know, but think about your own experience. Don't you think better after coffee than after vodka? After salad than fries? After a jog and a hot shower than an afternoon at a desk? All those actions impact the mental horsepower you enjoy at any given moment. What my doctors did was figure out what the body needs to optimize cognitive function."

"Something other than healthy food and sufficient rest?"

Perceptive question, Grigori thought. "Picture your metabolism like a funnel, with raw materials such as food and rest going in the top, cognitive power coming out the bottom, and dozens of complex metabolic processes in between."

"Okay," Korovin said, eager to engage in a battle of wits.

"Rather than following in the footsteps of others by attempting to modify one of the many metabolic processes, the doctors in Kazan took an entirely different approach, a brilliant approach. They figured out how to widen the narrow end of the funnel."

"So, bottom line, the brain gets more fuel?"

"Generally speaking, yes."

"With what result? Will every day be like my best day?"

"No," Grigori said, relishing the moment. "Every day will be better than your best day."

Korovin cocked his head. "How much better?"

Who's the rabbit now? "Twenty IQ points."

"Twenty points?"

"Tests show that's the average gain, and that it applies across the scale, regardless of base IQ. But it's most interesting at the high end."

Another few millimeters of smile. "Why is the high end the most interesting?"

"Take a person with an IQ of 140. Give him Brillyanc—that's the drug's name—and he'll score 160. May not sound like a big deal, but roughly speaking, those 20 points take his IQ from 1 in 200, to 1 in 20,000. Suddenly, instead of being the smartest guy in the room, he's the smartest guy in his discipline."

Korovin leaned forward and locked on Grigori's eyes. "Every ambitious scientist, executive, lawyer ... and politician would give his left nut for that competitive advantage. Hell, his left and right."

Grigori nodded.

"And it really works?"

"It really works."

Korovin reached out and leveled the buttons, stopping both timers and pausing to think, his left hand still resting on the clock. "So your plan is to give Russians an intelligence edge over foreign competition? Kind of analogous to what you and I used to do, all those years ago."

Grigori shook his head. "No, that's not my plan."

The edges of the cornflower eyes contracted ever so slightly. "Why not?"

"Let's just say, widening the funnel does more than raise IQ."

Korovin frowned and leaned back, taking a moment to digest this twist. "Why have you brought this to me, Grigori?"

"As I said, Mister President, I have a plan I think you're going to like."